THE LOST REGIMENT

MEN OF WAR

William R. Forstchen

A ROC BOOK

ROC
Published by New American Library, a division of
Penguin Putnam Inc., 375 Hudson Street,
New York, New York 10014, U.S.A.
Penguin Books Ltd, 27 Wrights Lane, London W8 5TZ, England
Penguin Books Australia Ltd, Ringwood, Victoria, Australia
Penguin Books Canada Ltd, 10 Alcorn Avenue,
Toronto, Ontario, Canada M4V 3B2
Penguin Books (N.Z.) Ltd, 182–190 Wairau Road,
Auckland 10, New Zealand

Penguin Books Ltd, Registered Offices:
Harmondsworth, Middlesex, England

First published by Roc, an imprint of New American Library,
a division of Penguin Putnam Inc.

First Printing, December 1999
10 9 8 7 6 5 4 3 2 1

Cover art by San Julian

 REGISTERED TRADEMARK—MARCA REGISTRADA

Printed in the United States of America

PUBLISHER'S NOTE
This is a work of fiction. Names, characters, places, and incidents are either
the product of the author's imagination or are used fictitiously, and any
resemblance to actual persons, living or dead, business establishments, events
or locales is entirely coincidental.

For the men of all the Lost Regiments of the American Civil War, North and South, who gave the last full measure of devotion and, in so doing, set an undying example of dedication and valor.

ACKNOWLEDGMENTS

This series has spun its web around me for more than a decade and it is now difficult to part from it. The desire to write a story in this genre with a Civil War theme formed over fifteen years ago, and I am eternally grateful to John Silbersack, my first editor with Penguin, for embracing an idea that other editors thought a bit mad. My sincere thanks must go as well to my agent, Eleanor Wood. When I became her client twelve years ago the Lost Regiment was the first thing I dropped on her desk, and it was she who saved it and moved it forward.

This series started just as I entered graduate school and is now finished after obtaining tenure at Montreat College, so it has been a constant companion through a lot of changes in my life. My most humble thanks must go to Professor Gunther Rothenberg. Gunther was, and still is, my mentor, and it was an honor to study under him. Dennis Showalter, President of the Society of Military Historians, was a hero of mine years ago, and thus my shock when he called me one day, me a lowly graduate student, to express his delight in *Rally Cry*. Dennis's input ever since has been invaluable and his studies of technology, logistics, and war are an inspiration. Mention must be made of Professor David Flory as well, a professor second to none. Another inspiration was the role model of L. Sprague de Camp when it came to combining history with science fiction and fantasy.

Numerous friends were advisors and of tremendous help on this project and others, and are deserving of thanks, especially John Mina, Kevin Malady, Maury Hurt, Bill Fawcett, Elizabeth Kitsteiner, Monica Walker, Donn Wright, Tom Sesy, Tim Kindred, Dr. David Dellecroce for discussions on the finer points of the "Moon

Fest," Newt Gingrich, and Jeff Ethell. Any relation to those who served in the 35th is purely coincidence. The community of Montreat College, students, faculty, and administration has been remarkably tolerant of my idiosyncrasies and story writing. It is a rare college today that indulges its professors thus, and I am thankful for their understanding and support.

Of course there is my family, who had to live through all of this, Sharon, Meghan (who learned to sing the "Battle Cry of Freedom" before she was three), and my parents, who encouraged my interest in history from the start.

There are numerous other names to mention, but publishers are not into acknowledgments that run for pages, nor as a reader do I often take the time to check them out, so we shall close it here. So if you are reading this, my thanks, but it is time to move on with the tale!

—William R. Forstchen
Montreat, NC
June 1999

MEN OF WAR

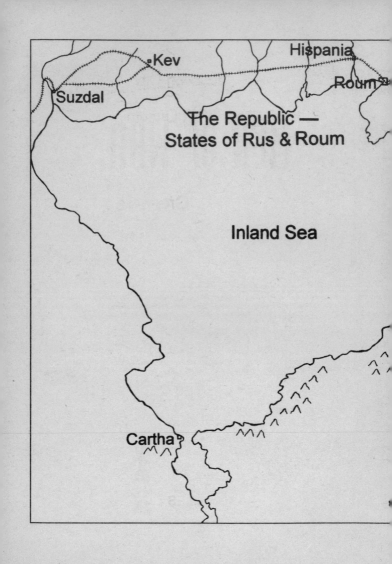

Hispania

Kev

Roum

Suzdal

The Republic —
States of Rus & Roum

Inland Sea

Cartha

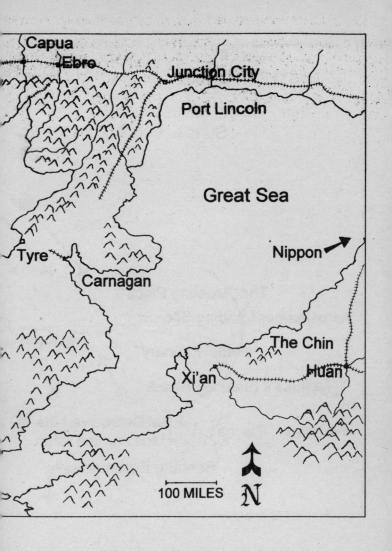

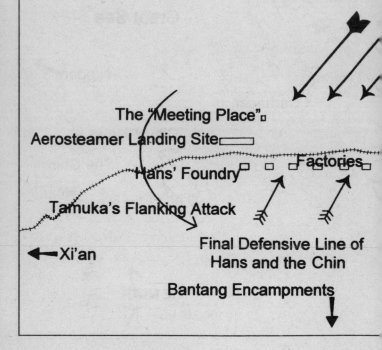

BATTLE OF HUAN

The "Meeting Place"

Aerosteamer Landing Site

Hans' Foundry

Factories

Tamuka's Flanking Attack

◄— Xi'an

Final Defensive Line of
Hans and the Chin

Bantang Encampments

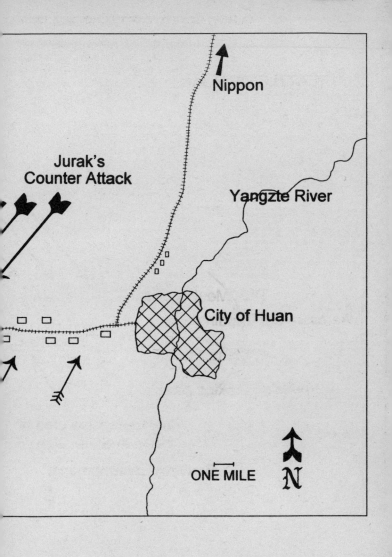

Nippon

Jurak's
Counter Attack

Yangzte River

City of Huan

ONE MILE   N

Chapter One

Colonel Andrew Lawrence Keane reached up and reverently touched the silken folds of the flag of the 35th Maine. Aged and bloodstained, the fabric was as fragile as the wings of a dying butterfly.

A hundred nameless fields of strife, he thought wistfully. *My own blood on that standard, my brother's, all my comrades. How many of us left? Less than a hundred now.* He slowly let his hand drop.

It was early morning, the air heady with the scent of late spring. The grass was up, thick, a lush green, sprinkled with a riot of flowers—blue, yellow, and strange purple orchids unique to this alien world that was now home.

Nature was already hard at work covering over the scars of the bitter winter battle. The deep trenches cut by the besieging Bantag were beginning to erode away, collapsing in on themselves under the incessant drumbeat of the heavy spring rains. Scattered wreckage of battle, discarded cartridge boxes, broken caissons, shell casings, tattered bits of uniform, and even the bones of the fallen were returning to the soil.

His gaze swept across the field, lingering for a moment at the great city of the Roum, looking like a vision of an empire lost to his own world far more than a millennium ago. Pillared temples adorned the hills, the new triumphal arch commemorating the great victory already half-raised in the center of the old forum. Even in the city the scars of the bitter winter battle were beginning to disappear, new buildings rising up out of the wreckage, the distant sound of sawing, hammering; a city being reborn echoed across the fields.

He turned his mount, nudging Mercury with his knees, shifting his gaze to the long lines deployed out behind him, a full corps drawn up for review before heading to the front. It was the glorious old 9th Corps, so badly mauled in the siege. The corps was deployed in battle formation, three divisions, with brigades in column, colors to the fore, occupying a front of more than half a mile. The formation was obsolete for battle use; in an open field it would be torn to shreds by modern firepower. But old traditions died hard, and such a formation could still inspire the ranks, giving them a sense of their strength and numbers.

"They're starting to look better," Hans Schuder announced. Andrew looked over to his old friend and nodded, urging Mercury to a slow canter, the flag bearer of the 35th following, as he paraded down the length of the line, saluting the shot-torn standards of the regiments, carefully eyeing the men.

Most of the wear and tear of the winter fight, at least on the exterior, had been repaired . . . new uniforms to replace the rags that had covered the men by the end of the winter, rifles repaired and well polished, cartridge boxes and haversacks bulging with eighty rounds per man, and five days' rations.

Here and there the ranks had been replenished with new recruits, but most of the men were veterans; rawboned, tough, lean, eyes dark and hollow. Far too many of the regiments were pitifully small, sometimes down to fewer than a hundred men. Andrew had considered combining units and cutting the corps down to two divisions, but there had been a howl of protest. Regimental pride was as strong on this world as with any army back on the old world, so he had let the formation stand.

Reining in occasionally, he paused to chat, making it a point to single out men who wore the coveted Medals of Honor. Eighteen had been awarded for the siege of Roum, and another five for the units that had flanked the Bantags with Hans Schuder. Self-consciously he looked down at his own medal, given to him personally by President Abraham Lincoln. It still made him feel somewhat guilty that he had thus been singled out. Taking command of the old 35th at Gettysburg after the death of Colonel Estes, he had simply held the line, refusing to budge, the same way the other regiments deployed along Seminary Ridge had fought on that terrible first day of the battle. He had bled the 35th white, lost his only brother, and awakened in the hospital minus an arm. *And for that they gave me a medal.* He looked over at Hans riding beside him. It wasn't fair, he thought again. If anyone deserved the medal for that day, it was Hans.

His gaze shifted to a color sergeant from the 14th Roum who had won his medal the hard way, killing over a dozen Bantags in hand-to-hand fighting. Andrew nodded to the sergeant and, as tradition demanded, saluted first in recognition of the medal. The sergeant, really not much more than a boy, grinned with delight and snapped off a salute in return.

"Sergeant, ready to go back up to the front?" Andrew asked, still stumbling over the Latin.

"I think we're ready, sir."

Andrew smiled and continued on.

"I think we're ready," Andrew said in English, looking over at Hans. "They'll fight, but they're worn out."

"Who isn't, Andrew?" Hans replied laconically. "The years pass, the fighting continues, the faces keep changing in the ranks. They just keep seem to be getting younger; that boy with the Medal of Honor couldn't be nineteen."

"Actually just turned eighteen," Andrew replied. He looked back again at the boy with the old eyes, and saw the looks of admiration from the others in his company, for Keane had singled him out.

The old game, Andrew thought, "with such baubles armies are led," Napoléon had once said. Two new awards had been created at the end of the Battle of Roum, and many of the men now wore them, a dark purple stripe on the left sleeve denoting a battle wound, and a silver stripe, also on the same sleeve, for having killed a Bantag in hand-to-hand combat or for a conspicuous display of gallantry. A good third of the corps wore the purple stripe, and several hundred the silver. It just might motivate a frightened boy to stand while others ran.

Coming to the head of the formation Andrew reined in and returned the salute of Stan Bamberg, commander of the 9th Corps and an old gunner of the 44th New York Light Artillery, who today was relinquishing command to head south and take over the 3rd Corps in front at Tyre. Jeff Frady, a redheaded gunner from the 44th had been promoted to take command, and in part this ceremony was the pomp and circumstance for a change of leaders.

"Nice day to be heading up to the front," Stan announced, looking at the pale blue morning sky. "This is a good corps, Andrew."

Andrew caught the undercurrent of concern in Stan's voice. The 9th had been shredded at Roum, and some said the unit had simply broken. The survivors, including Stan, felt that something had to be proven.

"How's the arm?" Andrew inquired. Stan smiled, flexing it with barely a grimace, a souvenir of the last minutes of the battle for Roum, when the corps commander had gotten a little too enthusiastic, ridden to the front lines, and received a Bantag bullet as a result.

"Ready to head south?"

Stan smiled. "I'll miss these boys." He was staring at Jeff, who had been his second for well over a year. "Take good care of them."

Jeff nodded, not replying.

A steam whistle echoed in the distance, interrupting their thoughts. Looking past Stan, Andrew saw a train coming down the broad open slope, its flatcars empty after delivering half a dozen land ironclads to the front. The corps would need thirty trains to take the ten thousand men and their equipment up to the front lines. Once they were in position everything would be in place for what he prayed would be the blow that cracked the Bantag position wide-open.

He had taken the trip up there only a week before, to see the situation in front of Capua and arrange the final plans for the next offensive. The Bantag withdrawal back to the destroyed town, ninety miles east of Roum, had been thorough and brutal, not a single building, barn, hovel, bridge, or foot of track had been left intact by the retreating Horde. Over the last four months his railroaders had worked themselves to exhaustion, repairing, as well, the damage done by the two umens that had raided between Hispania and Kev.

Even with the reconnected line, Pat O'Donald, up at the front, could barely keep five corps supplied, and though he was screaming for the 9th to move up as quickly as possible,

Andrew half wondered if their arrival would be more of a burden than a help.

They were at a stalemate, and he feared that this was a stalemate the Human forces would eventually lose. Though the Battle of Roum, in a tactical sense, had been a victory, in an overall strategic sense he feared it might very well have proven to be a dark turning point of the war.

He remembered his old war back home, the summer and autumn of 1864, when Sherman and Sheridan had laid waste to Georgia and the Shenandoah Valley, crippling the breadbasket of the Confederacy. That, perhaps far more than the bitter siege in the trenches around Petersburg and Richmond, had truly broken the back of the Rebel cause.

Here, in the present, the Bantag ravagings were a blow so severe that he had been forced temporarily to demobilize nearly twenty thousand Roum infantry who had been farmers. If they didn't get some kind of crops in, the Republic would starve the following winter.

Beyond the physical devastation of the Bantag winter offensive there was the human toll as well. Another forty thousand casualties for the army, more than a hundred thousand civilians lost and a million more homeless. The war was wearing them down, even as they continued to win on the battlefield.

He sensed this new Bantag leader understood that far better than any foe he had ever faced across all the wars with the three hordes. The others had always perceived victory as a prize to be won on the battlefield. Yet in the reality of war that was only one component.

What was needed now was not just a victory but a shattering and overwhelming triumph, an annihilating blow on the battlefield that broke the back of the Bantag Horde. He hoped that the forthcoming offensive would be that blow.

"Sir, are you all right?" Jeff asked.

Andrew stirred, realizing he had been gazing off in silence.

He smiled, saying nothing for a moment. He was still weak, a hollow fluttery feeling inside, as if his heart, his body had gone as brittle as glass. The pain, thank God, was gone, though the dark craving for that terrible elixir, morphine, still lingered, the memory of its soothing touch drifting like a fantasy for a forbidden lover.

"Just fine, Jeff, let's not keep the boys standing here. Reviews might be grand fun for generals, but they can be a hell of a bore for privates."

"Yes sir. I'll see you up at the front, sir."

Jeff snapped off another salute and turned his mount, barking out a command. The fifers and drummers deployed behind him started in, commands echoing across the field as the densely packed columns wheeled about to pass in review and from there deploy out to the depot where the trains waited.

The "Battle Hymn of the Republic" echoed across the open fields as the long sinuous columns marched past, the bayonet-tipped rifles gleaming in the morning sun.

Stan, obviously moved by sentiment for his old command, cantered back and forth along the ranks, reaching down to shake hands and wish the boys well.

"This has got to be the last campaign," Hans announced. Andrew shifted in his saddle, looking over at his old friend.

"Another battle like the last and it's over with; either they will break us, or Roum will crack, or maybe even our own government. Andrew, you've got to find a way to end it now."

Andrew looked away, watching as the ranks passed. There had been a time when this army, his army, so reminded him of the old Army of the Potomac. No longer. It had the look, the feel of the Confederate Army of Northern Virginia. The men were lean, too lean. His army was beginning to unravel from having fought one too many battles and knowing it would be forced to continue to fight, the only escape being dismemberment or death.

It was evident all across the Republic, not just here, or at the front, but back in Suzdal, and to the smallest village hamlet. The vast infrastructure he had attempted to build to support this war was stretched like a bowstring and beginning to fray.

"You see it, too?" Andrew asked.

The columns swayed past, dust swirling up so that they looked like shadows passing even though it was noon. He could sense the lack of enthusiasm, the almost boyish excitement that went through an army when it finally broke camp and headed back up. No, these were grim veterans

who would fight like hell, but the enthusiasm was damp-
ened by the knowledge of reality.

"I see it in you as well, Andrew Keane. You're still not
over your wound."

Andrew chuckled dismissively. "Breath comes a bit
short, but other than that I'm fine."

"Right."

He looked over at his old friend and smiled.

"You should talk. How many wounds is it, five now?
And that heart of yours. Emil keeps telling you to slow
down a bit and to cut out chewing tobacco."

As if in response Hans fished into his haversack, pulled
out a plug, bit off a chew, and, playing out their old ceremony, offered the plug to Andrew. He took it and bit a
chew as well, and Hans smiled.

"We're two worn-out old warhorses Andrew. But hell,
what's the alternative, go to the old soldiers' home and sit
in a rocking chair on the porch? Not I. Down deep, I kind
of hope I get shot by the last bullet of the last war."

"Don't even joke about that."

"Superstitious?" Hans chuckled.

"No, it's just something you don't joke about. But you're
right, we're both wearing down. Everyone is."

In the dust-choked column a passing regiment raised
their caps in salute. Andrew let go of Mercury's reins and
took off his hat to return the gesture.

"You know, there is part of me that would actually miss
this," Hans drawled as he leaned over and spat. "Nothing
in peacetime can equal this, a full corps of infantry drawn
up to march off to war."

Andrew nodded. It wasn't just the sight of them, it was
the sounds, the smells . . . the rhythmic clatter of tin cups
banging on canteens, the tramping of feet on the dusty
road, the snatches of conversations wafting past, the scent
of leather, sweat, horses, oil, even the staticlike feel of the
powdery dust. It was something eternal, and it was one of
the few things the gods of war gave back in exchange for
all the blood offered up on their altars.

After so many years he could close his eyes, and it could
be anywhere, here on this mad world, or back in Virginia.
And he could sense as well the differences, the grimness
of purpose, the quiet resignation, the feeling that this was

some sort of final effort. He wondered, if, at this very moment, his rival less than a hundred miles away was engaging in the same exercise, towering eight-foot Bantag warriors marching past. Was he judging his troops as well, knowing that a final cataclysmic battle was coming?

"And what about them? What does he have? What is he feeling at this moment?" Andrew whispered.

"Who, this Jurak?"

Andrew nodded again.

"I rarely saw him, can't recall if I ever even talked to him. He's changed the war though, that's certain. Almost makes me wish we still had Ha'ark."

Escaped Chin slaves confirmed the rumors that Ha'ark had died in front of Roum, most likely murdered by his own followers. For a brief moment Andrew had hoped beyond hope that with the death of the so-called Redeemer, the war would be over, and the Bantags would simply retreat. They had indeed retreated, but it had been to dig in and go on the defensive throughout the waning days of winter and into the spring.

For the first month he was glad of the breathing space, giving them a chance to do repairs, especially to the railroads, evacuate Roum civilians westward to Suzdal, bring up supplies, and get ready.

By the second month he was actually hoping they'd come out of their defensive positions at Capua . . . and by the third month he knew this new leader, Jurak, had changed the nature of the war.

He could sense a difference, a more methodical mind, calculating, not given to rash moves.

"I hate the fact we have to dig him out," Andrew said, Hans nodding in agreement. "It's as if the bastard is sitting there, just begging us to come in."

"Could always count on them attacking up till now," Hans replied, "but you're right, he's waiting for us to kick off the ball."

Andrew grunted. Though Hans had taught him how to chew, he had never really mastered it and was embarrassed as he tried to spit and half choked instead.

Damn, the hordes could always be counted on to attack. The trick then was to find a narrow front, dig in, and tear them up. Jurak had reversed the tables. Capua was a damn fine defensive position, flanked by marshes and heavy forests to the north, more marshes and sharp jagged hills to the south. It was a front fifteen miles wide and fortified to the teeth.

Yet it seemed there was no other way. All indicators were that during the spring Jurak had invested a massive effort on building up his infrastructure, and his factories were churning out guns, ammunition, and supplies most likely at a faster pace than that of the Republic. If Andrew let this pace go on for another six months to a year, Jurak could swarm them under. He had to strike, like it or not.

The last of the swaying columns of infantry drifted past, blue uniforms already turning dirty gray-brown from the dust, men covering their faces with bandannas soaked in water. Jeff emerged out of the dust, cantering back down the line, followed by his guidon bearer. They reined in and saluted.

"I'll see you up at the front, Jeff. Tell Pat not to get overanxious and start the show without me."

"Yes sir. And sir, please do all of us a favor."

"What's that, Jeff?"

"Don't push yourself too hard."

Andrew smiled. How strange the role reversal of late. Prior to the wound he had been the father; now he was feeling like the aging parent whose children were increasingly solicitous about his well-being.

Offering a casual salute, Jeff spurred his mount, shouting for the column to increase its pace. Fifers squealed, picking up the "Battle Cry of Freedom," the song rippling down the ranks, a strange mix as some sang the words in Latin, others in Rus. The column wound past, rank after endless rank, the strange rhythm of rattling canteens and tin cups, the squeaking of leather, the scrape of hobnailed shoes on the hard-packed ground all blending together. More dust swirled up as a battery of three-inch rifles clattered past, the air thick with the smell of horse sweat, leather, tar, and grease, the men riding the caissons waving cheerily.

The dust thickened, obscuring the view. Andrew reached up to wipe his eyes. But it wasn't just the dust; to his surprise he was in tears. It was as if he was watching an ageless ritual for one last time, a sense that here was a final moment, the army going forth one last time, hopefully to victory. But the pageantry, the flags snapping in the rising breeze, the dark columns of infantry, rifles glinting, all of it was the passing of the armies into a dark and unknown land. It was an army of ghostly apparitions, and again he thought of the dream that had consumed him while he had lain in the twilight world that bordered on death, the tens of thousands who had gone ahead, sent there by his orders. How many of these boys were now marching to that destiny? When, dear God, would it ever end?

Jurak Qar Qarth of the Bantag Horde walked along the battlements lining the east bank of the river just above Capua. The midsummer twilight cast long shadows across the river, silhouetting the human fortifications on the opposite side of the river. He peered intently, raising his field glasses to scan the lines, oblivious to the warnings about snipers. An occasional shot fluttered overhead, a round smacking into the embankment above the firing slit, sending down a shower of powdery dirt.

An enemy flyer lazily circled above the lines, waiting in challenge for any of his own airships to come over, an offer he would not take since airships were far too precious to waste in foolish dueling that served no strategic purpose.

He slid back down from the firing slit and looked back at the gathering of umen Qarths, the commanders of his twenty-five divisions committed to this front.

In the hours after his killing of Ha'ark he had assumed that he, too, would die. But led by Zartak, the oldest of the clan Qarths, the council had declared him as the rightful successor, the one of legend sent to redeem the world, while Ha'ark had been a false usurper.

It was a position he had never desired, but the simple fact of the matter was that he either take it or die. He knew that if there had actually been a blood challenge, he would have been lost, but there was still enough of the superstitious fear of him and the others who had come through the Portal of Light, to ensure his acceptance as a demigod sent to save the hordes.

Being stuck on this world, fighting this war, none of it was what he desired, but saddled with the responsibility, he would see it through to its conclusion. Ha'ark had been far more the adventurer, the seeker of glory and power, while he had stayed in the background.

Even on the old world he had not sought the shock of battle. Drafted to serve in the War of the False Pretender, he had spent eight years in the ranks, never rising because such power was not what he wanted. Solitude, a good book, a conversation with some depth to it were far more to his liking, and the others of his unit, though they knew he was dependable in a fight, found little else in common with him.

Regarding the humans of this world he felt no real hatred; the visceral loathing and dread shared by all of the hordes for this hairless race since the start of the rebellion of the cattle was beyond him in any true emotional sense. On an intellectual level he fully understood the fundamental core of this war; it was a fight for racial survival. After all that had happened only one race could expect to survive, while the other would have to be destroyed. That is what he now fought for, survival. He was of the race of the hordes, they had made him their leader, and he had to ensure that this world would be safe for them.

He smiled, remembering, a refrain from a poem from his old world:

"Those I fight I do not hate, those I defend I do not love."

His gaze scanned the umen chieftains. Barbarians, all of them barbarians, clad in black leather, human finger bones strung as necklaces, one of them casually drinking fermented horse milk from a gold-encrusted human skull. Yet they were now his, perhaps the most capable warriors he had ever seen, razor-sharp scimitars that could cut a human in two dangling from waist belts, more than one of them carrying revolving pistols, a few with carbine rifles casually slung over their shoulders.

All of them were scarred, most sporting old saber slashes across cheeks, brow, and forearms, reminders of a simpler and happier age when the enemy were the other hordes and war was the sport of warriors and not a question of survival or total annihilation. Many bore the ritual cuts on forearms or across foreheads, slashes that were self-inflicted at the start of a battle in order to lend a more fearsome appearance. Several were missing limbs, hands, arms blown off or amputated.

Zartak, the eldest, was legendary throughout the Horde, a rider of four circlings of the planet, eighty years or more of age. At Rocky Hill, it was said that his left leg had been blown off just below the knee and he had not even flinched. After wrapping a tourniquet around his thigh he continued to lead his umen on the last desperate charge to take the hill, and then, in spite of the injury that normally would have killed someone half his age, he actually survived.

The ancient warrior looked straight at him then, and nodded. Strange, Jurak thought, he had often heard of the ability some claimed to be able to sense and probe the thoughts of others. Ha'ark had claimed the skill, but lied. Zartak had it, though, and in the months since becoming Qar Qarth Jurak had felt an increasing bond with this ancient one who had seen the world from one end to the other four times over.

That must indeed have been a dreamworld, the endless ride eastward toward the rising sun. The daily cycle of rising, mounting, following the slow pace of the wheeled yurts, herding the millions of horses that were the wealth of the clans, the arrival at yet another city of the cattle, there to exact tribute of gold, silver, cunningly wrought weapons, and the flesh of four-legged cattle and the delicacy of the two-legged variety as well. Then moving on the next day, riding forever, breaking the tedium by raiding northward into the realm of the Merki Horde, or to the far north and the domains of the dead Tugars.

But Keane had changed all that. Keane and his Yankees from another world.

Those changes were spreading like a plague around the world faster than a Horde could ride, and if he, his race were to survive, there was but one answer now: total annihilation. This was a war of no quarter. Either the rebellion and this human dream died, or within a generation not a single rider of the hordes would still be alive. They would be hunted by the victors, with machines ever more cunning and complex. The memory of the thousands of years of the Endless Ride, of the joy of the Riders, of the misery of the cattle, could be forgotten by neither side, and the time of reckoning had come.

Jurak had promised them that when victory was complete, when the last of the Rus and Roum were dead, and for good measure the Cartha, Chin, and Nippon were systematically slaughtered as well, so that there was no living memory of what happened, then the Golden Age would return. The machines would be destroyed. Bow, lance, and scimitar would again rule, and again they would ride eastward, resuming the endless journey of their ancestors.

He knew the promise was a lie. Such knowledge once released could not be returned. As he gazed silently at those gathered around him, he could sense that change already. Many of the Qarths, the clan and umen commanders, had already started to adapt themselves, speaking of enfilading fire, advancing by fire and cover, the use of artillery for suppressive fire. They understood how one locomotive could move in a single day what once required ten thousand horses, and the advantages of that. No, the machines would triumph in the end, and in a way the thought pleased him, for he knew it was a vital necessity.

For if Keane and his Yankees had come to this world via the Portals of Light bearing the knowledge that they did, it meant that somewhere in this universe there was a world of cattle who had mastered steam. The natural progression of such things would lead them forward to more, and greater, discoveries. Eventually, as well, they would discover that their world was studded with the lost Portals of Light left behind by his own fallen race, and how such gates could be used to span the universe.

No, there would come a day when more humans might very well arrive with yet more advanced weapons, and on that day his own race must be ready or, better still, rediscover the portals for themselves and use them.

That was but part of the reason why he had moved so aggressively throughout the last of winter and the spring to stop offensive action, to build up reserves, to spend more on the making of more factories and newer weapons. With the millions of slaves at his disposal, as distasteful as that was, he would outproduce the Yankees and then destroy them.

But such musings were not for now. There was still this war to be won. It was fitting that the Qar Qarth, the new Redeemer, have moments of silence, as if praying to the ancestors, but they waited for his pronouncements.

"You are right, Zartak," he said, finally breaking the

silence, "they are building up for an attack. New gun emplacements, more sniper fire, the report of troop trains carrying ironclads."

Zartak, who would be known as a chief of staff on his old world, grunted an acknowledgment. Jurak looked at the old one, mane nearly gone to white, balanced precariously on his peg leg, and felt a bond of affection. Here was one who during the long months after the defeat before Roum had educated the new Qar Qarth as to the ways of the world, the history of the Bantag clan and of all the hordes that rode the world in the north, or who sailed the great seas of the southern hemisphere.

"I know the inactivity of the past months has weighed heavily upon all of you," Jurak continued, "as it has weighed upon me. Victory was within our grasp before Roum and lost in the blinking of an eye for but one foolish mistake, the failure to protect our transport for supplies.

"That is why we have waited for so long. We have built those supplies back, but we have done more, occupying half of the lands that were once of the cattle of Roum. This is causing them to starve, and sooner or later they will be forced to attack, and it will be here."

"Directly across the river?" Tukkanger, commander of the elite umen of the white horse, asked. "Even we have learned the folly of that."

"Yet they will come. The river is low, fordable now for much of its length." And he pointed back west. The river, the only barrier separating the two lines dug in on opposite banks six hundred yards apart, was reduced to a muddy trickle.

"Keane must attack; it is the only front available. Their southern pocket leads but to open steppe, and without a rail line advancing behind them, they cannot support an operation. We, in turn, are building a rail line across the narrows between the two seas to support our efforts against Tyre. That city has become a trap for them, one which they now cannot abandon for fear that we will use it as a base once our rail line is completed. Yet for them to attack us there would be a useless thrust into empty land.

"The path up through the mountains where they flanked us last time is now secured and heavily fortified by us. No, they must cross the river here. He will seek a battle of annihilation, a final desperate lunge to break our strength and our morale."

There was no sense in explaining the political pressure to these warriors, though he and Zartak had spoken of it often enough. Part of his strategy, in fact the major part, was to try and drive a wedge between the alliances of Roum and the Rus, to emphasize their military helplessness.

"They must take back this land which belonged to the Roum or lose face. So we will let him attack; he will fail. Then, when the time is right, we shall attack in turn. And this time, I promise you, we will not stop until Roum, and beyond that Suzdal and all of Rus, are in flames."

He said the words not as some grandiose vision or prophecy, but rather as a simple statement of the campaign to come, and those around him nodded one by one in agreement.

This would be a new kind of war for them, he realized. They had been bloodied in the long campaign all the way from the Great Sea to the gates of Roum, learning how all things had changed. Now they would see it in action. All he needed was for Keane to step into the trap, and in his heart he knew that Keane was about to take that step.

Varinna Ferguson, widow of the famed inventor who had done so much to ensure the survival of the Republic, walked through the vast hangar, gazing up in wonder at the air machine that filled the cavernous hall. This machine was special, with the name *Ferguson* painted on the port side, just behind the pilot's cabin. Work crews were busy putting the final coat of lacquer on the double-weaved canvas of the wings. Tomorrow the machine would be ready for its first rollout.

"You checking this one off, too?"

She looked over at Vincent Hawthorne, chief of staff of the Army of the Republic, and smiled. He was directly responsible for all ordnance development, and thus her boss. But the relationship of Ferguson's widow to the Republic was a strange one. She held no official rank or title. As she was heir to the memory of the great inventor, all showed her deference, for in the final months of his life she was the one who increasingly served as his eyes, his ears, and finally even his voice. It was as if some part of him still survived through her.

What few had grasped was just how unique their pairing had been. The attraction wasn't just that of a shy eccentric inventor for a beautiful slave in the house of Marcus, former Proconsul of Roum and now the vice president of the Republic. The beauty was long gone, and she was no longer even conscious of the frozen scar tissue that made her face a mask, or the twisted hands that still cracked open and bled after hours of writing. It had always been something more than the simple attraction, as if Chuck had sensed the brilliant light of the mind within. When he had first started to share his drawings, his plans, his daydreams with her, she found she could strangely visualize them in their entirety, the parts on the sheets of paper springing into three-dimensional form, fitting together, interlocking, working or not working.

Though she might not have the leaps of imagination he did, there was within her the concrete ability to carry out what he had visualized, to sense when to reject the impractical and when to mold the practical into life. Only a few, the inner circle of Chuck's young apprentices and assistants, fully realized just how much it was Varinna running things toward the end. She had the natural mind of an administrator who should be paired with a dreamer. Her dreamer was dead, but his notes, his sketchbooks, his frantic last months of scribblings were still alive, lovingly stored away, and she would make their contents real.

He had recognized that in her, and in so doing had not just been her lover but her liberator as well. In any other world she would have lived her life out as a servant in a house of nobility, a mistress most likely in her youth, as she had in fact been to Marcus, and then married off to another slave or underling when the prime of beauty began to fade. That, indeed, had been her fate, but instead she married a free man, a Yankee who had loved her for what she was, and she knew there would never be another like him in her life.

She looked over at Vincent and smiled, suddenly aware that she had allowed her thoughts to drift again. Even after all these years, he was still slightly embarrassed around her, unable to forget the day they had first met, when a very young Colonel Vincent Hawthorne had come to Roum as a military attaché and Marcus had casually suggested that she make sure that the guest was comfortable in every way that a guest of a Proconsul should be.

The young Quaker had been in a panic over her advances and now, with the memory of Chuck, she was glad it had turned out as it did, for though Chuck was able to deal with her relationship to Marcus, there was something about the way the Yankees thought about sex that might have made difficulties between her husband and Vincent if anything had indeed finally happened.

"What did you say?" she asked.

"This machine. Is it getting checked off for the front?"

She shook her head.

Vincent looked around for a moment at the vast hangar. Over a hundred feet long and forty feet high it was like a cathedral for the new age of air, high timber-vaulted ceiling, skylights open to admit as much light as possible for dozens of workers lining the scaffolding, carefully inspecting every double-stitched seam, searching for the slightest leak of hydrogen from the four gasbags inside the hull. It had been Varinna's idea to mix in a small amount of pungent coal gas with the hydrogen for this test so that the smell would be a tip off of a leak. She watched as one of the inspectors called over a crew master who leaned over, sniffed a seam, and then gave the go-ahead to lacquer on a patch.

"Let's step outside where we can talk," Vincent suggested, and she nodded an agreement.

The evening was fair, the first hint of a cooling breeze coming up from the Inland Sea to the south, rippling the tops of the trees, and with the sleeve of her white-linen dress, she wiped the sweat from her brow.

The crew down at number seven hangar was carefully guiding its machine, E class, ship number forty-two, out of its hangar, a crew chief swearing profusely as a dozen boys worked the guidelines attached to the starboard side, keeping the ship steady against the faint southerly breeze. As the tail cleared the hangar they cast off, letting the 110-foot-long airship pivot around, pointing its nose into the breeze. Carefully they guided the ship over to a mooring post, in the open field where ships number thirty-five through forty-one were anchored as well. The production run of the last four weeks, all of them going through the final fitting out, engine checks, test flights, and crew training before being sent up to the front.

She had nearly ten thousand people working for her. An entire mill had been set up just for the weaving of silk and canvas, then stitching the panels together on the new treadle sewing machines. Hundreds more worked in the bamboo groves, selecting, harvesting, and splitting the wood that would serve as the wicker frames for the airships.

Canvas, silk, and framing came together in the cavernous sheds to make the 110-foot-long ships, while in other workshops the bi-level wings were fashioned. From the engine works the lightweight caloric steam engines were produced, brought to the airfield, mounted to the wings, hooked into the fuel lines for kerosene, and mounted with propellers.

Only within the last six months had one of her young apprentices, after examining the remains of a captured Bantag ship, announced that the propellers should not be made like ship's propellers, but would work far better if shaped like the airfoils Chuck had designed for the wings. The new designs, though difficult to make, had resulted in a significant increase in performance.

Finally, with framework completed, wings mounted and folded up against the side of the ship, forward cab, bomber's position underneath, and topside gunner positions mounted, tail and elevators added on, and all the controls and cables correctly mounted, it was time to gas up the ship.

The center bag was hot air, hooked into the exhaust from the four caloric engines mounted on the wings. Forward and aft were the hydrogen gasbags, filled from the dangerous mix of sulfuric acid and zinc shavings, cooked in a lead-lined vat, mixed with a bit of coal gas for scent.

Ten thousand laborers produced eight Eagles and four of the smaller Hornets per month. And the average life expectancy was but ten missions. She wondered, given the current state of affairs, how much longer she'd be allowed such resources, yet in her heart she sensed that it was there, not with the vast arrays of army corps and artillery, that the fate of the Republic would be decided.

All of this from my husband's mind, she thought with a

wistful smile. *Ten years ago I would have thought it mad wizardry, or the product of gods to fly thus.*

Of all of Chuck's projects it was flight that had captivated him the most, inspiring his greatest leaps of creative talent and research. The Eagle class airships were the culmination of that effort. With a crew of four and three Gatling guns, it could range over nearly five hundred miles and go nearly forty miles in an hour.

A low humming caught her attention, and she looked up to see a Hornet single-engine ship diving in at a sharp angle, leveling out at less than fifty feet and winging across the field, the evening ship returning from patrol of the western steppes on the far side of the Neiper, keeping a watch over the wandering bands from the old Merki Horde. They weren't enough to pose a truly serious threat, but they were sufficient in number to tie down a corps of infantry and a brigade of cavalry to make sure they didn't raid across the river.

The Hornet banked up sharply, the pilot showing off for the audience on the ground, and Varinna winced slightly at the boyish display. The fault with the rear-mounted engine had killed half a dozen pilots before it was figured out, and though the problem had been solved, she wished the pilots were a little less reckless.

Out in the field where the seven new Eagles were moored, ground crews were double-checking the tie-downs for the evening and getting ready to settle in for the night in their camp, each crew of twenty-five sleeping in tents arranged around the mooring poles. They had to be ready to react instantly, day or night, to any shift in the wind or weather. Far more ships had been lost to thunderstorms than had ever been shot down by the Bantags.

Another airship, a somewhat battered Eagle—number twelve, a veteran of the winter campaign and sent back for refitting—came in, banking erratically, a cadet pilot most likely at the controls. She watched anxiously as it turned to line up on the vast open landing field of several dozen acres.

"The boy's crabbing, not watching the wind vane," Vincent announced.

Varinna nodded, saying nothing, as one wing dipped, almost scraped, then straightened back up, the boy touching down hard, bouncing twice, then finally holding the ground. She could well imagine the chewing out he'd get from Feyodor, her assistant now in command of the pilot-training school, made worse by the withering sarcasm of the crew chief for the machine, who would make it a point of stalking along with the pilot for the postflight checkoff, blaming the novice for every crack and dent the machine had ever suffered since the day it had first emerged from a hangar.

"How many more machines can you have up within the next five days?" Vincent asked.

"For what?"

"Varinna, you know it really isn't your place to ask. I'm ordered to send up every available machine, and that's what I'm out here to check on."

"I know the plan as well as you do," she replied sharply.

Vincent started to sputter and, quickly smiling, she held up an appeasing hand.

"Colonel Keane shared it with me when he was here in the city last week. But even before then I knew about it."

"I don't even want to ask." Vincent sighed, gesturing back to the west, where the distant spires of the cathedral in Suzdal stood out sharply against the late-afternoon sky. "That damn city is a sieve when it comes to keeping a secret."

"And that's just one of the reasons I don't think the attack should be launched in front of Capua."

She could see her statement had caught his attention, and he had learned long ago not to dismissively wave off her opinions. That was another thing Chuck had taught her. When you prove yourself right on the big issues, you can get away with one hell of a lot. It was Chuck's insistence on continuing the rocket-launcher program that had saved everyone's hide at Hispania, and that little feat had been performed in direct contradiction to orders.

"So go on, madam general, explain," Vincent pressed.

She bristled for a second, then realized that he wasn't being sarcastic and was in fact listening respectfully.

"Capua is so damn obvious that this new chief of theirs must know it as well. For that reason alone I think we should avoid it."

"Don't you think Andrew and I have argued out that

point a dozen times in the last three months?" Vincent replied, a slight flash of temper in his voice.

"Ah, so you don't agree either then?"

He flushed, his eyes turning away for a moment, and she nodded slowly. Vincent always had been too transparent. But now she knew she was in.

"I've talked with every pilot who's come back here throughout the spring. One of them, Stasha Igorovich, told me that he flew a reconnaissance flight just two weeks ago and reported signs of numerous land ironclads having been moved into the forests north of town."

"I read that report, and you know then as well as I do that when Andrew sent up two Hornets the following morning to check on these tracks this eagle-eyed pilot claimed he saw, there was no sign of them."

"The Bantag are learning concealment, Vincent. The same as we have." She pointed back up toward the all-important offices and machine shops for the Ordnance Department. The once attractive whitewashed buildings had been covered with a coating of dirty brown paint. Netting with woven strips of green-and-brown cloth had been draped over the buildings so that from the air they were all but invisible.

"Need I remind you that we got the idea for that netting from the Bantag? Yet another thing this Ha'ark and his companions most likely brought over from their own world. In fact, I suspect that from the air we are far more visible than they are. And if so, the Bantag must be blind not to have noticed the buildup along the Capua front, the number of guns moved up, the dozen pontoon bridges and hundreds of canvas boats, rocket launchers, all of the equipment needed for a direct assault across a river. They're waiting for us."

"Maybe they are, but the war has to be decided, and decided now. If we can only come to grips with them, beat them on their own field, we'll turn the tide. Damn it all, woman, they're still parked less than one hundred miles from Roum. We have to get them out of there now."

"Or if we don't Roum leaves the Republic? Is that the sole motivation now for this attack?"

"Or the Republic, or what we want to call the Republic, will leave Roum." Vincent sighed, wearily shaking his head.

"Varinna, you know as well as I do this country's finished. One more winter of war, and we fall apart. Even if we win now, it'll be a near-run thing at best."

Vincent looked away again, watching for a moment as the pilot who had so clumsily landed endured a good chewing out from Feyodor while the crew chief pointed at what was most likely a broken wheel strut and exploded into a torrent of swearing.

"Tell me where we have shortages right now," Vincent snapped, looking back at her.

She said nothing.

"Where do I start then? Fulminate of mercury for percussion caps? Our source of quicksilver is playing out, six more months and we might have to start rationing cartridges, or go all the way back to flintlock guns. How about silk for these airships? We're out. Oil for kerosene, the Bantags overran the last oil well eleven days ago. Sure we can substitute coal oil, but that's just one more example. And men ..."

His voice trailed off for a moment.

"How many hundred thousands dead? If we had five corps more, even three corps, I'd break the back of this war in a month. But even if I did have the extra men, where the hell would I get fifty thousand more uniforms, cartridge boxes, tents, smallpox inoculations, and rations for a summer's campaign, let alone the rifles and eighty cartridges per man for one afternoon's good fight?"

Again he sighed, extending his hands in a gesture of infinite weariness.

"One of the things I'm supposed to order is the reduction of the workforce for the airships."

"What?"

"You heard me right. You and I played a good little game of doctoring the books, but some of our congressmen finally figured it out and hit the ceiling. They want the resources put into artillery or land ironclads."

She waved her hand dismissively.

"Taking one for the other is illogical. Those people are trained for this job. We'll lose production on both ends if we switch them off."

"Well, they want five thousand of them transferred before the month is out. Sent to the fields if need be to try and harvest more food. Lord knows we're falling short of that as well."

She wearily shook her head.

"Varinna, we can't keep what we have in the field much longer. That's why Andrew's making this lunge."

"They must be in the same boat as we are," she replied.

"Maybe so, but then again maybe not. Remember, they have slaves, millions, tens of millions if need be, spread all across this world. I think the newcomers, Ha'ark and the others, brought with them the understanding of how to harness that labor to their own ends. So they outproduce us, and in the end they overwhelm us. Our only hope was to kill so damn many of the Bantag warriors that they'd finally turn aside. We destroyed a good third of their army during the campaign of last autumn and winter, but it wasn't enough."

"So destroy their supplies."

Vincent smiled, and for an instant he caused her temper to flare, the dismissive look reminiscent of ones far too many men would show when she first stepped forward to make a suggestion. The smile finally disappeared.

"Sorry, Varinna, it's just that every damn senator and member of the cabinet, and even the president comes at me with their war-winning suggestion."

"I'm not one of them. I was Ferguson's wife first, then I was his assistant, then his partner, and finally in the end I did it myself, including holding him while he died."

"I know. I'm sorry."

She lowered her head. She didn't let it show much anymore, the memory of the pain. With an effort, she forced it aside.

"To go all the way back to your original question, I could force ten more ships into the air and have them up at the front for the offensive."

"But you don't want to."

"They'll most likely all get shot down the first day. You saw the way that boy just landed. I agree with Jack Petracci that these ships need to be used en masse. We saw that last month when forty of the Bantag machines bombed Roum and sank three supply transports in the harbor."

"And they lost half their machines in the process," Vincent replied. "Not much of a trade-off in my book."

"Still, it showed what could be done. But there's no sense in having the mass if the poor dumb fools fly straight into enemy fire. After all the work it takes to build one of these, sending it up with a boy who's got twenty, maybe twenty-five hours of flying time is suicide. Hold these machines back from this fight. Give us time to train more pilots. Twenty more Eagles and Hornets won't make a difference."

"I have my orders."

"For flightworthy machines. Listen to me in this, and while you're at it keep those bastards from Congress and their investigating committees out of my way. I'm telling you, my friend, after the attack on Capua, these ships might be the deciding factor for this war."

"After Capua?"

"You'll see, Vincent. You'll see."

Chapter Two

Pulling aside the blanket that served as a door, Andrew stepped down into the dank confines of the bombproof that doubled as headquarters for the Capua Front.

A smoky coal oil lamp suspended over the map table by a piece of telegraph wire tied to an overhead beam provided the only illumination. He looked over at the pendulum clock tacked to the broken lid of a caisson and leaned against the opposite wall . . . 3:10 in the morning.

The long twilight of dawn was just beginning, and through one of the view slits he could see a tinge of scarlet to the northeast, silhouetting the Bantag earthworks on the opposite bank of the river. The fact that he had managed to get any sleep at all surprised him, but ever since the wounding near this very same spot six months ago, he found that he tired easily and needed far more rest. The ability to get through a sleepless night and then fight a daylong pitched battle was gone for him.

Going over to a smoking kettle resting atop a leaky woodstove, he poured a cup of tea and sipped the scalding drink. He looked over at Pat, Hans, and Marcus, who were huddled over the map debating some minor detail.

The fact that the three were thus engaged was a clear indicator that they were nervous. The plan had been laid over two months ago. Everyone was in place; there was no changing it now. All that was left was the one word of command that would set the complex assault into motion. He had learned ages ago that there came a point in an operation where it was best to step back and let those farther down the chain take over. A nervous commander, at such a moment, was much more a burden than a help.

Andrew put down his cup and moved to join his friends. "Anything new?"

"There was a skirmish down by the river a half hour ago, a Bantag patrol trying to slip across," Pat announced.

"And I think they're on to it," Hans replied. "Not just this patrol, the whole thing; they're on to it, they want us to try this crossing."

"And you want me to call it all off?"

Hans said nothing.

"Damn it, Hans," Pat replied, "we've been stuck on this line all spring. My God, man, if we don't break this stalemate, we'll be here till Judgment Day. We break his back here, today, and we end this standoff and end this damn war."

Hans wearily shook his head and looked up at Andrew with bloodshot eyes.

"Son, you're making this decision out of political concerns rather than for military objectives."

"The president ordered it," Andrew replied, his gaze fixed on Marcus.

Marcus stared straight at him and was silent. Andrew knew the Roum vice president was fully committed to this assault. The Bantag were still in possession of some of the most fertile lands of Roum, a million of his people were displaced, and he wanted the land back.

Marcus's gaze shifted toward Hans.

"I remember Andrew once saying that war was an extension of politics."

"My God, I've got a Roum proconsul quoting Clausewitz to me," Hans groaned.

"Who the hell is Clausewitz?" Pat asked. "Does he live here?"

Andrew could not help but chuckle, then, more soberly, "This war transcends politics."

"Maybe externally," Marcus replied, "as far as the Bantags go. But internally, for the Republic, it has become an ever-present concern: Which one of the two states will abandon the other first?"

"Not while I'm alive," Andrew replied, jaw firmly set, his voice gone quiet.

"Nor I, my friend, you know better than that. But the people of Roum want their land back, and this morning we're going to get it, and drive those bastards from the field. You, I, all of us here have planned this battle for months, down to the finest detail. I fear the only thing we might be lacking here is the nerve to see it through."

Hans stiffened and leaned forward over the table.

"I can't believe you would think that of me," Hans snapped.

Marcus extended his hand in a conciliatory gesture.

"I'm not doubting your courage, old friend. We've planned our best, now let us trust in the gods and in the courage of our men."

Andrew swept the group with his gaze.

"It goes as planned," he announced, and without waiting for comment he left the underground room, finding it far too claustophobic.

Ascending the steps of the bunker, he stepped onto the grassy knoll under which the headquarters was concealed. A faint breeze was stirring from the north, cool air coming down out of the hills and distant forests. Sighing, he sat down, kicking up the scent of sage with his boots. *Strange smell; never knew it up in Maine,* he thought. Hans had mentioned it, though, saying it reminded him of his days out on the prairie before the Civil War.

He plucked up a handful of the thick coarse grass, crushing it in his hand, letting the pungent smell fill his lungs. Leaning back, he looked up at the stars, the Great Wheel, wondering as he always did if one of the specks of light might be that of home.

So strange, home. Maine, the Republic, the memory of peace. Even in the midst of a civil war, everyone knew that there would be a day when it would come to an end, when both sides, North and South, would go home to their farms, villages, towns, and pick up the threads of their lives. Perhaps that was some of the uniqueness of America, the sense that war was an anomaly, an interruption of what was normal, a tragic third act of a play that had to be waded through so there could be the final resolution and running down of the curtain. Then the audience could get up, go home, and resume their lives.

He knew so much of the old world was not that way. Strange, though he had never been there, this place made him think of Russia. It wasn't just the Rus, descendants of early medieval Russians, that he had found here and forged a nation out of. No, it was the land itself, the impenetrable northern forests, and out here the vast open steppes, the endless dome of the sky, the scent of sage and dried grass, or the cold driving wind of winter. *This is what Russia must be like,* he thought. The history, the same as well. A land of ceaseless bloodletting, of vast armies sweeping across the dusty ocean of land. War, when fought, was with implacable fury, no quarter asked or expected! Here it was the norm, the ever-present reality.

He wondered yet again if his dream of the Republic could ever take root in this land. The necessity of war and survival had united Yankee, Rus, and Roum together, at least for the moment, but would that hold if they ever won and drove the barbarians back? Could the Republic survive peace?

He heard someone approaching, but didn't bother to turn. The limping stride and smell of tobacco indicator enough of who it was. Hans settled down by his side with a groaning sigh, reached over, and, like Andrew, plucked up a handful of sage, rubbing it between his hands, inhaling the scent.

"Long way from Kansas to here," Hans announced.

Andrew said nothing, knees drawn up under his chin as he looked off to the east. The light was slowly rising, only a matter of minutes now. He heard the clatter of a rifle dropping, a muffled curse, and looked to his left; down in the ravine below a column of troops waited, more felt than seen, the hissed warning of a sergeant barely audible as he tore into the fumble-fingered soldier. At the head of the ravine engineering troops had positioned bridging pontoons and dozens of the flimsy canvas assault rafts. He couldn't see them, but he knew they were there; the men of the 9th Corps had rehearsed this assault a score of times along the Tiber over the last two months.

To the right he heard the hissing of a steam engine, one of the land ironclads, Timokin's regiment, deployed in the next ravine. He wondered if the sound carried across the river, so still was the air. *We should have gone yesterday,* he thought. *The fog cloaking the river was thicker then. There's still time to call it off, wait for fog, rain . . . maybe we should go an hour earlier, in the complete dark.*

"Nervous, son?"

"Huh?" Andrew looked over at his old friend.

"I am."

Startled, Andrew said nothing. Hans was always the rock, the pillar; not once had he ever expressed fear when battle was nigh. Andrew remembered Antietam, his first fight, waiting in the predawn darkness of the East Woods. He had been so frightened that after trying to choke down a breakfast of hardtack and coffee, he had crept off to vomit. But until five minutes before the assault went in, Hans had made a great display of sitting with his back to an elm tree, fast asleep. The old sergeant latter confided that it had all been an act, he had been wide-awake, heart racing like a trip-hammer, but figured that such studied indifference was a better tonic to the boys than going around whispering nervous encouragements.

"You don't think it will work?" Andrew asked.

Hans looked over at him. "We did plan it together, but a frontal assault across a river, Andrew? Risky business. I fear at best it's an even chance. From what little we've figured of Jurak we know he's damn smart. He must have figured this one out as well, knew we'd finally have to come in frontally."

"And you have another suggestion," Andrew asked, trying to mask the note of testiness in his voice.

Hans put his hand out, letting it rest on Andrew's shoulder.

"Responsibility of command, Andrew. At Gettysburg you held when I would have pulled out. It shattered the regiment but saved the old First Corps. You led the assault at Cold Harbor when I would have told Grant to go to hell and ordered the boys to lie down. Maybe you've got more nerve than me."

Startled, Andrew said nothing.

"I'm getting far too old for this." Hans sighed, taking off his hat to run his fingers through his sweat-soaked wisps of gray. "There always seems to be one more campaign, though, always another campaign."

"But there are times we do love it," Andrew whispered. "Not the killing, not the moments like this one with the doubt and fear. But there are moments, the quiet nights, the army encamped around you, the moment of relief when you know you've won, the pride in the eyes of those around you."

Surprised Hans looked over at him and nodded. "If this is the last campaign, what becomes of us then?"

Andrew chuckled softly. "I wish."

"Your instinct is telling you don't attack this morning, isn't it?"

"Yes."

"Then listen to it."

Andrew sighed, "We've been over it before, Hans. We can't flank, we can't break out from the southern pocket, they won't attack. We have to end the stalemate. The president ordered this assault. And remember, we planned this one, and all the time we planned it we figured we could pull it off."

"So why the cold feet at this last minute?" Hans asked.

Andrew looked at his friend.

"You first. Why you?"

Hans sighed. "Gut feeling that they're on to us over there. That this is what they want us to do and fully expect us to do."

Andrew plucked up another twist of grass, taking pleasure in the scent of sage.

"There are no alternatives now," Andrew said.

"What Vincent suggested, it is a thought."

Andrew shook his head.

"Maybe six months from now, with four times the amount of equipment to even hope that it'd work. Right now it would be nothing more than a mad suicidal gesture. Vincent's dreaming if he thinks we could deliver the killing blow that way. There simply isn't enough to do it."

"It's because you know I would do it—that I'd have to go. That's what's stopping you from considering it."

Andrew looked over at his friend in the shadows.

"Hans," and he hesitated for a moment, "if I thought that sacrificing you would end this war, would save your child, my children, I'd have to order it."

Hans laughed softly.

"I'm not sure if you're just a damn good liar or you really mean that. Strange though, I do hope you're not lying. We're soldiers, Andrew, we all know what the job means, and I hope that from the beginning I taught you the sacrifice required of command, even when it comes to your closest friend."

"I sacrificed my brother, didn't I?"

Hans said nothing in reply.

Andrew dropped the fistful of grass, reached out, and let his hand rest on Hans's shoulder for a moment, then shyly let it fall away.

"So why the butterflies in your stomach now?" Hans asked, shifting the subject.

"I'm not sure, and that's what troubles me. At Cold Harbor I knew it was suicide but I went in because it was an order. I knew if I refused they'd take the Thirty-Fifth from me and the boys would have to go anyhow. I saw Chamberlain do the same damn thing two weeks later at Petersburg. He knew it was senseless, but he led his brigade in anyhow."

"And he damn near got killed doing it if I remember correct."

Andrew nodded. "It's just that this battle is different. Most all of them were either meeting engagements like Rocky Hill, or we were on the defensive and well dug in, like Hispania or Suzdal. Now they're the ones dug in, and you're right, I have to assume that Jurak has this one figured.

"It's more than that though. We both know we're all but finished. Its becoming evident that Jurak is outproducing us. You saw those reports Bill Webster sent us from the Treasury and Vincent from the Ordnance Department."

Hans spat a stream of tobacco juice and grunted.

"They'd change their song if the Bantag were at the gate."

Andrew shook his head.

"We're running out, Hans. The pace of production, it's exhausted the nation. The same thing we saw with the rebs by the autumn of '64. There are too many supply bottlenecks, too many men in the army, too many people making weapons, not enough making the basics for living, and a million people from Roum driven off the land. In short, we're collapsing."

"And that's your reason for attacking here and now?"

Andrew leaned forward, resting his chin on his drawn-up knees.

"No, Hans. I think I'd have enough sense to stop it if I understood that was the only reason for attacking. But

Marcus is right, we have to do something. The people of Roum have to know that the Rus will fight to help them take back their land. So there is the politics. We have to find a way, as well, to end this war before we either collapse or Kal succumbs to the pressure that's growing in the Senate to accept Jurak's offer for a negotiated settlement."

"If Kal accepts that, he deserves to be shot," Hans snapped.

"He's the president," Andrew replied, a sharp edge to his voice.

"And you wrote the bloody Constitution. So change it. I tell you I smell something in this."

"Are you accusing Kal?"

"No, damn it, of course not. If anything he's a rotten president because he's too damned honest and simple."

"We used to say that about Lincoln, but under that prairie-lawyer exterior there was a damn shrewd politician."

Hans nodded, spitting a stream of tobacco juice and wiping the bottom of his chin with the back of his hand.

"We have to end this war now," Andrew announced, shifting the topic away from matters that he felt bordered on treason. Hans was right; he had indeed written the Constitution for the Republic. But once that Constitution had been accepted by the people of Rus and Roum, it had gone out of his grasp, and it now must bind him as it bound any other citizen who swore his allegiance to it, and thereby accepted its protection.

He stood up. Raising the field glasses that hung from his neck, he turned his attention to the opposite shore. The eastern bank was lower than the western, the terrain flat, not cut by the ravines of the western bank. Jurak should have drawn his line farther back, not here. It was almost as if he chose a weaker position to tempt them in. Andrew could see the outlines of the fortifications lining the opposite bank.

Wisps of smoke, morning cook fires, rose straight up in the still air. Again the shiver of a thought. The monthly moon feast had been two days ago, the cries of the victims echoing across the river throughout the night. He wondered if what was left was now roasting on those fires.

Originally he had planned the attack to go in then, but it was too obvious a night for them to strike, and, besides, the bastards usually stayed awake throughout the feast night and might sense something.

There's still time to stop, the inner voice whispered. The battlements along the eastern bank were clearly silhouetted. This was the precious moment, the west bank draped in darkness, the east bank highlighted. He heard footsteps behind him . . . it was Pat, followed by Marcus.

"Andrew, it's three-thirty."

Andrew looked at Hans, almost wishing he could defer the decision. Hans was staring at him.

Andrew lowered his head, whispering a silent prayer. Finally he raised his gaze again.

"Do it."

Jack Petracci, circling five miles back from the front, took a deep breath, not sure if he was glad that the moment had finally come, or dreaded the fact that the show was really on.

"There's the signal flare," he announced to Theodor, his copilot. "Make sure the others follow."

Banking his aerosteamer over to a due easterly heading, he scanned to port and starboard. The formation appeared to be following. Leaning over, he blew into the speaker tubes.

"Romulus, Boris, report."

"One airship, turning back," Romulus announced, "think it's number twenty-two. Rest are forming up."

Better than expected, Jack thought; forty heavy aerosteamers and thirty of the new Hornet single-engine escorts, it would be the largest air strike ever launched, the dream of more than five months of planning. Not exactly the way he wanted it done, but it would prove once and for all that the tremendous investment in airpower was worth it.

More flares were soaring up along the front line, marking the beginning of the assault, slowly rising heavenward in the still morning, catching the scarlet light of dawn. Seconds later sheets of fire erupted, climbing rapidly and filling the sky with curtains of flame and smoke as more than three thousand rockets thundered across the river, smothering the Bantag in an inferno of explosions. Long seconds later the dull concussion washed over him, clearly audible above the howl of his ship's engines and the wind racing through the rigging.

Another volley rose up, several errant rockets twisting, corkscrewing back toward his formation, which was now less than two miles from the front. The shells detonated in the air, leaving white puffs of smoke drifting.

He was now over the rear lines of the fight.

Long snakelike columns of troops were below, black against the landscape, waiting to head down into the ravines lacing the riverbank, which were the assault paths to the front. Pontoon crews were already out into the river, floating their barges into place, dropping anchor lines, while hundreds of assault craft, water foaming about them as the men paddled furiously, were already approaching the far shore.

It looked like the first wave was making it, men swarming out of the boats, struggling up the muddy embankments. Mortar shells were impacting on the river, foaming geysers erupting.

"Colonel, sir?" It was Romulus, his top gunner.

"Go ahead."

"Formation is spreading out as planned, sir."

"Fine, now keep a sharp eye for their ships up there, son."

He caught a glimpse of half a dozen of his airships breaking formation, turning to the northeast, and was startled as four Hornets passed directly overhead, moving fast, forging straight ahead to penetrate deep into the rear, ready to interdict any Bantag airships that dared to venture up.

They were over the river, thickening clouds of dirty yellow-gray smoke obscuring the view.

"There's our target!" Theodor shouted, pointing off to starboard. Jack picked it out, an earthen fort on a low rise that jutted out into the river. It looked just like the sand table model of the front that he and his force had spent days studying and planning over. Smoke was rising up from the position; the rocket barrage had hit it hard, but he could see where dark-clad Bantags were pouring into the position from a trench connecting the battery position to the rear. Two fieldpieces were already at work, spraying the river with bursts of canister.

"Hang on, boys. Here we go!" Jack shouted, as he

pushed the stick forward, the heavy four-engine craft rapidly picking up speed. Slipping out of his seat, Theodor dropped down below Jack's legs, fumbling to open the steam cock to the forward Gatling gun.

A dark shadow slipped overhead, and, cursing, Jack jammed the throttles to his four engines back as he stared up at the underbelly of an aerosteamer slipping across the top of his ship, the bottom gunner and bomb dropper gazing down at him in wide-eyed fear. Jack pushed the nose down, praying his tail wouldn't slam into the ship above. Romulus, in the top gunner position, cursed wildly in Latin.

For an instant he forgot the fight below until a rifle ball slammed up between his legs in a shower of splinters. Looking down, he saw the ground racing up and pulled back hard on the stick. The aerosteamer nosed up, swinging in almost directly astern the ship that had almost collided with him. The Bantag trenches raced by, several hundred feet below, and Theodor opened up, .58 caliber Gatling bullets stitching the earthworks.

He felt his ship surge up and at almost the same instant Boris, his bomb dropper in the cabin slung below, cried that their load had been dropped. Ten canisters, each weighing a hundred pounds, tumbled into the fort. Jack violently swung his craft over into a sharp banking turn. He caught a glimpse of his bomb load slamming in; the first two tins burst open but the percussion fuses which studded them failed to ignite. The third one, however, blew, sparking the load of benzene to life. The fort disappeared in an incandescent fireball as nearly two hundred gallons of benzene exploded, the concussion rocking his ship.

Bright orange-red flares of fire ignited along the entire front as one after another the aerosteamers unleashed their new weapon. He caught a brief glimpse of one ship, folding in on itself. *Too low, damn it, you bloody fools!* he silently cried as the ship's hydrogen air bags, ignited by the burst of flame from below, flared with a pale blue flame, the wings folding in, flaring as well, the wreck spiraling down and disappearing into the inferno.

The heavy airships turned, racing back to the west, heading for the airfields twenty miles behind the front to reload and rearm. Jack swept low over the river, passing over the second wave of assault boats and pulled back hard, going into a spiraling climb, turning to head back over the front for a closer look at the action.

He watched as the squadrons of Hornets swept in, dodging around the fires, raking the enemy positions with their Gatling guns. On the river he could see several land ironclads, loaded onto rafts pushing off into the river, dozens of men slowly poling the ungainly cargos across, geysers of water erupting around them. Blue-clad bodies bobbed in the swirling confusion.

On the eastern shore, the lead regiments of the 9th Corps were up into the wire entanglements, cutting their way through. He caught a glimpse of a regimental standard going up the embankment of the fort he had just bombed. Other flags were going forward, men spreading out around the fires ignited by his aerosteamers. Damn it, it looked as if they were actually making it!

A Hornet passing below him suddenly went into a tight spiraling climb, seemed to hang motionless, then started a slow sickening backwards slide, crashing tail first into the ground next to an ironclad, rupturing into a fireball as its gasbag ignited.

Another rifle ball cracked through the cabin, showering Theodor in splinters.

"Damn it, Jack, if you're going to float about up here, at least go higher."

Embarrassed, he realized his copilot was right. He had allowed the spectacle below to capture his attention. Pulling over into a tight corkscrew turn, he started upward, looking down at the ironclad as it churned past the flaming Hornet. The top of the machine's turret had a white cross painted on, signifying that it was a regimental commander's machine, most likely Timokin's. At least the kid was safe for the moment, he thought grimly, turning back to survey the layers of defense still to be penetrated. They had breached the first line, but there were still three more lines to go before they would be across the rail line to the rear.

"Put that next shot through the embrasure damn it!" Brigadier General Gregory Timokin, commander of the First Brigade of Land Ironclads roared, looking down from his perch in the top turret to his gunnery crew below.

Without waiting for a response he turned his attention

back forward, then slowly rotated his turret aft, sweeping the shoreline with his gaze. The first wave of assault boats was ashore, at least what was left of them, men hunkered down low on the riverbank, most of them still half in the water, hugging the protection of the low rise. He could see columns of fire rising up from Jack's firebomb strike, but directly in front the enemy were still holding. Half a dozen ironclads to his right were up over the bank, crushing down the wire entanglements, the lead ironclad already into the first line of bunkers and entrenchments, its Gatling gun shredding the Bantags who panicked and climbed into the open to run. Back across the river everything seemed an insane confusion. Dozens of broken canvas boats littered the muddy waters that were still churning up from mortar rounds and shells detonating. Men floundered about in the chest-deep water, some struggling forward, others flaying about in panic, trying to head back to the west shore, while others bobbed facedown, no longer moving.

It looked like a disaster but experience told him that at least the first stage of the assault, the gaining of a foothold on the eastern shore, was apparently succeeding. When first approached by Pat O'Donald with the proposal that he and his ironclads would attempt to ford the river in a frontal assault he had thought the scheme insane.

"Damn it all, even if we don't sink, we'll get hammered by their artillery before we're halfway across," he had argued. "Make the shore, and their rocket crews will slaughter us on the muddy banks as we wallow about."

Well, he had made it across. As for incoming fire, precious little had hit yet, the human's barrage of weaponry all but incapacitating or panicking the Bantag forward defense.

Another wave of boats came out of the swirling smoke, men paddling hard. He turned his turret forward again as the crew below shouted with triumph, their next round having torn straight into the Bantag bunker.

"Take us forward," Gregory shouted. "Everyone look sharp, gunner load with canister."

He slowly pivoted his turret back and forth, scanning the ground ahead as they inched up over the river embankment. Crushing down the wire, he caught glimpses of blue-clad infantry surging forward to either side of his machine, leaping into the trenches. Cresting up over the top of a

bunker, he saw a mob of Bantag running along a communications trench, heading back toward the second line. A
well-placed burst from his Gatling dropped half of them
before the survivors disappeared around a cutback in the
trench.

The ground ahead was open and flat, the second enemy
line now clearly visible as a rough slash in the ground a
quarter mile ahead. The plan called for the ironclads to
lead a direct assault and overrun the position, supported
by Hornets and ground troops armed with rocket launchers.
By the time they approached the strongest defenses, the
third line a mile farther back, Jack's airships were to have
landed, rearmed, and returned to plaster a mile-long stretch
of trenches with over four thousand gallons of flaming benzene. But at this moment the key to the plan was to keep
moving, to keep the Bantag off-balance and running until
their supply depots to the rear were overrun and destroyed.

Flashes of light were igniting from the second trench line,
and bullets and mortar fragments started to ping against
the armor. Cracking open the top hatch, he stuck his flare
pistol out and fired, sending up the green signal indicating
he was across the Bantag riverfront position. A second,
then a third ironclad crept into view on his right, the turret
of one turning, the machine's commander sticking a hand
out of the firing slit to wave.

Timokin grinned. *Mad fool, I'll put you on report for that
once we get this over with,* he thought, trying to remember
the name of the young lieutenant aboard the *St. Galvino.*
The lead company started to form around him, deploying
out to either side. A rocket slashed past his turret, startling
him. He caught a glimpse of a Bantag launcher team falling
back into a trench, torn apart by the fire of the ironclad to
his left.

Cautiously he reopened the hatch and stuck his head out
for a quick look around. Nearly a dozen machines were up,
hundreds of infantry deployed into the trenches behind
him. There was no telling what the hell was going on to
either flank, but straight ahead the way looked clear. He
saw a regimental standard, a brigadier's guidon beside it.
Catching the general's eye, he motioned forward; the brigadier waved in agreement. Back on the shoreline he saw
more waves of the flimsy canvas boats coming in, some of

them bearing mortar and rocket-launching crews. A Hornet flashed overhead, Gatling gun roaring, tracers tearing into the position forward. The sun broke the horizon straight ahead, silhouetting the enemy line.

July Fourth he thought. The Yankees put great store in that day; Independence Day they called it. It was also the anniversary of the Battle of Hispania. He had been too young to fight in that one. *Will this day be as glorious?* he wondered. He felt a moment's hesitation. Somehow the shoreline felt secure, a haven to pull back to, where you couldn't be flanked, but he knew the thought was senseless. The whole plan, a plan which he had helped to design, was predicated on speed. Cut through the lines of defense, get into the open country, and slash down to their major rail depot and destroy it. Victory was five miles ahead, and the longer he waited, the more remote the chance of grasping it.

Reloading his flare pistol, he fired it again, rapidly reloading and firing off yet another shell, the signal that he was moving on the second line.

He slipped back down into his turret, slamming the hatch shut.

"Engineer, full power; driver, straight ahead!"

"I'm going over," Pat announced.

Andrew stood silent for a moment, leaning over, eye glued to the tripod-mounted telescope staring intently toward the ruins to Capua on the east bank and several miles downstream.

"The message dropped from Petracci was on the mark," Andrew announced. "There're definitely plumes of smoke over there."

"Well, we did expect some sort of countermove," Pat replied. "It's less than two dozen ironclads. Timokin can handle that."

Andrew stood back up, stretching, trying to ignore the occasional shell that hummed overhead. In the two hours since the beginning of the attack they had forced a lodgment nearly two miles across and in some sectors were already through the third line. Considering the nature of the assault, casualties had been light, so far twenty-five hundred. Marcus had already gone forward, insisting over Andrew's objections that he should be up forward with his boys from 9th Corps.

The first of the pontoon bridges was nearly completed, and he watched for a moment as his engineer troops, laboring like a swarm of ants, anchored the last boat in place, while half a regiment of men armed with picks and shovels worked to cut down the low embankment on the east side and fill in the labyrinth of trenches just beyond. A column of infantry, rifles and cartridge boxes held high overhead, slowly wended their way across the river at a ford, a long serpentine column of blue standing out boldly against the muddy brown river.

The surviving canvas boats were now being used to ferry boxes of ammunition, mortar and rocket-launching crews, medical supplies, and even barrels of fresh water since the day promised to be hot and with all the dead and refuse littering the river Emil had issued the strictest of orders against using it. Andrew looked over his shoulder to where a casualty-clearing station was already at work. Those who could survive the trip were loaded into ambulances for the hospital train that would have them back to Roum before noon.

Casualties had been heavy in the first two waves, nearly fifty percent of the 1st Brigade, 1st Division, 9th Corps had gone down. He kept trying to console himself that the losses had just about been what was expected, but it was small solace for the nearly twenty-five hundred dead and wounded. He thought of the review held just a week ago, remembering faces, wondering which of them had been part of the sacrificial offering.

Andrew looked over at Pat. "I'm going with you. Hans, you stay here at headquarters."

"Now, Andrew, we agreed on this," Pat protested.

Andrew nodded, forcing a smile. It was more than just being at the front, getting close to get a feel for what was going on, and to inspire the troops. Ever since his wounding, only a few miles from this place, he had not been under heavy fire. Inwardly he was terrified; it was hard not to jump every time a mortar shell slipped overhead or a bullet snapped past, and this was the rear line. He had to see for himself if he could take it.

He looked over at Hans. His friend was staring at him

appraisingly. Pat had turned as well, arguing his point to Hans, trying to get the old sergeant major to agree that Andrew had to stay back from the fighting. Andrew knew that Hans understood the real reason he had to cross over that river. Hans wordlessly nodded an agreement.

"Well damn all," Pat growled. "Don't blame me if you get your fool head blown off."

"What about you then?" Andrew asked. "What about your fool head?"

"Bullet hasn't been cast yet," Pat replied with a twinkle in his eyes, backing down from the argument.

Leaving the top of the bunker, Andrew motioned to his orderly, who was holding the bridle of his favorite old mount, Mercury. He rubbed the horse's nose, then shook his head. No, it would be hot up there, and Mercury was getting on in years. Besides, after all the campaigns together he wanted him to survive this one.

"Bring up another mount," Andrew said.

"Can't risk your old horse but it's all right to risk you, is that it?" Pat asked peevishly.

"Something like that."

Andrew swung up awkwardly into the saddle of a massive mare, a mount bred from the horses captured in the Tugar Wars. It was nearly the size of a Clydesdale, typical of nearly all the mounts in this army—and damned uncomfortable, he thought as he picked up the reins and nudged the horse down toward the nearest ravine.

Reaching the edge of the shallow gorge, he hesitated for a second. Even though the engineering troops had cut a road into the side of it, it was still a steep descent. Then he urged the horse forward, falling in with a column of infantry, noticing by the red Maltese Cross on their slouch caps that they were men of the 1st Division, 5th Corps.

"Hot up there, sir?" one of the sergeants asked, looking up nervously at Andrew.

"We got a firm foothold, Sergeant. Ninth Corps is driving them."

"Well that's a switch," came a comment from the ranks.

Andrew continued forward, ignoring the insult, even though Pat turned, ready to offer a good chewing out. There was still some bad blood between the Rus and the Roum Corps, especially toward the 9th and 11th, which had broken during the siege. It was part of his reasoning for giving the assault job to the 9th, a chance to clear their reputation and break the jinx.

Strange, he thought; back with the old Army of the Potomac the 9th had been jinxed there as well, damn good fighting men but something always seemed to go wrong for them.

Reaching the bottom of the ravine he followed the contours of the twisting washout. Wreckage littered the rocky sides, broken equipment, empty ammunition boxes, a scattering of dead who had been caught by the Bantag counterbarrage. The last turn in the ravine revealed the river straight ahead.

It was said that whether you were winning or losing, the rear area of a battle always looked like a disaster, and he hesitated for a moment, steeling himself while taking it all in.

Shattered canvas boats littered the shoreline, dozens of bodies, and parts of bodies lay along the beach or floated in the muddy water, washed back up to shore by the slow-moving current. Fragments of bodies, blackened by fire, were plastered against the side of a ravine, most likely what was left from a caisson igniting. The air was thick with the stench of muddy water, powder smoke, and that unforgettable clinging smell of death, a mixture of excrement, vomit, and raw open flesh. In another few hours the cloying stench of decay would be added until finally one would feel as if he could actually see the hazy green smell of death.

He straightened in the saddle, moving his mount out of the way as the infantry column, without hesitating, splashed into the river by columns of fours, holding rifles and ammunition pouches, haversacks filled with rations over their heads. A line of cavalry were deployed downstream, ready to fish out any man who might lose his footing and go under.

Andrew rode along the edge of the water, heading up to the next ravine, where the pontoon bridge was going in. A mortar shell whistled overhead. impacting against the top of the cliffs that rose up on his left, sending down a shower of rock fragments and dirt. He tried not to flinch, and then looked over sheepishly at Pat.

"You'll get the nerve back," Pat said softly, "I was the same way after I took that ball in the stomach."

Andrew nodded, saying nothing. Straight ahead, the bridge was rapidly taking shape. The last boat had already been anchored, and stringers between the boats were nearly halfway across the river, the crews working feverishly to anchor the heavy timbers to the reinforced gunwales of the pontoon boats. Dozens of men, most of them stripped to the waist, were hauling up the four-by-ten planks, which were laid across the stringers and serve as the roadbed. Once completed, the heavy artillery, a second regiment of ironclads, and hundreds of tons of supplies could be rushed forward.

Turning his mount, Andrew splashed into the river, the water surprisingly cool as it spilled into his boots. The mare surged forward, stepping nervously for footing as they reached the middle of the river, Pat at his side.

Fifty yards downstream an artillery shell slapped into the water, raising a geyser. He studiously ignored it, keeping his eyes on the far shore. His mount shied nervously, nearly throwing him as it quickly sidestepped. A body, which the horse had trod on, tumbled up out of the murky water, then sank, dragged back down by the weight of the pack harness that had three close-support rockets strapped to it.

He said nothing, wondering about the human packhorse who had drowned thus. He tried to make a mental note, to balm his soul, that if there was another river assault, the first waves were to go in with rifles and personal ammunition only. But then how many die because of no close-in rocket support . . . again the equations of death.

They finally gained the shore. The litter there was far worse than the west bank. Dozens of waterlogged assault craft, which had barely made it across, lay abandoned, many of them bloodstained, bodies still inside. Scores of dead littered the embankment, dead twisted into every impossible angle the living could never assume, bodies torn by rifle shot, shells, fire, tangled in with the Bantag who had defended this position. Casualty-clearing stations, marked with green banners, were packed, the seriously injured men being sorted out for the trip back across the river by boat, the less seriously injured and those who were doomed being detailed off to wait until the pontoon bridge was finished.

As he rode up over the embankment the roar of battle seemed to double. Straight ahead was obscured in yellow-gray clouds of powder smoke and dust, the front line dully illuminated by flashes of gunfire and the sudden flare of another load of benzene dropped by an Eagle.

Ghastly weapon, he thought as he rode up over the forward line of Bantag trenches and saw where such a strike had incinerated dozens, their giant bodies curled into fetal balls, a few outstretched, blackened clawed hands raised to the heavens in a final gesture of agony. The stench was horrific, and he struggled not to gag.

"Bloody bastards, good to see 'em like this," Pat snapped. Andrew looked over at his old friend and said nothing. No, the hatred was far too deep to express pity, to wonder if there was any sense of humanity in these creatures. Interesting that he had chosen that word in his thoughts . . . *humanity. Does it mean I consider them to be human? Strange, old Muzta of the Tugars, I had shown him pity, spared his son, and he in turn spared Hawthorne and Kathleen, even went over to our side in the Battle of Hispania and turned the tide of battle. He's most likely a thousand miles east of here by now, but if I saw him, I would offer him a drink from my canteen. Yet still I hate his kind in general.*

Don't think about this now, he thought. *There's a war to be fought.*

He turned away from the trench, dropped the reins of his mount, and awkwardly scanned the action with his field glasses. The ground was too bloody flat, hard to get above the fight and get a feel for it. It seemed to be spread out in a vast arc sweeping a mile or more to the north, then several miles in from the river, and then arcing back around into the ruins of Capua.

Spent rounds slapped past him, kicking up plumes of dirt like the first heavy drops of rain from a summer storm. From out of the smoke ahead two aerosteamers appeared, both of them Eagles, one with two engines shut down, broken fabric and spars trailing from its starboard wing. The second Eagle was above and behind it, protecting it; as they reached the river the second steamer turned, started back to the front, then turned yet again and began to circle above Andrew, a blue-and-gold streamer fluttering from its tail marking it as Petracci's command ship.

A message fluttered down, marked by a long red strip of cloth. An errant breeze had picked up, and the streamer fluttered down into the edge of the river behind them. One of Andrew's staff who had been trailing behind him urged his mount back to retrieve it from a soldier who had already picked it up.

The orderly who had retrieved the message reined in, holding the leather cylinder, the muddy ribbon dragging on the ground. Andrew motioned for him to unstrap it and open it up, a task impossible for him to do with but one hand.

The orderly popped the lid, unfolded the sheet of paper, and handed it over. Andrew's glasses were splattered with water and mud, and it was difficult to focus as he carefully read the note, written in English in Jack's clumsy printed hand.

> Count twenty plus ironclads coming up from Capua. Three to four divisions, half mounted, deploying out from reserve depot on rail line. Watch your left, numerous plumes of smoke at point F=7. Going back for closer look. . . . J.P.

Andrew handed the message over to Pat while calling for another orderly to unroll a map. The young Rus lieutenant pulled the map out and held it open for Andrew.

He cross-referenced the coordinates. F-7, a ruined plantation, a square-shaped forest at the north end, a woodlot of maybe forty to fifty acres. The heavy belt of forest marking the edge of the open steppes several miles beyond. Could they? His aerosteamers had carefully swept the front line for weeks, looking for buildups, concealed positions, wheel marks.

Well there were bound to be surprises, but Jack had a good nose for spotting trouble. *Is the plan too obvious,* he wondered. *Too obvious that we break through here, then pivot in a right hook, sweeping down behind Capua and their rail line. Might the counterpunch be concealed to the north of us?*

Even as he wondered, the sound of battle started to pick up from the north, and, reining his mount around, Andrew rode toward the roar of the guns.

Bent over the map table Jurak watched as one of the Chin scribes leaned forward, having taken the message from a telegrapher who was also a Chin and traced a blue line onto the map, marking where the Yankees had broken through his third line and were now driving straight toward this position.

Stepping out of the camouflaged bunker, which was concealed in a grove of peach trees and covered with netting, he turned and looked to the northwest. Mounted riders were coming back, many of them wounded. Straight ahead he could hear the staccato bursts of Gatling-gun fire and the whistle of a steam engine. The enemy column of steam ironclads was approaching.

How damn primitive, he thought. *Most likely can't make three leagues in an hour. Hell, on the old world there'd be hundreds of them, thousands, breaking through at ten, twenty leagues to the hour, jets by the hundreds blasting the way clear.*

Yet this is my war now. Ha'ark never understood the nuances of tactics, how to adapt to what was here, how to lay the trap, and then have the patience to let it spring shut. It was always the attack, the offensive. He was right in that these primitives have no concept of defensive warfare but let them see victory today and it will all change.

He raised his field glasses, scanning the line, catching glimpses of dark black masses, the Yankee ironclads, advancing slowly, methodically, brief glimpses of blue, the infantry deployed behind them.

A stream of tracers snapped overhead, one of the ironclads firing at long range. He ignored it, looking across the grove and back toward the rail line behind him. A single train was on the track, one of the heavily armored units. On the siding were dozens of cars, some of them burning from the air attacks, but most still intact, their deadly cargo concealed within. The trenches weaving through the grove, and around the rail track were a masterpiece of concealment, the raw earth carted off at night, the deep bunkers cunningly placed, everything covered with camouflage netting, something that his warriors had first thought was some sort of bizarre joke.

He could clearly see them now, range less than a league away, the thin line of troops he had deployed were just enough to let the enemy think that there was resistance and that it was now breaking up. *"The best time to strike is when your opponent is flush with victory for then the collapse of his morale shall be complete." Master Gavagar made that pronouncement three thousand years ago,* Jurak thought. *Ha'ark had never had the subtlety to think of that, to think of the best way to break their will . . . now we shall see.*

"Jack, to the north, where we were looking earlier."

Petracci turned his attention to port, to where Theodor was pointing. The same spot as before, F-7, the plantation near the northern rim of forest. Vertical plumes of smoke, a few before, but now dozens of them. The smudges of smoke were puffing . . . damn, machines.

"Take the controls," Jack shouted. Letting go of the stick he raised his field glasses, braced them, finding it hard to focus in as the machine surged up on an early-morning thermal, then leveled back out. He caught it for a second, lost it, then caught it again. . . .

"Damnation, ironclads, fifty . . . a hundred of them!"

Chapter Three

General Gregory Timokin never even saw the shot that took him out of the fight. One second he had been watching the retreat of the Bantag infantry and mounted units, eager finally to get in range of the rail line, the next instant an explosion of steam blew up into his turret. He could hear the screams of his crew down below, men being scalded alive from the burst boiler.

Clawing at the turret hatch, he pulled himself up and out, gasping for breath. Just as he rolled clear of the turret and hit the ground his ironclad blowtorched as nearly a hundred gallons of kerosene poured from the ruptured fuel tanks into the boiler and ignited. Horrified, he could hear the dying screams of his men inside, one of them fumbling at the latch on the starboard entry port.

He stood up, staggering to the machine. Grabbed the handle to try to turn it, screaming with pain—it was already scalding hot. He felt someone jiggling the handle spasmodically, but the door wouldn't give. Damn, they were turning the latch but hadn't unbolted the locks inside.

"Open the locks, God damn it, open the locks!" he screamed.

He felt as if he was trapped in a cursed nightmare, the door wouldn't open, the screaming inside wouldn't stop . . . and he was terrified of what he would see if the door did open.

He heard the screams inside and then he was down, someone pushing him to the ground.

"Stay down, you damn fool!"

Bullets snapped past, machine-gun fire, slower than a Gatling but a machine gun nevertheless, the bullets tattooing against the side of his ironclad where he had been standing only seconds before.

A rocket snapped overhead. Turning, he saw it slam into another ironclad, the *St. Yuri,* which had been on his right flank. The round struck a glancing blow and detonated, scoring the armor.

"My men!" Gregory screamed. "I've got to get 'em out!"

"They're dead already." Then he was being dragged back, another soldier coming up out of a shallow ditch behind the burning machine to help pull him in.

As the three rolled into the ditch the ammunition in the *St. Malady* burned off, ten-pound shells bursting, the top turret tearing loose, tumbling skyward and then crashing down, a pile of twisted wreckage. Tracer rounds soared upward, oily black smoke blowing out from the turret mount as if the ironclad had been turned into a blast furnace.

Numbed, he stared at his beloved machine, still not believing that his comrades inside were dead.

"What hit us?" he asked vacantly.

Even as he asked the question he saw a flash of light straight ahead, the muzzle blast of a gun, and a split second later the *St. Yuri* went up, the turret blowing clear off from the shot.

Stunned, ignoring the danger, he stood up. Only seconds before he had been leading nearly forty ironclads, advancing in line abreast, supporting a full division of infantry. Half of them were now burning. Impossible; the ground ahead, all the way to the railroad track, was open, the enemy on the run. He saw more flashes, as if the guns were firing from out of the ground . . . a concealed line, camouflaged, invisible from the ground and from the air. God damn, how did they do this? How did they learn it?

"Sir, if you want to get killed, damn it, do it someplace else. I'm not going to risk my ass again to save you."

He turned and saw a colonel by his side, crouching low. At nearly the same instant something plucked at his shoulder, his epaulette snapping off, tearing his uniform. He squatted back down and stared at the officer, saying nothing.

The colonel uncorked his canteen and offered it over. Gregory took a drink, grimacing. It was vodka laced with just a hint of muddy water.

"Your hands; you better get back to the aid station; I'll send a man with you."

He saw that his hands were already puffy, bright pink. The flesh of his right hand was blistering, and the sight of it made him realize just how damn much it hurt. Looking down he noticed that his trousers were scorched black, the leather of his boots burned. Not as much pain there at least.

"In a minute," he gasped, handing the canteen back.

"Out of nowhere," the colonel announced, obviously shaken. "Thought we had a clear run, then the ground ahead just exploded."

He paused, looking back over the edge of the ditch. Timokin followed his gaze and saw dozens of men down on the ground, in a line so neat it was as if they had been ordered to drop together. Some of them were still alive, trying to crawl back, puffs of dirt kicking up around them, and above the roar of battle he could hear the barking laughter of the Bantags who were picking them off. A desire to do something, anything, urged him to climb out and try to help, but instinct told him it was now a deadly killing ground, and he was amazed that someone would be so insane as to pull him away from the *St. Malady,* which was a dozen yards forward and still burning.

"It just exploded with fire," the colonel continued. "It looked like your ironclad rolled over some sort of infernal machine, the back end just lifted right up from the blast. Then you got hit from the front a second later."

The dirt on the lip of the ditch sprayed up as machine-gun fire swept them. Seconds later the mortar rounds started, whistling in, bracketing the depression that was rapidly filling with men who were crawling back from the inferno ahead. He caught a glimpse of a lone ironclad driving back in reverse, a rocket flaring up from ahead, streaking past the machine's turret.

Puffs of smoke were igniting along the Bantag train track which was so tantalizingly close, less than a quarter mile ahead. Motioning for the colonel's field glasses, Gregory took them, grimacing with pain as he cupped them in his hands and clumsily focused them on the rail line. Rhythmic lights were snapping from the armored cars, the rate of fire was slow, maybe a hundred rounds a minute, but it was a machine gun, and he cursed silently.

What was far more startling, though, was the sight of ironclads emerging, as if rising up from out of the ground on the far side of the track and from a peach-orchard-covered knoll. The bastards had dug them in, the saints only knew how long ago, and covered them over and waited. Now they were stirring to life, rising up out of concealment. They looked heavier, a newer model, with turrets just like his own machine. Along the rail track, farther back, he could see several dozen small specks, apparently hovering in the air, but gradually taking form. Bantag airships, coming in to support. Several Hornets harried the edge of the formation; a Bantag machine went down in flames, but a Hornet plunged to earth as well.

"My God," he whispered. "We're losing."

"Andrew, I think we better get the hell out of here!" Pat roared, leaning over to grab the reins of Andrew's horse.

Andrew shook his head, motioning for Pat to let go, but his friend refused.

Sitting upright in the saddle, Andrew raised his field glasses, fixing his attention to the north. Less than a quarter mile away he could see them coming, a wall of Bantag ironclads, forty or more advancing nearly side to side.

Jack, who only minutes before had dropped a message warning of the breakthrough was circling above them, oblivious of the ground fire, all three of his gunners firing their Gatlings.

Surviving ironclads that had been supporting the left flank of 9th Corps were backing up, engaging the enemy machines, but it was apparent the armor on the Bantag machines had been reinforced, bolts that had once so easily sliced through at two hundred yards were now careening off the enemy machines in a shower of sparks.

Four ironclads stopped after backing into a shallow depression, and Andrew watched intently as they waited for the Bantag to close in. Knots of infantry fell in around the ironclad behemoths, and Andrew nudged his mount, wanting to ride up to join them.

"Are you crazy!" Pat roared. "A mounted man won't last three seconds up there."

"Well, damn it, I've got to do something!" Andrew shouted.

Pat looked over at the half dozen staff and couriers who still trailed them. Most of them were wide-eyed with fright, but they knew what to do, moving up to surround Andrew and shield him.

"Back away, damn you!" Andrew shouted, but they ignored his protests.

The battle erupted straight ahead as the four ironclads opened up at less than a hundred yards. Two of the enemy machines exploded. A hail of fire slashed back. Deployed as they were directly behind the action, solid shot bolts, machine-gun fire, and shell fragments screamed past Andrew and his companions. Pat visibly flinched as a solid bolt sucked the air between them, the round screaming past like a demented banshee.

The turret was torn off one of the ironclads, steam and flame blew out the back of another. The two survivors fired back, destroying two more of the enemy machines. The Bantag continued to press in, yet another machine exploding as a rocket crew fired into its flank at point-blank range. And then they were through the line, followed by hundreds of Bantag infantry swarming forward. Several of the enemy machines were towing wagons, which were now unhitched. Mortars were already set up inside the wagons and within seconds their crews were sending dozens of shells aloft.

"We've got to get back!" Pat shouted, and he pointed to the left.

Down by the riverbank a solid wall of Bantag infantry were racing forward at the double, oblivious of losses; the thin line of blue trying to contain them cracking apart.

"They must have had five umens or more concealed on our flank," Pat shouted. "They're going to cut the pontoons and our crossing point. Andrew, you're getting out of here now."

Andrew wanted to knock Pat's hand away, as his friend again grasped the reins of his horse, turned, and broke into a canter, dragging Andrew along.

"Give me the reins, damn it," Andrew shouted.

Pat looked back at him.

"I'm not doing anything stupid."

Pat nodded and finally let go.

Andrew gathered up the reins and followed as Pat weaved his way down a farm lane, that in a different age had connected a villa to the road running parallel to the river. As they reached the river road Andrew was stunned by the chaos.

Some officers still had control of their units, ordering men to dig in. A battery of ten-pounders was pushing its way up through the ever-increasing mob of refugees heading to the rear. Pat broke away, rode over, and ordered them to unlimber alongside the ruins of a small temple, the toppled-over columns of limestone offering some protection.

Andrew turned to watch, surveying the ground, wondering if this could be a breakwater to stop the unrelenting assault. A regiment, still in semblance of order and falling back down the road, slowed as Pat galloped up to them, ordering the men to fall in on the flanks of the guns.

The enemy ironclad assault was clearly visible, less than a quarter mile away, coming across the open plain, hundreds of men running in front of it, trying to escape.

Terrified soldiers crashed through the line Pat was trying to form up. With drawn sword Pat rode back and forth, screaming for the men to rally. Some slowed, falling in; others dodged around and kept on going, crying that it was impossible.

The advancing line of Bantag ironclads slowed and ground to a halt two hundred yards away.

"God damn them," Pat cried. "They know the range we can kill them at and are sitting just beyond it!"

Andrew nodded, saying nothing.

A ragged volley erupted from the line of enemy machines, and a gale of canister swept the position. Gunners dropped at their pieces, two of Andrew's staff collapsed, one of them shrieking in agony, clutching a shattered arm.

The gunners opened up, six pieces recoiling back with sharp cracks, but the bolts simply ricocheted off the front armor of the enemy machines.

The one-sided duel lasted for several minutes, the slow-firing machine guns of the enemy ironclads stitching back and forth along the line.

Conceding that a suicidal gesture was meaningless, Andrew urged his mount behind the wall of the temple, Pat and the surviving staff joining him.

Mortar rounds began to rain down, bracketing the position, and Andrew struggled to control his own fear as the deadly messengers whispered overhead and detonated with loud cracks.

"Why don't they charge, damn it?" one of the staff cried.

"They don't have to," Pat snarled. "Not until they're damn good and ready."

A ragged cheer erupted from the battery, and, looking up over the wall, Andrew saw a lone enemy machine exploding, most likely a lucky shot through an open gun port. Three of the six guns of his battery were out of action, and more than half the crew was down.

Andrew was startled as a flyer, skimming overhead, engines roaring, blocked out the sun for an instant.

A message streamer dropped less than a dozen feet away. He looked up, saw smoke pouring from one of the Eagle's engines—another engine had been shut down.

An orderly handed the message up.

> Sir, get the hell out! Entire front collapsing. Ten umens and hundred ironclads attacking you. South flank gone, Bantag about to take pontoon bridge. Must pull out. My ship is finished. . . . Jack.

"Here they come!"

Andrew nudged his mount around and came out from behind the temple. The enemy ironclads were advancing again. Their tactics were changing; they smelled victory. Bantag infantry, thousands of them, were swarming forward, all of them heavily armed with rifles, rocket launchers, mortars. Ignoring the losses, they broke into a swarming charge. The regiment Pat had deployed fired a single ragged volley, then simply melted away, officers shouting for the men to fall back. There was no semblance of order to the pullout; men simply turned and started to run.

Andrew rode up to the battery commander, who had miraculously survived the enemy barrage.

"Major, abandon your guns, get your men the hell out of here!"

"Sir?"

"You heard me, son. Get your wounded on the limber wagons and save yourself. Now move!"

The gunners, hearing Andrew's command, needed no persuasion. Turning, they started to run, though discipline held long enough for them to help the wounded onto the limber wagons. Drivers lashed their teams, swinging the wagons out onto the road.

A blast of canister dropped the entire lead team of six horses into a tangled heap, blocking the road. Chaos erupted as the other limber teams tried to maneuver around the pileup.

Pat, hat gone, saber dropped, was waving a pistol, standing in his stirrups, bawling orders. Andrew looked back, saw Bantag infantry less than a dozen yards away, piling up over the guns, catching those who had not moved quickly enough, bayoneting the wounded on the ground.

Andrew rode up to Pat.

"Come on!"

"The guns. God damn them, I've never lost a gun!"

"Come on!"

Pat suddenly turned, lowering his pistol, apparently aiming it right at Andrew. He fired, dropping a Bantag who was between them, clubbed rifle poised to knock Andrew from the saddle.

Pat spurred his mount forward, Andrew following, his mount staggering, nearly falling, as it was shot in the haunch. It regained its footing and in a panic broke into a lopsided gallop.

Andrew looked back, horrified. The Bantag were into the traffic jam of limber wagons, tearing the wounded down off of the caissons, bayoneting drivers. He saw a man being flung into the air, shrieking, falling back down on upturned bayonets. The Bantags seemed to have reverted, caught up in the blood frenzy, some of them literally tearing men apart with their bare hands.

Behind the insane swarm the ironclads pressed in, not hesitating, one of them rising up and over a twisted tangle of men and horses, crushing them under.

Ahead the road was packed with thousands heading to the rear. And there was nothing for Andrew to now do but ride with them into defeat.

Gregory could sense the rising panic in the troops packed in around him. Minutes before the men had advanced jauntily, feeling the worst of the assault was over, the trench lines cleared, and they were into the open ground beyond. He was beginning to feel the panic in his own heart as well, the easterly breeze blowing back into his face the stench of his machine burning, a mixture of kerosene, hot iron, and human flesh.

He started to shake. He had seen it often in others, after getting hit, no pain at first, then the shaking, the feeling that all the blood had drained out of you. Suddenly, with no warning, he leaned over and vomited.

"Sergeant, get the general the hell out of here."

He didn't want to accept the offer of help but was grateful when he felt strong hands grabbing him by the shoulder.

"This way, sir."

He looked into the eyes of the infantryman. About his own age, early twenties, but harder, muscles like whipcords, a scar creasing his jaw, an ugly red slash that seemed to double the size of his mouth lopsidedly to one side.

The sergeant led him down along the ditch, head bobbing up occasionally, scanning the land.

"Defile there, sir, about a hundred yards farther back. We'll have to move quick to get to it . . . Ready?"

He found he couldn't speak, his entire body was trembling. Fear, exhaustion, the pain, he wasn't sure which. Another convulsion hit him, and he vomited again. The sergeant held him by the shoulders until the spasm passed.

"Ready to make a run for it?"

Gregory nodded weakly.

"Now sir!"

Together they went up out of the ditch, Gregory still gagging, the sergeant half-dragging him along. Bullets whip-cracked overhead, they reached the next ditch, rolling in amongst the packed tangle of men who were cowering there for cover, several of them cursing the pair, ignoring the star that was still on one epaulette.

A mortar round thudded into the packed crowd less than twenty feet away, and Gregory winced as a fine mist of blood sprayed into his face. He started to cry, not exactly sure why, sick with himself that he was breaking down in front of the men, but the sight of a lieutenant who the shell had landed on caused him to think of his crew. By now, they were blackened charred bits of greasy dirt, not blown apart like the body in front of him.

"It's all right, sir, let's keep going."

The sergeant fell in with a carrying party using the shallow ravine to move the wounded back. It was a procession of tears, some of the men moved along easily on their own, clutching a blood-soaked arm, obviously glad to be out of it with, at worst, the loss of an arm. Others moved along silently, features a ghastly green-tinged pale. No stretcher party would carry them—they were the dying and time could not be wasted—but by some herculean effort they dragged themselves back, believing that by doing so, by staying with this river of half-torn bodies that they could somehow remain in the ranks of the living.

Medical orderlies with green armbands to identify them to the provost guards, struggled to carry the rest, some on stretchers, others bundled into a ground cloth or blanket.

He was a veteran of half a dozen hard-fought engagements, but until this moment, locked up in his iron machine, he had never really looked closely at what could be done to men, or to himself. Some were burned, faces, hands blackened, others parboiled by steam like him, features puffing up, eyes swelling shut. Others clutched at holes torn in the chest, mangled faces, or shattered limbs.

The procession was strangely silent, and he staggered along with it, feeling as if he was a fraud, not really wounded, a coward who was allowing himself to be led away, hiding under the protection of a sergeant ordered to take him to the rear.

He would rise from his inner woe occasionally to realize that there was a mad battle swirling about him. Hundreds of shells were arcing overhead, the worst mortar barrage he had seen, far worse than the Battle of Rocky Hill. Nothing was moving forward. Men were bunched up in ditches, sprawled flat behind the ruins of abandoned villas, barns, sheds, or behind burning ironclads, some digging frantically with bayonets, scratching holes to hide in. The rifle and machine-gun fire was continuous, but increasingly he noticed the men were not firing back, but instead were hunkering down, unable to go forward and too frightened to get up and sprint for the rear.

He looked back toward the front and gasped. A dozen

enemy ironclads were moving up, the lead one within spitting distance of his own destroyed machine. Machine-gun fire erupted, stitching the shallow ravine he had been dragged into. Men were bursting out of the cover, running, collapsing. A rocket crew to one flank stood up, fired off a round. It slammed into the side of the enemy machine and skidded off. Seconds later the men were dead.

He spotted one of his machines pivoting, a lone David fighting a dozen Goliaths. It slammed a shot into the rear of a Bantag machine, blowing it apart, and then was torn to shreds in turn, half a dozen bolts slicing it apart. The entire front was breaking apart, falling back. Dark forms were emerging out of the ground, Bantag infantry, bent double, moving quickly, sprinting forward, dropping, then rising and racing forward again. Their movements were different, not the upright charges of the past. He sensed that these warriors were different, trained in a different type of combat, and the sight of them was terrifying.

His sergeant pulled him away and pushed on down the ravine, heading back to the rear. Several times officers started to close in on the sergeant, but when they saw he was helping a general to the rear they backed off, yet again redoubling Gregory's shame. Without the star on his shoulder he would have had to make it back on his own, and at the moment the terror was so great that he knew he couldn't walk, let alone crawl, without the strong arms of the sergeant around him.

The ravine finally played out, but they were now a good six hundred yards from the front and the sergeant ventured up the side and out onto the open ground. Gregory looked around and saw a green flag fluttering behind the ruins of a plantation house with a white rectangle in the middle, the insignia of the field hospital for 2nd Division, 11th Corps. The low stone walls provided some protection from the incoming fire, and several times the sergeant pulled him down as mortar rounds crumped in the open field they were traversing, their progress hindered by the torn-up tangle of untended grapevines and arbors.

Well over a hundred men were lying behind the building, most of them from 11th Corps but a sprinkling of 9th Corps and even a few wearing the distinctive black jackets of the

ironclad Corps, the men looking up at him expectantly as
he came in.

The sergeant eased him down, announcing that he was
going to fetch the doctor. The soldier to his right was unconscious, a bandage covering most of his face, blood seeping out; to his left was one of his ironclad men, hands and
face blackened, the flesh cracked and peeling. He could see
the boy was blinded and didn't have the heart, or the courage, to speak to him.

A hospital orderly came up, led by the sergeant, and
squatted down.

"How you doing, sir?"

Gregory looked at him, unable to form the words, to
tell him to go away and tend someone else who needed
him more.

The orderly held up his hand moving it slowly back and
forth in front of Gregory's face, watching intently.

"Can you see my hand, sir?"

Next he took Gregory's hands, turning them over, pressing gently, watching Gregory's reaction.

"You'll do all right, sir. You got scalded. From the sound
of your voice you might have taken some steam in. I'll get
some ointment, then the sergeant here can take you back
to the river."

Even as he spoke a courier came galloping up, crouched
low in the saddle, reining in hard, a bloodstained doctor
turning to face him. Words were exchanged. The courier
saluted, reined about, then started forward, heading up to
the front.

The doctor stepped back, shouting for his staff to form
up. Gregory watched silently, sensing something as orders
were given with hushed voices. The orderly never came
back with the ointment as the men raced off. The doctor
seemed to shrink visibly as he looked at his charges.

"Everyone listen up," he shouted in Latin, trying to be
heard above the incessant roar of battle. Gregory listened
intently, unsure if he was hearing the words correctly. The
doctor paused, crouching low as a flyer passed low overhead, smoke trailing from an engine, then stood back up.

"We have to evacuate this position now! Anyone who
can move on his own, start heading for the rear immedi-

ately. If you have the strength to help a comrade do so. Let's get going."

He turned away. Gregory struggled to his feet, looking around. Men staggered up, others tried, then slipped back down. Far too many didn't move at all and he could see there were nowhere near enough orderlies to move them all. He looked over at his sergeant.

"Give a hand with someone else; I can make it from here."

"You certain, sir?" and he could sense a genuine concern that touched him deeply.

"Certain, Sergeant. Kesus be with you."

"And the gods with you too, sir," the sergeant hesitated, then looked back. "Sir, I'm sorry about your crew. My younger brother's on one of them machines. Do you think he's all right?"

"I pray so."

The sergeant nodded, looked down at an unconscious man with a bandaged face, and, reaching down, he hoisted him, cradling him in his arms like a child, and started for the rear. Gregory went up to the doctor. At his approach the doctor's eyes shifted to the star on his shoulder.

"Why are you pulling out?" Gregory asked.

"Didn't you hear?"

"Hear what?"

"We're being flanked, cut off."

"What?"

The doctor pointed to the north, and for the first time Gregory was aware of the roiling columns of smoke, punctuated by fires, and dull flashes of light. It was like a curtain stretching from horizon to horizon. He caught a momentary glimpse of a dark machine slowly moving up over a distant hill, dozens of dark towering forms behind it . . . Bantag; above them an aerosteamer was spiraling down in flames. The image reminded Gregory of a painting that terrified him as a child, in the great cathedral of Suzdal, *The Day of Judgment,* the world was in flames, the damned consigned into the hands of demons, who, of course, were of the Horde. It looked the same now. Turning to look back from where he had come, he could see the survivors of the assault pulling back, some of the men running headlong for the rear, others turning, trying to fight, going down under the hail of fire.

"Better get the hell out of here now," the doctor said, turning to the operating table to scoop his instruments into a carrying bag. A lone ambulance was being loaded up with wounded.

"These men?" Gregory asked.

"Those who can't walk are left," the doctor announced grimly, and to his horror he saw an orderly drawing out a revolver. It was never spoken of, but all knew that orders were never to leave wounded behind for the Bantag if they couldn't be evacuated.

Horrified Gregory stepped around the doctor and struggled to pull a man up.

"Leave him, he's dying anyhow," the doctor announced calmly.

"Like hell."

Tears of pain and frustration streaming down his face Gregory grabbed a corporal who had lost a leg and was still unconscious, hoisted him, and started for the rear.

Chapter Four

Brakes squealing, the train glided to a halt. Wearily, Andrew stood up, looking down at his dress uniform, nervously brushing at a stain just below his breast.

"Long ride," Hans groaned, sitting up from the narrow bunk where he had slept for the last hundred miles of the grueling seven-hundred-mile transit.

Andrew nodded, vainly trying to stretch the kinks out of his back.

"Ready for this?" Hans asked, standing up and, with an almost fatherly gesture, brushing some soot off Andrew's shoulder.

"Not sure. Almost feels like going into a battle."

"It is, and maybe just as dangerous."

There was a final lurch of the cars, then a blast of the whistle. Looking out the window, he saw an expectant crowd waiting in the hot early-morning sunlight. A military band, sounding tinny, struck up "Battle Cry of Freedom."

He stepped out onto the back platform, looking around. A small delegation was waiting, but his eyes were focused on but one group, Kathleen and the four children. Madison, his oldest, broke free and rushed forward with delighted cries, the twins following. Kathleen, dressed for once in a civilian dress, the traditional Rus smock and blouse, with her red hair tucked under a kerchief, looked absolutely delightful, their youngest son in her arms, looking at him wide-eyed. It had been over half a year since he had last seen him, and the boy had obviously forgotten though he did smile tentatively as Andrew stepped off the back of the car, Madison tugging at his pants leg, Jefferson and Abraham grabbing the other. She came forward, leaning up to kiss him.

"You look exhausted."

"I am."

Looking down the length of the platform, he saw anxious families swarming around the three hospital cars that made up the rest of his express train, the first casualties back from the front since the disaster in front of Capua.

"There's no one here," she whispered. "He didn't come down."

Though he was not one for pomp and ritual, the fact that the president had not come to meet him, or at least have an honor guard, was a clear enough indication of the mood. It was also a very public and visible statement by his old friend that there was serious trouble ahead.

"Colonel. How was it?"

He turned to see Gates, editor of *Gates's Illustrated Weekly,* standing expectantly, pad of paper in hand, pencil poised.

"No comment for now, Tom."

"Come on, Colonel. I'm running an extra on the battle, and there's precious little information out other than a partial casualty list and rumor that it was bad."

"You'll have to wait."

"Is it true you've been summoned back by Congress to report before the Committee on the Conduct of the War?"

"Tom, why don't you just back the hell off," Hans snarled.

"I need something, anything," Tom pressed, ignoring Hans.

"Gates," Hans snapped, "I remember how you peed your pants at Gettysburg, you were so damn scared, and hid behind the Seminary building till I dragged you back out. Why don't you print that."

Andrew shook his head at Hans, feeling sorry for Gates, who stood abashed, face turning red.

"Your first fight, Tom. We all peed ourselves at one time or another," Andrew said reassuringly, patting him on the shoulder. "It's all right."

He guided the editor off to one side.

"Look, Tom, it was bad, very bad. In short, they tore us apart, but for the moment you can't publish that."

Tom looked at him, obviously torn between his old loyalty to his colonel and the demands of his new profession.

"Let me report to the president first. Come over to my

place later in the day, and I'll tell you everything I can. Is that fair?"

Tom nodded. "I'm sorry, sir. It's just that this place is going wild with rumors. There's talk that if it's true we lost at Capua, that Congress will vote that the Chin ambassadors sent by Jurak are to be formally received and given the offer of cease-fire."

Andrew sighed and lowered his head.

"Andrew, be careful going in there. That's not the only rumor floating around town this morning."

"What then?"

"Senator Bugarin is calling for Rus formally to secede from the Republic, establish its own state again, and make peace with the Bantags."

"Damn all," Andrew hissed.

It was, of course, illegal according to the Constitution. Given the experience back on his home world, he had written a clause into the document strictly forbidding secession unless three-quarters of Congress, and all the voting citizens, agreed to a new Constitutional convention.

"I told you before we should have hung every last boyar after the revolution before the Merki War," Hans announced, having come up to join the conversation. "Bugarin was in with that crowd then."

"He was formally absolved," Andrew replied sharply, "and remember, he is a senator of the Republic."

"Yeah, sure," Hans snarled, letting fly with a stream of tobacco juice.

"Flavius, the Speaker of the House, is hopping mad, too," Gates continued. "With word that Marcus is missing and presumed dead, a hell of a lot of pressure is on him now to stop trying to be even-handed and think more like the senior representative from Roum."

"He's also now the next in line to the presidency," Hans announced.

Andrew found himself wishing he could block this all out. He had left the battlefield less than a day ago; too much was flooding in too quickly.

"I've got a carriage waiting for us," Kathleen announced, breaking in. "Tom, let Andrew meet with the president, then they'll most likely make a joint statement. Why don't you come over after dinner."

Andrew could not help but smile at the way she could switch on the charm when needed, and the publisher finally relented, backing away and darting off to catch a lieutenant who was being carried off the hospital car on a stretcher.

Kathleen led the way, Madison grabbing her father's hand and chattering away, Andrew replying absently to her conversation. Reaching the carriage, she pried the children loose from their father and handed the baby over to a nurse, who led them away, Andrew waving good-bye as the carriage lurched forward, feeling guilty about his role as a father who was never home and was now too preoccupied to offer them any attention.

They drove past the long row of ambulances drawn up by the station. There was a time when he would have insisted upon stopping, getting out to talk to the men and their families, but he could so clearly sense the mood. In spite of the brilliant sunshine it felt as if there was a dark shadow over the city. Official censorship or not, news was clearly out that the offensive had turned into a bloody disaster.

Reaching the inner gate, they passed into the old city of Suzdal, and for a brief instant he relaxed, enjoying yet again the exotic medieval flavor of the city. Though this section had been twice destroyed in the wars, each time the residents had built it back as it was, though somehow the woodwork now seemed more crudely done and hurried, as if the pace of the new world he had created would not allow time for the ancient Rus art of woodcarving as it was once done. The old gaily painted window frames and decorative designs were gone as well since the lime for whitewash and the lead for paint were both designated as precious war materials.

The carriage finally reached the great square of the city, going past the cathedral, Kathleen making the sign of the cross as they did so. He was tempted to stop, to go in and see if Casmir, the Holy Metropolitan and head of the Rus Orthodox Church, was there, for he knew that the priest would be his staunchest supporter to the bitter end, and at this moment he needed to hear some form of encouragement. But the white banner was not flying over the central onion dome, meaning that the holy father was elsewhere, most likely at the military hospital to help as the first wounded came in.

The carriage turned across the square, the scene of so many triumphal parades, and the place where twice he led the old 35th into battle, first against the Boyar Ivor, and then in the final charge against the Tugars. Memories rushed back of so many who had marched or fought across this square and were now but dust, and Kathleen, as if sensing his mood, reached over and squeezed his hand again.

"Remember the first time we went for a walk here?" she said, as if trying to divert his thoughts from more melancholy contemplations.

He smiled, looking into her eyes, remembering that first wondrous day together, when they had visited the court of Ivor then roamed the city till dusk, having no idea, as yet, of the terror of the hordes.

Straight ahead was the White House. A strange blending of the old and the new, the former palace of a boyar, with all its ornate and intricate stone carvings, high narrow windows, and fairy-tale domes, whitewashed by order of the president in imitation of the legendary place where Lincoln had once resided. He could see a crowd gathered near the steps, a twin line of infantry drawn up to clear the way. A color guard was waiting, bearing the flag of the Republic, and as the carriage stopped at the base of the steps they came to attention. Andrew and Hans stood up, each of them saluting the colors as they stepped down to the cobblestone pavement. A small band of half a dozen drummers and fifers now sounded ruffles and flourishes and then went into "Hail to the Chief." At the top of the steps the president, Andrew's old friend Kal, appeared, wearing his traditional black frock coat and stovepipe hat, beard cut like Lincoln's, always a slightly absurd sight since he stood barely five and a half feet tall, yet touching nevertheless in its respectful imitation of a legend from another world.

Kal slowly came down the steps, the small crowd of bystanders respectfully silent, the few soldiers in the group coming to attention and saluting, civilian men and boys removing their hats and one old woman making the sign of the cross.

Andrew, curious, watched, knowing that protocol demanded that he ascend the steps, not forcing the president to come down to greet him. But Kal had never stood on such foolish protocol, and normally would have been at the station, eager to embrace his friend in a traditional Rus bear hug and kiss. The fact that he had not done so indicated so much to Andrew, and it was such a strange paradox for Andrew had so often lectured the old peasant on the dignity of office and the precedents that needed to be set. Now they were caught in that very game.

Kal stopped midway down the twenty steps, hat still on, and there was a long pregnant pause.

"Don't push it," Kathleen whispered.

Finally, Andrew climbed the steps, trying not to let his fatigue and stiffness show. He came to attention and saluted, Kal nodding a reply but no embrace or even a slap on the shoulder. The effect was immediate, whispers running through the crowd of onlookers. Behind the president Andrew caught a glimpse of several senators, all from Rus, one of them Vasily Bugarin.

"Let's go inside to talk," Kal finally announced.

Andrew nodded in agreement, saying nothing. There was a moment's hesitation as Kal looked over at Hans.

"I want my second-in-command with me," Andrew said, and Kal turned without comment, leading the way up the stairs.

Andrew looked back at Kathleen, who flashed a smile and turned without comment, getting back into the carriage. He felt guilty, not having said more, not feeling more, and that realization was troubling. His feelings were almost an abstraction, a memory, as if he had become so brittle inside that there was no room at the moment for the love and devotion he knew he should feel for his family.

Though it was still early morning, he was glad to step through the ornately carved doors and into the cool dark interior of the executive mansion. Once out of sight of the crowd he hoped that Kal would drop the role and show some warmth, but there was no relenting as the president led the way down the corridor, past the old audience chamber of the boyar and into a side room which served the president as his office.

The room was simply appointed, as was typical of the old Kal. Icons of Perm and Kesus, the half-pagan manifes-

tation of Orthodoxy which had been transplanted to this
world dominated the far wall, with smaller icons of a variety of saints, some of them men of the old 35th and 44th
New York, surrounding the centerpiece. The other walls
were covered with maps studded with red and blue pins
marking the situation on the western front, where remnants
of the Merki were raiding, the coasts of the Inland Sea and
the shadowy war which had resumed against Cartha, and
the Eastern Front from which he had just come. In the
center of the room was a battered oak table around which
a dozen straight-backed chairs were set. Andrew was delighted to see the Holy Prelate Casmir sitting at the far
corner, the priest coming to his feet as Andrew came in.

"Good day to you, Andrew," he said in fairly good English, and Andrew smiled, taking off his old kepi hat with
a show of genuine respect. Across from him was Vincent
Hawthorne, a mere shadow of a ghost, his uniform hanging
loosely on his narrow frame, still sporting the Phil Sheridan
look of pointed goatee and mustache.

Without comment Bugarin took a chair next to Casmir,
and Kal beckoned for Andrew to sit next to Vincent, Hans
taking the chair to Andrew's right while Kal sat down next
to Bugarin.

Andrew was tempted to voice a protest, to ask to be
allowed at least to freshen up and get a bite to eat before
going into this meeting and then somehow get a few minutes alone with Kal to probe out what was going on, but a
cold look from Kal stilled his protest, and as he sat down
he made do with a cup of tea that Casmir made a point of
pouring for the two new arrivals. The prelate then insisted
upon a prayer which ran on for five minutes and which
placed a heavy emphasis on his thankfulness for the safe
return of Andrew and Hans, the need for divine guidance
and strength in the trials to come.

As the three Rus made the sign of the cross Andrew
raised his head and stared straight at Kal.

"Andrew, we need an honest report of what happened
out there and why," Kal said, opening the meeting without
comment or one of his usual witticisms designed to break
the tension.

"I've never been anything but honest with you, Mr. President," Andrew replied coolly, deciding to be formal and avoid the use of the informal nickname of Kal.

Strange, he thought, *you were once a peasant, a storyteller and jester for the Boyar Ivor, hiding your cunning behind the mask of a fool in order to protect your family and yourself when the Tugars came, hoping against hope to thus spare your daughter from being sent to the slaughter pits. Hawthorne, who is now your son-in-law, taught you about the ideals of a Republic, it was you who triggered the rebellion, and for years afterward I taught you all I know about how to rule and wrote the very Constitution which put you in power.*

Andrew could not help but feel a flicker of resentment now, the mentor who found himself outranked by a student, but was this not as it should be, he told himself. *Across all these years I kept demanding that the military must answer to the civilian, and here now are the results.*

"Andrew, please tell us what happened," Casmir interjected. "The entire city is in turmoil with fear, some are even claiming the front has collapsed and the Bantags will be at the gates."

"No, they haven't broken through, the front is the same is it was before the attack."

"In other words you did not gain a single inch of ground," Bugarin interjected.

Andrew shifted his gaze to study the senator. It was rumored that he had tuberculosis; his skin was almost china white, laid flat against the bones of his face. Dark eyes seemed to burn like coals as he returned Andrew's look. In spite of the senator's current stance Andrew found he did have a certain amount of respect for the man. He had avoided the infamous "Boyars' Plot" to overthrow the government before the Merki War and had briefly commanded a regiment and then a brigade before Rus was evacuated. Stricken with illness he left the army and was immediately elected senator.

Yet, in the last year protest against the war had increasingly centered around him, first as a general concern about the progress of the fight, and then increasingly as a voice of separatism and mistrust of the Roum and their ability to fight. That was the one thing Andrew could not comprehend, this damnable wedge being driven between Rus and

Roum. If it succeeded in splitting them apart, the Republic would fracture, and they would all die. How men with the intelligence of Bugarin could not see that was a mystery.

"If you are asking if we held the opposite bank of the river," Andrew replied. "No."

"What are the total losses?" Casmir asked. "I want to know the human cost first."

Andrew sighed, looking up for a moment at the ceiling.

"At least twenty-seven thousand five hundred men killed, wounded or captured out of the forty thousand who crossed the river. Just over nine thousand wounded made it back; all the rest of the casualties were lost."

"Merciful Perm bless them," Casmir intoned, making the sign of the cross.

"And equipment?" Kal asked.

"Every ironclad engaged was lost, that's fifty-three machines. Nineteen light aerosteamers and eleven heavy machines lost as well. Eight field batteries lost, and almost all the equipment for three corps along with two regiments of engineering and pontoon equipment, three corps field hospitals, and somewhere around fifty regimental stands of colors."

Kal blew out noisily and leaned back in his chair.

"How, damn it?" Bugarin cried. "What did you do wrong?"

"Just tell us," Kal said, cutting Bugarin off.

"It was a trap," Andrew said. "Plain and simple. This new leader, Jurak, is different. I fear that the world he came from is far more advanced than mine. He has a better grasp of how to use the new weapons being created, his army is transforming itself into something far different that what we faced with the Tugars and Merki."

Andrew drew in a breath; the room was silent except for the ticking of a small wooden clock on the wall near Kal's desk. He remembered that the clock was the same one Vincent had carved for him long ago before even the Tugars had come.

"They had a new model of land ironclad. Heavier armor and with that the knowledge to keep back out of range of our own ironclads and rocket launchers. There was a new airship, twin engine, faster than our Eagles and almost as fast as the Hornets. Also, they have a new type of gun, like our Gatling, slower firing but still deadly."

"Didn't you anticipate any of this?" Bugarin asked.

"Not directly," Andrew had to admit.

"What do you mean 'not directly'?"

"As commander I had to assume that things would change with their new leader. Also, that they undoubtedly would have new weapons. Jurak, however, was shrewd enough to keep all his cards hidden until we were fully committed, then he unleashed them all in one killing blow.

"Tactically, as well, he presented a new front. I would estimate that at least five of his umens were armed with better rifles, but beyond that they had obviously trained as much as we had. These were not Horde warriors charging blindly—they came on with a skill and purpose we haven't seen before."

"What actually happened," Kal interrupted. "Tell me that."

"We launched the assault following the plans I reviewed with you the week before the attack. Losses in the first stage were less than anticipated, just over two thousand killed and wounded. Six hours into the assault our advanced column was within striking distance of their main depot, five miles east of Capua, when the counterattack struck."

"And you did not anticipate that they would counterattack?" Bugarin asked sharply.

"Of course we expected a counterattack," Andrew replied, trying to keep the weariness and frustration out of his voice. "All of the hordes were masters of mobile warfare and knew enough to keep a mobile reserve positioned behind their lines, either as a force to seal a break or as reserve to deliver the final blow."

"So why were you not prepared?" Kal asked.

Andrew hesitated for a moment, surprised by the coldness in Kal's voice.

"We were prepared. Ninth Corps led the breakthrough supported by the First Ironclad Regiment. Eleventh Corps followed next, anchoring the left flank, while elements of two other corps crossed to anchor the right flank and provide reserves. The Second Ironclad Regiment was held in reserve for the follow-up advance once the pontoon bridges were laid and we felt we had achieved a breakthrough.

"What surprised us was the sheer number of ironclads in their reserves, reports estimate there were upward of two hundred compared to fewer than a hundred of ours, of which we committed only fifty in the first wave, the number of new aerosteamers, their introduction of a machine gun, and finally the tactics of concealment and concentration of ironclads in large striking columns."

"In other words, you were caught unprepared," Bugarin pressed.

Andrew said nothing, and Hans finally interrupted.

"No plan ever fully survives first contact with the enemy, and in war no one can ever prepare for all eventualities."

"You were against this offensive, weren't you, Hans?" Kal asked.

Now it was Hans's turn to hesitate.

"Yes, he was," Andrew said. "The responsibility is mine."

There was a long silence again, and Andrew half wondered if Kal, for a variety of reasons, would ask for his resignation and turn command over to Hans. That was indeed part of the reason he had insisted that Hans leave the front and return to Suzdal with him. There was even a bit of a wish that indeed such a decision would be made, relieving him of all that was pressing in.

"The retreat, I heard it was a rout," Bugarin said, breaking the silent tension.

"Yes, there is no denying that. The river was at our backs, the men quickly realized that the enemy was breaking through on both flanks and rolling the line up with the intent of creating a pocket. Yes, they ran, ran for their lives as even the best troops will."

"So they ran," Bugarin continued. "Ninth and Eleventh Corps ran, troops primarily made up of men from Roum."

So that was it, Andrew now realized, and he felt a flicker of anger. No senator from Roum was present.

"I don't see Tiberius Flavius, Speaker of the House, present here," Andrew replied coolly. "As Speaker, isn't he entitled to be here as well, Mr. President?"

"This is an informal discussion," Kal replied.

"It seems more like an inquiry by the Committee on the Conduct of the War," Hans snapped.

"I wasn't asking you for comment, Sergeant," Bugarin growled.

Hans started to stand up, but a look from Andrew stilled him.

"I will accept no aspersions on the gallant soldiers who crossed that river, whether they were Rus or Roum," Andrew said, his voice cutting through the tension.

It was impossible for him to try and explain now all that had happened. Though he would not admit it here, the army had indeed broken, the worst rout he had seen since the disaster along the Potomac.

It was almost like Hispania in reverse, his army disintegrating, falling back to the river a disorganized rabble. But in this room, under the cool gaze of Bugarin and Kal, that was impossible to explain. How to explain the exhaustion, the fighting out of the army as an offensive weapon? He knew that to try and explain that now would be an admission of defeat.

Yet was this not defeat? He could admit to the loss of the battle at Capua and take responsibility for it. Yet was this the beginning of the end he wondered? Would the army continue to disintegrate and fall back, or was there some desperate way to wring one last victory out of the situation and save what was left?

"Why did you let the vice president go into the attack against my orders?" Kal asked.

Andrew was silent. The memory of the broken body of his old friend, carried back across the river by men from the 11th, was still too fresh.

"I could not stop him," Andrew replied sadly. "He insisted that he go forward with 'his boys,' as he called them. I understand that was part of the reason for the rout. When the counterattack was launched he was caught by the opening barrage of rockets and killed instantly. Word quickly spread through the ranks . . ."

His voice trailed off. Still hard to believe that Marcus was dead. Yet another part of the political equation he had not anticipated.

"And your own actions?" Bugarin asked. "Did you personally try to rally the men?"

Hans bristled yet again; there was a certain tone to the statement, an implication. Andrew did not respond for a moment, never dreaming that someone might actually question his own behavior under fire.

Kal was the first to react. With an angry gesture he cut Bugarin off.

"This is an inquiry," Kal snapped, "not an inquisition."

There was a flicker of eye contact, and Andrew felt at least a small sense of relief. Some of the old Kal was still there and was not comfortable with the way things were going.

"I'm willing to answer," Andrew said, breaking the silence. He looked past Kal, staring at the ceiling.

"I'll admit here that going under fire again left me nervous, though it did not affect my judgment. I crossed to the east shore and stayed there until it was evident that the north flank had completely caved in."

"Why didn't you call up reinforcements?" Bugarin asked.

"Always reinforce victory, never reinforce defeat," Andrew shot back.

"Wasn't the defeat perhaps in your own mind?"

"I think that after more than a decade of campaigning I know the difference," Andrew replied sharply. "Any unit, even First Corps, would have broken under the pounding inflicted on the left and center. As to a counterstrike, I have to ask with what?

"Three corps went into that assault. I have a total of three left to cover all the rest of that front from the tangles of the Northern Forest down into the mountains of the south. That was our total offensive striking power. If that was blunted, there was nothing left."

"In other words, as an offensive force in this war, the Army of the Republic is finished," Bugarin replied sharply, staring straight at Kal.

Andrew inwardly cursed. It was exactly what he did not want to admit to but had now been maneuvered into saying.

"And if the Bantag now launch a counterattack?" Bugarin pressed. "Can you stop it?"

"We have to stop it."

"You didn't answer my question."

"There is no alternative," Andrew snapped.

"Perhaps there is."

"There is no alternative," Andrew repeated, his voice sharp with anger. "We cannot make a deal with the Bantag; that will divide us and in the end kill all of us. We must fight if need be to the bitter end."

Bugarin stood up and leaned over the table, staring directly at Andrew.

"You have been nothing but a disaster to us, Keane. We have fought three wars, hundreds of thousands have died, and now we are trapped in a war that we are losing. Beyond that we are trapped in an alliance with an alien people who can't even defend their own land. As chairman of the Committee on the Conduct of the War, I hereby summon you to give a full accounting of this disaster."

With barely a nod of acknowledgment to Kal, the senator stalked out of the room. Casmir, rising from his chair, motioned for Kal to stay and hurried out after Bugarin.

Andrew sat back down, realizing that Kal was staring at him coldly.

"Now you see what I am dealing with here," Kal announced. "You'd better prepare yourself for what you'll have to face over the next couple of days."

Andrew nodded. "Kal, you at least know the boys out there tried their damnedest to win."

"I know that, Andrew, but it doesn't change the fact that nearly twenty thousand more families lost a son, or father, or husband. How much longer do you think we as a people can take this?"

"Until we win," Hans replied coolly.

"Define victory to me when we are all dead," Kal whispered. "Andrew, we have to find a way out of this war."

"Kal, there's only one way," Hans interjected.

"You, old friend, are a soldier, and that is the path you must see to victory," Kal replied, his voice filled with infinite weariness. "I, as president, am forced to consider alternate means. I might not like them, I might not even trust them, but I do have to consider them, especially when Bugarin has rallied a majority of senators."

Andrew looked over at Vincent, who nodded. That bit of news was a shock. If Bugarin held the majority, the Senate could force the issue to a vote at any time.

"Kal, we can't surrender. Nor can we allow the Republic

to split. Jurak is obviously outproducing us. Any agreement, even a temporary cease-fire, will play to his hand."

"I hear that from you, Andrew. From Bugarin I hear threats of breaking the Republic apart if need be to end the war. From the Roum representatives I hear complaints about our supposed suspicions regarding them. From Webster I hear that the economy is tottering into collapse. Tonight, as the casualty lists come in, I will sit and write letters until dawn, sending my regrets to old friends who've lost a loved one."

His voice seemed near to breaking.

He lowered his head, put on his stovepipe hat, and slowly walked out the room, moving as if the entire weight of the world was upon him.

Andrew, Hans, and Vincent stood respectfully as he left.

Andrew sighed, settling back in his chair and looking over at Vincent, who smiled weakly.

"Hawthorne, just what the hell is going on back here?" Hans asked, going around to the side table and taking the pot of tea from which Casmir had poured earlier and refilling his own cup. Taking a fruit vaguely resembling an apple but closer in size to a grapefruit, he settled into the chair Kal had occupied, pulled a paring knife from his haversack, and began to peel off the thick skin from the fruit.

"It's madness here," Vincent began. "Kal is losing control of Congress, which is fracturing between representatives of Rus and Roum. The Roum bloc is claiming the war is not being pressed hard enough to expel the invader from their soil. Beyond that there are some who are claiming it is deliberate in order to cut down the population and thus establish an equal balance in the House."

"That's insane." Andrew sighed. "Damn all, who the hell could even think that?"

"And the Rus side?" Hans asked.

"Well, you heard it straight from Bugarin. The Roum can't fight and the burden is resting on the old army of Rus. We lost tens of thousands pulling their chestnuts out of the fire last winter and now, in this last battle, they panic again."

"Never should have named them the Ninth and Eleventh Corps," Hans said. "It was unlucky with the Army of the Potomac, and the same here."

"Funny, even that legend is spreading around," Vincent said, "some of the Roum claiming it's a jinx we deliberately set on them."

Andrew could only shake his head in disbelief.

"So the bottom line?" Andrew asked.

"Word is the Senate will vote a resolution today asking for your removal from command."

There was a quick exchange of looks between Andrew and Hans as the sergeant cut off a piece of peeled fruit and passed it over to Andrew.

"It won't happen of course. You'll stay, and there'll be a staged show of support for you, but the mere fact that it happens will weaken your position."

"Figured that, but what's the real game?"

"Far worse. With Crassus dead, and no vice president, the Roum representatives are increasingly nervous. Speaker Flavius is next in line but remember he isn't of the old aristocracy of Roum. He was once a servant in the house of Marcus who rose through the ranks, was disabled after Hispania, and found himself in Congress."

Andrew nodded. He had tremendous admiration for Flavius. A true natural soldier. If he had not been so severely wounded, he undoubtedly would have risen to command a division, or even a corps. His selection as Speaker had been something of a surprise, but then the House was dominated by old veterans, both Roum and Rus from the lower classes. But he didn't have the blind support and instant obedience Marcus could command. Marcus could merely snap his fingers, and all would listen. Flavius lacked that, and though he was now but a heartbeat away from the presidency, Andrew knew he could not stem the growing friction between the two states of the Republic.

"Bugarin will hold hearings about the battle at Capua. He'll declare the war lost and push for a cease-fire."

"An agreement with the Bantag?" Hans asked. "Damn all to hell I keep telling you, Andrew, we should be shooting those Chin envoys they keep sending through."

"I can't. Congress specifically ordered that we receive them and pass them along."

"And they're nothing but damned spies."

"Don't you think I know that?" Andrew snapped hotly.

Hans settled back in his chair, saying nothing at the tone of rebuke and frustration.

"Are there the votes for a cease-fire?" Andrew asked.

"No, not yet, but the real maneuver is to break the Republic. Reestablish an independent state of Rus, cut Roum off, and pull the army out."

"And after the Bantag crush Roum they'll be at our gates."

"You know that, I know that," Hawthorne replied, "but for a lot of folks here, any offer of peace, even if but for six months or a year, with the boys back home, and the crushing work in the factories eased off . . . well that seems all right with them.

"Bugarin's already floating around a plan to build a fortified line at Kev, claiming that even if the Bantag did betray the agreement, without having to worry about Roum or holding Tyre, we'd have more than enough to stop them."

"They're fools," Hans cried, his anger ready to explode as he glared at Vincent.

"Yes, but remember I've been stuck back here since last year being your liaison, so don't blame me for the bad news."

Andrew could see that being cut out of the action was still wearing on Vincent but on the other side his exposure to all the administrative work as chief of staff was seasoning Hawthorne, training him for a day when, if they survived, he would take the mantle of control.

"You should go into the factories," Vincent said. "I'm in there damn near every day now, trying to keep production up. They're hellholes, old men, women, children as young as eight working twelve-hour shifts six days a week. Emil is pitching a fit, about conditions. Tuberculosis is up, and a lot of the women working in the factory making percussion caps are getting this strange sickness; Emil says it has something to do with mercury, the same as with hatters.

"There's shortages of everything, especially since we're feeding nearly a million Roum refugees who lost their land. A lot of folks are getting by on gruel and watery soup with a hint of meat dipped into it. The prosperity we saw building two years ago is completely out of balance now. A few folks, mostly old boyars and merchants are getting filthy rich on the war industries, but the ordinary workers are slipping behind."

"So get Webster in, have them figure out some new kind of tax. Hell, he's the financial wizard who figured it all out in the first place," Andrew said, always at a loss when it came to the finances of running a war.

"He's trying, Andrew, but these same people have the ears of Congress and block any changes in the taxes. We cobbled together an industrial war society. The Union could take it back home; we had two generations of change to get used to it. The Confederacy didn't, and remember how they were falling apart. Well, it's the same here. We're producing the goods but barely hanging on, in fact it's slipping apart. Rebuilding the railroads after last winter's campaign, and the buildup for this last offensive meant too many other things were not done. Webster said it's like pouring all the oil we have on only half the machine. Well, the other half, the installations, morale, political support, they're all seizing up and falling apart."

Andrew did not know how to reply. During the early spring, after his recovery from the wound, he had tried to understand just how complex it had all become, attending meetings with Webster that would go half the night. He'd demand more ironclads, locomotives, better breechloaders and flyers, and ammunition, always more ammunition, and Webster would repeat endlessly that it meant scrimping on something else equally important if they were to keep the machine of war running.

"You want to understand disenchantment with this war, go into the factories at two in the morning and you'll see. There have even been rumors about strikes to protest the war and conditions."

"It's that or the slaughter pit," Hans growled, cutting another piece of fruit and this time tossing it to Vincent.

"It's been what, more than six years since this city was the front line," Andrew said wearily. "We've taken well over a hundred thousand more casualties in this war. I can understand people back here grasping at any straw that's offered."

"In fact even the good news from the western front seems to be hurting us," Vincent said.

"What's that?"

"Sorry, I guess you didn't hear. We got reliable intelligence that Tamuka was kicked out by what was left of the Merki Horde following him."

"That bastard," Hans growled. "I hope they made him a eunuch or better yet killed the scum."

It was rare that Andrew heard a truly murderous tone in Hans's voice, but it flared out now. It was Tamuka who first held Hans prisoner. He could see his friend actually trembling with pent-up rage at the mere mention of the name.

"What happened?" Andrew asked.

"You know that the skirmishing has died off on the western frontier. So much so that I'm recommending relieving a division posted out there and shifting it over to the eastern front. A couple of weeks back a small band of people came into our lines, refugees from what apparently are folks descended from Byzantine Greeks living to the southwest. They said that a umen of the Merki came to their town, killed most of them, but the survivors witnessed a big blowup, the bastards were killing each other and a one-handed Merki who was the leader was driven out of the band."

"That's got to be him," Hans snarled. "Even his own kind hated him. And he wouldn't have the guts to die with some honor rather than run."

"The rest of them took off, riding west; the one hand, with maybe a score of followers, rode east."

"I wonder where to?" Andrew mused.

"Straight to hell I hope," Hans interjected.

"Word got back here, and Bugarin said it shows that we will now have more than enough troops to defend ourselves."

There was a long moment of silence, and yet again he was troubled by all the changes he and his men had created here. Industrialization was the only hope for survival in their war against the hordes, to stay ahead of them in technology and use that to offset their skill and numbers. But ever since the arrival of Ha'ark and Jurak, their hope for that edge was disappearing, and in many ways had clearly been lost in front of Capua. Though on his old world, America had embraced technology and what industrialization could provide, he knew there was a dark side to it, the teeming noisome hellholes around the factories, children laboring in smoky gloom, the mind-numbing dullness of a life of labor. He could balm his conscience with what the alternative was, but for most peasants what had happened in their lives?

Ten years ago they waited in dread for the arrival of the Tugars but resigned themselves to that fate, knowing that but one in ten went to the slaughter and then the Horde rode on and the cycle of life continued the dread of the return twenty years—a lifetime, away. Though he could not truly comprehend it, he could indeed see where some might say the old ways were preferable to what they had now.

Through the high window he could hear a stirring outside, distant shouting, and he froze for an instant, wondering if indeed there was already rioting in the streets over the defeat at Capua. He stared off, unsure of what to do next.

"Andrew, we have to end this war," Vincent announced.

"You talking surrender, too, boy?" Hans asked, his voice icy.

"No, hell no," Vincent replied. "But it's my job to tell Andrew and you what is going on at the capital. Hell, I'd rather be at the front than here. I know what you two saw at Capua. The difference here is that since this campaign started no one in Rus, except for the soldiers, has seen a Bantag, except for those raiders around Kev. All they know is the hardship and shortages without seeing the enemy face-to-face. Those damn Chin ambassadors are talking sweet words, and some are listening, and then the rumors get spread out."

"My people, are they working on the ambassadors?"

Andrew found it interesting how Hans referred to the three hundred Chin whom he had led out of captivity from Xi'an as "my people." In a way they had become his own personal guard. There was even a Chin brigade now, made up of those who had escaped during the winter breakthrough into Ha'ark's rear lines, and shortly they would go to the front. In a way they were Hans's personal bodyguard, his status with them as liberator raising him to a godlike position in their eyes. It was his idea to make sure they were put in contact with the human ambassadors representing the Horde.

"I have their reports waiting for you," Vincent said. "Sure, they admit that if they fail to return with a peace agreement their entire families will be sent to the slaughter pits. Some have even whispered it's all a crock what they're saying but none will do so publicly out of fear that word will get back to Jurak. But this Jurak is shrewd, damn shrewd. His last messenger said they would offer to stop the slaughter pits, the same as the Tugars did."

"Damnable lie," Hans cried. "I was there; I saw what they did."

"The Tugars stopped," Andrew said.

"We haven't heard from them in years; they might very well be back at it," Hans replied.

"I'm not sure. They learned our humanity—that changed it."

"And you believe this Jurak?" Hans asked heatedly.

"Of course not. He and I both know one clear point. This is a war of annihilation. After all that has happened, it is impossible for this world to contain both of us. Anything he offers is the convenience of the moment to buy breathing time, to split us apart."

"I wish we did have a year's breathing time," Vincent interjected.

"It'd be a year's breathing time for him, too, and never at the price of losing the Roum."

"Andrew!"

Surprised he looked up to see Kathleen standing in the doorway, face red, breathing hard, as if she had been running.

"What's wrong?" and for an instant he thought it was something with the children.

"You're all right, thank God."

"What?"

"Someone just tried to assassinate Kal!"

Andrew was out of his chair, followed by Hans and Vincent. He suddenly realized that the clamor outside the building had risen in volume, and with the door open, the shouting in the corridors was audible as well.

"Where is he? Is he all right?"

"In his quarters; Emil was sent for and I followed."

Furious that he hadn't been told immediately Andrew pushed through the growing turmoil in the hallways, shov-

ing his way past the crowd in the old audience chamber
and back around to the rear of the building and the private
apartments. Andrew caught a glimpse of Tanya, Kal's
daughter and Vincent's wife. Crying she ran up to Vincent,
who swept her up under his arm, shouting questions.

Andrew forced his way through the troops assigned as
the presidential guard and into the bedroom. Emil looked
up angrily from the side of the bed and for a moment
Andrew froze at the sight of the black frock coat, covered
with blood, lying crumpled on the floor, the battered stovepipe hat beside it, just above the brim an ugly blood-soaked
gash cut along the side. Kal, eyes closed, features pale, was
lying on the bed, the pillow beneath him stained with
blood, his wife kneeling on the other side, crying hysterically, Casmir behind her, hands resting on her shoulders.

For a flash instant he remembered a nightmare dream of
years ago in which he had seen his hero, Abraham Lincoln,
in the same pose, dead from an assassin's bullet.

"Out, all of you out!" Emil shouted.

Andrew did not move.

Emil rose from the side of the bed and came up to him.

"Please, Andrew, I need his wife out of here; if you go,
she'll follow with the others."

"What happened?"

"I don't know, I wasn't there," Emil said wearily.
"Casmir said they were walking across the plaza when a
shot was fired from atop the church. Thank God at the
same instant someone called his name and he started to
turn. The ball creased his head. He might have a fractured
skull, I'm not sure, but I've seen worse who lived."

"But he's unconscious," Vincent said nervously.

"Hell, you'd be, too, if someone cracked the side of your
head like that. Like I said, I'm not sure if it's fractured. I
just want quiet in here, so please leave."

Andrew nodded, withdrawing, motioning for Casmir to
follow. The priest gently guided Tanya out with him, her
cries echoing in the hallway, creating a dark tension that
was ready to boil over as everyone was asking who and
why.

Andrew caught the eye of the captain of the guard and
motioned him over.

"Secure this building, Captain. Six guards on this door,

then sweep the building, everyone outside, send them home or, if they live here, they're to go to their rooms and stay. Send a messenger over to the barracks of the Thirty-Fifth, mobilize them out, secure a perimeter around this building and Congress."

"There's no need to surround Congress."

It was Bugarin, features flushed with excitement.

"Senator, as commander of the military I am responsible for security, and I ask you not to interfere."

"And it sounds like it could be the start of a coup to me, Colonel."

"Follow your orders, Captain," Andrew snapped. "Report back to me within a half hour."

"I said there is no need for this now."

Andrew finally turned back to face Bugarin.

"I'll be the judge of that, sir."

"The culprit has already been caught."

"What?"

"And hung by the crowd outside; it was a Roum soldier."

"Merciful God," Andrew whispered in English.

Though all urged him to launch the attack, still he refused, counseling calm, the gathering of strength before the final unleashing of the storm.

"As your own ancestor Vigarka once declared, 'When the portal of victory appears open, gaze twice before entering.'"

Jurak saw several of the clan leaders nodding in agreement, chant singers who stood at the back of the golden yurt exchanging glances of pleasure that their new Qar Qarth could so easily quote from the great history of the ancestors.

"We know we have destroyed three of their umens," and as he spoke, he pointed to the Corps commanders' guidons hanging from the ceiling of the great yurt, shot-torn and stained regimental flags by the dozens clustered around them.

"That leaves but three on this front; surely our twenty-five umens can overwhelm that," Cavgayya of the 3rd umen of the black horse replied.

"Yes, we can overwhelm that, but why spend so needlessly of our sacred blood. More than fifty thousand yurts mourn their sons and fathers from the war before the great city of the cattle. Though we won this battle, still another fifteen thousand mourn. Our seed is not limitless like that of the cattle; each of your lives is precious to me.''

Again he could see the nods of agreement. Ha'ark had been a profligate with the lives of the Bantag. It wasn't just the fifty thousand before Roum, it was another seventy thousand casualties to bring the army to Roum, nearly a third of their total strength of warriors lost. Yes, he suspected he could break through even this evening, but let it simmer just a bit longer, he reasoned. Keep the pressure on with raids, shows of strength. And most of all let the dozens of new ironclads, that even now were being sent to Xi'an and from there shipped across the Great Sea, come up to the front. Then he would launch the final push.

But perhaps that might not even be necessary, he thought with a smile. *Their will is cracking.*

"There shall be time to finish this war forever and with but a few more drops of blood compared to the buckets spent already.''

Chapter Five

Suzdal was seething with rumors of plots and counterplots as Andrew stepped out of his simple clapboard house on the village square, the guards standing to either side of his porch snapping to attention.

After the battle against the Tugars, and the destruction of the lower quarter of the city, the men of the 35th had been given this section of the city as a place to live, and there they had built a fair replica of a New England town square, complete with Presbyterian and Methodist churches, a monument in the center of the square to the men who had come to this world, and a bandstand, where in the brief periods of peace, evening concerts had been held.

Andrew allowed himself the indulgence of a cigar while Hans, hands in his pocket, leaned against a pillar of the porch, anxiously looking around for a place to spit before settling on a bare spot of ground next to a bush covered with exotic yellow flowers. Emil came out a moment later, slapping his stomach.

"First halfway decent meal I've had in days," Emil announced.

Andrew smiled. How Kathleen had managed to scrounge up a piece of corned beef and what passed for cabbages on this world was beyond him. Upstairs he could hear the children settling into bed, and again he felt guilt for not going upstairs to spend a little time, to play with them and forget, but too much had happened today, and there was still more to be done.

"You can almost sense it in the air," Emil said. "This place is ready to explode."

It had come close to a riot in the hours after the assassination attempt. Emil declared that Kal stood a chance of making it even though his skull had indeed been fractured by the glancing blow of the bullet. Most of the citizens of the city, though, were convinced that Kal was already dead no matter what Emil or anyone else said. It had almost come to a fight when Andrew personally led a detachment to cut down the broken body of the Roum soldier who had been dragged out of the cathedral and strung up from a tavern sign. It took the intervention of Casmir to still the mob, and the body was taken by a detachment of soldiers to the Roum temple for burial in the catacombs. A guard was now on that temple, and orders passed that any Roum citizens in the city were to remain inside for the time being.

The only good thing to come out of it all was the cancellation of the meeting with the Committee, but that ordeal would come later in the week.

"Here comes Hawthorne," Hans announced, and Andrew saw Vincent come around the corner of the square, limping slowly, still using a cane, accompanied by the rest of the men Andrew had summoned, Bill Webster, who was secretary of the treasury, Tom Gates from the newspaper, Varinna Ferguson, and Ketswana, who was Hans's closest friend from their days of captivity and now served on his staff.

As the group came up the steps Andrew motioned for them to stand at ease and led the way into the small dining room, which had already been cleared of the evening meal. The group settled around the table, Andrew playing the role of host and passing around tea and, for those who wanted something stiffer, a bottle of vodka.

"All right, we've got to have it out," Andrew said. "Perhaps I've been out of touch," and he hesitated, "what with getting wounded and staying up at the front. I need to know just what the hell is going on back here."

No one wanted to open, and finally his gaze fixed on Webster. Years behind the desk had added a bit to his waistline, and his face was rounder, but the flag bearer who had won a Medal of Honor leading a charge still had the old courage in his eyes and the ability to talk straight when needed.

"The economy is in a shambles, sir."

"You were responsible to make sure it kept running," Hans interjected.

"Yes sir, I was. Now I could go into some long-winded lecture on this, but the plain and simple fact is we've tried ever since we've arrived here to pull these people across a hundred years of development in less than a generation. We've created a top-heavy system here, and the strain is now showing."

"Top-heavy? What do you mean?" Andrew asked.

"Well sir. Back when this all started all we needed to build was a factory, actually several factories, that could turn out lightweight rails, steam engines, and a few small locomotives, and works to make powder, smoothbore muskets, light four-pound cannons, and shot. That didn't take much doing once we got the idea rolling. Primitive as we thought them to be, the Rus can be master craftsmen, and they quickly adapted."

"And the Tugars were breathing down our necks to spur us along," Hawthorne interjected.

Webster nodded in agreement and pushed on.

"We had a couple of years of peace after that to consolidate. In fact that was our boom period thanks to the building of railroad installations and the mechanization of farming with McCormick reapers, horse-drawn plows and planters. We produced surpluses that weren't going into a war, but rather were going to generate yet more production. We even had enough surplus that it started to improve people's lives as well, things like additional food, clothing, and tools. We started schools, literacy went up, and with it even more productivity."

"Don't forget medicine and sanitation," Emil interjected, and Webster nodded.

"Right there for example, sir. We had close to a thousand people working in Suzdal alone to install sewers and pipes for water. The same in Roum and every other city. We had thousands more building hospitals, training as nurses, midwives, and doctors. They were taken out of the traditional labor force, but the economy could afford that and in fact benefited directly by it. People had immediate benefits with lower mortality, particularly with children. Such things had a major impact on people's morale and willingness to work.

"Then the Merki War comes along. Sir, as we all know, Rus was devastated from one end to the other in that fight.

We scorched earth like the Russians did against Napoléon; the only thing we evacuated were the machines to make weapons and tools. After the end of that war the rebuilding normally would have taken a generation. Barely a home, other than in Suzdal, was left standing, and in addition we had to help Roum with the building of their railroads.

"Beyond all that we had to change our industry completely to outfit a new kind of army. Now it was rifles, breech-loading guns, more powerful locomotives, aerosteamers, ironclads, new ships for the navy, heavier rail for the track. Tolerances on all machinery had to be improved a full magnitude or more.

"For example our old muzzle-loading flintlocks were nothing more than pipes mounted on wooden stocks; if they were off a hundredth of an inch in the barrel no big deal. The caliber of the ball was three-hundredths of an inch smaller than the barrel anyhow.

"When it comes to our new Sharps model breechloaders, however, we're talking thousandths of an inch tolerances on each part. It took tremendous effort, precision, and training to reach that. We had to take thousands of men and women and train them from scratch, and that took time, surplus, and money. Remember, they still have to eat, have housing, and the basics of life, even though while they are learning new skills they aren't directly contributing anything to the economy."

Andrew nodded, trying to stay focused on what was being said but already feeling frustrated. His point of attention had always been the battlefield, and the politics of shaping a republic, having to deal with this aspect, was troubling to him.

"All our production energy went into improving our military," Webster continued without pause, "rather than things directly needed to build a broader base of wealth for everybody. Even though we were at peace, we were still running a wartime economy. Living standards, both here and in Roum, actually started to drop as a result even though people were working harder.

"If we had had five years, better yet ten, we could have adjusted, eased off, produced things like housing, schools, churches, hospitals other than for the military, improved roads, made better farm tools, laid track for the transport of goods rather than for items of military priority, trained doctors for the villages rather than the army, and for that matter had hundreds of thousands of young men building these things rather than carrying rifles. So when this new war started the strain redoubled.

"Add into that the fact that more than half of Roum is occupied territory. Some of our richest land is in the hands of the Horde, with more than a million refugees having to be provided for."

"Wait a minute," Hans interjected. "I keep hearing about how nearly half the Rus have died as a result of the wars."

"That's right," Webster replied quietly.

"Then give that land to the Roum refugees."

"They still have to have places to live, seeds for crops. Some of the fields have been fallow for five years or more and are overgrown. We're trying that, but still, what they're producing is maybe one-tenth of what they grew a year ago."

Hans grunted, looked around, and finally spat out the open window. Andrew could not help but grin and made certain not to make eye contact with Kathleen.

"The point is," Webster pressed, "the economy is brittle. The best analogy I can give is that we're like the Confederacy in late 1864. Sherman is cutting the heart out of Georgia, Sheridan has burned the valley, the rail lines have been pounded to pieces by overuse and undermaintenance. I remember Sherman saying that war was not just the armies that fought, it was the entire nation, and he was taking the war into the heart of the enemy nation."

"That's what the Bantag have done, though I don't know if they're actually aware of it or not."

"From what I suspect of Jurak he's aware of it," Andrew replied.

"I hate to say this, sir," Webster replied, "but no matter how gallant our army the folks back home are just plumb worn-out. People no longer trust the paper money we introduced. The women that make fuses for shells, we were paying them five dollars a week a year ago, now it's fifty. I'm printing money twenty-four hours a day, and no one wants it anymore. Andrew, the tens of thousands who work in the factories have to eat since they're no longer growing their own food. We have no gold or silver reserves, so what do we pay them with?"

He fell silent looking around guiltily as if he had created the bad tidings. Everyone knew he had wrought a miracle just managing to build the system up, and for Andrew it was frightful to hear that it was on the point of collapsing.

"And the Bantag, isn't that reason enough to work?" Hans replied. "Damn it all, their sons and husbands are dying up at the front. Isn't that reason to go and work?"

"A growling stomach, your children crying because they're hungry can blunt the argument," Gates replied. "I'm out there every day talking to people, getting news."

"And what are they saying?" Andrew asked.

"Maybe if the Bantag were pouring over the White Mountains by Kev, maybe that would rouse them up again. But then again, Andrew, how many times have they already endured that since we got here? It's these damn Chin ambassadors talking peace and the word going straight from the floor of Congress to the streets that's helping to undermine it."

"And can't they see it's a damned lie?" Hans cried. "I was there, damn it. The Bantag are no different than the Merki, or even the Tugars for that matter."

"We have to talk not about what we wish or desire, but rather what is," Hawthorne replied.

Andrew looked over at his young chief of staff.

"Go on, Vincent."

"I think Webster and Gates are right. War weariness is eroding our ability to fight. All these people went into this war with little if any concept of what freedom was, other than a vague ideal. Next they expected that it would be one short hard fight and decided. No one, not even us, anticipated a series of wars that would drag on for close to a decade."

Andrew found that idea alone to be troubling. The question had been raised more than once during his old war back home as to whether a republic had the ability to maintain a long-term conflict. It was through the personal strength of George Washington alone that the Revolution had not finally degenerated into a military dictatorship.

In the war with the Confederacy if victory had not been so evidently close in 1864, the Democrats most likely would have won the elections and accepted a divided country, thus squandering the blood of more than a quarter million Union men who had died to hold the United States together. Given that knowledge he wondered if a republic could endure this continual battering?

"Politics in Congress," Vincent continued, "is dividing the Republic not just between Roum and Rus, but also between those who are accepting the bait of terms and those who are not. Finally, there is the simple military question we must all face."

"And that is?"

"Can we still win in the field?"

Andrew looked around the room. Kathleen stood in the doorway, hands tucked into her apron pockets. Upstairs he could hear one of the children engaged in some mischief, their nanny trying to shush him to silence. All eyes were upon him, forcing the question that had burdened his soul long before the start of the doomed offensive.

"It's not a question of can we win," Andrew offered, "rather it's a statement that there is no alternative to victory. Even if we had lost the war back home, we would have gone on living. Sure, we all remember the stories about Andersonville and Libby Prison, but even then we knew that if cornered, surrender was still an option, and most Rebs would share their canteen with you and bandage your wounds. We were fighting a war where surrender for either side was an option. If we had lost that war, we would not have liked the results, but we would have gone home and continued to live.

"We'll most likely never know if indeed we did win the war back on Earth. I think it was evident that we would. As for the Confederates, defeat did not mean annihilation or even enslavement, so we were all seeing that many of them were willing finally to have peace and to accept the consequences. Here there is no such luxury."

"You haven't answered the question, sir," Vincent pressed.

Andrew bristled slightly at the cold, almost accusing tone in Vincent's voice but knew that the boy was doing his job, and besides, he would be forced to answer the same question before Congress.

"If it continues as it is," he hesitated, looking down at his clenched fist, "no, we will lose the war."

There was a stirring in the room, looks of fear, shock. All except Hans who didn't stir, his jaw continuing to move mechanically as he worked his chew of tobacco.

"Why?" Gates asked.

"It was always the edge of superior technology that offset their numbers. We had barely a corps of men armed with smoothbores when the Tugars came. We were outnumbered ten to one, but it was enough to stop them. Against the Merki we fielded six corps, about the same size army that fought at Gettysburg. We were outnumbered six to one there, and that was a damn close run for they had smoothbores and artillery the same as we did, but we had moved on to rifles, rockets, and better airships.

"Even last fall we had an edge. They had the land ironclads, but we quickly made one that was better and armed with Gatling guns. But in one short year they've caught up with some sort of rapid-fire gun, their airships are as good as ours, and their new ironclads heavier than ours and able to outgun us.

"As to the numbers. One corps is wasted guarding the frontier to the west. Two more corps are ringing the territory to the southeast of Roum. We have three corps in the pocket down on the eastern coast of the Inland Sea, and—until three days ago—we had eight corps on the main front. Now we have little more than five corps on that front."

He hesitated for a moment.

"So we've lost the edge. They're outproducing us. They outnumber us six to one on the Capua Front. We can assume that within a fortnight they will force a crossing the same as we tried, the difference being that they will succeed. At that moment, in a tactical sense, we will be exactly where we were back at midwinter. Strategically, however, the difference will be that their weapons are better, their commander more prudent, and we will be down well over fifty thousand men compared to what we had the last time."

"And so that's it?" Gates asked.

"I think the political ramifications are clear enough," Andrew continued. "Marcus, God rest him, is dead. Though he was bloody difficult at times, he was a friend I could trust. That strong leadership from Roum is now a vacuum.

Flavius is good as Speaker of the House but doesn't have the following Marcus did. I fear that once the line is broken, Jurak will shrewdly offer terms yet again, the fears between the two states of the Republic will explode, the Republic will fracture, and then we shall be destroyed."

Andrew stopped talking. As he reached over to his glass of tea he realized his hand was trembling.

"Are you suggesting that we stage a coup d'état?" Gates asked.

"I didn't say that," Andrew replied sharply.

"It has to be considered," Hawthorne replied forcefully.

Startled, Andrew looked over at him.

"Sir, the army knows what it is fighting for. They see what the enemy can do. For that matter damn near every veteran who is no longer in the service because of disabilities understands it as well. Yes, they're war weary, we all are, but they'll be damned if they'll ever bare their throats to the Bantags' butchering knives.

"And as for Congress. If those bastards are willing to sell us down the river, if they're maneuvering to splinter the Republic, then they deserve to be hung as traitors, every one of them."

"What you're saying is treasonous," Andrew snapped.

"If this be treason, make the most of it," Hawthorne cried.

Vincent looked over at Hans. "Ask Ketswana to tell us what he learned."

Hans nodded and quickly spoke to Ketswana in the dialect of Chin which the captives had used while in slavery.

Ketswana replied in broken Rus.

"Roum soldier, one who hung. Was in tavern five minutes before shot fired."

Surprised, Andrew looked at Hans.

"I have my own intelligence net here; they answer to Vincent when I'm not around."

"This was never authorized by me."

"It was by me. The Chin and Zulus were neutral; they could talk to both sides, Rus and Roum. With the stress developing between the two sides I thought it best to act, so I got this going last autumn."

"Something about that shooting didn't sit right from the start," Vincent replied. "I checked that poor boy's record.

Promoted to corporal for heroism at Rocky Hill. Invalid due to dysentery and the last nine months in hospital. But everyone said he was a good soldier, eager to get back. Not the assassin type."

"But he was found in the church?" Kathleen asked.

"Yes, he went running in to try and catch who did it. Then a mob grabbed him, claimed he had a gun, and he was dragged out and hung."

"According to who?"

Hans looked over at Ketswana.

"One of my men drink with him, follow, see all, get away before he hung, too."

"So who was leading this mob?"

"It might have been a crowd carried away with frenzy. It might have been more, though," Hans said.

"Go on."

"Kill the president. There's no vice president; therefore, the Speaker of the House, Tiberius Flavius, becomes president. Either he was plotting to do it or someone else."

"Flavius is an honorable man," Andrew replied sharply. "I knew him as a damn good officer who came up through the ranks, and he's a wounded veteran of Hispania. He's not the type."

"Or then a countercoup," Hawthorne replied. "Blame Flavius for the death of Kal, claim it's a plot by Roum to seize the government, and break the Republic in the process."

"Bugarin?"

"My likely candidate," Hawthorne snapped bitterly.

"Damn all." Andrew sighed. So that's why Hawthorne is thinking coup, strike first in order to prevent one.

There was too much to assimilate. He had been far too preoccupied with the preparations for the offensive and the dealing with the results to give serious consideration as to what was going on seven hundred miles away in the capital. He knew there were tensions but prayed that a successful attack, even one that was just a partial success, would quiet the differences and create the resolve to push the war through to its conclusion. He wondered self-critically if that concern had clouded his decision-making to go ahead with the offensive.

He suddenly felt exhausted, unable to decide what to do

next. He knew that a mere nod of his head would mean that Vincent would get up, walk out of the room, and within the hour Congress would be arrested. Besides the training school of cadets who were now the 35th Maine and 44th New York, there was a sprinkling of forty or fifty men from the original units in the city, holding various key positions. There was a brigade of troops garrisoned there and thousands of discharged vets in the factories who could be called out in an emergency. He'd have the government by morning, straighten out the mess, then go from there.

And, damn it, destroy forever what I wanted to create here. Of that he was certain. Once the precedent had been set, it would be forever embedded in the heart of the Republic. Washington had resisted the temptation knowing the history of Rome and Greece when it came to coups. He would rather have seen the Revolution go down to bloody defeat than betray it. Napoléon, rather than Lincoln and Washington, would then be the model for this Republic, this entire world. The concept of a republic which he had so carefully nurtured since first setting foot upon this world would be lost forever.

Yet even if I did seize control, then what? The war is still being lost. We might hold on for a while, maybe even create a stalemate on the Capua Front, but still Jurak will wear us down, for he has the labor of millions of slaves to support him, and if need be feed him with their own flesh. Either way we lose.

He looked at his friends. How to admit it, that after ten years of valiant effort, they were losing. *Have we been losing all along,* he wondered, *and were just not willing to admit it? If that's true, then is the dream of a republic one that is ultimately doomed to failure?* Though he wanted to believe in Kal, he sensed that his old friend was weakening under the stress, and for the time being he was out of the picture. The other side promised peace. And the greater complexities of the issues—well, tragically, the average person just didn't seem to grasp them.

He had been in the army too long, he realized. In the military issues were far clearer—there was survival or death, that was drilled in from day one. You did the right thing, you survived, make a mistake . . . you died, or worse yet, good men died because of you.

A hell of a lot of good men had just died because of his mistake, his not realizing that the very nature of the war was changing yet again.

It's changed again, so we have to find a way to change it back in our favor. He looked over at Emil.

"I want the truth from you, my friend."

"Go on."

"Since I got wounded, I mean since I came back to command," he hesitated.

Emil leaned forward in his chair. He sensed Kathleen's watchful gaze on him.

"I'm not the same. Something's changed in me."

"We're all changed," Emil started soothingly, but an angry wave from Andrew silenced him.

"No, I don't mean that. It's deeper than that. I feel like I've lost something. Not just my edge, far deeper, the very mettle of my soul. All along I sensed a problem with our assault at Capua, I sensed it but failed to clearly get ahead of the problem and reason it out before it happened."

"No one could have anticipated the response from their new leader," Emil replied.

"But I should have. There's no damn room for a mistake in my position."

He looked around the room at his old friends, wondering for a moment if he was about to dissolve into tears. *Do that, though, and we've all lost.* In the end, he realized, all of it, from the moment they had come through the Portal of Light, back so many years, so many ages ago, all rested upon him.

Damn, I never wanted this, and then he hesitated with his inner remorse as the truth surged up from within. The self-humility was a lie, a damnable lie. He had indeed wanted it.

He had wanted command of the regiment, Hans knew that as far back as Fredericksburg. He loved his old commander, Colonel Estes as a father, but like any son of ability, inwardly he longed to transcend what his father was and could be. And when Estes fell at Gettysburg he had mourned him, yet he had sprung to take his place.

He had wanted a brigade, knowing he could do better than far too many of the damned fools Meade and Grant allowed to command. Here was a harsh realization. One is taught to have humility, to admire one's elders and emulate them, and a display of raw ambition is somehow immoral.

Yet he knew in the core of his soul that he was blessed with something, and that something was the ability to lead . . . and to dream of all the greatness that a republic could be. Yet so unfortunately a republic, and a volunteer army of a republic, far too often drew into its folds the weak, the venal, those who were ambitious for their own sakes.

He looked around at his friends.

"I fomented a rebellion against the natural order of this world," he said slowly. "When we realized what the hordes were, the men actually voted to take ship, to find some safe haven and sit it out, but I talked them into fighting and convinced the Rus they could fight.

"And now it is all crashing down around me.

"Emil, I think I've been sick. Sick within my soul. Ever since this winter the stress of it has paralyzed me. I feel like a puppet. The strings are moved, I woodenly follow into the next step, and thus I've numbly wandered to this point. The government is collapsing, I allowed an offensive to be launched that my inner heart told me not to allow, and now I sit here numbly as the end closes in around us."

Emil said nothing, staring straight into his eyes. The moment seemed to stretch out.

"I believe there are two paths to this world, to any world," Andrew said slowly, his voice thick with emotion. "The one is to believe what the masses believe. To make yourself part of them, and to follow, to follow even as you claim to lead."

"And the other path?" Emil asked.

"If God gave you the ability, even if everyone else thinks you are mad, then use it."

Emil chuckled softly.

"We shall either meanly lose or nobly save the last best hope of mankind," Emil finally offered.

"I'm taking control of this situation," Andrew said. "We're all frightened right now, me most of all. Either we become mad and fight back, or we die. But if we are doomed to die, let's die as free men."

"The dogmas of the quiet past are inadequate to the stormy present."

Surprised, he looked up at Kathleen, who had just spoken. She smiled knowingly, as if having sensed every thought that had crossed his mind.

"And as our case is new," Gates continued, "we must act anew and think anew. We must disenthrall ourselves and then we shall save our country."

Andrew smiled at the recitation of Lincoln's famous words. The room was hot, silent except for the ticking of the grandfather clock in the corner of the room, the only other sound the laughter of one of the children upstairs.

We must disenthrall ourselves . . . but how damn it, how?

"We have to end the war now," Kathleen said. Her voice was hard, cold. It wasn't a statement of speculation or hope, it was merely hard honest fact.

He looked up at her.

"You mean negotiate?"

"No, damn it. No! We all know where that will lead. It will merely postpone our deaths. If you do that, I'll go upstairs and poison our children rather than have them live with the death we all know will come. Jurak cannot rest until all in this room, and all touched by you, are dead. He understands us too well, and thus understands the threat that we are."

"So what is the alternative then?" Andrew sighed. "Another offensive? The government will block it. For that matter I wonder if we'll even have a government or a united effort in another few days."

"Exodus, go north," Webster ventured quietly.

"You mean just leave?" Andrew asked.

"Exactly. We did it before, we evacuated all of Rus against the Merki. Well, maybe the mistake was we tried to hold on to the steppe region. Lord knows how far north the forest belt extends. Pack it up, and go into the forest until we find a place where they won't follow."

"We've talked about that before," Vincent replied. "It's impossible. First off, the government will break apart on that one. Second, they'll follow us, and we'll be burdened down with hundreds of thousands of civilians, children, old people. It will turn into a slaughter."

"Well if the government does surrender, that's where I think we should all head," Webster replied. "I'll be damned if I stay here and wait to have my throat slit. At least there's some hope in that."

"If I were Jurak," Andrew replied, "I wouldn't care if it took twenty years. I'd hunt down the survivors. There is no way they can ever dream of continuing their ride until they know we are all dead, for once they turn their backs upon us we'll rebuild. The fundamental issue, besides the moon feast, the enslavement, is that they are nomadic. They cannot leave a cancer behind that will spread in their wake."

"He'll kill everyone once we're dead or fled," Hans said. "You people seem to have forgotten something in all this. Andrew, I remember the dream was there for you at the start, but it seems to have blurred. This is not just about us. We started a revolution on this world. The only way it will survive is if we spread the revolution around the entire planet. We must free everyone or no one. I left millions of comrades in slavery when I escaped, and I vowed upon my soul to help set them free and if need be to die doing it."

Andrew was surprised by the passion of Hans's words. He was normally so reticent, and so rarely was an idealism allowed to creep out from behind the gruff Germanic exterior of the old sergeant major. He could not help but smile at the revolutionary passion that moved his oldest friend.

"Then free them," Varinna Ferguson said in flawless English.

For the first time since the meeting had started Andrew took serious notice of the woman sitting on the chair by the doorway. Kathleen's hands slipped down to rest on the woman's slender shoulders. As she spoke it seemed that the voice almost came from somewhere else, so horribly scarred were her features, the skin that had grown over the burns a taut expressionless mask. And yet he could still sense the graceful beauty that was locked within, that had caused Chuck Ferguson to see beyond the torn exterior to the beauty and strength of the soul.

"I didn't know you could speak English," Gates exclaimed, looking over at her in surprise.

"You never asked," she replied, her words causing a round of chuckles from the others. "You were always too busy talking to my husband to notice me."

"My apologies, madam," Gates quickly said, his features turning red, "my most humble apologies."

"You said 'free them,' " Hans said, the slightest tone of eagerness in his voice. "How, may I ask?"

"How did we first know that you were alive?" she replied.

"Jack Petracci flew over us."

She looked inquiringly at Andrew, who nodded. She slowly stood up. In her hands was a battered notebook.

"These are some of my husband's writings. How do you say . . . ideas, dreams. That is why he taught me English, so I could read them after he was gone."

She put the book upon the table and all looked at it with a bit of reverence, for without the mind of Chuck Ferguson they knew they would have died long ago.

"Right after you were rescued, before the war started on the eastern front, he made some notes here." And she opened the book, skimming through the pages until she finally came to the place she wanted. "Just a few pages, but on the night before he died he pointed them out to me, told me to work upon them."

She passed the book over to Andrew. He carefully took the bound volume, scanning the page, wondering how she had managed to master Chuck's infamous scrawled crablike writings.

She reached into her apron pocket, pulled out a sheaf of papers, carefully unfolded them, and laid them out on the table. It wasn't a bundle of papers but rather a large single sheet of drafting paper, half a dozen feet across and several feet wide, taking up most of the table. Andrew noticed just how badly her hands had been burned as well—two of the fingers on her left hand were little more than stumps. As he scanned the paper he saw that half of it was a detailed map, the other half covered with a different kind of handwriting than Chuck's, simple block lettering, some of it calculations, the rest commentary with lines drawn to the map while the far right side of the sheet had sketches of airships.

"I did," she hesitated, "calculations. I think it is possible to do, but the chances? It is win all or lose all."

Andrew stood up and went over to her side, the others gathering around him. He stood silent, scanning the map, then the plan written out, and finally the calculations. It was the details of the plan Vincent had forwarded to him just prior to the assault. He looked over at Vincent; there was the slightest flicker of a smile tracing the corners of his mouth.

"Impossible," Webster announced sharply, breaking the silence.

Andrew looked over at Hans and saw the eyes of his comrade shining brightly, and he felt a stab of fear, knowing what it undoubtedly meant.

"I rejected this idea out of hand less than a week ago," he finally announced.

"That was a week ago," Varinna replied. "Today is today, the day after a defeat. Just minutes ago I heard you admit that we shall lose the war. If we are to lose the war, then this plan should go forward."

"Why?" Emil asked, leaning over the table to study the lines on the map. "I think anyone who goes on this, particularly the airship operation is doomed to die."

"Because it won't matter then," she announced smoothly. "The men who go would die anyhow if they stay home. If they go and die, and lose, then it is the same. If they go, and die, but change the path of the war to victory, then it is a sacrifice that is worth it."

Andrew marveled at her cold precise logic, which cut straight to the heart of the matter.

As if from a great distance he could hear the grandfather clock chiming the hour—it was midnight.

All waited for him to speak. He was torn. He so desperately wanted to grab this, to cling to it, to see it bring them to a change in fate. Yet he feared it as well and all that it suggested and held, especially for Hans.

"This is what I've dreamed of all along. I say go," Hans finally said, breaking the silence. Andrew turned, looking into his eyes again.

Andrew finally nodded.

"We do it. Start preparations at once."

Who was it? Kal stirred uncomfortably, the pain was numbing but he had known worse, losing an arm, the beatings old Boyar Ivor, might his soul burn in hell, had administered.

Yet who did it?

He opened his eyes. His wife, sitting at the foot of the bed, roused from her sleep and started to get out of the chair. Her features were pale, heavy cheeks looking pasty in the candlelight.

He motioned for her to sit back down, but she was already at the side of the bed.

"Water, my husband?" she whispered.

He started to shake his head, but the pain was too much. "No, nothing."

"I made some broth, beef, your favorite."

"No, please."

He looked around the room.

"Emil?"

"He left. Said I was to fetch him if you wanted."

"Where?"

"He's at the colonel's home."

"Ah, I see."

He knew she would not relent with her attentions until she could do something, so he finally let her pull the blankets up, even though the night was so hot. He remained quiet, staring at the candle as she finally settled back into her chair and picked up her knitting which had fallen to the floor when she had dozed off.

Why would Emil be at Andrew's? Were they planning something?

Not Andrew. Never Andrew. In the beginning he could have so easily become boyar himself. No one would have objected, least of all me, he reasoned. *I was just peasant, he was already officer, like a noble and he was the liberator. Instead he propped me up, trained me, made me the president.*

But was that so I could always follow what he desired. Bugarin said as much, that a Yankee could never rule for long, so he had chosen a dumb peasant to be his shield. He wondered on that thought for a moment. *There was a certain wisdom to it, for in the end never did I go against what Andrew desired; therefore, in a way he did rule without all the bother of it.*

"Not Andrew," he whispered.

She stirred, ready to get up again and he allowed his eyes to flutter shut. She settled back down in her chair.

Bugarin? Logical. Blame it on Flavius. I'm dead, Flavius

is killed by the mob, Bugarin becomes president and then boyar again. So guard against Bugarin. But it just might have been Flavius after all. Yet if I had died, we would not have lived an hour in the city of Suzdal.

Who then?

I have lost Congress. Bugarin has the votes of those who want an end to it. The Roum congressmen are in terror, lost with the news of Marcus's death. If I continue the war as Andrew wants, then they will block it, splitting the Republic. If I try to stop it, what will Andrew do?

An inch to the right Emil said. But one inch, and I would not have to worry about this. I would be standing before Perm and his glorious son Kesus, all cares forgotten. Yet Tanya would still be here, the grandchildren, their half-mad father Vincent.

Ah, now there is a thought. Vincent is the warhawk. Could he be the mask behind the mask? Andrew would never do it, but Vincent was capable. If Bugarin tried a coup, Andrew would block it but might fall as well. Then it would be Vincent.

No. What was it Emil called it? A word for too much fear. But it was troubling, and he could not go to sleep.

The fact that he had asked for the meeting had caught him by surprise. Walking into the main hall of the Capitol Building he stopped, looking to his right toward his own chambers. The building was empty except for the lone military guard posted under the open rotunda. It had been started in the year before the start of the Bantag War. Though Keane insisted that construction must go forward in spite of the war, the less than half-completed dome was now covered with canvas.

He turned to his left and walked into the meeting chamber of the House of Representatives. Often he had heard the shouted debates coming from this room, and he found it distasteful, a rowdy mix of foreigners and lowborn peasants. At least the fifteen members of the Senate were, except for one or two, of the proper blood, even those from Roum, in spite of their being cursed pagans.

"Senator Bugarin. Thank you for coming."

The chair behind the desk turned and the diminutive

Flavius was staring at him. He was lean and wiry, a mere servant in the house of Marcus and now the Speaker.

Though he loathed the type, Bugarin could sense that Flavius was a soldier's soldier, one whom the veterans who predominated in Congress could trust whether they were of Rus or Roum. And since the pagans were the majority, of course their man would control this half of Congress.

Bugarin said nothing. He simply approached the chair, waiting for this one to rise in front of a better. Flavius, as if sensing the game, waited, and then slowly stood, favoring his right leg, giving a bare nod of the head in acknowledgment of the man who controlled the other half of the legislators.

"I'll come straight to the issue," Flavius said in Rus, his accent atrocious to Bugarin's ears. "We both know that poor soldier who was murdered today had nothing to do with the assassination attempt."

"How do you know?" Bugarin asked politely.

Flavius extended his hands in a gesture of exasperation.

"We might disagree on a great many things, but to assassinate the president. Never."

"Are you saying he acted alone then?"

"You know precisely what I am saying. The boy was innocent. He should have been standing in these chambers receiving a medal rather than being hung by a Rus mob."

"So you are saying we murdered him?"

"Damn you," Flavius muttered in Latin, but Bugarin could sense what was said and bristled.

"The Republic is dying; we can still save it," Flavius continued, gaining control of his temper.

"Republic? It is already dead," Bugarin snapped. "It died when your soldiers ran at Capua, unable even to retake their own territory."

"I had a brother with Eleventh Corps," Flavius announced coldly. "If he is dead, he died fighting, not running. I've been a soldier most of my life, and I know my people. They are as good in battle as those from Rus. I wish I could strangle with my own hands whoever started these rumors, these lies about my people."

"Understandable you would react that way."

Flavius stopped for a moment, not sure of what to say next.

"If that is all you wish to discuss?" Bugarin asked haughtily.

"No, of course not."

"Then out with it. It's late, and I have other concerns."

"Will you pull Rus out of the war?"

"My position is well-known."

"And that is?"

"The war is unwinnable now. We must seek a way out."

"And that means selling Roum to the Bantag?"

"Are you not contemplating the same deal with Jurak?"

Flavius said nothing for a moment.

"You have spies as do I. I know that Marcus, before his death, was secretly meeting with the ambassadors before they were forwarded to the Senate. And remember, Flavius, the issues of war and peace rest with the Senate. The great colonel designed it that way, did he not?"

"There is nothing more to be said," Flavius replied coldly.

Bugarin smiled.

"It was a feeble attempt," Bugarin ventured just as he was starting to turn to leave.

"What?" And there was a cold note of challenge in Flavius's voice.

"Just that. Too bad you missed."

As Bugarin turned the sound of a dagger being drawn hissed in the assembly hall. Bugarin turned, dagger drawn as well.

"Come on you lowborn bastard," Bugarin snarled. "Spill blood here and show what a lie this place is."

Flavius was as still as statue, dagger poised low. Finally, he relaxed, letting the blade slip back into its sheath.

"Yes, it's true I know not who my father is. My bastardy is of birth, not of behavior."

Bugarin tensed, ready to spring, but knew that before he even crossed the few feet that separated them the old veteran would have his blade back out and buried to the hilt.

Forcing a smile, Bugarin stepped back several feet.

"It will be settled soon enough. I think the question is now, who will betray whom first."

"As I assumed, Senator," Flavius said with a smile.

Chapter Six

Andrew slowed as they rode past the station, reining in his horse for a moment to let the long string of ambulances pass. The hospital trains had been coming in throughout the night, more than three thousand men over the last week, and with each casualty unloaded a new story was blurted out about the disaster at Capua.

In the predawn darkness he knew no one would recognize him. In the past he would have stopped to talk with the wounded as they were off-loaded, offer encouragement, but not this morning. On this of all mornings there were other things to be done before the sun rose.

Hans, riding beside him, bit off a chew and passed the plug over to Andrew, who nodded his thanks and took a bite of the bitter tobacco.

They rode in silence. Hans, slumped comfortably in the saddle, carbine cradled in one arm. Andrew looked over at him, wondering, wanting to say so much but not sure how to say it.

"Hans?"

"Yes?"

He sounded so relaxed.

"Are you afraid?" Andrew whispered.

Hans smiled.

"A slave doesn't have the luxury to be afraid. Remember, I was a slave, and then I was freed, at least in body. I wonder if this is how Lazarus felt, having seen what was beyond and then returning."

He shook his head, as if the dark thoughts of the years of imprisonment weighed him down.

"Every day I've had since has been a gift. Now it's time to pay for the gift."

"I wish it was different."

"I know, son. It's all right, though," Hans said soothingly. "You were the one that had to make the decision to do this and now bear the responsibility for our lives. This might very well be the hardest command decision you've ever made."

Andrew nodded.

"Once we take off, the commotion will certainly be noticed, and you'll have to tell Congress. If we lose"—and he chuckled—"well, there goes the last hope I guess."

Andrew didn't want to think of that alternative yet. It would mean every single airship and ironclad was gone. Without them, Jurak would slice through the Capua line like a hot knife through butter. As it stood now, if he second-guessed what was truly up, he might do it anyhow.

"Damn tough decision," Hans said, "and here you were worried if you'd lost your nerve."

"Just before we went in at Capua, I lied to you, Hans."

Hans chuckled and spat. "You mean about willingly sacrificing me if it meant victory."

"Yes, I've sacrificed too many. I still think I should go on this one, not you."

"Can you speak Chin?" Hans asked. "How about the Bantag slave dialect, or even Bantag for that matter?"

Andrew sighed and shook his head.

"Well that kind of settles it, doesn't it?"

"I know."

"Andrew. Sometimes it's the staying behind and doing nothing that's the hardest thing of all."

They stopped as a diminutive switching engine, one of the old 4-4-0 models wheezed past them, pushing a flatcar loaded with two freshly made ten-pound breechloaders.

"I've been thinking on that, too," Andrew said.

"What?"

"The doing nothing."

Hans chuckled. "Actually, my friend, given my choice, I'm glad I'm going rather than staying here and dealing with this snake pit of politics."

Andrew could not help but smile as they urged their mounts forward after the train passed.

Once clear of the yard they rode up through the rows of roughly made brick homes that housed the thousands of workers who labored down in the valley of the Vina River.

Past one of the burial mounds of the Tugars they continued their climb up the hill, Hans stopping for a moment to watch the inferno of steam and smoke cascading up from the foundry as a new batch of molten iron was released from its cauldron.

"It's almost beautiful," Hans exclaimed, pointing to the towering clouds of smoke caught and illuminated by the first light of early dawn. Andrew found himself in agreement. It made him think of the school of artists back on the old world, who worshiped the beauty of nature and painted the scenery of the Hudson River valley.

The smoke and steam had the same quality as the billowing afternoon cumulus, cloaking a mountaintop, but this mountain was man-made, the clouds man-made as well. The lighting, however, was unworldly, the deep morning reds unique to this world.

He smiled at the thought of the word *unworldly,* unworldly for home, but then this was home now, after all these years the sunlight normal, the twin moons normal, the lighter feel when one walked normal as well.

"I take it yesterday's session with the Senate was bad?" Hans asked.

Andrew nodded. "It's deadlock. Kal is nowhere out of the woods yet. Flavius refuses to step in as acting president since it would mean that a pro-peace man would take his place, and Bugarin is badgering to sign the agreement presented by the Chin ambassadors."

"Well, in an hour I'll be beyond it all," Hans announced.

"I know," Andrew whispered.

"Maybe by doing nothing at all you might be doing the best thing possible," Hans said.

"What do you mean?"

"You'll figure it out."

Hans chuckled, and Andrew knew his friend had presented him with a little something to dwell on and was not about to say anything more on the subject.

Their path led them through what had once been the grove where he had first admitted to Kathleen that he loved her, long since gone and replaced with warehouses and yet more brick homes. Finally, they crested the road leading along the banks of the reservoir and were out of the new city of Suzdal. The waters of the lake were still, a mirror surface reflecting the morning sky, a soft welcome relief.

Directly ahead were several low clapboard buildings covered with camouflage netting and painted a dark green and brown. Lights still glowed in the windows and there was a bustle of activity inside. Out around the building dozens were racing back and forth.

Riding up, the two dismounted and hitched their horses. Varinna stood in the open doorway, and it was obvious she had been up all night, as she wearily came down to greet the two.

Since the decision to launch the mission all of her people had worked at a frenzied pace, made more difficult because of Andrew's decision to clamp down a tight lid of security on the whole operation. It was a near-impossible thing to contain, with the city only a couple of miles away but by some miracle no one in Congress had found out, most likely because they were too preoccupied with their own squabbles to notice the round-the-clock insanity up at the aerosteamer field.

As for the dozens of messages sent to the front and to Roum, ordering the redeployment of aerosteamers and the remaining regiment of land ironclads, that had all been done using a book code. Admiral Bullfinch had personally overseen loading the ironclads during the night. The two ships carrying the machines and a transport hauling hydrogen vats, ammunition, and ground crews had all sailed under cover of night. If everything was going according to plan, they should have arrived during the night at Tyre and also alerted Stan Bamberg that things were suddenly going to get very hot.

Varinna smiled and extended her hand.

"Everything's ready," she announced. "Any word from Roum?"

"Nothing. The front's quiet."

"Good."

Andrew took her hand and squeezed it, pleased by the light that seemed to sparkle in her eyes. This effort had triggered something within her, and he felt a surge of confidence that she was the mastermind who had conceived so many of the details. The death of Chuck had deeply shaken him, so much so that he had failed to realize the capabilities that were alive in her.

"Let's go to the field." And leading the way, she walked down the slope and out onto the flat open landing field. Crews were dragging out the last of the airships from the hangars, and engines were beginning to turn over.

He was awed by the panoramic sight laid out before him. Sixteen Eagle airships were lined up wingtip to wingtip. Twelve of them brand-new, four having come back from the front for repairs and engine replacements. In the shadowy light they looked ghostly, giants out of some forgotten age of the past, or a foretaste of the world to come.

The men chosen for the mission were already lining up beside their machines, ten to each airship in addition to the crews. Nearly all of them were Hans's old companions, survivors of his liberation last year, or the winter flanking assault down into the valley of the Ebro.

Three hundred of their comrades from the Chin brigade had been loaded on trains the morning after the decision was made to launch the assault and sent by express to Roum, there to take transports to Tyre. With them went equipment to refit the twenty-eight Eagles and thirty Hornets that would fly from Capua to Roum, and from there down to Tyre as well. If all went according to plan there, those airships would lift off shortly before midday.

"You know, Varinna, you were holding out on me," Andrew said, looking over at her and trying to appear cross.

"The airships? Some needed repairs, the rest, well there were problems, adjustments, and several were finished ahead of schedule."

"They could have made a difference at Capua."

"I don't think so. If Chuck had been alive, he would have told you not to do it and then done the same thing I did."

"So that justified holding back on these Eagles?"

"No sir, but you are glad now that I did."

Andrew could not argue with her on that point. And he knew eight, twenty, fifty airships would not have made a difference that day.

The morning silence was shattered as more engines turned over, stuttering up to a humming throb.

He saw Jack Petracci slowly walking toward them, moving stiffly. Andrew motioned for him to stand at ease.

"Everything ready?"

Jack laughed softly.

"I guess so, sir."

Andrew said nothing. With most men he would have torn into them over such a lackadaisical air, but there were some, especially those like Jack, who danced so closely with death for so long, that one had to understand their fey attitude, especially at a moment like this.

"Numbers forty-seven and fifty-two, we should check them both off the list. I think forty-seven is leaking too much gas; the inboard starboard engine on fifty-two is shot."

Jack looked over at Varinna, who shook her head.

"Everyone goes," Andrew said. "Order those two to hug the coast as long as possible but everyone goes."

"What I figured, sir. I already told them that."

"These new pilots, you think they have the ability?" Andrew asked.

Jack again chuckled softly. "Well, sir, as long as there's no storms, the sky is clear, we don't get jumped by any of the Bantag aerosteamers. I sort of figure half of them will be dead within the week anyhow, even if this doesn't work, but that goes with the job."

"All right, Jack," Andrew said quietly, but his tone conveyed that Jack's fatalism shouldn't be pushed too far.

Andrew looked around at the assembled group, then put his hand on Jack's shoulder and led him off so the two could talk alone.

"I haven't had a chance to talk with you about this plan."

Jack said nothing, leaving no opening.

"You don't like the plan."

Again the laugh. "Don't like it. Well, I always figured I'd die ever since I got myself drafted into this damn fool air corps. You see, sir, I was just thinking yesterday that if I had kept my mouth shut about having flown in a balloon back on the old world, none of this would have happened." And he waved vaguely toward the assembled ships.

"And we would have lost the war long ago. The missions you flew made the difference."

"Sir. We're going to die. I mean all of us. I saw the

fight at Capua from a mile up. The reserves they have, the numbers. They just keep coming and coming. And I thought about all that we were taught when we were young. Remember the poems, 'Old Ironsides,' even that Tennyson fellow and the 'Charge of the Light Brigade.' We believed it was good to die the heroes' death. But I wonder now, maybe it's all meaningless. You die, and that's it. So you lose."

Andrew said nothing. Anyone with a mind had dwelled on this idea, just that it was poison when it took hold on the eve of battle.

"You ever have the feeling they had just made the bullet with your name on it?"

Andrew nodded. "Sure, plenty of times. Remember Cold Harbor. We wrote our names and pinned them on our backs before we went in? At Hispania, the morning of the third day, I knew I was going to die."

"And the winter, at Capua?"

Andrew felt a cold shiver. No, no real premonition then, and yet it had all but killed him. Yet far too often he had seen men like Jack, the darting eyes, the inner agony, made worse by the sense of futility that seized some.

As he looked at Jack the thought came yet again about the nature of courage. Some men, those like Vincent, for some strange reason truly lacked the imagination to contemplate just how agonizing a wound or death could be. They simply went about their duty, mind at ease. Vincent had suffered a horrifying wound, yet it seemed not to have scarred his soul. The scar in that boy was different, an inner woe triggered long ago because of the conflict over his Quaker upbringing and his innate talent for leading men in battle. Vincent's answer was to let his soul sink into a cold indifference to all suffering, his or anyone else's.

There were others though, like Jack, who were continually tormented by their imaginations, inwardly flinching as each bullet flickered past, who awoke in the middle of the night, sheets sweat-soaked, the nightmare of what could be twisting into their fluttering hearts. As he looked at Jack he felt a surge of admiration, knowing that Jack's type of courage was far more difficult to grasp and maintain. Every day he had to mask that terror and go out to face death yet again.

Jack, his hand trembling, reached into his jacket pocket and pulled out a folded slip of paper.

"I was never much of one for being a gentleman with the girls. Remember the Oneida Society back before the war? Actually tried to join it, I did, but they said I was too young then."

He laughed softly, and Andrew smiled.

"She's a girl in Roum, works in Ninth Corps main hospital. Took care of me right after I crashed back in the spring. Funny, she's suddenly very important to me now, so see that she gets this."

Andrew solemnly took the letter, knowing it was senseless to try and talk differently at a time like this.

"Jack, I wish I could let you stand down from this one. But you're the only one who can lead it. That's why I asked you to fly back here. These boys are so green I was afraid they couldn't find Tyre unless you were there to shepherd them along."

Jack smiled weakly. "I know, and believe me, I'd take the offer if I thought I could."

"Jack, in all honesty, is there a chance for this one? I mean Vincent seems to believe in it. Hans, well of course he'd do it. We've done desperate things in the past, but this is a throw in the dark."

Jack looked at him silently, and Andrew regretted his few seconds of weakness. He had pulled Jack aside to gently tell him to brace up in front of the others, and he was asking for reassurance instead.

"As long as we limit it to what we agreed on. I know Hans wants to push it all the way, but sir, the ships simply don't have the range. I can't ask the boys flying the ships to go on a one-way trip with no hope of survival. Stick to the original idea, and there just might be a chance. If we had three or four times as many airships, a real fleet of a couple of hundred of them, I'd guarantee we'd do it. That'd mean we'd have a full brigade of troops rather than barely a regiment. At the very least, though, it will throw one hell of a punch into their supplies and might take the pressure off at the front."

Andrew nodded. That had been the big fight argued out all week. Varinna's plan called for a two-step approach, the second phase not being launched unless the first half went flawlessly and a truly secure base was seized to operate out of. The morning after the decision was made to go Hans started the argument that it had to be done all at once. Andrew could understand the argument about surprising Jurak and not giving him time to react, but he knew as Hans most certainly knew that it was suicide to try.

And yet he could sense what Hans would indeed do once he was out there. The first phase was, at best, a spoiling raid, to swoop down on the Bantag port city of Xi'an, smash things up, sink ships, and destroy supplies. Vincent's mission was to act as bait to draw troops and better yet ironclads out of Xi'an before the air attack hit. The goal, if it could be achieved, was for Vincent to cut all the way to the Great Sea and secure a base for airships and perhaps even for oceangoing ships captured at Xi'an.

But it was still only half a victory. If they could actually hold Xi'an, transferring troops by sea from Vincent's force to reinforce the captured city, Jurak would be cut off from his supplies and forced to abandon all of the Roum territory all the way back to the Great Sea. He'd have to pull back all the way to Nippon. It would be a tremendous victory . . . but the Bantag army would still be intact, the war machine still working and ready to come back yet again. What Hans wanted was to take it all the way, but he felt he could never order that, for such an action would surely result in the death of all those who attempted it. It could mean, as well, that in attempting to reach for everything, Jurak could counterstrike and smash the plan apart.

Andrew took Jack's hand and grasped it tightly.

"Fly carefully."

"The soul of caution I've always been. It's how I've made it to twenty-eight very old years."

Coming stiffly to attention Jack saluted. "Sir, I think it's about time we got the show moving, so if you'll excuse me."

Andrew returned to his small group. While he had been talking with Jack, Vincent rode in. As usual he was dressed in his "Phil Sheridan" uniform, oversize riding boots, snowy white gauntlets, uniform with a bit too much gold braiding, rakish kepi, and still the ridiculous pointed goatee and mustache.

Andrew could see the boy was eager to be returning to

the front. He would have preferred that Vincent stay in Suzdal, but given the assassination attempt on his father-in-law Andrew now felt that it was best to get him out of town for a while. If not the target of an assassin's bullet, Vincent could, on the other hand, do something rash. And besides, given what he was contemplating doing, Vincent's presence in the city simply wouldn't fit into the plan.

It was indeed getting to the time for departure. For days he had agonized about this moment.

The engines on most of the airships were now turning over, shattering the predawn quiet as pilots revved each one up in turn, let them run full out for several minutes, then throttled them back down to idle.

Vincent was eager to be off. He had already said his good-byes to his family; it was part of his nature never to let that side of his life show anymore. There was no sense in going over the plan one more time. Vincent had conceived part of it, especially the land ironclad assault out of Tyre. He knew it far better than Andrew.

The salute was casual, as if he was leaving for morning inspection of a company.

"It'll work, sir," Vincent said. "I promise you that."

Andrew nodded, and the boy was off, heading to his airship, his chosen staff following. He had abandoned his cane and walked slowly, with a pronounced limp. Now it was just Hans and Varinna and she mumbled something about going to check one of the ships and left the two alone.

Hans sighed and slowly sat down on the grass, motioning for Andrew to join him.

Hans smiled and Andrew suddenly felt a terrible longing, somehow to turn the clock back, to make it all as it once was so many years before, and to hide from the knowledge of all that would be. Hans had aged, his hair going to white, his teeth crooked, stained dark yellow, several of them gone or turned to black, his skin no longer tanned and leathery but now waxy. He had never really admitted to himself just how much the years of prison had changed Hans. In so many ways they had softened him, made him more open to saying what was in his heart, but be had lost his tireless vitality as well. Yet, at this moment he felt as if Hans was summoning back that strength for one more effort.

"The war's lost, Andrew. We've fought the good fight for God knows how many years. We've held three empires at bay, but now they're closing in. But in order for them to do that they had to change, too, and that is where they are vulnerable.

"Before, it was like striking at a nest of bees. We had to cut them down one at a time until there were none left. Andrew, we've forced them in a way to become like us, and in so doing we now have the opening. We can reach into the nest, crush the queen, and the eggs and the nest dies."

Hans became animated as he spoke, his eyes locked on Andrew's.

"Don't you think he's figured that," Andrew replied, "and taken the necessary precautions?"

"Surprise will be on our side. We maintain that element, and we win. The part of the plan involving Vincent seems like folly, but it will be the focus for just long enough that it will keep them off-balance. Then the rest of it goes in. He'll suspect the air support is for Vincent. By the time he realizes, we'll be on him.

"We've got to do this, Andrew; otherwise, it isn't just us who lose, it's the Chin, it's the entire world. Now that's something I'm willing to risk my life for. The question is, now do you have the guts to risk it as well."

Andrew looked over angrily at Hans.

"It isn't a question of my courage."

"Yes it is. The courage to let go. If it wasn't me going, maybe it'd be easier somehow."

He wanted to deny it. Lord knows how many he had sent to certain death going all the way back to his own brother. But Hans was different.

Andrew lowered his head.

"Yes, damn it. I think when that aerosteamer takes off that is it, I never see you again. I can deny it, say it's the committing of our remaining air fleet to a mad venture. But it's really you."

"And I am the only one that can lead it."

Andrew finally nodded.

"Go." He whispered.

Hans leaned out, his hand tentatively taking Andrew's, and then he grasped it tight.

Andrew looked up to see tears in his friend's eyes.

"You'll do fine, son, just fine."

Andrew started to break. What could he say, how could he say it? The words finally spilled out of him, contained for so long.

"I love you, Hans, as I loved my own father."

Hans smiled.

"I know. We've always loved each other, you as the son I never had; it's just that the way we both are, who we are, makes it impossible to say what we feel."

The two sat in silence for a moment, eyes locked. There was such a flood of memories for Andrew, of Antietam, the lonely nights on picket, the cold winter mornings sharing a cup of coffee, the dusty marches, the moments of fear and of triumph, the pain of losing him and the indescribable joy of finding him again.

"And Hans."

"Yeah?"

He had not breathed a word of it to anybody over the last week, but now was the true moment of letting go, of turning back the lie he had whispered at Capua. He knew what had to be done . . . and both of them were soldiers who understood that.

He unbuttoned the top of his uniform, reached into his breast pocket, and pulled out an envelope, handing it to Hans.

"I want you to go all the way," Andrew whispered.

Hans, looking straight into his eyes, understanding what Andrew was asking, simply nodded.

"This is my written authorization in case Jack or anyone else disagrees. Hans, you've got to go all the way with this one, no half measures."

Hans smiled. "You know I would have done it anyway."

"I know that." Andrew sighed.

"It's just you wanted me to know you were behind my decision."

Andrew nodded, unable to speak.

Hans patted Andrew on the shoulder.

"Like I've always said, I'm proud of you, son," he said, hesitating, "and thank you. Ever since the day I escaped, leaving my comrades behind, it has haunted me. I have to do this."

There was a moment of silence between the two, both lost in their memories.

"I think they're waiting," Hans said gruffly, trying to hide the emotion that threatened to overwhelm him.

Andrew finally looked over his shoulder and saw all who were waiting, standing respectfully, some with heads lowered. All was silent except for the aerosteamer engines powering up, propellers cutting the still morning air.

Andrew nodded and ever so slowly let go of Hans's hand. Andrew tried to smile, fighting to hold on to what little control he had left.

He stood up shakily, Hans grunting as he stood as well.

"Well, they sure as hell haven't gotten us yet. You lose an arm at Gettysburg, get your lung shot out at Roum. Hell, the Comanche couldn't get me, a Reb sniper tries to take my leg off and a Merki arrow in the chest and then shot up again escaping. Shit, we'll get through this one, son; there ain't nothing left to shoot up."

Andrew chuckled as Hans put his arm around Andrew's side as if helping him along, two old battle-scarred warriors, hobbling along. The others waited, and Andrew felt as if all of them could sense what was exchanged between the two.

Andrew was surprised to see that Father Casmir had just ridden up and was dismounting. How the priest found out was beyond him, but then he always seemed to know everything.

He came up to Andrew and Hans, shaking their hands.

"Hawthorne told me about the plan."

Andrew shifted silently, angry that Vincent could be so loose-tongued.

"Don't worry, I haven't breathed a word of it. Brilliant, it's absolutely brilliant."

He looked over at Varinna.

"Perhaps you should be a permanent part of our war councils."

"Chuck would like that," she said with a smile.

"No, you're your own person now. Let the dead sleep, my daughter. You have a mind and a heart of your own."

"Your Holiness, a good blessing sure would help," Hans said, and Andrew looked over at his friend in surprise.

Hans reddened slightly. "Well, it's never too late to get a bit of religion."

Casmir chuckled and, reaching into his robes, pulled out a small vial filled with holy water. Uncorking it, he motioned for Hans to kneel and sprinkled a few drops over his head while softly chanting a prayer in the ancient language of the Rus, unchanged across a thousand years of exile.

The deep melodious chant rose in volume, all who were gathered around falling to their knees, even the Chin and Ketswana. Though of old Presbyterian stock, Andrew felt overwhelmed by the moment and fell to his knees as well, head lowered in prayer for his friend, for the mission, for all who were fighting or longing to be free.

Casmir turned away from Hans, holding the vial up, sprinkling the holy water over the assembly, the chant continuing, Andrew managing to understand a few words . . . "and for those of the old world and all those of the Diaspora in exile upon this world we beg your mercy and protection . . ."

The Diaspora, an ancient Greek word carried to this world. *We of the Diaspora,* he thought, *but if we win this fight it shall no longer be thus. We will have finished our wanderings, our enslavement, our exile, and this shall forever be our home.*

He looked over at Hans again, and it was as if a strange light was gathered about him, about all those who were leaving. He remembered now and understood, that if ever there was a cause worth dying for, this was it. It wasn't a war to take something, or even to defend the property or country one had. Hans was right. It had been, it always would be, a war to set men free, the most noble of all causes that one could ever sacrifice oneself for. That was why Hans had to go, and that was why Andrew had to let him go.

The chant died away and there was a long drawn-out moment of silence. Andrew looked up and saw Casmir staring straight at him, smiling. The priest offered his hand, and Andrew took it, coming to his feet.

"Load 'em up!" Andrew shouted, surprised by the power of his own voice.

Hans went up to Ketswana, the two exchanged a few words, slapped each other on the back, and Ketswana started to detail off the Chin in groups of ten, pointing each group in turn to one of the machines.

With a grin Ketswana started for the machine directly behind *Flying Cloud,* then angled over to Andrew.

"Don't worry, sir, I bring him back for you," Ketswana announced. Andrew took the Zulu's hand with a firm grasp.

"Godspeed and good luck, my friend."

Ketswana, obviously delighted with the mission, slapped Hans on the shoulder, turned, and sprinted off.

"Other than you the closest friend I have," Hans said.

The two went over to Jack, who was briefing the pilots gathered round, with Varinna and her assistants standing to one side.

"Remember, you have no bottom gunner now. If we do get jumped, you head right to the deck and hug it. The fake stinger might throw them off for a while, but if they ever figure it out, that's the spot they'll go for."

Andrew looked over at one of the ships. The compartment which had once held the bottom gunner and bomb dropper had been removed, replaced with a wicker basket affair fifteen feet long and six feet wide. What was nothing more than half a dozen broom handles, bundled together and painted black now extended from the back of the basket. The squads of Chin soldiers were lining up by the doorway into the baskets, most of them obviously unnerved by the size of the airships, the noise of the engines, and the prospect of what they were about to do.

There had been no time, or surplus fuel to give any of them even the briefest of orientation flights; this would be their first time aloft. They chattered nervously amongst themselves, waiting their turn as the first man climbed the rope ladder into the wickerwork compartment. By the time the sixth to seventh man had climbed aboard, the airships had settled down onto their wheels and now it was not much more than a high step to board.

After the last man was aboard the ground crews passed in their carbines, which had been thoroughly checked to make sure they were empty, cartridge boxes, two blankets per man, tins filled with rations, and two five-gallon barrels of water. Slung along either side of the compartment were four boxes roped in place carrying the additional gear.

"All you have to do is stay behind me," Jack announced,

continuing his briefing. "If I should fall out, well you'll have to navigate yourselves in. You're divided into squadrons of four ships, so squadron leaders, it'll be up to you. The navy's given us good maps of the coast with all prominent landmarks, so once you hit the coast again fix your position and either head north or south into Tyre."

He looked around at the group.

"I'll see all of you this evening."

The pilots, nearly all of them not much more than twenty, grinned nervously. There was a scattering of laughter, some gallows humor, and the group stood up.

"Hold it!"

It was Gates. Andrew felt a flash of annoyance when he saw what the newspaperman wanted, but then the historian inside took hold and he nodded approval.

Gates already had the camera out of the wagon and up on its tripod. The sun was just breaking the horizon, casting long shadows.

"You'll all have to stand very still, there's not much light."

Gates moved the camera slightly so that he could get part of an airship in the background, then motioned for Andrew to join the group. He felt a presence to his side and saw that Hans had come back from his ship to join in the moment, followed by Ketswana and several of the Chin. Vincent strolled over and stood beside Varinna, who had a chart rolled up under her arm, with Casmir on her other side.

"Hold it now." Gates took the cap off the lens and started to count down the seconds.

All stood silent, striking their most formal pose, Andrew realizing that as always he had turned slightly to hide the empty sleeve. From the corner of his eye he saw Hawthorne, always the young Sheridan with right hand slipped into his open jacket. Pilots stood casually in their baggy coverall pants, wool jackets open, several with their hands in their pockets. Then there was Hans, slouch cap pulled low, shading his eyes, jaw working a plug of tobacco so that his face would look blurred.

Again the moment of crystal clarity came, the realization of just how precious this all was, how this was a moment as fragile as a glass figurine.

" 'We few, we happy few, we band of brothers,' " he whispered, his voice carrying.

"That's it," Gates announced, replacing the lens cap.

Jack broke the tableau, stepping in front of the group, turning, and facing Andrew.

"With your permission, sir. Air's heavy and still. All machines are loaded. It's time to go."

Andrew returned the salute.

"Good luck, son."

Jack smiled wanly and without another word started for his machine. The group broke up, the men setting off at the run, and suddenly he was alone.

He turned to say a final farewell to Hans, but his friend had already set off, falling in alongside Jack. Andrew felt a shudder of disappointment but knew instantly that Hans was right.

Hans climbed up the ladder into the forward crew compartment without looking back, followed by Jack, who pulled the rope ladder up behind him and closed the door. He could see Hans climb into the seat normally occupied by the copilot but Theodor was now the backup commander of the air corps and so was flying in the second airship.

Ground crews stepped back from their airships, crew chiefs each standing in front of his machine, right hand raised, red flag held aloft. The chief in front of Jack's machine twirled the flag overhead in a tight circle. One after another each of the engines revved up, propellers turning to a blur, then idled back down. Stepping away to the port side of the aerosteamer, the chief waved the flag again and pointed it forward.

All engines revved, and the machine slowly lurched forward. The bi-level wings on the port side passed within a few feet of Andrew, and as it passed the twin engines kicked up a swirl of dust around him, the air heavy with the smell of burning kerosene. The second and third aerosteamers followed, engines roaring. The column, looking like ungainly birds, taxied down to the eastern end of the grass airstrip, a line of slender hydrogen-filled ships, wings seemingly added on as an afterthought.

The lead ship turned, facing into the gentle breeze stirring out of the west. The heads-on silhouette, illuminated from behind by the rising sun, caught Andrew as a stunningly beautiful sight, wings mere slivers of reflected light. The machine lurched forward, seconds later the sound of the engines coming to him.

He tensed, watching as the airship lumbered down the runway, not seeming to move at first, then ever so slowly picking up speed. Gently, gracefully, it lifted off while still a hundred yards away.

Jack expertly leveled off not a dozen feet off the ground, letting his machine build up speed before climbing. It came straight on, some of the crowd around Andrew ducking. He came to attention, saluting as the machine soared overhead, engines roaring, wind strumming the wires sounding like a harp floating in the heavens. He caught a brief glimpse of Hans, perched in the copilot's seat, a childlike grin lighting his features. Their eyes held for a second, and in that instant it was as if all the years had stripped away and he was now the old man and Hans was the boy, embarking on some grand and glorious adventure, and then he was gone.

Nose rising up, *Flying Cloud* started to climb, followed by *Heaven's Fire,* and *Bantag's Curse.* One after another they passed, some wagging their wings in salute, others coming straight on, their pilots too nervous to try anything other than getting off the ground.

Jack led the way, spiraling heavenward, waiting for the last ship to form into a long, straggling column. Finally, he turned due east, rising up through a thousand feet, and sped off, catching the breeze aloft.

Andrew watched as their shape changed from that of slender crosses to a round indistinct blur and then a mere dot of light that finally winked from view. Around him the ground crews finally began to break up, talking softly among themselves, walking back to their hangars, some looking back longingly to the east as if wishing they could go.

"I think that was one of the hardest decisions you've ever made."

Andrew turned to see Casmir by his side.

"Yes, Your Holiness, it was," he whispered.

"I remember you once saying that in order to be a good commander you must love the army with all your soul. The paradox is that there will come a time when you must then order the very destruction of the thing that you love."

"Yes, I said that a long time ago."

"Do you think it will work?"

"Hans believes in it."

"But do you?"

"I don't know. There are too many variables. The weather turns bad. The Bantag have warning and send airships up to meet them. As it is there's barely enough fuel, if they don't capture additional stores, or the advance position for the second wave ..." His voice trailed off. "Far too many things can go wrong."

"Life is a process of things going wrong. That is how Perm made the universe. It is our challenge then to find the faith to remake them into what is right and pleasing to His eye."

Casmir smiled and put his hand on Andrew's shoulder.

"I wish I had your faith."

"You do, it's just hidden at the moment. Best we head back to the city. Who knows, by the time we get back there might not even be a government."

He said it so casually but Andrew felt all the worry of that other problem returning.

Varinna, who had launched this entire effort, stood wistfully, crippled hand cupped over her brow to shade the sunlight as she continued to gaze eastward, tears streaming down her face. She sensed him looking at her, and, turning, she faced Andrew, and he knew he had to resume his strength.

He forced a smile.

"Chuck dreamed it, you made it possible. It will work."

"You think so?"

"I wouldn't have ordered it," Andrew said. He looked around at those gathered around him, Casmir, Varinna, Gates, the technicians and ground crews, all of them wanting to believe, and he knew that he had lost his own faith ever since the moment he had been cut down by the mortar shell. It was needed now, needed for all of them.

He smiled.

"I have faith," he whispered. "It will work."

"My Qarth."

Jurak stirred, looking up at the entry to his yurt. Zartak

stood in the open doorway, silhouetted by the dawning light.

"The time?" Jurak asked, embarrassed that he had slept past sunrise.

"No matter, you were up half the night. I ordered the guards not to disturb you, but this cannot wait."

"The Yankees, they're moving," Jurak said even as he stretched and came to his feet.

"How did you know?" Zartak asked cautiously.

Jurak shook his head. "Don't go running off proclaiming I have the ability of far seeing. It's just that I had a dream. I saw Yankee airships. My back was turned, and they fell upon me by surprise."

Zartak stared at him intently until Jurak nodded toward what he was holding. The old warrior stirred and handed him two telegrams, and Jurak scanned the contents.

"Three Yankee ships carrying land ironclads spotted late yesterday by a flyer out of Tyre patrolling the Inland Sea between Tyre and Roum. First light this morning ships seen in harbor at Tyre. New airships at Tyre already behind our lines and attacking."

"When did this come in?"

"The second report just minutes ago. The first report the middle of the night."

"Why the delay?" he asked angrily.

"Apparently a problem with a relay station. Then when it arrived here the Chin who transcribed it simply put it in with the other reports on train movements and supply shipments."

"Damn all."

"Should I have an example made of him?" Zartak asked.

Jurak thought on it for a moment, then shook his head.

"If I killed every telegrapher who made a mistake, the line would be down in a day."

"He might have done it deliberately," Zartak pressed.

"Tell him another such mistake and it won't be the moon feast, it will be slow impaling," Jurak replied.

Zartak gave a noncommittal grunt in reply.

Jurak looked around the yurt. Though it was the yurt of a Qar Qarth, piled with gold and every luxury known to this world, he still would have traded it all for running hot water, privacy when relieving himself, and music, music that could be heard at the touch of a button rather than the wailings of the chant singers and the nerve-tearing screeches of the single-string *basha*.

Zartak offered to help him dress, but he waved the old warrior aside as he slipped into leather trousers that felt cold and clammy, riding boots, a leather jerket, and a lightweight shirt of chain mail, nothing that would be much good in a battle but here in the rear lines was worn as a matter of course to protect against an assassin's blade in the back.

As he did so he continued to think about the two telegrams.

"Moving their ironclads down to Tyre," he said. "I wonder if they stripped everything off this front."

"We could send up our airships to look behind their lines here."

He nodded in agreement.

Why Tyre though? He walked over to a map drawn on the tanned hide of one of the great woolly giants that wandered the steppes. The map was stretched out on a wooden frame, showing the entire world from Nippon to Suzdal.

The mapmaking of the Bantag had intrigued him as soon as he had come to this world. With the endless circlings they had drawn out every step of their march, every watering hole, river ford, cattle settlement, place of good grazing, and places where the land was barren. The great scroll, when stretched end to end, measured well over two hundred paces. What hung before him was but one small part of the great fabric of this strange world that was now his home.

He stared at the map.

"From Tyre, two days of hard marching could bring them up to the head of the rail line we are running from this small port here." He pointed at the map. Zartak nodded.

"Carnagan the cattle call it," Zartak replied.

"Our warriors at Tyre, except for a few regiments, have yet to be armed with rifles. If he flings his ironclads into them, there will be no stopping such an advance. Take our rail line, push to the Great Sea, and establish there a base to harry our supply shipments."

"Audacious. Typical of Keane."

Keane. Did Keane dream of this he wondered. If so, it

was a desperate bid. Most likely he had stripped all his ironclads and his surviving airships for this attack. He just couldn't send the ironclads. It would have to have infantry support, at least a umen of their troops as well.

He traced the route out on the map. Send an order to Xi'an, have them divert the next shipment of ironclads, rush the machines to Carnagan. Though the distance was long, move up some airships as well, and also some airships from Capua. There were eight umens surrounding Tyre. Even with just bows that should be enough once the ironclads and airships were moved into place.

"We let them get their heads well into the trap," Jurak announced, "make sure we don't attack too soon. Then snap it shut and annihilate what is left of his advanced weapons."

"Suppose that isn't the true goal?"

"What?"

"Suppose it is something else."

Jurak turned back to the map. The ironclads were too far south even to think of attempting a march to the northeast. From there it was nearly 150 leagues to his main supply depot at what the Yankees once called Fort Hancock.

Xi'an? Two hundred leagues southward and then east to the narrows of the Great Sea, and even there it was a mile-wide channel to cross to the eastern shore and then another hundred leagues back up to the northeast.

No. Not Xi'an.

"You dreamed of airships, my Qarth," Zartak said, his voice barely a whisper, "not ironclads."

"I know."

He continued to stare at the map.

"Well, it was only a dream, my friend."

Chapter Seven

"There's the coast," Jack shouted, trying to be heard above the roar of the engines. "That looks like Tigranus Point, means we're about twenty miles north of Tyre."

Jack lowered his field glasses and passed them to Hans, but at the moment Hans really didn't care. For the last hour he had been far to busy suffering from an acute bout of airsickness.

"I can still see the Hornets, though." He pointed down and to the right. Hans vaguely looked in the direction Jack was pointing and nodded bleakly, though he saw nothing.

"We'll have to wait out here another ten minutes or so, give them a little more time to cut up the Bantag telegraph lines just to make sure." Even as he spoke he turned the wheel hard over to the right.

Hans grasped the edge of the forward panel, sparing a quick glance to his right as the aerosteamer went into a sharp banking turn. A mile or more below the ocean sparkled, catching the light of the late-afternoon sun. He tried not to contemplate just how far down it was, how long the fall would take.

Jack grabbed the speaking tube to his topside gunner and blew through it.

"You still with me up there? Tell me if everyone turns on me, and I want a count off."

Hans uncorked his own speaking tube to listen in as the Roum gunner counted off the ships, still holding at eleven Eagles, and all were turning.

As Jack had predicted the one with the leaking hydrogen bag had turned back after only an hour. After leaving the coast of Rus behind and crossing out over the Inland Sea for the run to Tyre the topside gunner had excitedly reported that one of the ships had burst into flames and gone down. Two more just seemed to have wandered off.

The ship bumped through another bubble of air, and Hans was again leaning out the side window, gagging.

They spiraled through half a dozen banking turns. Hans looked around bleakly. He guessed it should be a beautiful sight. Puffy clouds seemed to dance and bob around them, the aerosteamers pirouetting in circles like butterflies in a field of white flowers. They slipped through the edge of a cloud, the world going white, the air colder, the ship bobbing up and down. Suddenly the world exploded back into blue, the turquoise blue of the ocean below, the crystal blue of the horizon, the darker sky above.

He could hear a moaning curse echoing through the speaking tube connected to the compartment holding their passengers. A small hole had been left in the floor for the men to relieve themselves but from the shouts and curses only minutes after they had taken off he could figure easily enough that it didn't work thanks to the forty-mile-an-hour breeze whistling through the compartment. Someone apparently had missed the target yet again. Jack chuckled at their distress.

"We should have papered over the compartment at least. Those boys must be freezing back there."

Jack pushed his ship through one more slow banking turn, gaze fixed on the eastern horizon.

"They must have cut the telegraph lines by now; we gotta head in if we want all these ships down by dark."

Hans sighed with relief as they leveled out, again picking up a southeasterly heading.

After several minutes he could finally distinguish the eastern shore of the Inland Sea, recognizing the point north of Tyre and the gentle curving coast of shallows and mud flats that finally led down to the rise of ground and narrow harbor. Jack edged the elevator stick forward, easing back slightly on the four throttles. They thumped through another small cloud, which was beginning to glow with a pale yellow-pink light. The summits of the Green Mountains, fifty miles to the north and east, were cloaked in the clouds and what appeared to be a dark thunderhead.

Jack pointed out the storm.

"Get caught in one of those, and you're dead," he shouted.

Hans nodded, breathing deeply, struggling against the urge to get sick yet again.

Scanning eastward, he wondered if his eyes were playing tricks or could he actually see the distant shore of the Great Sea nearly a hundred miles farther east. The two oceans, back on the old world they'd more likely be called great lakes, were closest together at this point. Long before the wars there was even a trade route going overland from Tyre eastward to the small fishing village of Carnagan.

Back in the old days of the Great Ride, the eternal circling of the world by the hordes, this region between the two seas was usually disputed by the Tugars to the north and the Merki, making their long ride farther south through Tyre and from there around the southern end of the Great Sea and then up into Nippon and the edge of the vast populous lands of the Chin.

He took the field glasses, which rested in a box between his seat and Jack's, checked the map, then raised the glasses to scan the coast. After months in the siege lines of Tyre he knew it all by heart, the outer circle of the Bantag lines, half a dozen miles from the city, the inner line of his own works, the ancient whitewashed walls of the town clustered around the harbor. He caught a glint of sunlight reflecting off the wings of a Hornet out beyond the enemy line, held it for a second, then lost it, wondering how Jack could so easily spot such things from ten, even twenty miles away. He again looked eastward with the glasses, but they were lower now. It was hard to tell just how far he could see out across the open brown-green prairie.

He studied the harbor again, bracing his elbows on the forward panel containing the pressure and temperature gauges for the four engines. The machine was bobbing up and down too much, though, for him to keep a steady lock, and another wave of nausea started to take hold. Taking a deep breath, he settled back in his chair.

The air was getting warmer, humid.

"I see transports in the harbor. Hope they're the right ones, or we're finished."

Hans nodded, closing his eyes for a moment, breathing deeply, wishing they were higher up again, where the air was cooler. The minutes slowly passed. He finally got his stomach back under control. He opened his eyes again. They were just a couple of miles out from the harbor, flying parallel to the coast.

He spotted the aerosteamer landing field, south of town, right on the coast. There was already one airship down.

"We got more ships to the north." It was the top gunner.

Hans looked over anxiously at Jack. Several seconds passed.

"Four engines, must be the ones from Roum." Both breathed a sigh of relief. The Bantag had committed only a couple of ships to that front, and both had been aggressively hunted down over the last week and destroyed, but there was always the prospect that Jurak had moved reinforcements down there.

From due east he could see two Hornets coming in as well, one of them trailing a thin wisp of smoke. They passed directly west of the harbor, and Hans saw half a dozen ships tied off at the docks. Several land ironclads were on the dock, puffs of smoke rising as they slowly chugged along, joining a long column of machines weaving up through the narrow streets of the town. *At least that phase of this mad plan seems to have gone off,* he thought.

They passed the airfield on their left and a quarter mile in from the coast, Jack looking over at it, then at the ocean below.

"Bit tricky, crosswind coming off the sea, about ten knots or so. Keep both your hands on the throttles. Remember the two to the left are for port engines, the two on the right for the starboard. It takes several seconds for them actually to change anything, so be damn quick."

Hans shifted uncomfortably, doing as ordered. Jack started into a shallow banking turn to port, altitude still dropping. As they got halfway through Hans looked up through the topside windows, which were now angled down toward the horizon, and saw the other aerosteamers bobbing along like moths, following in a ragged line stretching back half a dozen miles or more.

Jack gradually started to straighten out, having drifted past the airfield, turning slightly to port to compensate for the crosswind. Hundreds of antlike figures ran about along either side of the field—the ground crews. It was going to be a tricky balancing act.

They had started out heavy, but after close to fifteen hours of flying they had burned off hundreds of gallons of fuel. They could have dumped some of their hydrogen to compensate, but orders were not to do that since it would be impossible to cap off all the hydrogen needed if the ships were to be turned around quickly. The center air bag was filled with hot air, drawn off the exhaust of the four engines. On the way down Jack had dumped all of it. In the fine balancing act between hydrogen bags, hot air, and the lift provided by the bi-level wings, the ship should have a stall speed of only ten knots or so, about the same as the crosswind. That meant they would touch down almost standing still, then ground crews would have to snag lines and secure tie-downs. If not, the ship would start drifting backwards, drag a wing, and within seconds be destroyed.

Jack kept the ship nose low, coming in over the edge of the field, then continuing down most of its length to leave plenty of room behind for all the other airships to touch down. Hans, nervous, kept both hands tight on the throttles, never quite matching up to what Jack wanted as he shouted commands to throttle up on one side, then the other, ease back, then throttle up again.

The airship bounced down once, gently, soared back up, Jack cursing sharply, quickly slapping Hans's death grip on the throttles, knocking all four of them back. The ship hung in the air for a moment, then settled back down, harder this time, as Jack spun the crank to his left, which opened and closed the vent to the top of the hot-air bag.

Hans saw someone darting up toward their cab, disappearing underneath to grab the forward hold-down line; a dozen others swarmed in to either side. Jack seemed to have three arms and four hands all at once, making sure the throttles were back, but not all the way, so that if the ground crew lost grip, he could slap them forward and try to claw back up into the sky. The hot-air vent was opened again. The machine lurched, ground crew under them becoming visible again as they spliced on a long pull line and a dozen men took hold, allowing the ship to weather-vane into the wind, and then pulled it off the field.

A pop that sounded more like a dull whoosh than an

explosion startled Hans. Jack looking back out the portside window, cursed softly, then settled back into his seat.

"Looks like number twenty-eight; I knew the boy was too green."

"What?"

"Burning, what's left of it. Most likely jammed a wing into the ground, snapped it, fuel line sprays, then the fire hits the hydrogen bags."

He said it matter-of-factly, but there was a deep, infinite weariness in the tone.

The crew chief in front of their machine held up a red flag, spun it in a tight circle several times, then slapped it down to his side.

"Throttles off," Jack announced even as he pushed them all the way back. "Fuel valves off, controls neutral . . ." He continued down the list, announcing each step as he did it, leaning over to Hans's side to perform several of the tasks.

"Fine, that's it. Open the hatch."

Hans opened the bottom hatch, dropped the ladder, and, feeling very stiff and old, slowly went down the dozen feet to the ground. The air felt different, the memory of the long months in Tyre triggered by the scent of the ocean mingling with the dry musky sage. As he stepped away from under the ship he looked back and saw the flaming wreck of one of the airships. A wagon was drawn up, a crew working the pumps, laying down a feeble spray of water. More airships came in, pilots wisely swinging to windward so no errant sparks caught them.

Some of the ships came in easily, touched down as gently as hummingbirds; others plodded in, slamming down hard, bouncing. A few came in without enough speed, hung motionless, and started to drift backwards, one of them digging its tail in. Jack cursed soundly as the machine just hung there, ground crews frantically jumping up and down, trying to grab the hold-down lines. The pilot threw on full throttles, the machine started back up, hung in the air, finally stalled, and this time the nose dropped, most likely from his having opened the forward hydrogen bag. The machine slammed down hard, undercarriage wheels snapping, driving up into the wings, while the cargo compartment seemed to disappear. Even though they were upwind, Hans could hear the screams of the men trapped within.

As the ground crew around him secured the tie-down ropes to bolts fastened into heavy concrete blocks, the crew chief finally gave permission for the top gunner and the men in the cargo compartment to dismount. One by one they came down the ladder and were a pitiful sight, obviously half-frozen, covered in vomit, disgusted with themselves and the world in general. The last two had to be helped down and laid out on the grass. Hans realized he most likely didn't smell too good himself.

He was relieved to see Ketswana coming up with Vincent right behind him, and together, as the shadows lengthened, the last of the airships from Suzdal landed. Then several minutes later the first of twenty-eight more ships, Eagles all of them veterans from the Roum Front, came in, the more experienced pilots having no problems with the crosswind landing. Several of them simply bypassed the landing strip and, ignoring the shouted protests of ground crews, picked out a tie-down location, slowed to a hover, then gently floated in to a touchdown.

Last of all were the twenty-five Hornets from Suzdal and Roum, buzzing in like tiny insects after the heavy cumbersome four-engine machines. Mingled in were half a dozen more Hornets that had been fighting throughout the day in front of Tyre. Powder-smoke stains from the forward Gatling gun blackened the undersides. One of the ships was badly shot up, streamers of fabric fluttering from a starboard wing.

The display made Hans's pulse quicken. Here, obviously, was one of the most remarkable sights in history. Over seventy flying machines, all of them gathered together in this one place. And though it was a wild, mad scheme, it gave him hope for the moment. Nature seemed to be adding to the display, the long shadows of late afternoon lengthened, exaggerating the size of the machines so that they looked like giants skimming over the ground. The bloodred sun hung heavy in the western sky, while to the north the towering thunderstorm, which everyone had been eyeing nervously, marched on in stately pageantry to the east.

The last of the Hornets, stripped-down versions with no

forward gun, replaced by a small compartment underneath which could hold one man, came in and landed. There was barely any room left on the open field as the last ship rolled to a stop.

A young major came up to the group, and in the shadows Hans recognized the sky-blue jacket and silver trim of an officer in the air corps.

"Welcome sirs. Sorry I couldn't come over earlier but I was kind of busy," the boy announced, obviously from Roum and struggling to speak in Rus.

Jack clapped him on the shoulder.

"Varro. Good job, son, your people did a damn fine job."

"Thank you, sir. It helped to have those extra ground crews brought down by transport from Roum but still all the hold-down crews were infantrymen yesterday. I'll pass the word along."

"The Hornets that flew down from Roum yesterday"— he nodded to the half dozen machines that had the unusual baskets underneath—"started out this morning as ordered. Two haven't come back, but the first reports are that they've cut the telegraph lines at twenty or more places from here all the way up to the Green Mountains."

"Damn good news," Vincent announced.

Hans nodded in agreement. Yet another idea of Varinna's. One of the first objections he had raised when the plan was presented was that the moment they touched down with so many airships in Tyre, Jurak might surmise the real target. She immediately countered with the sketch of how to convert the light fighting airships into a two-man unit. Strip out the Gatling gun, put in a small crew compartment. The ship touches down along some isolated stretch of the telegraph line, the crew member hops out, climbs the pole, cuts the line, and if there's enough time rolls up a couple of hundred feet of wire and takes it with them while a second Hornet, this one fully armed, circles to keep back any riders posted to patrol the wire.

Hans was delighted with the simple ingenuity of the proposal. Telegraph lines had always been so damn vulnerable. Back in the old war on Earth a couple of dozen cavalry men could play hell with a line, and it took regiments of men, posted damn near at every pole to keep a crucial line up and running. The Bantag umens at Tyre were now completely out of touch with Jurak, and it'd take at least a couple of days for word to be carried by horse. The trick, of course, was in the timing. To let Jurak get word of the ironclads' landing in order to draw his attention to Tyre, but not the entire air fleet.

"Are General Timokin and Stan Bamberg here?" Vincent asked.

"Follow me, sirs; they're waiting over at headquarters."

Hans fell in with the group as they strode across the field. The passengers from the airships were out, nearly all of them a sorry-looking lot.

"Major, are copies of *Gates's Weekly* making it down here?"

"Ah, yes sir, we just got the issue about what happened up at Capua. They came in on the transport carrying the ironclads."

"Well detail off some men. I want every copy you can find rounded up. Then find some glue, if need be take some flour and mix it into a paste. Then paper it on the outside of those wicker troop carriers."

The major looked at him confused, then called to a sergeant who had been tailing along and detailed him off.

"In all the rush we never thought of it," Jack said. "Damn foolish mistake, type of thing that can lose a war."

As they passed the line of Hornets Hans slowed to inspect the machines. More than one was holed, a couple had hydrogen bags that were completely deflated, a patching crew was working by feel since no lighting of any kind was allowed near a ship that could be leaking hydrogen.

Several of the Hornet pilots came up to Jack, saluting.

"We really grabbed their tails out there," one of them announced excitedly. "I came over a low rise, must have caught a hundred of them camped out in the open, about fifty miles back from the front. Damn did I tear them up."

"The landings, did they work?" Vincent asked.

The pilot was startled to see the chief of staff of the army standing in the shadows and snapped to attention and saluted.

"Ah, yes sir. The Hornet I was escorting, he landed three times along a ten-mile stretch of the wire and tore out a good long piece at each." The pilot nodded to a slight boy standing beside him.

"Tell him, Nicholas."

"Like he said, sir. We took down wire between two poles at three different places."

Hans could see that the boy was shaken, left hand clasping his right arm in the evening twilight, the black stain on the arm obviously blood.

"Your crewman?" Jack asked.

The boy shook his head.

"I lost him on the third landing. Some of them bastards were hiding in a gully, no horses. They shot Petra as he was up on a pole, then came rushing out. I got hit, too, but managed to get off."

He lowered his head.

"I think Petra was still alive when I left him," the boy whispered.

Jack patted him lightly on his left shoulder.

"You did the right thing. You had to save your Hornet."

"No sir, I was scared. I might have been able to get him in."

"No you couldn't," the other pilot interjected. "I had no more ammunition, so all I could do was try and scare them by flying low. That's when they shot up my ship as well."

"I was scared and ran."

"We're all scared," Jack replied softly. "Now get some rest. I want both of you back up tomorrow at first light, wounded or not. Anyone who can fly has to be in the air tomorrow. You saved your ship, so don't think about anything else now."

They continued on, Hans catching a glimpse of a bottle being passed around as soon as they had passed.

The headquarters hut for the airfield was nothing more than a brown-walled adobe shack, typical of Tyre, where lumber was in such short supply. It was the only light on the field as the men labored under the glow of the twin moons that were breaking the eastern horizon.

As they stepped in Hans was startled to see Gregory Timokin. His face was still puffy, pink, blistered. Hands were wrapped in bandages, and it reinforced yet again just how desperate this venture was. Stan stood beside him, grinning, obviously eager for the operation to begin.

Though his stomach was still in rebellion over the flight

he quickly took up the bottle of vodka sitting on a rough-hewn table, uncorked it, and took a long drink.

"All right. What's the bad news first?"

Gregory snickered.

"You want the long or the short version?"

"Go on."

"Fuel first of all. If we were burning coal, there'd be more than enough. Fifty-two ironclads. I'll need twenty-five thousand gallons if you want them to get to Carnagan."

"I have first priority," Jack interjected.

"And that's at least another forty thousand gallons for one way."

"We supposedly had it stockpiled," Hans said, rubbing his forehead as the vodka hit him.

"The oil field is lost. We had enough stockpiled through our coking of coal and getting the coal oil," Vincent said. "What's the problem? And what do you mean 'fifty-two ironclads'?"

Gregory sighed, staring at the ceiling. "One of the ships carrying more coal oil and ten land ironclads hasn't docked."

"What the hell? There was supposed to be a monitor escort for you people."

"Fog. Yesterday and the day before. We came out of it, near Tigranus Point, and the ship was missing. I asked a Hornet to go up the coast, and the pilot thinks he found the wreck. It went straight into a shoal and foundered."

"Damn all," Hans snapped. "So we're short how much?"

"Fifteen thousand gallons."

Hans looked over at Vincent, who shook his head.

"We could make that up in a week from the coking plants at Roum and Suzdal. It's getting it here, though."

An argument broke out between Jack and Gregory over who got priority on the fuel; Hans just sat woodenly, staring at the bottle for a moment, while meditatively munching on a piece of hardtack to put something back into his stomach.

"Ground the Hornets that got shot up. Pull off the Eagle that cracked its undercarriage, then detail off four more Eagles to stay behind."

"What?" Jack snapped. "That's ten percent of my remaining force."

"Our force, Jack, our force. We need fuel for the ironclads. The Eagles can be used locally for support. Once more fuel comes in they can be used to haul what, a couple of hundred gallons each out to the column to keep it supplied. Gregory, I'm taking five thousand gallons from you for our remaining airships."

Now both Gregory and Jack were on him, but he sat silent, his icy stare finally causing them to fall silent.

"I know that won't give you enough fuel to reach your objective with any margin to spare. Figure this though. Half your machines will break down before you even get there. Do like we did on the Ebro. Drain off the remaining fuel, load it into the ironclads still running, then move on."

The two started to object again, and Vincent slammed the table with his fist.

"Damn all. There's no time to argue now. This operation is supposed to kick off tomorrow morning. The argument's over. Gregory, your machines, are they ready?"

"If you mean off-loaded, yes sir. Like I said, we're down to fifty-two."

"And did the Bantag see them before the lines got cut?"

"Certain of it."

Hans smiled. "Good. That's what we wanted."

"I don't get it," Gregory replied sharply. "Why didn't you cut the telegraph wires first before we brought the ironclads down here. Now they'll know and be on us."

"That's what I wanted," Vincent replied. "We're the bait."

"The what?" Stan asked. "And what do you mean 'we'?"

"Because I'm going with you, Stan."

"Fine, but what the hell is this about bait?"

"We had to cut the lines before we flew all the airships in here to Tyre. The moment we did I assumed Jurak would figure what the real target is. I didn't want him to guess the true intent, so I wanted him to get word that all our ironclads had been moved down here. He'll assume that we are trying to break out of Tyre and take Carnagan. After all, it is a logical move. We take Carnagan even briefly and we could threaten his supplies moving over the Great Sea. Beyond that we could tear up that rail line they're building from there over to here. I want him to focus on here while Hans presses the main attack."

Both Stan and Gregory nodded, but it was obvious that

they were less pleased with this role, and the definition that they were to be a diversion rather than the main attack.

"So it's Third Corps and nothing else?" Stan asked.

"Yes. We have to keep a minimum of two corps here in Tyre to hold this base. I think one corps is more than enough."

"You ready?" Hans asked.

Stan smiled, shifting the plug of tobacco in his cheek, looking a bit like a younger version of Hans.

"We scraped up ten days of rations per man, one hundred rounds of ammunition with an additional hundred in the supply wagons. New shoes have been issued. We're ready."

"And your feelings on this one?" Timokin asked.

Stan smiled. "Oh, about the same as everyone else, I guess. But what the hell. Kinda figured we all should have drowned off the coast of Carolina ten years ago. Every day since has been a bonus. If we're going to go down, let me do it out in the open fighting. Tell me where to go, Hans, we'll get there."

Hans smiled and looked over at Vincent. The three corps cut off in Tyre had developed a unique spirit. In the one sense they felt abandoned, cut off on a useless front while the big actions were fought up around Roum. But on the other side they had a blind faith in Hans and any sense of difference between Rus and Roum had been burned out of them during the harrowing retreat from the Green Mountains down to this coastal port and the long months in the trenches afterward. These men were battle-hardened but not battle-exhausted as were the survivors of Roum and the nightmare assault at Capua.

"Effectives?"

"Ten thousand two hundred men with the corps ready to march. Six batteries of breech-loading three-inchers, and one mounted regiment."

"What about supply wagons?" Gregory asked. "That's the crucial thing. We need healthy horses and good strong wagons that can keep up."

"About a hundred," came the reply, and again there was the look of exasperation from Gregory.

"Hell, four hundred wounded in a fight, and we're in trouble." He looked over at Hans.

After the horror of leaving over a thousand wounded behind during the retreat of last year, Hans had made a firm statement that never again would wounded by abandoned. He shifted uncomfortably.

"Ammunition and coal oil have to come first. With luck we'll capture a lot of horses at the start. That'll alleviate food and transport for lightly wounded. Wounded that can be saved get wagon space; those who can't make it . . ." He lowered his head, leaving the rest unsaid, that the man would be left behind with a few rounds of ammunition.

"What I figured," Stan replied. "Just I think of old Jack Whatley at times . . ." His voice trailed off.

"Anything else?" Hans asked.

The group was silent, looking one to the other.

"Fine, we start up in six hours. Try and get some sleep."

One by one the group headed out. He knew Jack and Gregory would be up all night, double-checking on each machine. Finally, only Vincent was left. He settled down in a chair across the table from Hans, eyed the bottle, and finally uncorked it and took a drink. Hans said nothing.

"War's changed too much." Hans sighed, stretching out his stiff leg. "I miss the old ways. God, there was something about a division, an entire corps on the volley line. It was hell, but I'll never forget Fredericksburg, watching the Irish brigade going up the hill. Damn what a sight."

"Even Hispania," Vincent replied. "When we pivoted an entire division, closing off the flank, the men cheering, shoulder to shoulder, perfect alignment, over four thousand men. Wonder if we'll ever see the likes of that again."

"Not with these new machines. Changed everything. Guess it's inevitable. Back on the old world, bet they have 'em as well by now."

Vincent took another drink and passed the bottle to Hans, who nodded his thanks, shifted his chew, and enjoyed another gulp.

"Don't go getting yourself killed out there," Hans said.

"Goes with the job."

"No, there's more to it."

He leaned forward, staring into Vincent's eyes.

"Son, my generation, Andrew, Pat, Emil, we've played out our part. A chapter's closing with this war. If we win." He shook his head. "No, when we win, I pray that will be the end of it for us. But that doesn't end it on this world. You and I, perhaps even more than Andrew and Pat, are the real revolutionaries. I was their prisoner. You, well you had your own torment from them."

Vincent said nothing.

"We both know this war will have to sweep the entire world. The Bantag are of the great northern hordes, but there must be more out there. We only know of one small part of this world. We have no idea of what is southward beyond the realm of the Bantag, what's on the other side, what threats there still are. The only hope is to free all of humanity on this world, then build from there. It will be your war then."

"So stay alive, is that it?"

Hans smiled. "After this is over you'll have Andrew as your mentor. He thinks he wants to let go of the reins, but knowing Andrew that will change. There's supposed to be an election at the end of the year. Who knows, he might even run if we still have a country and are still alive. If he does, well you'd be the choice for who would run the army."

"What about you, or Pat?"

Hans smiled and waved aside the question.

"You can't have a better model than him to follow. And watch out for him, too. It will be tough at times."

"As he followed you," Vincent said, and Hans was surprised to see a softening, something so rare in this boy who had come of age too early in the crucible of war.

Hans cleared his throat nervously.

"You talk like you don't expect to come back," Vincent said.

"Well, when you planned this mad operation, what chance did you give to the air operation?"

Vincent said nothing for a moment.

"Well?"

"Varinna was a bit more optimistic than I."

"I see. But you know, it's what I wanted, what I said from the very beginning. That's why Andrew decided it was me who should lead it rather than you."

"I know that now."

"And Vincent."

"Yes?"

"I'm going all the way with this one."

He didn't mention Andrew's authorization; he'd only play that if he had to.

"Kind of figured you would," Vincent replied calmly.

Hans looked up at the simple wooden clock hanging over a tattered picture from *Gates's Illustrated*, a full-page print of Jack Petracci with four smaller images, one in each corner of the illustration, showing airships fighting.

"Well past ten," Hans announced. "We're up at three, so let's get some sleep."

Vincent nodded. He was never one to be able to hold his liquor, and the three shots of vodka had made him noddy. Within minutes he was snoring peacefully. Hans stepped outside. By the light of the twin moons he could see the shadowy forms of the airships lined up, men laboring about them in the dark. A wagon clattered past him, trailing a heavy scent of kerosene. He heard muttered snatches of conversation in Rus, Latin, Chin, even a few choice expletives in English. Overhead the Great Wheel filled the sky. It was a comforting sight. *A good world this. Maybe we can go beyond the mistakes of the old one, build something better. But first we have to survive,* he thought.

He went back into the hut and quietly lay down on the other cot. Strange memories floated for a moment, not of the war, even of the prairie, but long before, Prussia, the scent of the forest wafting through the open window at night when he was a boy. The shadow of his mother coming in to check on him, then drifting away.

Why that? he wondered. His hand rested on his chest, feeling the quiet beat. Steady now, not the hollow drifting sense that came too often. Emil kept talking about the need to take it easy. Old Emil, God just how old was he? Must be well over seventy. Hard to keep track of the years, real years as counted back home.

The clock quietly ticked, his thoughts drifted, and he knew there would be no sleep tonight. Far too much to think of, not of what would come . . . but rather of what had once been.

Jurak sifted through the reports, carefully reading the roughly printed Rus letters taken down by the Chin telegraphers. All lines south of the Green Mountains had been cut by airship attacks.

That was not the concern of the moment, though. It was the airships that were troubling him. Along the entire Capua Front there was only one airship.

It was supposed to represent ten ships, and it was the clumsy deception that gave it away. The humans had taken to the use of symbols which were known to be numbers in their English language. Observers along the front were given the strictest of orders to note down such symbols when they reported sightings. The same ten numbers kept appearing for the last seven days but it was only this afternoon that one of his warriors, a lowly commander of ten, had been allowed into his presence, claiming that he was convinced there were not ten ships but only one. When questioned he said he remembered the one particular ship since it had almost killed him during the river battle and that it had a slight stain along the underside of its left wing and a triangle-shaped patch not much more than a handspan across on the right wing. All of the supposed ten ships now had the identical stain and patch.

With that Jurak had made it a point to observe the ship as it flew over twice during the day and the commander of ten (who was now commander of a hundred) was right. They were pasting different numbers on the ship. It was an old trick, and the fact that the humans resorted to it must mean that their airships were all somewhere else.

He had already sent faster riders southwest from the nearest garrison to the breaks in the line, demanding a full report. News, though, would be a day old.

In the morning he thought he had a clear grasp of the plan. Now he wasn't sure. Such an operation would not require every airship of the Yankee fleet. There were several scenarios possible, a couple within the capability of what the humans knew of war. There were several beyond them, or had they realized that airships could be used for more than just reconnaissance and bombing?

He felt a cold shiver at that thought and called for a guard to summon Zartak.

Chapter Eight

"Hans, time we got moving."

It was Ketswana, his towering bulk filling the doorframe. First light was tracing the horizon, dawn still more than an hour off. Engines were already warming up on the airstrip, distant voices echoing.

"Come on, Vincent, let's roll."

The boy was fast asleep, curled up on the coat, his over-size riding boots still on, making him look even more like a child who had insisted upon falling asleep in his play uniform. Vincent stirred, and then was bolt upright, a brief instant of panic until he realized where he was. Hans said nothing, understanding. Old instincts from the field.

"Everything all right?" Vincent asked a bit too loudly.

"Just that it's time."

"Right."

Ketswana came back into the room carrying a wooden plank. Two steaming tins of tea were on it, along with pieces of hardtack topped off with slabs of cold salt pork. Hans blew on the rim of the cup between gulps of the scalding brew, then quickly consumed the cold breakfast.

Vincent was up, eating a bit more slowly. Gregory Timokin came in.

"Everything's ready, sir," he announced to Vincent. "We better get up to the front."

Vincent nodded and started for the door, taking his cup of tea with him. He stopped by Hans's side.

"Not much at sentimental good-byes, Hans."

"Nor I."

Vincent chuckled. "Sure, Hans. See you in a week."

"You too, son. Gregory, don't let him bang his head."

Gregory smiled and offered Hans his hand. Hans took it gently, and even then Gregory grimaced from the pain.

"Wish you were coming along, too. It'd be like the Ebro all over again," he said, forcing a smile.

"Once was enough," Hans lied. "Besides, I like flying."

Vincent started out the door, then stopped.

"Save a little glory for me, will you?" he asked light-heartedly.

Hans laughed softly.

"And for God's sake please come back." And now there was a note of concern in his voice. Before Hans could reply, he was gone.

"Everyone seems to think we're going to get killed, my friend," Hans said to Ketswana.

"Not us, we're immortal. As long as I'm with you, you're safe."

Finishing his tea, Hans left the cup in the hut, stepped outside to relieve himself, then started for the flight line. More and yet more engines were turning over, warming up. Crews were loading into the cargo compartments, and Ketswana mentioned that nine men, after the flight over from Suzdal, absolutely refused to get back in. Volunteers from the ground crews had replaced them.

All around them was a bustle of activity. They passed several Hornets revving up their engines, a crew chief shouting obscenities in Rus. A wagon clattered past, again the smell of kerosene. With a thousand men working as ground crews, most of them pressed into service and only given a couple of days training, it was a near miracle, Hans realized, that the entire place hadn't exploded with some darn fool having smuggled in a box of matches for a smoke, or from the accidental discharge of a gun.

They passed an Eagle, the ten Chin gathered in front of it, squatting around a bucket of steaming grits and a smaller bucket of tea. They didn't even notice their commander passing, and continued to chatter in their singsong voices. A ground crew trotted past, carrying coils of ropes, and then several boys darted around Hans, lugging skins filled with water to be loaded on board a ship.

"The training pays off here," Hans said. "There was part of me thought Varinna mad to think it could be pulled off, but here it is. Men, equipment, fuel, food, ammunition, all of it coming together in this place."

"They know it's this or defeat," Ketswana replied. "We

know as well that this is something special, a new thing, something we will always remember."

It was hard to sort out which flier was which in the darkness, and finally they had to grab one of the ground crews to guide them to Jack's ship. As they approached the aerosteamer, Hans was glad to see that *Gates's Illustrated* had finally been put to a good use, enough copies had indeed been found to paper over the front and sides of the cargo compartments to block out the wind.

Ketswana started for the crew compartment under Jack's ship.

"I thought you were on number thirty-nine," Jack observed.

"Didn't like the pilot."

"Suppose something happens to me," Hans interjected. "You're to take over, remember?"

Ketswana laughed.

"And suppose something happened to me on the other ship. Where would you be? No, I stay with you, my friend."

Hans wanted to argue but he could see Jack standing by the ladder to the forward compartment, arms folded, grinning.

"Kinda logical actually," Jack announced. "I'll get you in. Besides, the boys know what to do; the company commanders are all briefed."

"All right, go on, get in," Hans said, and Ketswana gave a final wave before ducking under the airship and climbing aboard.

"How is everything?" Hans asked.

"One more machine down. Engine caught fire about an hour ago when they started it up, and part of the wing burned. This takeoff in the dark, a bit tricky."

"I know. It's a balance. Would have preferred to come in at dawn, but that meant night flying, and most of these boys would have gotten lost or wound up in Cartha or back in Suzdal. We've got to get down with enough daylight to get the job done."

"Then we better get moving."

Jack climbed the ladder first and a moment later one of the ground crew, who had been sitting in the forward cab watching while the engines ran on idle, scrambled down the ladder. Hans ascended into the cab and climbed into the copilot's seat, suddenly aware again of the lingering stench from the previous day's bout with airsickness. He wondered if there was something perverse about pilots, and they took a secret delight in the smell. For a moment he was worried that his stomach would rebel, leaving him without a breakfast. Opening the side window he stuck his head out and took a gulp of air.

"Let's hope everyone's on his toes," Jack shouted. "I taxi out first, then each airship down the line follows. We circle out to sea and form up, then head out from there."

Opening up both speaking tubes, he blew into them.

"Topside. Bottom side, hang on, we're heading out."

Hans caught some moans and a burst of laughter from below. Ketswana actually was enjoying himself. Any chance to get into battle, in a land ironclad, aerosteamer, if need be crawling through a cesspool, it didn't matter to him, as long as he could kill Bantag.

Jack took hold of the throttles, edging them up until all four engines were howling. Finally, the ship lurched forward.

"We're heavy, damn heavy, and no wind to help us lift off."

He spun the wheel, closing the hot-air-bag vent atop the center air bag. They reached the center of the landing strip, following a ground crewman holding a white flag aloft, which stood out like a pale shimmer in the early-morning light. Hans felt as if somehow the machine was beginning to feel lighter, and he mentioned it to Jack.

"The center bag, depending on outside temperature, provides several hundred pounds of lift. Hell, I'll make an airman of you yet. You seem to have the feel for it. Starboard throttles idle, keep port side at full."

Hans put his hands on the throttles, Jack quickly guiding him, then letting go as he turned the wheel for the rudder. With ground crew helping, the airship slowly pivoted and lined up on a faint glimmer of light, three lanterns at the end of the field marking the takeoff path. The crew chief held his flag aloft, twirled it overhead, and let it drop while running to the port side to get out of the way.

"Here goes, full throttles, not too fast now . . . that's it."

Hans fed the fuel in, the caloric engines slowly speeding up. They held still for what seemed an eternity, then started forward again. The takeoff seemed longer than the day before, the ship slowly lurching and bouncing, bobbing up once, settling, then finally clawing into the air. The three lanterns whisked by underneath, Jack holding the ship low to gain speed, the hot exhaust going into the center air bag, heating it up even more, lift increasing. He banked gently to starboard, and in the darkness Hans sensed more than felt the ocean open out beneath them. Jack continued his slow climbing turn, the top gunner reporting a second, third, and fourth ship lining up behind them. As they spiraled upward Hans wondered how anyone could see where the other ships were, but as they completed one full circle and the eastern horizon came back around he saw several airships clearly silhouetted against the red-purple horizon.

The air was gloriously still, reminding Hans of the sensation of sliding with skates on the first black ice of winter when he was a boy. They went through another circle and another, the ships spiraling up like hawks, slowly climbing on a summer thermal, soaring into the dark heavens.

The vast world spread out below them, faint wisps of ground fog now showing dark gray, the second of the two moons slipping below the western horizon, to the east the sky getting brighter. Each turn took them farther out to sea, the coast receding, part of the plan in case watchful eyes on the ground had somehow reestablished communications during the night.

"Losing another one," Jack announced, breaking the silence, and he pointed to where a ship, streaming smoke from one of its engines, was breaking away, heading straight back to the airfield.

Two Hornets came up, climbing far more steeply than the Eagles, soaring upward, their escort but also a signal that the last of the Eagles was off the ground.

"Any count?" Jack asked, calling up to the top gunner, whom Hans truly pitied, stuck atop a flammable bag of hydrogen in an exposed Gatling mount. It was also his job to crawl around atop the bag and plug any holes shot through it in a fight. No silk umbrellas had been issued to the crews for this flight—the weight considerations had ruled it out—but even with such a device for jumping the top gunner rarely made it, since as soon as a ship caught on fire the heavy weight of the gun plunged the man straight down into the burning bag.

"Hard to count. I figure at least thirty ships are up, sir."

"Well try and get me the right number," Jack snapped.

"Damn. If we only got thirty up, we'll be slaughtered." Jack sighed, looking over at Hans.

"We go with what we got even if it's only one at this point," Hans replied absently, straining to catch a glimpse of the ground east of Tyre. Dawn was just breaking down there; Vincent would most likely be kicking off his move. Hans thought he could catch glimpses of smoke, a flash of light.

They continued through their final turn, the aerosteamer coming out of its gentle banking climb. Jack leveled them off, commenting that they were up over three thousand feet and climbing. The air was noticeably cooler, still calm and smooth. There was a glimpse of an airship several hundred feet lower, passing directly beneath them, the gunner looking up and waving. Jack lined up the compass on a southeasterly heading, pulled the elevator back slightly higher, pitching the nose upward. Tyre was now off the port side, a dozen miles away, impossible for Hans to see in his starboard seat.

"We level out at nine thousand, should be able to catch the current coming out of the west. That'll help us along a bit. Now remember, Hans, this is all from memory. I've only been there twice, so the charts aren't good."

"I trust you."

"You've got to; there's no one else."

The climb continued and gradually, through the glass view port between their feet, down in the position of the forward Gatling mount, Hans spotted the coast as they headed back to shore.

"Take the wheel, hold it steady for me on this heading," Jack ordered. "Watch the compass, but also line up on some feature on the horizon. Also you can use the sun, but remember it keeps shifting, so don't follow it around."

Hans tentatively put his hands on the wheel.

"That's it, just hold it steady. Let me ease back a bit on the throttles—we need to conserve fuel."

The steady thump of the engines, the vibrations running through the ship, changed pitch, and though still loud, the change was a blessed relief. Still, there was the sensation of gliding on ice. The beautiful light of the dawning sun suddenly exploded across the horizon, flooding the cabin with a deep golden glow.

With the plane's nose pitched high, he felt as if he were climbing to the heavens and was filled with a deep abiding peace. The moment was worth holding on to and savoring. He looked sideways, Jack had settled back in his chair, eyes half-closed, and his hands were off the controls, arms folded across his chest. There was a momentary fear, and Jack smiled.

"Hans, actually it's not all that hard. Just keep the heading, as we clear through nine thousand feet, the mercury in that gauge in the middle will tell you when, ease the nose down slightly. That's a while off, just relax and hold course." And he closed his eyes.

He felt suddenly as if he was alone in the ship, a joyous sensation, piloting it through the upper reaches of the sky. What waited ahead was forgotten for the moment, all of it washed away . . . and he was content.

"Andrew."

The dream had been of long before, of Mary. Long before her betrayal, long before all the pain when it had all been so innocent, so fresh and alive, walking hand in hand along the shore. Even in the dream he had been cognizant of the fact that he had one day found Mary with another man while he was still in Maine, that Kathleen was the center of his life now, but still there was such a pleasure in seeing his first true love again in spite of all the pain she had given him. Kathleen's gentle touch stirred him from the memory, and he felt a pang of guilt as he looked up into her worried eyes, as if afraid she could somehow sense what he had been dreaming.

"What time is it?" he whispered.

"Just before dawn."

He heard a distant rattle of musketry and was instantly awake.

"What is it?"

"I was at the hospital in the church when it started, and came back here. I don't know."

Even as she helped him to get his trousers and jacket on

he heard the hard clatter of hooves on the cobblestone pavement below his window, a rider reining in, the horse blowing hard, the messenger shouting to the guards at his door. He looked out the window and saw one of his staff, a young Roum lieutenant, another one of old Marcus's innumerable "nephews," leaping from the saddle and running up the steps of the front porch, to pound on the door below.

From the next room one of the twins stirred, crying softly, and Kathleen looked to Andrew. He nodded, and she left as he stepped out into the dim hallway and went down the stairs. He could see the shadow of the messenger beyond the glass panes of the door and called for him to enter. The boy came in, stiffly snapped to attention, and saluted, speaking so rapidly in Latin that Andrew had to motion for him to slow down.

"Sir. There's gunfire in the Congress halls. It's reported that the Speaker is dead and Bugarin has declared himself to be acting president."

Andrew sighed wearily, leaning against the wall. *Poor Flavius. Most likely went to meet Bugarin alone and died for it,* he thought.

"Andrew!"

Emil came through the door, breathing hard.

"Andrew, they've taken the White House!"

"What? I was just there." He paused, trying to remember. He had sat up with Kal till after midnight. The president was still drifting in and out of consciousness but apparently on the mend. But that was four hours ago.

"Well it was just stormed by some of the old boyars," Emil gasped. "Bugarin's proclaiming that he is president."

"If Flavius is dead, then he is," Andrew said quietly, staring off, eyes no longer focused on the messenger or Emil.

"What the hell do you mean?"

"Just that. The Constitution places Bugarin fourth in line of succession. The president is still incapacitated. Flavius wanted to avoid the crisis but not be declared acting president. Bugarin wants it, and with Flavius dead he has it."

"And you'll let him take it?"

Andrew said nothing.

"Andrew, at this very moment, that bastard's most likely

proclaiming an armistice, passing the order for the armies to stand down."

"I know."

"And what are you going to do?"

"Do? My God, Emil, what the hell have I been doing here for the last ten years? We didn't want to be here. We didn't want to get dragged into this war. Damn near all the men of our lost regiment have died in this godforsaken hellhole."

He turned away and backed up to the staircase.

"Kathleen, get the children up."

"Why, Andrew?"

"We're getting them out of here for the moment."

He looked back at the young Roum staff officer.

"Get down to the office of *Gates's Weekly*. Find Gates, let them know what's happening, round up some men if you can to hold that position, and don't let anyone you don't know into this part of the city."

He looked up to the top of the stairs where Kathleen was standing, ushering the children out of the bedroom.

"Take the children over to the armory of the Thirty-fifth. They'll be safer there."

"Where are you going?"

He reached over to the stand by the door and, taking his sword, clumsily snapped it on, reluctantly allowing Emil to help.

"I'm going to the White House."

"Why, for God's sake? Bugarin will kill you."

Andrew shook his head.

"No. There's too many old veterans still with him to allow that. We're going to have a talk."

"What?"

He paused, looking into his office, where framed over his desk were his two most prized possessions, his commissioning papers as colonel of volunteers, signed by Lincoln, and his Medal of Honor won at Gettysburg, presented by Lincoln as well. Going over to the display case he tore it open, taking out the medal, holding it reverently in his hands for a moment before clumsily pinning it on and heading out the door.

Several more men had come on horse, others were gathering in the town square that looked so strangely like a small piece of New England transported to this alien world.

One of his orderlies, as if reading Andrew's mind, was leading Mercury out from the stable behind the house. Andrew mounted, Mercury moving easily beneath him, two old companions who had been together for over a decade. Word was spreading rapidly, and from the clapboard houses lining the square he could see the last few of his old companions who were in Suzdal coming out, Webster fumbling to button a uniform that was far too tight among them. From the northeast corner of the square a small detachment came into view, moving at the double . . . they were boys, cadets serving in the 35th Maine, which was now a training regiment, the West Point of the Republic, the boys too young to be pressed into action at the front. One of them proudly carried the regimental standard. Emil came up by Andrew's side, having taken a horse from one of the couriers.

"Going to the White House now is madness, Andrew. If Bugarin has indeed seized the government, he'll kill you on sight."

Andrew felt a building rage.

Webster came running up, breathing hard.

"Is Kal all right?"

"We're not sure," Emil replied.

"Damn all, Andrew, this has gone too far. Seize control of the government now. The men will follow you!"

He delivered the last words with a rhetorical flourish that echoed across the plaza, and a cheer went up in response.

Andrew reined Mercury around hard, his steely gaze silencing the group. Turning, he headed toward the southeast corner of the square, saying nothing as Emil urged his Clydesdale-sized mount up beside him.

As Andrew rounded the corner onto the main street to the great plaza and the White House beyond, he saw that the street was already filling. He rode past the boarded-up theater, a tattered post hanging from the side billboard announcing a performance of *King Lear*. It caught his attention for a moment, the strangeness of watching Shakespeare performed in Russian on this alien world. The Roum soldiers stationed in Suzdal had been fascinated by *Julius Caesar,* since the real Caesar was from a time on Earth long after their ancestors had been swept to this world. He remembered as well a final night just before the start of the Merki War and the performance of *Henry V*.

He rode past, following the broad open boulevard flanked on both sides by ornately carved log buildings three and four stories high, the few older ones that had survived the fires and wars still adorned with gargoylelike images of Tugars. The crowd moved uneasily as he passed; there were no cheers today. Nor was there anger . . . rather it seemed to be an exhaustion of spirit and soul. It was easy to spot veterans, for nearly everyone was very old, very young, or female, veterans standing out as men on crutches or with empty sleeves. Those that could came to attention and saluted as he passed, but he kept his eyes fixed straight ahead.

"Are you going to fight them?" Emil finally asked, and Andrew said nothing.

"The men are with you. You know that?" Emil nodded behind them. He didn't need to turn; he could hear the steady tramping of the cadets, the voice of Webster shouting out orders, urging even the veterans by the side of the road to fall in and "support their colonel."

They passed the office of *Gates's Illustrated Weekly*. The publisher was in the street, mounted, waiting, apprentices, printers, the rest of his staff pouring out, some of them carrying rifles or pistols. Gates fell in on Andrew's flank.

"I thought the press was supposed to be neutral," Andrew quipped. "What ever happened to the pen being mightier than the sword?"

"Like hell we're neutral," the publisher snapped angrily. "He has some senators with him, all of them armed."

"Any troops?"

"No organized units. But there are some men, a few old boyars and former men-at-arms mostly. I knew we should have killed all of them after that last rebellion."

"What happened?" Andrew asked.

"Flavius is dead. I know that for a fact; one of my reporters was in the building when it happened. Bugarin didn't do it, though, at least not by his own hand. Again, it was like the shot at Kal. We don't know. But once it happened Bugarin rounded up some followers and made straight for the White House. Apparently a few shots were fired there."

"Kal?"

"No idea. But word is Bugarin dragged in one of the justices and Casmir."

"So he's getting himself sworn in," Emil replied. "If he's president, we've got to fight them, Andrew."

"I realize that," Andrew said quietly.

Sometimes the hardest thing was to do nothing, Hans had told him, and he smiled at the thought.

The great central plaza of the city of Suzdal was directly ahead, already filling with the citizens of the city. As he rode to the edge of the square a buzzing hum rose up from the crowd. Behind him Andrew heard Webster shouting for the company of cadets to move forward at the double and clear a path.

Andrew reined in sharply, then turned Mercury sideways. He looked back down the street and saw that several hundred men were now with him. Behind them a crowd was pressing up the street to watch the drama.

Drama, so much history and drama in this square, he thought. *The first time we marched in. The day the envoy of the Tugars arrived. The charge against the boyars' army and then the stand against the Tugars in their final assault. Grand moments, too, the victory parades, the first reading of the Constitution I penned myself, its public ratification and the declaration of the Republic and the inauguration of President Kalenka.*

Now this.

He held his hand up, motioning for Webster to stop.

"I want this formation to halt and ground arms," Andrew said. He spoke softly but firmly.

Webster looked up at him, confused.

"Mr. Webster, you are secretary of the treasury and no longer a soldier of rank with the Thirty-fifth, but I expect you to obey my orders nevertheless. Halt and stand at ease."

Webster still did not react.

"William. Do you understand me?"

"Yes sir."

Reluctantly Webster turned and shouted the order. There was a tense moment, several of the men shouting their refusal, but the order was finally carried out. He caught a glimpse of Kathleen in the crowd and forced a smile to try and calm her fears.

"Mr. Gates, you might as well come along as a member of the fourth estate. Emil, well I just want you along as well. Once you get the chance, go inside to check on Kal."

He saw the colors of the 35th Maine hanging limp in the still morning air. A gentle nudge with his heels, and Mercury edged forward to the head of the column, where the color-bearer stood. The boy came to rigid attention at Andrew's approach. He looked down and smiled at him.

"Son, do you know the responsibility you have?"

"Yes sir, the souls of the men who died beneath these colors"—he nodded up at the blood-soaked folds—"they float about us now. Their spirits live in the flag."

The answer caught Andrew off guard and he stiffened. Of course the boy would believe that, he was from Roum. Two thousand years ago their soldiers believed their dead gathered about the standard of the legion.

Was Johnnie now here, Ferguson, Mina, Malady, Whatley, and Kindred, so many others?

Slowly he raised his right hand, eyes focused on the flag, his mind filled with all that it represented. He saluted the colors.

Quickly, before the men could see the emotion that was about to flood out, he turned Mercury about with a nudge of his heels and a whispered command, picked the reins up, and quickly urged the horse to a slow canter. Emil fell in behind him, the doctor cursing under his breath since he hated to ride.

The crowd gathered in the great plaza parted at Andrew's approach; he could hear his name echoing across the square. As he passed they closed in behind him, surging forward toward the White House.

It was really nothing more than an oversize log structure, typical of ancient Rus, window shutters painted with gay designs, wildly fantastic ornamentation adorning the corners and steeply pitched tile roof. At Kal's insistence the entire thing had been whitewashed, since after all that was the house a president lived in, a house painted white.

He wondered if poor Kal was still alive in there. His old friend, his first real friend on this world, had changed so much in the last year. It was almost as if a dementia, an exhaustion, had broken him. He at times wondered if Kal had simply been too gentle, too filled with compassion to be a president. Every single death at the front told on him. Barely a day went by when he was not in the cathedral at noonday, attending yet another memorial service for the boy of a friend, an old drinking comrade, or simply because he felt that a president should be there when someone mourned a life given for the Republic.

Andrew remembered how shocked he had been the last time he saw Lincoln, face deeply etched, eyes dark and sunken. When Lincoln noticed the empty sleeve, just a quick sidelong glance, then looked back into his eyes, he felt as if the president was filled with a fatherly desire and prayer that Andrew would be spared from any more agony in service to his country. That was Kal, even more so, and all the man wanted now was for the killing to stop.

And there was the paradox of war, that there were times that in order to save lives the killing must go on.

He reined in by the steps of the executive mansion. A cordon of troops ringed the last few steps into the building, the crowd nervously edging up on the lower level. Emil suddenly blocked his view, swinging his mount in front of Andrew.

"Doctor, just what the hell are you doing?" Andrew whispered.

"Damn all, Andrew, there could be a sniper in any of those windows up there."

"I know that, Doctor; now kindly move. The last thing I want at this moment is to see you get hurt."

Emil reluctantly drew his mount around beside Andrew, but he continued to look up at the building, squinting.

Andrew was motionless, and the seconds dragged out.

"Andrew?"

"Yes?"

"What the hell are you doing?"

"Waiting."

"For what?"

"Just waiting," Andrew snapped, his tone making it clear that he didn't want to talk.

The crowd was pressing around him, an old woman tugged at his leg, he looked down, she spoke too rapidly in Rus for him to understand, her voice drowned out by the rising clamor of the anxious crowd.

Finally, a captain came out the front door, leaving it

open, stepped through the cordon of guards, walked down the steps, smartly snapped to attention, and saluted. Andrew recognized him as the officer in charge of Kal's personal guard.

"Colonel, sir?"

"Good morning, Captain."

The soldier looked up at him, obviously a bit confused.

"Captain, President Kalenka, how is he?"

"Sir, he is still alive. I have placed a double detachment of guards at his door, two officers in his room armed as well."

"And they're good men?"

"Sir, I picked them," the captain announced, hurt by the implication.

Andrew stared at the young officer, gauging him, then nodded.

"And his condition?"

The captain drew closer, coming up to Andrew's side, the crowd drawing back slightly.

"Not good I'm afraid, sir; the fever's coming back, his wife says."

"Damn all," Emil mumbled.

Andrew nodded, lifted his gaze, staring again at the building.

"Sir?"

"Yes?"

"Sir, is there anything else?"

"Has Bugarin been sworn in as acting president?"

"Yes sir. Sir, I was ordered by one of his people to remove the guard from President Kalenka and place them around the room Bugarin is in."

"And you refused?"

"Yes sir, I most certainly did."

"As colonel in command of the army, I am giving you a personal order, Captain. You are to guard Kalenka with your life."

"I would do it anyhow, sir."

"No matter what orders you receive afterward my order to you right now comes first. President Kalenka is to be protected at all cost."

"I will die before anyone harms him, sir," the young captain replied fiercely.

"Good, son. Now please go inside and announce to Mr. Bugarin and Metropolitan Casmir that I request to see them, out here."

This order he announced with raised voice, the command echoing out over the crowd. The square grew hushed.

The captain saluted, hurried inside, and long minutes passed. Finally he returned, alone.

"Colonel Keane, Mr.," and he hesitated for a second, "Acting President Bugarin says that you are to report to him inside."

Andrew stiffened.

"As commander of the army I request a public meeting, here in front of the citizens of Suzdal, and tell him I will wait here all damn day if necessary."

The captain scurried back, and Andrew pitied him, caught between two fires.

"Andrew, are you going to do what I think you're doing?"

Andrew looked over at Emil and smiled.

The bell in the church tower tolled, marking the passage of time, and finally someone appeared in the door. It was Metropolitan Casmir. He turned, looking back into the White House, obviously shouting something that was unintelligible, then turned and strode down the steps, black robes billowing. He stopped several steps above Andrew, raised his staff, and looked out at the crowd, then made the sign of blessing. Instantly there was silence, everyone going to their knees, blessing themselves. Remaining mounted, Andrew was at eye level with him.

"Has Bugarin been sworn in as acting president?" Andrew asked.

"Yes, Andrew." His voice was low, barely a whisper. "It was your own Constitution that forced me to do it. Kal, I'm not sure if he will survive. Marcus is dead, Flavius is dead. Bugarin is next in line. The Constitution requires it; I had to bless the ceremony."

Andrew knew instantly from his tone that Casmir loathed what he had to do.

"Since you are the chief justice, I request that you initiate an investigation into the attempted assassination of the president and the assassination of the Speaker. I doubt seriously if the executive branch will do so. I doubt as well if you could muster the votes in the Senate to remove Bugarin."

"I will do everything I can, both as a justice and as a priest."

There was a stir in the crowd. Casmir looked back over his shoulder. Half a dozen guards were in the doorway.

"I told Bugarin I would denounce him as a coward if he didn't come out to meet you," Casmir whispered.

Andrew could not help but chuckle.

"Are you going to overthrow him?" Casmir asked, and Andrew sensed the conflict in his friend's voice.

He said nothing, watching intently as Bugarin appeared in the doorway, strangely wearing the stovepipe hat of Kal, which to this world had become the ceremonial symbol of the president. The guards, all of them older senators, came down the steps, Bugarin in the middle of the group.

They stopped behind Casmir.

Andrew stared at him intently. There was a defiance, but he could sense the fear as well. Was this the man who could engineer not just the assassination of the Speaker but the attempt on the president as well? Did he believe so passionately that the war must end that he would kill, or was he just a pawn as well?

Regardless of what Andrew suspected about how Bugarin had come to power, he was at least for this moment the president of the Republic.

With deliberate slowness Andrew raised his hand and saluted. A hushed whisper ran through the crowd. It was an acknowledgment, they all knew that. He could sense the tension easing out of Bugarin, but there was still a wariness. He heard a mumbled curse; it was Emil who remained defiant, unable to bring himself to salute.

"I wish to see President Kalenka now," Emil announced, addressing his statement to Casmir and emphasizing the word *president.*

"I'll see to it, Emil," the prelate replied, "and you are under my personal protection."

Emil looked over at Andrew.

"Just a second," Andrew whispered.

"For what? To see you kiss his bloody boot?"

Andrew ignored his friend's defiance.

"May I inquire of the acting president if there are any

orders for the army in regards to operations both offensive and defensive."

He said the words slowly, deliberately, so that all could hear.

"All offensive operations are to cease. I am asking for a cease-fire immediately. We will end this senseless war."

Again the ripple of voices erupted in the square. This was the moment. The crowd was confused. There was a ripple of cheers, but it lacked depth and enthusiasm. He could hear the rustling of arms back across the square, a muffled order, most likely Webster telling the men there to get ready.

"Sir, if you are ordering me to have the army stand down, I cannot obey that order."

There was an expectant hush.

Andrew slowly reached down to his side, placing his hand on the hilt of his sword. One of the senators started to raise a pistol, cocking it. Casmir turned to face the senators, shouting for them to remain still.

Andrew carefully drew out his sword, a ceremonial blade given to him by Kal and the Congress in recognition of their victory over the Tugars. He made it a point of now saluting with the blade, hilt drawn up before his face, blade vertical, but as he did so he looked up toward the flag gently fluttering atop the White House.

He took a deep breath, steadying himself for what would come next.

Quickly he inverted the blade in his grasp, fumbling slightly with his one hand since he was nervous.

With hilt pointed toward Bugarin he tossed the sword onto the steps so that it clattered by Casmir's feet.

"I hereby resign my commission with the Army of the Republic," he cried, voice carrying to the farthest corners of the plaza. "I retire to private life and shall leave this city and the Republic."

The crowd fell as silent as the grave. Bugarin looked at him startled, unable to react.

Andrew took a deep breath; to his surprise, he felt as if a horrible burden had been lifted.

He half turned his horse away from Bugarin. In his mind the man simply no longer existed.

Andrew looked at the crowd, the upturned faces.

"I gave ten years to this country," he shouted, his voice echoing. "We came to this world, more than five hundred of us. Over four hundred of them are dead, dying to give you freedom. In those ten years of service and sacrifice, I have learned something."

He waited a moment, the crowd in the square as silent as the tomb.

"You cannot give freedom to anyone. Each man, each woman must earn it themselves, and then guard it from others who would take it away. Guard it from the hordes, guard it from those who would bow again to the hordes." As he said the last words, he nodded toward the White House.

He looked straight back at Bugarin.

"I am now a private citizen and as a private citizen I say this to you. I expect the health of our beloved President Kalenka to be guarded at all cost. If he should die, for whatever reason, you will have to answer to me personally."

Bugarin blanched at the direct threat but said nothing. With a deliberate show of contempt, Andrew turned his back without waiting for a reply and again faced the crowd.

"To those who were my friends, who fought for freedom, I thank you. As for the rest." He hesitated remembering Davy Crockett's famous farewell statement. "Well, I pity you, for if you surrender, you will surely die. Farewell."

With head held high he started to ride back toward his home and felt a lightness within he had not known in years. He had done his duty, he had wrestled with the desire to take it all, an act he knew he could have done. He had not stained himself, and he had not destroyed the Republic. If the Republic was doomed to die, it would be other hands that destroyed his dream and not his own. By doing nothing more at this moment he felt that he had performed one of the most important duties of his career.

As he passed the spell around him broke, voices erupting, some shouting for him to stay, others calling to fight, others shouting that the war was over. Gates, riding by his side, looked at him, gape-mouthed.

"What about the war?" Gates finally asked.

Andrew smiled.

"They have three days down in Tyre before word can ever get to them. It's beyond my control now."

"God protect Hans and Vincent." Gates sighed.

"Yes," Andrew replied, lowering his head. "God protect us all."

"Where are you going?"

"North; I'll leave the city tomorrow."

Chapter Nine

Hans had told him he would enjoy it, and he was right. He had never liked horses all that much. An officer was expected to ride, and so he did, but trying to keep a comfortable seat aboard a monster the size of a Clydesdale was impossible, especially after the wound to his hip.

Riding an ironclad was different. It bounced the guts out of him as they rumbled up and down over the vast undulating plains, but at the moment he didn't care . . . he was back in action, and that's what counted.

Cresting a low bluff the driver down below halted their machine. To Vincent's left, sprawled on the ground, were half a dozen Bantag, torn apart by Gatling fire, their mounts dead as well. The Hornet that had done the job came sweeping back from the east, wagging its wings as it passed overhead, most likely returning back to base, its ammunition spent.

Moving stiffly, Vincent turned, holding the side of the turret, letting his legs dangle over the side of the machine, and he dropped clumsily to the ground. It was good to be out of the machine. The open hatch atop the turret tended to act as a chimney, drawing heat up from the main deck below, where the boiler was. The dry sage crackled beneath his feet, the pungent smell clearing away the stench of hot oil and kerosene.

He raised his field glasses. Far ahead, several miles away, he could see them, six umens identified so far, sixty thousand mounted warriors of the Horde . . . and all of them confused as hell.

The breakout had started at dawn. A rocket barrage of five hundred rounds had preceded the attack, and then fifty-two ironclads led the way. They'd lost six in that opening assault, but within minutes their firepower, combined with the support of twenty Hornets, had torn a gaping hole in the Bantag lines a mile wide, the enemy fleeing in disorganized panic.

Following them had come the entire 3rd Corps, moving by regiments in a huge block formation, the same system Hans had used the year before during the withdrawal from the Green Mountains. But this time they had additional artillery with them, wagons for supplies, in addition to the Gatlings aboard the ironclads and in the air.

It was a different kind of warfare for a different age, Vincent realized. Varinna had grasped that, and it was beginning to crystallize in his own mind. This was more like ships maneuvering at sea than the old style of battles on land. Keep the ironclads together except for a dozen scattered around the square of 3rd Corps to provide fire support and to act as rally points.

An ironclad ground up the slope beside him and came to a stop, steam hissing from the safety valve, the top door open, a head sticking out.

"Bastards don't know what to do!" Timokin grinned, sitting up in the turret of his machine and wiping his face with a sweat-stained rag. He climbed out and dropped to the ground next to Vincent. Other machines were climbing the slope behind them, moving in a giant V formation a half mile wide. It was a grand sight, smoke billowing, cleated wheels cutting into the dry turf, gun ports open, three-inch rifles and Gatlings protruding and ready for action.

Behind them all of 3rd Corps was marching in open block formation. Just inside the giant square six batteries moved at an easy pace, ready to swing out and deploy if needed, while in the center of the vast square were the wagons loaded down with extra fuel, ammunition, and medical supplies. The lone regiment of mounted troopers weaved back and forth outside the square along the flanks and rear, troopers occasionally reining in to trade a couple of shots with Bantag riders who ventured too close to the formation. Overhead four Hornets circled lazily, ready to swoop down if the Bantag should try to venture a charge.

He could sense the exhilaration in the ranks. Third Corps had stayed in Tyre throughout the winter, avoiding the gutting of the army at Roum and the disaster at Capua. If anything, the men had felt abandoned, forgotten on a secondary front, and after nine months in the siege lines were glorying in a chance to prove something.

Gregory offered Vincent his canteen, and he gladly took it. He had drained his own canteen hours ago and pride had kept him from asking for more water from his crew below, who were suffering in far worse heat. Too many months behind a desk he realized.

The water was hot, but he didn't care, rinsing the oily taste out of his mouth and then taking a long gulp.

"This is a damn sight better than Capua," Gregory said, wincing slightly when Vincent tossed the canteen back. "Type of country these machines were made for, not the tangle of trenches and traps up north."

Vincent nodded in agreement.

He continued to scan the enemy. Plumes of dust were rising from the west several miles behind the column. *They are most likely detaching more troops away from Tyre to follow,* he thought. *Maybe even abandoning the siege completely except for a small covering force, figure to pin us out here with everything they have and wipe us out.*

In spite of Gregory's enthusiasm and the fact that he had planned this operation himself, Vincent did feel a shiver of nervousness. It was one thing to calculate all this out on paper and maps; it was another thing to be out here now. Hans had been right, it was different down here. North, in Roum, the land was settled: There were roads, villas, towns, the typical orderliness of the Roum, everything squared off and proper. This was vast unsettled land, undulating prairie as far as the eye could see, like what he imagined Kansas or the Nebraska Territory to be. A place for the ironclads, but not for a column of infantry on foot.

It was a strange balance. The Bantag did not have a single ironclad on this front. The few rocket launchers they had were expended, and none of their artillery could stand in the open against the attack. Yet once mounted they could ride rings around the machines and the marching column of 3rd Corps. He looked back to the west, where 3rd Corps, nearly eleven thousand men, were moving through the dry knee-high grass, looking like an undulating blue wave traversing a green-brown sea.

Neither side could now come to grips with the other.

The Bantags did have one serious advantage, though—they could chose the place to stand and fight. He could not. They had mobility both tactically and strategically, his side had the firepower. If they could bring up firepower as well, it could turn deadly. And that was part of the plan as well.

He walked in front of his machine, surveying the ground, remembering the maps he had studied so intently that they were etched clearly in his mind. They were just under twenty miles out from Tyre, a damn good march for the first day. A shallow stream was directly ahead, several hundred yards down the slope, its water dark and muddied by the passing of the Horde riders.

"We camp here," Vincent announced.

"We've still got four hours or more of daylight, we could make another eight to ten miles."

Vincent shook his head.

"No. This is far enough. Besides, I want the men dug in, stockade with sod walls, and we've got water down there for the night. The next stream is six miles farther on, and if the Bantags have any sense, they'll fight us for it."

"Grand, and we chew them apart."

"There's time for that, plenty of time," Vincent said absently. "Let the pressure build some more first. Besides, we're not the main show, that's Hans's job. Remember, we're the diversion, the bait. We bed down early tonight, do a hard march tomorrow, and should nearly reach the head of the rail line they're driving west from the Great Sea. Jurak has undoubtedly figured by now that we are attacking here. He might already have dispatched troops and ironclads from Xi'an and Fort Hancock to converge and meet us in defense of that rail line. Let's give him time to get there and make the show easier for Hans."

Hans. He pulled out his watch. *He should be hitting just about now,* he thought. *God help him.*

It wasn't the time to vomit but the last two hours had been pure hell. Leaning over weakly, he retched, but there was nothing left to give. The ship bucked and surged, rising up on another thermal of hot air, then plunging back down.

"Is that Xi'an?" Jack shouted.

"What?"

"Damn it, Hans, pull yourself together."

He nodded bleakly, looking forward. They'd been over land for the last hour, bisecting the arcing curve of the river up to Xi'an. The cloud cover had been building since early afternoon, forcing them to drop lower, Jack expressing increasing anxiety about the prospect of a thunderstorm. If a storm did come up, it could wipe out the entire mission.

Hans raised his field glasses, bracing his elbows on the forward panel, trying to compensate for the unceasing motion of the airship, which was bobbing like a cork on a windswept sea.

It had to be it. In spite of the surging motion of the ship he caught glimpses of a vast walled compound, ships anchored, and for a brief instant a place that looked all too chillingly familiar, the small fortress village half a dozen miles below Xi'an, where he had holed up after escaping from the slave camps. The aerosteamer steadied for a moment, and the world beneath him seemed to come into sharp focus. The city was spread out along the east bank of the river, ancient brick walls glowing red in the late-afternoon sun.

Dozens of ships lined the docks below the bluffs, most of them galleys, several steamers, the rest traditional Chin junks. A dark seething mass swarmed the docks, looking like a stirred-up nest of ants . . . Chin slaves. From the air the city had a fairy-tale quality to it, a towering pagoda in the center, buildings with steeply pitched red-tile roofs, dozens of small temples dotting the skyline. Yet as he steadied his field glasses he could sense, more than actually see, that a fair part of the city was abandoned, derelict homes, weed-choked streets, collapsed roofs. Even as they labored for their masters the pathetic residents of Xi'an were dying, chosen for the moon feast, transported to work on the railroads, factories, and supply lines, or simply worked to death.

Checking again on the village where he had fought off the Bantag till help arrived, he gauged the distance up the river. There was no doubt about it: They were approaching Xi'an, main supply base for the Bantag Horde, the transition point for supplies coming from the heart of the Chin realm.

Two hundred miles eastward was that black heart of the Bantag Empire, the vast prison camps and factories where millions of Chin slaves labored to support the war. That heart was his ultimate goal, but first he had to seize this city. Everything the Bantag made to support their war effort had to come through here, off-loading from the trains to be loaded on ships that would transport it across the Great Sea, five hundred miles northward to be off-loaded yet again for the final run to Capua. This was the weak link in that vast chain.

This was the linchpin of Varinna's plan. A raid deep into the realm of the Bantag to seize the docks, sink the ships, burn the supplies—to cut the precious lifeline. Vincent was the diversion, to present Jurak with two threats, the prospect of their seizing a base on the Great Sea and with luck draw off some forces before his own raid struck. If Vincent was successful, all the better.

"Where do we land?" Jack cried.

"Damned if I know," Hans replied. "Can't you remember?"

"I only flew over the damned place once, and that was a year ago. The second time I flew to where you were, then got the hell out. Damn it, Hans, we should have sent in at least one reconnaissance flight before doing this."

Hans shook his head. One such flight might have tipped their hand. This one was going to be blind.

"Think they're on to us?" Jack asked.

"Have to be by now; they must have coast watchers reporting us coming in."

The city was just several miles out. Hans anxiously scanned the riverbanks, looking for a place to touch down that was close enough that they could directly storm the harbor area.

Nothing.

"We're losing another ship."

It was their top gunner calling in.

"She's going down. Damn, it's a Bantag flyer!"

His voice was drowned out by the staccato roar of a Gatling, the vibration of the topside gun firing shaking the cabin.

Jack held the ship steady, still aimed straight at the city, while anxiously scanning the sky above, looking for the enemy ship.

"There, north of the city wall, looks like an airfield!" Hans cried.

"That's it then! We're going in!" Jack shouted. He nosed the ship down, picking up speed.

"Got him! He's breaking to starboard. He's burning!"

Hans leaned forward, looking out the side window and caught a glimpse of a twin-engine airship, trailing fire, going down.

"Topside, how many still with us?"

"Somewhere around thirty-five I think."

Hans said nothing. Better than he hoped but still only 350 men.

They dropped through two thousand feet, the wires on the wings singing.

Hans cleared the speaker tube to the cargo department. "Ketswana, get ready!"

"About time."

Engines howling, the airship leveled out a hundred feet above the marshy western shore, then turned as they reached the river just south of the city and started to race straight in. Straight ahead he could see startled faces looking up, Chin slaves on the docks and around the warehouses, hands raised, pointing at the incoming assault. A scattering of Bantag were running along the walls. A stream of tracers snapped past the open window, startling Hans, it was one of the gunners flying behind them sweeping the walls.

"Fly us over the ships, then bank around into the airfield," Hans shouted.

"Why?"

"I want the Chin on the docks to see our insignia so they know what the hell is happening."

Jack banked the ship, turning more easterly, heading straight in toward the city, then banked over sharply, portside wing dropping down. They were directly above the docks lining the river below the city walls, white stars of the Republic exposed on the bottom side of the wings, an insignia clearly different than the human skulls of the Bantag. In spite of the howling of the engines and the shriek of the wind, he distinctly heard thousands of voices rising up, excited cries of hope.

The nausea was gone, he hung on, watching as land,

river, city, and sky wheeled in front of him. A bullet snapped through the cabin, shattering a window, glass flying.

They leveled out, heading straight toward a row of galleys berthed side by side, each of them loaded down with two land ironclads. A steamer, looking vaguely like an old-style Mississippi riverboat, towing two barges was out in the middle of the river, barges loaded down with crates behind it, heading downstream. Again the staccato roar of the Gatling from above; tracers tore into the first barge. It ignited in a towering fireball, debris soaring hundreds of feet heavenward.

"God damn that idiot!" Jack screamed, banking away from the explosion. "Cease fire up there!"

The boy was shouting with joy, tracers sweeping into the second barge, igniting the ammunition aboard that one as well. It looked like a vast fireworks show gone berserk. Jack continued to turn away, flying up over the top of the city wall, gape-mouthed Bantag looking straight up. Swarms of Chin on the docks were running, panic-stricken.

Hans was filled with a mad exhilaration, holding on to the side railing as Jack banked sharply in the opposite direction, leveling out, sweeping along the city wall, Bantag so close below that Hans could not resist the urge to stick his hand out the side window and offer a universal rude gesture. He was tempted to man the forward gun but knew he had to stay focused on the battle. Down in the narrow twisting lanes of the tightly packed city he could see hundreds pouring out of buildings into the streets, pointing.

They reached the northwest corner of the wall. The airfield was less than a quarter mile ahead, but now they were coming in at a right angle to the long axis. A Bantag air machine was starting to lift off, crawling into the sky, turning toward them.

Jack slammed the throttles back, banked to the west out over the river again until they reached the opposite shore. He then slapped the wheel in the opposite direction. The airship seemed to stand on its starboard wing as it pivoted, turning to line up on an easterly heading, aiming straight at the airfield. Jack eased the throttles back even farther.

Hans lost sight of the Bantag airship, felt a shudder, and caught a glimpse of a tracer snapping past, return fire from above. As they turned, he saw one of their aerosteamers going down, port wing folding up, caught in the fireball explosion of the barges, the machine falling like a moth with a wing torn off. The ship crashed into the river, the blue glow of a hydrogen fire soaring up, consuming the canvas and wicker framework.

The sky was filled with airships, flying about like a swarm of confused and angry bees, heading in every possible direction. The Bantag airship flew right through the middle, tracers streaking in from all points of the compass as a score or more gunners fired on it. The Bantag machine exploded and crashed into the dock, striking down dozens of Chin. Another ball snapped through the cabin past Hans's head, fired from one of their own ships in all the confusion.

"This is gonna be tight!" Jack shouted, as they lined up on the airfield.

It wasn't much, Hans realized, nothing more than a narrow swath of grass, the west side ending at the bluffs of the river, the other three sides surrounded by a jumbled sprawl of warehouses, slave encampments, and round wooden buildings that looked like oversize Bantag yurts.

The airship bobbed down, dropping below the rim of the bluff, Jack slammed in throttles, nosed up, cursing. They seemed to hang in midair, drifting in toward the bluff. Hans caught a glimpse of a red streamer fluttering in the wind at the end of the strip. They were coming in to land with the wind at their backs.

The ship barely climbed over the rim of the bluff and there was a sharp blow. They were down!

The ship bounced, rolled down the length of the airfield. Hans saw several dozen Bantag standing to one side, all of them motionless, completely surprised.

Jack let his ship roll out to the very end of the airstrip, clearing the way for the rest to come in, turning at the last second, slamming the throttles down.

"Everyone out! Get out, damn it!"

Hans unstrapped from his seat, stepped down, pulled open the bottom hatch, grabbed his carbine out from under his chair. It was a drop of a dozen feet, and he suddenly realized he couldn't negotiate the ladder while holding on to his gun.

"Move, damn it, move!" Jack was crying.

Hans dropped his weapon through the hatch and slid down the rope ladder, holding on to either side, burning his hands. Hitting the ground hard he clutched at his carbine, came up to his knees and levered it opened, pulled a cartridge from his pocket, and slammed it in. Some of the Bantag were still standing along the edge of the strip, watching. He stood up and came out from under the machine, moving along the wing, almost stepping into a propeller that was still spinning.

Ketswana was by his side, carbine raised. At a walk Hans started toward the Bantag, for a moment not really sure of what to do. They were mostly gray pelts and young. Another airship skidded past him, turning, spinning about as it ground to a halt. He looked down the airstrip. Airships were lining up, coming in, one after the other, one of them trailing smoke from a burning wing. It never made it, slamming into the bluff just below the airstrip, exploding. The ship behind it rose up, banking hard, nearly clipping the city wall with its wing, leveled out, then flew down the length of the field to come around again for another try.

He continued to walk toward the Bantag. They stood frozen like statues, most likely not even comprehending what was happening. Their inactivity told him volumes . . . the attack was a complete and total surprise, the arrival of the air fleet a complete shock. He was so close he could almost talk to them in a normal voice. He paused, and in spite of his hatred he couldn't bring himself to raise his gun; it was too much like murder.

Suddenly they came to life. One of them fumbled at his belt, pulled out a pistol, and raised it. Others started to draw their weapons as well. Ketswana leveled his weapon, fired, pitching one of them over backwards. Shots erupted, Hans continued forward, a bullet snipping past his face. He took steady aim on the forehead of a gray pelt and dropped him clean. Levering open his carbine he reloaded, looked up, and saw the last of them running toward the wall.

Hans looked back over his shoulder. More men were swarming out from under the grounded airships. Eight were already down, two more came in, landing almost wingtip to wingtip, one of them coming straight at him. He sprinted to get out of the way, dropping to the ground as the ship veered, its starboard wing clipping the side of a shack, a propeller popping off, spinning across the field like a berserk toy of a giant child, tearing up great gouts of dirt, then disintegrating into splinters. The ship lurched to a stop, port-side wing pivoting over Hans's head. The crew compartment underneath was already open, Chin soldiers spilling out, jabbering, cursing.

One of Ketswana's men raised a bugle, sounding the rally call, and men came sprinting from all directions. An airship screamed past overhead, coming from the opposite direction of the landing traffic, its topside and forward gun firing upward. He caught a glimpse of a Bantag machine turning away, fire billowing from its hydrogen bag, pilot tumbling out of the forward cab, a silk umbrella opening. The Bantag pilot drifted toward the airstrip. Before Hans could say anything, guns were raised, riddling the warrior, who hung limp in his harness.

More men were falling in around Hans. Someone had his guidon. He had completely forgotten about bringing that along.

He scanned the wall facing the airstrip. There was a gate, but it was already closed. *No, get lost in the warren of streets. It was the docks, get the docks, round up the Chin out there, then take the city from that side.*

He looked back over at the airstrip. More ships were still coming in. *What's on the other side, those wooden yurtlike buildings? Barracks for the Bantag. If so we could lose our ships.*

"Jack?"

"Right here."

"Round up fifty men or so; I want a defensive perimeter on the other side of the field. Once the last airship lands and off-loads, start turning them around, get them back up in the air again to provide support."

He started off without even waiting for a reply, racing down the length of the airfield. More ships were landing; one was on its side, burning fiercely, survivors hanging out of the side of the cargo compartment, dropping to the ground and crawling away.

A rattle of shots erupted from along the wall. He looked up, saw more Bantag up there, firing at the aerosteamers on the field.

He detailed off a dozen men, shouting for them to suppress the fire, and at the same instant an airship, banking sharply, winged overhead, its topside and nose gunners pouring a stream of Gatling fire down on the wall. Good, someone up there was thinking.

He pushed on, breathing hard, not used to the running, feeling his heart pounding, fluttering. He slowed for an instant urging Ketswana to push forward. There was a brief slap of pain in his chest that almost stole his breath away.

Damn, not now. He bent over, a Chin soldier slowing, coming up face filled with fear.

"Hans shot?"

"No. No, I'm fine."

He stood back up, placing his hand on the young soldier's arm to steady himself. The shiver of pain passed.

He started forward again, rounding the northwest corner of the wall. The shipyard and docks were far bigger than he had realized from the air. To his right, on the north side of the landing strip, were a row of boat sheds, bows of what looked to be seagoing ironclads sticking out. If any of those ships could get up steam and make it out into the river, they were finished. *If we could capture them, though,* he thought with a grin, *Bullfinch could play hell with Bantag shipping.* Catching the eye of a Chin sergeant leading a detachment, he pointed toward the boat sheds. The sergeant didn't need to be told. He saluted, shouted for his men to follow, and ran off. Directly below his feet, less than a hundred feet away, was the burning wreckage of an aerosteamer sticking out of the river. He saw several survivors crawling up onto the muddy bank.

Down the length of the city were dozens of piers, anchored ships, several of them burning like torches. Ammunition from the burning barges in the middle of the river was still igniting, showering the dockside with flaming embers.

The river was low, nearly twenty feet below the level of the wall. The bluff that the city was built on extended about forty feet out from the wall, then sloped off sharply down to the docks twenty feet below the level of the bluff. A steeply sloping walkway, emerging from the main city gate a couple of hundred yards away, connected the upper and lower levels. Just south of the gate he noticed for the first time that a railroad track ran between the wall and the edge of the bluff, boxcars and flatcars lining the track, all of them swarming with Chin. Atop several of the boxcars Bantag were already in position, crouching low, firing in his direction.

The wide pier along the riverbank was a scene of absolute chaos. Thousands of Chin swarmed back and forth, Bantag visible in the crush, towering above their slaves. Ketswana had deployed a heavy skirmish line from the wall to the edge of the bluff. Hans came up to join him.

"We can't get separated!" Hans shouted, trying to be heard above the cacophonous roar. "I'll advance along the top of the bluff. Keep pace with me down on the docks. As you pass each ship anchored to the pier, sweep the Bantag off but don't get tangled up in them. We advance to the gate, then try and gain a foothold in the town. Now move!"

He started forward at a slow walk, followed by several dozen men, moving along the lip of the bluff, looking up warily at the wall above. Ketswana, leading several dozen more, slid down the clay embankment, alighting on the pier. The seething chaos of Chin and Bantag was backing up in confusion at the sight of this blue-clad line sweeping around from the side of the city. Puffs of smoke ignited from Bantag on the pier, along the embankment, from ships, and atop the parked train.

"Aim carefully!" Hans shouted.

The skirmish line fired back, trying to avoid hitting the frightened slaves caught in the middle of the chaos. They pushed forward, passing the first dead, tragically too many of them human. A scathing volley erupted from a galley tied to the pier, several dozen Bantag lining the side of the ship. A man next to Hans dropped without uttering a sound, face a bloody mass.

Hans knelt, aimed carefully, fired. The battle stalled for several minutes as they struggled to suppress the Bantag defending the anchored ship, the men around Hans kneeling and lying down to return fire. He lost two more in quick succession. It was taking too long. Ketswana, leading the way, scrambled over the bow of the ship, disappearing in the confusion. Seconds later he reappeared, swinging a heavy Bantag scimitar two-handed, cutting down a black-clad warrior. Screaming a wild battle cry, holding the scimitar aloft, he jumped back onto the dock and charged forward.

The next ship downstream was in flames, bundled-up sails burning like torches. Hans pushed his line forward; they had to gain the gate. He saw a dark column coming out of that gate, Bantag infantry, and his heart sank.

And then it happened. The Bantag infantry, hemmed in on all sides by thousands of terrified slaves trying to get away from the fighting slashed out, clubbing, bayoneting their way through the press.

Caught between two fires, the Chin finally exploded. The terrified mob turned on their tormentors and within seconds the entire dockside from one end to the other had dissolved into a frightful, bitter riot, a revolution of tormented slaves turning on their implacable, fearsome masters.

Bantag were dragged down, disappearing under the swarm.

"Keep together!" Hans roared to his men. "Don't get lost in this! Take the gate and hold there!"

He pushed the line forward, advancing slowly, keeping the pressure on, coldly and logically realizing that if he could push the Chin back, drive them together, panic would seize them and they'd turn on their foes. The ground was slick with blood, footing nearly impossible with the mass of bodies. His line finally broke in two between the embankment along the wall and the lower dock, Chin by the hundreds swarming through on the steep-sloping ground separating the two.

As he advanced he looked down on the ships to his right. More of them were burning, one of them flaring like a furnace, Bantag in flames plunging off the side. *Damn, loaded with kerosene most likely,* he thought.

Suddenly they were at the gates . . . which hung wide-open, bodies littering the entryway, most of them Chin, but there were a half dozen Bantag as well. The boxcars, which he feared might serve as a barrier to his advance, were in flames. He almost felt pity for a lone warrior running back and forth, obviously terrified, weapon gone, the surging mob of Chin below taunting and screaming at him. He suddenly crumpled and fell off the side, into the waiting arms of the mob. The fighting was exploding through the streets of the city, the venting of long-suppressed rage.

He turned, looking down at the docks. If it was possible to pity the Bantag, he did so at this moment. No longer were they the feared masters. Some still fought, several dozen of them forming a square, bayonets poised outward. Most were simply being swarmed under. He saw one rising up into the air, held aloft by a dozen Chin, kicking feebly while the mob tore at him, beating him with clubs, slashing with knives; one, holding a Bantag rifle, plunged the bayonet in the warrior's side, pulled it out, then plunged it in again.

The flames continued to sweep along the docks, jumping from ship to ship, feeding hungrily on canvas sails, tarred ropes and decks, stores of kerosene, crates of ammunition.

He leaned against the walls of the city, resting for a moment to catch his breath.

"Hans, you all right?"

It was Ketswana, obviously delighted with the slaughter, carbine slung over his shoulder, sword still in his hands and dripping with blood and matted hair.

He nodded. It was too damned hot, made worse by the fires and the press of the mob.

A flyer streaked overhead, skimming down the river, forward gunner firing at a lone junk that had managed to push off from the dock. Water foamed around the ship, tracer rounds walking onto the deck, dropping the Bantag crew, sails sparking into flames, a wild hysterical cheer rising from the thousands of Chin along the riverfront.

Hans watched it soar past, the thought forming, wishing he was on it, above all of this madness, blood, and chaos where he could still his pounding heart and breathe cool air.

"Easy, so damned easy!" Ketswana exalted.

"Not yet, damn it," Hans snapped, refocusing his attention.

"First. Detail off some of our Chin sergeants. Get the people down there on the docks organized and put out those fires. We want those ships and the supplies on board."

Ketswana looked at him.

"This is no longer a raid; we're going to hold this place."

His companion broke into a grin. He pointed to the south end of the dock, where he had first spotted two land ironclads. The ship was still there, fire licking along its bow.

"I want those ironclads saved. We can use them. Next, detail off a company, get into the city, find out if there are any pockets of resistance. Try and find the human chieftain or ruler in there. I'm heading back to the airfield; we've got to organize the flyers, and find out if anything's coming at us from outside the city."

He broke away from the press around the gate, motioning for his guidon bearer and bugler to follow. Moving back along the wall, he was horrified by the extent of the slaughter left in their wake. He had seen far too many a battlefield, but there was nothing worse than the wake of a bloody murderous riot. The dead were not simply shot, they were torn apart, humans and Bantags locked in deadly embrace, hands about each other's throats, clawing at each other's eyes; blood, brains, looping entrails covered the embankment. Hundreds of Chin wandered about aimlessly, many of them seriously injured, but still capable of falling on a Bantag if they saw the slightest sign of life.

He reached the northwest corner of the wall. The airfield was again in view. Burning airships littered the ground, patches of dried grass burning as well, thick white smoke swirling up. He could hear a scattering of shots in the distance. He caught a glimpse of the ironclad boat sheds; the buildings were in flames. He moved slowly, winded from the battle, reaching the shed which must have been the headquarters for the airfield. Jack was out front shouting orders and threw his hands wide in exasperation at Hans's approach.

"Damn all! Where the hell have you been?"

"Fighting a battle."

"It's your job to stay in one damn place and give orders. I'm not a ground commander, and that's what you've got me doing here."

Hans smiled at Jack's exasperation.

"One of my men who just landed said he flew several miles to the northeast. Do you know there must be several regiments of Bantag camped up there, and they're already forming up?"

"We had to expect that," Hans said, forcing himself to conceal his surprise.

"We did our job here, Hans. Let's get the hell out while we can."

"How many airships left?"

Jack looked around at the packed confusion of the airfield.

"We lost nine coming in, at least I think that's the count. Another half dozen got lost or turned back. We're down to twenty-five, with just barely enough fuel to get home. Let's off-load the weapons, hand them out to the Chin, so I can get our airships out of here."

Hans shook his head.

"The air fleet stays here."

"What?"

"Just what I said. Pick out one ship with a good crew that won't get lost, and send them back to Tyre with word that we're in. I'll write out the message before they leave."

Jack drew closer.

"Hans, you know and I know that wasn't the plan I agreed to fly. This was a raid to smash up Xi'an and, hopefully, trigger a revolt to tie Jurak down and cut his supplies. If you and your men were going to stay, I was to turn my fleet around and get back to Tyre. We've done that. I want my airships out of here now."

Both ducked as a bullet whined past. Turning, Hans saw a couple of Bantag on the wall. A volley of shots erupted from the Chin soldiers standing around the two, driving the Bantag down.

"Damn all, Hans, a dozen Bantags with rifles could riddle the rest of my ships. I've got to get them up and out of here. This place is just too hot."

"I know that. Get airborne, we still got a couple hours of daylight. Range east, up the track, get some other ships over that camp where their troops are forming and shoot it up. Let's get some panic going out there. If you can, have someone land twenty or thirty miles up the track and tear up some telegraph lines. Once dusk settles come back in and land here. We should have this place secured by then."

Again another shot snapped past them. Cursing, Hans raised his carbine, took careful aim at a Bantag on the wall, and dropped him.

"If I do that, we won't have enough fuel to get everyone back," Jack cried even while Hans was shooting.

"I know that," Hans said.

"Hans?"

The sergeant major stared at him, saying nothing.

"Damn it, Hans, you won. Jurak will choke up there at Capua. It'll take him weeks to get any supplies after this. If you want to stay here, well that was part of the plan if you thought you could hold. I can be back from Tyre by tomorrow evening with two hundred more men and supplies."

"No." He shook his head violently.

Jack stared at him, and their eyes locked.

"I knew you would do this," Jack finally whispered. "Damn you. I didn't think we'd even make it this far. Hans, I'm still alive. Do you understand that? I thought I was dead, and I'm still alive. For God's sake, all I want to do now is live out a few more days without being terrified."

As he said the last words his voice started to break.

"And you knew as well as I did what we have to do out here."

"You're talking bloody suicide for all of us," Jack cried. He backed away from Hans, cursing violently.

"I'll not order my men to die. God damn you, Hans, I've lost nearly half of them already." He pointed toward the flaming wrecks littering the field.

"You're not ordering them," Hans whispered. "I'm ordering them."

"Andrew said nothing of this to me," Jack shouted.

Hans started to reach for the letter of authorization tucked into his breast pocket and hesitated. No, that wasn't the way, he realized. He stepped up to Jack, putting his hand on the pilot's shoulder. Jack tried to shake it off, but Hans grasped him tight, forcing him to look into his eyes again.

"Jack, I'm going to end this war the only way it can be ended," he announced slowly. "We're going straight into the heart of this bloody empire and tear it out. We're not stopping with Xi'an. We're going to liberate all the Chin."

Jack said nothing.

"I can't order men to near-certain death, Jack. But you know this is the only way left, and someone has to do it."

* * *

"So, they found the weak spot."

Jurak turned away from the map in the center of the yurt illuminated by oil lamps looted from a nearby Roum villa.

He motioned for his aging friend to have a seat. Taking down a wineskin, he tossed it over. Zartak grunted his thanks, uncorking the skin and draining half of it off in long, thirsty gulps.

"This Roum wine, far better than the brew the Chin make. About the only thing I like in this damnable country is the wine."

Jurak said nothing, turning back to study the map and calculate his next move.

"There's a wine from the south, a land out across the great encompassing ocean," Zartak said. "Our cousins who live there make it themselves, delicious as nectar."

"Make it themselves?" Jurak asked.

Zartak nodded, motioning for Jurak to sit down. The expression on Jurak's face made it obvious that he did not want to be diverted at the moment, but Zartak simply chuckled and patted the camp chair.

"You already know what needs to be done, and so do I. Now relax for a few minutes before you go off."

Jurak grudgingly gave in and sat down, taking the wineskin.

"None of these humans down there," Zartak continued. "Oh, a few slaves are traded as we ride past. Five hundred leagues or more south of Cartha. The two oceans here are mere lakes to the Great Sea."

"Have you ever seen it?"

"I've ridden nearly four circlings," Zartak cackled. "I've seen everything of this world. Not like the stories you tell me of your world, my Qar Qarth."

Jurak looked up, annoyed at the honorific title. Zartak smiled as if joking.

"Cities that glow at night, flying machines that are as fast as sound. Now you are my Qar Qarth, but I must confess I find it hard to believe, for nothing can outrace the voice of thunder. So many strange things you've seen Jurak."

Zartak sighed wearily, shaking his head, running long, knurled fingers through his thinning mane.

"You're different, too," Jurak replied. "Not like the other clan chiefs."

Zartak laughed.

"The Merki had a position within their Horde, the Shield Bearer, believed to be the spiritual advisor, the other half of the soul of the Qar Qarth. The fallen Tugars as well had an elder general. I fought him once, the last one that is. He was good, very good."

"And you were thus to the last leader of the Bantag, before we, Ha'ark, the rest of my squad came here?" Jurak asked.

Zartak nodded.

"We're not all as primitive as Ha'ark believed, or wanted to believe. We were here long before the first humans trod this world. I, for one, believe this was the home world, the birthplace of the first ancestors who grasped the stars and then fell from greatness. How else is it explained that you came from another world through the Portal of Light."

Jurak nodded. The history of his own world taught that they were descendants of the first elders, godlike travelers who stepped through space and then became stranded upon his world. If so, they had to have come from somewhere. This world might very well indeed be the ancestor world of all of his race.

"The portals, I've wondered about that since we came here," Jurak said, staring up through the open flaps of his yurt, the Great Wheel overhead.

"Gates, I think," Zartak replied. "And may the gods and all the ancestors curse the day the gates into the world of the humans were created. The fools who built them, then left them unattended, were mad."

"Yet it brought you the horse, even the great woolly beasts, and of course the cattle?" Jurak said cautiously.

Zartak looked at him carefully and leaned forward. He picked the wineskin up, realized it was empty, and tossed it aside.

Jurak reached under a table and pulled out another sack, handing it over. The old warrior nodded his thanks.

"The air up in this region is chilled at night; this will warm my bones and help me to sleep."

He smacked his lips, sighing as he recorked the skin, which was now half-empty. Picking up the folding stool he had been sitting on, he moved it over to the open doorway of the yurt, motioning for Jurak to join him. They sat in silence for several minutes, gazing out at the steppes and the Great Wheel rising in the eastern heavens.

"The Endless Ride," Zartak whispered, gaze fixed on the heavens.

"Oh how glorious it was in my youth. You came long after these troubles had started, and all was changing. I think you would have liked it then, even though you are civilized."

Jurak looked over and saw that Zartak was smiling slyly.

"At dawn to see the vast multitude arise, facing to the east, chanting our greetings to the morning sky. The yurts, a hundred thousand of them, and that of the great Qar Qarth drawn by a hundred oxen with room for a hundred within. Our encampments blanketed the steppe for as far as the eye could see.

"And then we would ride, the wind in our hair, the thunder of a million hooves causing the earth to shake. Hunters sweeping far forward, bringing in game, the great wool-clad giants with tusks that could feed a thousand for a day."

He smiled, taking another drink.

"I remember my first hunting eagle. I named him Bakgar after the God of the Westerly Wind. His cry would reach to the heavens. We'd range far ahead, he and I. Have you ever truly been alone on the steppes, my son?"

Jurak shook his head, inwardly pleased that the wine had loosened the old one's tongue, causing him to drop the deference, the titles, to call him son. He realized that Zartak was not even aware of the slip.

"To be truly alone, the bowl of the blue heavens overhead, the great green sea beneath you, spring grass as high as your stirrups. When the god Bakgar sighed, the green sea shifted, rocking, the wind taking form as it touched the land. And the air, the smell, you know you were breathing the sweet breath of heaven.

"And I'd raise my wrist, setting my own Bakgar loose, and with a great cry he'd circle upward, bright golden feathers rippling. Alone, so truly alone, and it was worth everything to be alive and to know that, to know the joy of a fleet horse, an eagle on your wrist, and the wind in your hair."

He lowered his head for a moment, lost in his dreams.

"And you never knew the joy only the young can feel when they ride to war for the first time. Our umens would fill that green sea, ten thousand riding as one, turning as one, pennants snapping overhead, the great nargas sounding the charge.

"My first charge, ah there was a moment. It was the year before I completed my first circling, not far from here in the land of the Nippon. We and the Merki. When we loosed our shafts ten thousand arrows blotted out the sun, the dark shadow of them racing like a storm cloud."

He shook his head and sighed.

"Madness really. But we fought for different things then. The world was big enough for all of us to ride, to hunt, to have pasture. It was simply to match steel against steel and prove that we were still worthy of the blood of our ancestors and unafraid. It was not to the final death, to the slaughter of the young, the old, the bearers of young. No, just steel against steel. Not like this." And he vaguely waved back toward the west and the front lines.

"If you bested a champion, you took his *faka,* his glory, but would suffer him to live, even to feast him before sending him back to his yurt. That was as war should be."

He took another drink of wine.

"But always there were the humans."

"You don't call them cattle anymore," Jurak said.

Zartak laughed sadly.

"You know I once had a pet. It was when I was a child, a female. In those days, among those of the blood of the royal lines it was common to give to a youth a human pet to serve as companion, a teacher of their languages, a slave to do the menial tasks."

He was silent for a moment.

"Go on."

"Some, as they came to their first passions of youth, would become besotted by such a cattle female."

Jurak could not hide his disgust at the mere thought of it. It was a subject not spoken of, a dark infamy only whispered of, and punished brutally.

"No, not in that sense did I care for her," Zartak added, not even aware of his friend's reaction.

"Not in that sense?" Jurak asked cautiously.

"Her name was Helena. She was of the tribe called the Greek Byzantems, a thousand or more leagues to the west. But I did love her."

Zartak shifted uncomfortably.

"I think she genuinely cared for me, almost like a mother to a child. She was a gentle creature. I remember when I was not more than five years or so I was stricken with a fever that all but killed me. She sat by me day and night for nearly the passing of an entire moon."

"What of your mother?"

"I never knew her. She died giving me life. My father never took another to his bed and died mourning her. Thus there was only Helena to tend to me.

"She would tell me stories of her people, of human kings and princes of their old world, of a poet called Homer. She knew much of his great ballad by heart."

And for a moment Zartak drifted, speaking in an unknown tongue of House Atreides and black-hulled ships. The ancient song died away, and he took another drink.

"You know the ritual of the naming day, the day a warrior is accepted into his unit of ten and finally takes the name he will carry for the rest of his life?"

Jurak nodded, having seen it often enough since coming to this world.

"One is expected to make a sacrifice, usually a horse"— he paused for a moment—"but also a cattle. My cousins had taunted me that I was too attached to my cattle pet. My father was dead by then, so it was my eldest uncle who on that morning decreed that Helena was to be the sacrifice."

He stopped again, finishing the rest of the wine sack. With a low grunt he threw it out of the yurt, reached back under the table without bothering to ask, drew out another sack and opened it.

"Strange how this brew loosens the tongue to such foolishness."

"Go on," Jurak said softly. "Tell me."

"So I went to my yurt. She had laid out my warrior's garb, my first shirt of chain mail, the scimitar and bow of my father. I knew she was proud of me, even though I was of the Horde and she was merely a cattle. And she was wearing a plain white robe, as white as a morning cloud, the robe of a cattle sacrifice. She already knew.

"I could not speak. She smiled and said that today she would join her parents. We had slaughtered them years before, and yet she loved me. She went unafraid. I was the one who was afraid, as we walked to the circle where my family awaited.

"We entered the circle. She hesitated at the sight of the stake she was supposed to be tied to. My uncle, a cruel one he was, had wood piled about it. He wanted the old forms to be observed, so she was to be burned alive and then devoured."

Zartak hesitated and looked away.

"She turned and looked at me and whispered in her language. 'If you loved me as I loved you, do it now. Please don't let me burn.' "

He stopped again.

Jurak waited in silence.

" 'He maketh me to lie down in green pastures. He leadeth me beside still waters.' "

"What?"

"The last words she said," Zartak whispered. "It was a prayer of her people. She taught me to say it. She said her god taught it to her people, and my gods would hear it, too. When I was a cub we would say it together every night.

"She began that prayer. I stepped behind her so she could not see the blade."

He paused again.

"No. That's a lie. Because I could not bear to look into her eyes. I killed her with a single blow before she finished the prayer. I did that so it would catch her unaware and those were her last words.

"And so the feast of my naming day began. My cousins fell upon her body. I had lost face for my weakness, killing her thus, and I was taunted for years after that. I didn't care. I knew what was in my heart even if they did not."

Zartak's voice broke, and Jurak was unable to contain his surprise. Such a display of emotion before one not of your own blood was all but unknown.

After several minutes Zartak regained his composure.

"The drunken ramblings of a decrepit warrior," Zartak announced self-consciously.

"No, not at all."

"I knew then they had souls. That they were as good as us. Yes, I joined in the moon feasts and felt the passion of the slaughter when after a long and hungry ride we fell upon a great city of theirs and one out of ten were culled out to feed us. I remember three circlings back when one of the cities on the far side of this world rebelled. It was somewhat the same as here; some humans had come through a portal in a ship. They had weapons of powder, men with black beards, blue uniforms, and a great ship flying a flag of red and blue and white. They did not have the skill of these Yankees, though, in the making of machines. But they did field a great army of humans armed with pikes and bows, following those flags and golden eagles as standards. We slaughtered all of them, millions, the feasting lasted for weeks before we rode on, and I did love it.

"Yet always I was haunted by her."

"Your love of her?" Jurak asked, uncomfortable associating the word *love* with a human.

"No. That was inside here." He pointed to his stomach, the liver, where all feelings rested.

"No. It was the knowledge of what they truly are. When the first humans came here our ancestors slaughtered them out of hand."

He hesitated for a moment. "And that was good."

"Why?"

"Our ancestors had reverted to barbarism, becoming little better than the cattle they slaughtered. And then came the horse and we bred it to our size and the tribes started the Great Ride about the world. If only it had stayed thus, I would say that was good, too. But somewhere back then our ancestors decided not to slaughter all the humans, but to spread them out about the world instead. To place one of each of their tribes as a chief or king. Then, when we circled the world and returned in twenty years, there would be more of them.

"We thought ourselves so wise, for we reasoned, let the humans do the labor. Let them raise food for us, let them fashion saddles, lay down vineyards, make the boats, rafts, and bridges so that we might cross the great rivers in our path. Let the humans do all things and in addition offer up their flesh as food.

"We thought that would control their numbers, to harvest them as one harvests the great tusked beasts or the vast herds of the hump-backed bisons. So in that first circling of long ago there might be a village of a hundred humans by a river. Twenty years later two hundred and then by my time a city of a hundred thousand, two hundred thousand.

"They are fertile, and we are not. Perhaps our blood is old, and theirs is young. I don't know. But our numbers never seemed to increase; theirs did. Some in their wisdom urged that we harvest half, and at times we did, but then we would ride on and upon our return a generation later there'd be yet more.

"They spilled out of the Portals of Light. Oh, never many, perhaps in an entire ride we'd discover one new tribe. Sometimes they were but a few dozen, more often a ship or two. I suspect that upon their world the old portals are lost beneath several different seas. We'd scatter them about or settle them in one place, tell them to labor, and move on. Of late, though, in the last ten or so circlings we should have realized that something was happening on their world that was not happening here."

"What?"

"Their cunning, their skill with machines. That ship I told you of. I spoke once with the elder warrior of the Tugars who told me of a similar ship, filled with men wearing jackets of polished steel. The Tugars slaughtered them, of course, but we should have realized the threat and acted before it was too late. The Tugar elder also told me that near here there was a similar ship whose crew actually escaped and sailed south toward the ocean that circles the southern half of this world.

"We should have realized then that we had to somehow change the balance between us."

"And do what?"

"Either come to terms with them or slaughter them all."

"Terms? How?"

"I know. I think it is impossible now. My cousins, all my people, not one in a thousand do I think contemplated who these humans truly were. They were cattle, they were food, they were slaves. None heard the beauty of their languages, their poetry, their songs." Again his words lapsed into the ancient human tongue, speaking of the numbering of ships and the names of captains dead across three thousand years and the infinity of the universe.

"It was far more, though. We have become"—he hesitated for a moment and then spat out the word—"parasites upon the flesh and minds of the humans."

Jurak stirred uncomfortably, started to voice an objection but Zartak waved his hand, motioning him to silence.

"Think of it. Every weapon we carry, the clothing we wear, the food we eat, all of the new tools of war, none of it has been shaped by our hands. We do nothing but exist; it is they who have fashioned the world.

"It has gone to the very soul." Zartak sighed. "The division between us now. Imagine if the world was reversed, imagine if it was the humans who rode and who feasted upon our blood, who cracked our bones open to draw out the very marrow while we were still alive."

Jurak shivered at the thought. Impossible. The primal dread of being consumed, eaten alive, the fear that was even more dreadful than the fear of death filled him with darkness.

"No, it could never be. Could it?" Jurak laughed coldly.

"That gulf can never be crossed now," Zartak continued. "Too much blood has been drawn for them ever to forgive us. For that matter our own people cannot imagine it any other way as well. Oh, I have whispered at times and been rebuffed when I suggested such thoughts when I was young. My cousins taunted me, accused me of an obscene love for my dead pet, so I learned to be silent. I learned to hide such thoughts and thus did I rise through command of ten, to a hundred, to a thousand, to ten thousand, to eldest of the clan of the white horse. Now as an ancient one though I find I am as free as a youth to speak again."

"And that is why I value you," Jurak replied. He hesitated, looking at the Great Wheel, visible outside the open flaps of the yurt, wondering which out of all the millions of stars was his home world. He felt a cold shiver, a loneliness, and infinite sadness.

"So you see no chance then of a change?" he finally whispered.

"Go outside this yurt and shout for the west wind to go away."

Zartak sighed, then chuckled softly, the laughter sad, lonely.

"No, we are both trapped in this war. The Yankees freed these humans and with that freedom the inner dread, the paralyzing fear of being eaten alive was replaced with a blind all-consuming rage. You saw with your own eyes what they can now do, even with their bare hands if they have the chance."

Jurak nodded, remembering the carnage of Roum, and along the Ebro, where the slaves had rebelled and escaped, literally tearing warriors limb from limb in their frenzy.

"And now what?"

Zartak looked up at him and smiled.

"I'll be gone before it is decided. Perhaps the last of you will come early to join me above, where again there will be the Endless Ride. I fear, son, that either you must kill all of them or they will kill all of us. It is that simple."

"Even though you loved one of them?"

Zartak flinched.

"A weakness of youth," he fumbled.

"No. Perhaps an insight?"

Zartak sadly shook his head.

"Don't let it weaken you. This is not a time for weakness. Do you honestly think that after all we have done to them there could ever be peace, a place in this world for us and a place for them?"

Jurak found that he was again wrestling with that thought. If this campaign was lost, as he feared more than once it would be, then what?

"You're wondering what will happen if we lose this war," Zartak said. "This attack at Xi'an caught you completely off guard."

"Yes."

"It surprised me, too. I did not understand these flying machines. I did not ever think they could be used to transport hundreds of warriors across hundreds of leagues to fall upon our center of supply. Tell me, were such things done on your world?"

Jurak sensed the slightest tone of rebuke in Zartak's question.

"Yes. But the airships there could carry a hundred in their bellies. And there would be hundreds of such ships in the sky at once, warriors leaping from them, floating to the ground under the umbrellas made of silk."

"Such a sight it must have been."

Jurak nodded.

"The ships here, so primitive in comparison, I never considered that they would risk all of them. There cannot be more than three hundred of them in this attack."

"Joined by how many tens of thousands of Chin?"

Jurak was silent. Damnation.

"If you do not suppress this rebellion within the next day, two days at most, all is lost. You will have to flee east or south, south across the seas, for they will come after you."

"From all that I've heard of Keane, I wonder if he would if we did leave."

Zartak grunted.

"I wonder about him as well. I do have the sense you know. And of Keane I sense much. But consider the rest of the world. Let word come to all the other humans of this world that we have been beaten, and they will rise up, remembering their dead across all these thousands of years. There is no compromise with that I fear."

Jurak slowly nodded in agreement.

"I know. Perhaps we are alike in that, for I know if it was as you said, if it was they who rode and we who bowed, I would die to kill but one."

"See what we've created here?" Zartak laughed sadly.

"I know."

"And now?"

"They found the weak link. They've used their air machines to fly several hundred soldiers to Xi'an. The city is in chaos, rebellion, the last telegram before the line was cut said hundreds are being slaughtered, including females and cubs."

Zartak nodded.

"A brilliant move," Jurak whispered. "Damn all. I tried to consider every potential, every move and countermove. I knew if we went to the defensive and waited, we could build our forces up, train our troops, and even outproduce the Yankees. I knew if we held most of the territory of the

Roum we could perhaps even drive a political wedge between the two states of their Republic, maybe even get them to mistrust and turn on each other."

"The humans you sent in secret to kill their president and Keane, a masterful move," Zartak said.

Even now that might be working, Jurak thought. A few additional refugees slipped across the line, trained and conditioned, knowing that if they did not come back within three moon feasts their entire families would die in the next one.

"Yet never did I see this coming."

"Your dream of last night," Zartak said, "it was a portent. You have the power, you know."

If I have the power, he wondered, *then why do all the paths ahead now seem equally dark.*

"You told me that you have a weapon that can burn entire cities in one blinding flash. Could you make one now? That would end this."

Jurak was surprised at the casual mention of such a fearsome weapon.

"No, that is the work of thousands, tens of thousands," Jurak replied, his voice distant.

To get these primitives to the point where they could make a magnetic separator, let alone a breeder reactor, maybe in a thousand years perhaps. As for the science? I can figure out how to make explosives, even a lathe to turn out guns, but that?

And even if I did, he thought, *would I unleash such a horror on this world?*

"The Yankees will make one someday," Zartak announced.

That thought had never crossed his mind. Yes, they most likely would. They were makers of machines, and machines begot more machines.

"And this attack from Tyre?" Zartak asked, suddenly shifting the conversation back to more immediate concerns.

"It might be a diversion, but if they gain the western shore of the Great Sea, create a base, combine that with ships captured from Xi'an, we are finished on this front. That was masterful as well. Letting us see it coming. The ironclads we sent from Xi'an, if they were there now, tonight, we would crush the rebellion."

"But the new railroad coming up from Nippon and connecting across the north of the Great Sea is finished. We won't need the Sea."

Jurak shook his head. Here it was obvious that Zartak was thinking only as a warrior who fought on land and had never before faced a naval force.

"We must hold the Sea. If they take the rail line we were building toward Tyre and combine that with holding Xi'an, they can move reinforcements up. I suspect that is why they are moving one of their corps overland along with the ironclads. If they've captured ships at Xi'an, they could have that equipment in Carnagan within three days. Or they could strike us from behind, or even range northward, landing troops to cut the new rail line along the northern shore. We have to crush the rebellion in Xi'an and at the same time beat back this attacking force."

Zartak slowly nodded in agreement.

"Or send it straight into the heart of the Chin realm, toward Huan."

Jurak sighed, looking back at the map in the middle of the yurt.

"What will they do next?" Jurak whispered, more to himself than his companion.

Zartak stood up and looked at the map.

"I think the one they call Hans is leading this," Zartak said.

"Why do you say that?"

He smiled. "Call it that sense we believe in."

Hans. The thought chilled Jurak as he stared at the map.

"If it is Hans, what do you think he'll do next?" Jurak finally asked, looking back at his old friend.

Zartak walked up to the map and jabbed at it with a bony finger.

"He'll go here. Straight for the heart. Why they did not do that in their first strike is beyond me."

"Most likely their flying machines could not range that far and carry enough men."

"If that is so, then by flying out of Xi'an such a move would now be possible. He will do this come first light tomorrow. What you saw at Roum, what is happening today at Xi'an. Tomorrow it will erupt there."

Jurak felt a cold chill.

"We still have the railroad back to Nippon and from there back into the land of the Chin," Zartak said, tracing the route out on the map. "The humans most likely don't even know we completed that. Supplies can be shifted that way. Order every train on that line to reverse itself, to go back. There are two umens in Nippon with modern arms; send them down at once."

Jurak worked out the mental calculations, the number of trains that were moving those two umens up to the front.

"They could be back in Huan by tomorrow night."

"Alert the commander of the city. Have him round up the human leaders. Have him make it clear that if the Yankees land and the local population does not join in the rebellion, they will all be spared. If they do join, all will die."

Jurak was surprised by the forcefulness of his voice. He nodded in agreement.

"I'm going back there. I wanted to check with you first, but just in case I already ordered the track to be cleared and a train prepared."

The pieces seemed to be falling into place. He looked at his desk piled high with the messages of the day, and his thoughts focused on one in particular.

"Did you know that Tamuka rode into Huan this morning?" Jurak asked.

Zartak stiffened.

"The usurper. The old Qar Qarth of the Merki?"

"Yes."

"He is a mad beast. Why did he go there?"

"I had a report that the Merki who were following him finally rebelled and drove him out. I assumed he had been killed or taken the honorable path and fallen upon his sword."

"You should have told me of this, my friend. Tamuka has not the courage to rid the world of his presence."

"When I heard that he was seen this morning I assumed he was riding east, perhaps even to join the Tugars in the empty lands to the east."

"Or to make problems for you. That is the more likely path."

"And he has wandered straight to where the fight will

be tomorrow," Jurak replied. "Are the gods of our fate spinning a thread here?"

"I hope not. Order the commander there to seize him, kill him if need be."

Jurak nodded. He heard a train whistle sounding from the rail yard. Seconds later there was a clatter of hooves, his escort guards coming to tell him that the track ahead was clear and it was time to leave.

"I'd best be leaving, old friend."

"By train, it will take days."

"Only till dawn. I've ordered a flyer to be waiting for me 150 leagues east of here. The train will reach there by dawn, and I'll fly the rest of the way."

Zartak chuckled.

"Better you than me. The only time I intend to fly is when my ancestors summon me home."

He scratched his balding mane.

"Soon enough it will be, but not too soon. I wish to see how this all will end."

"I want you to command here, to press an attack."

"We're not ready."

"Get ready, and press it. I would prefer this morning if possible."

Zartak shook his head.

"The ironclads we diverted to Carnagan. We'll need those. You'll remember they started landing this afternoon."

Jurak sighed.

"I don't have time now for the details. Have the messages I've left on my desk sent. Send instructions to Huan as we discussed and one to Carnagan that they must press the attack there tomorrow and finish it. At least we can smash that army, then we launch the attack here. Win or lose at Huan, we smash their armies before they realize what they've accomplished and we can still win in spite of this setback."

Zartak formally bowed, and again the old roles were assumed.

"My Qar Qarth. The machine of steam awaits you." It was one of his guards, waiting respectfully outside the yurt.

"So you see no alternatives other than this," Jurak asked,

dropping his voice, gaze locked on Zartak. "A war of total annihilation of one or the other."

"For the sake of an old friend of my youth, I wish I could," Zartak whispered. "No. And I think she knew that, too. We and they are bound together in this world, and only one shall emerge triumphant."

"Then let it be us," Jurak said coldly.

Chapter Ten

Though numbed with exhaustion Hans still felt a fierce exhaultation. Grim though war was, there were indeed moments, that in spite of the tragedy, nevertheless held a soul-stirring drama to them.

During the night the Bantag had tried three assaults to break into the liberated city of Xi'an. The third assault had actually gotten over the walls until it was finally cut off by a reserve of several hundred Chin armed with revolvers hauled in by the airships. Most of them barely knew how to shoot their weapons, most of them died, but the Bantag died with them.

Standing outside the wall, he looked back at the city. It was burning out of control, a vast pillar of light, like out of some biblical story, marking a place of vengeance and liberation, the flames a holy purging that would wipe away the stain of bondage.

He felt strangely different this morning. It wasn't just the exhaustion, or the gnawing pain in his chest. It was the fact that with his decision to press the attack the very nature of the war had changed within him and within his men. It was no longer a desperate defensive lunge to hold on to what they held. It was now truly a war of liberation, an all-or-nothing throw of the dice. He was never one for the false heroics of battle—he had always felt himself to be beyond such idiotic notions—but at that moment, as he watched the city burn, he felt a strange exultation, as if his small army was an avenging host going forth to purge this world of its sin.

He nudged the flanks of his mount, a Bantag warhorse, the saddle far too big, the animal as exhausted as he was, and therefore docile. They slowly weaved their way through the wreckage of the rail yard east of the city. A string of boxcars still burned fiercely, thick oily smoke tumbling skyward, the air heavy with the smell of burning meat. Bantag rations. He preferred to think that it was salted beef, taken from the bisonlike herds that roamed the steppes in this part of the world, or even salted horse. The idea that they might actually slaughter humans, salt them down, and package them the same way his own army prepared rations was too horrid to contemplate.

The wind shifted, the black cloud enveloping him for a moment, and he gagged on the smell. He nudged his mount again, cleared the smoke, and reined in for a moment. A knot of Chin were gathered around a shed by the side of the track. They were shouting, cursing. He drew closer. Three Bantag had been cornered inside, all of them wounded. They were dying slowly under the kicks and blows.

Hans spotted one of his own men, a Chin in uniform, and roared at him to finish the wounded off. The soldier saluted, drew his revolver, and pushed his way through the crowd. Hans rode on, barely noticing the crack of the pistol behind him.

Discarded equipment littered the rail yard, broken rifles, an upended box of cartridges, an overturned caisson, shells lying on the ground, a fieldpiece on its side, a stack of saddles smoldering, bundles of arrows, smashed-open barrels leaking oil, kerosene, flour, what even smelled like the rice wine of the Chin, and everywhere bodies, Bantag and human. All of it was illuminated by the lurid red glare of the city burning, a glow so bright he could have easily read one of Gates's papers, reminding him of the night Fredericksburg burned just prior to the assault.

The troops he had brought in were hard at work. Each man was now in charge of a unit of ten, sheperding them along, organizing details to pick up discarded equipment that might be useful, a group of them on their hands and knees picking up cartridges spilled from an ammunition box. One sergeant, a survivor of the escape from the factory prison the year before, had his men broken into two-man teams. One man was supposed to stand stock-still while the second man rested the barrel of a Bantag rifle on his shoulder, aimed, and shot. It looked ludicrous but the damn idea actually worked, enabling the diminutive and emaciated Chin actually to use the enemy weapons. They gleefully fired away, sniping at a scattering of Bantag who still lingered on the far side of the rail yard.

If he had the time there was enough captured artillery here to field several batteries, but the thought was absurd. They might get one or two shots off, but anything beyond point-blank range was hopeless. Down deep he knew the entire idea was next to hopeless. It was one thing to come swooping in as they did, trigger a rebellion, and overwhelm the local garrison. If they ever had to face a disciplined umen of Bantag warriors, it would be a massacre.

The trick was to keep moving, to roll them up before they had time to react. He had to keep moving in spite of his exhaustion.

He rode around a line of half a dozen flatcars on a siding. A couple of hundred Chin were piled on board, half of them armed with the precious revolvers carried in on the airships, others simply carrying makeshift spears, poles with a knife strapped to the end. As he rode past the engine he recognized one of his comrades, yet another survivor of the prison.

"Ready to go back?" Hans asked.

The old man flashed a grin.

"I know this machine. Remember ride to there." He gestured off to the south, where half a dozen miles away they had holed up after the escape. "I run it good."

Hans leaned up, shook the man's hand, and rode on.

Four trains were lined up, four engines pulling a total of thirty flatcars and boxcars, all of them crammed with over fifteen hundred Chin. The vast majority knew damn little of what they were doing. A day ago they were slaves, knowing that they'd live only as long as they could work. Now they were loaded aboard trains heading east, straight into the heart of the Bantag realm. If they had any sense about it at all, they undoubtedly knew they were going to die. He could see the fear and resignation with many, torn away from a numbed life, but a life nevertheless. A few were afire with the desire for revenge, clutching the pistols given out, holding them up as Hans passed, making him nervous. Several men had already been killed by accident.

Reaching the forward engine, he returned the salute of

Seetu, one of Ketswana's men, who overnight had been promoted from sergeant to commander of an expedition.

"Ready?" Hans asked.

Seetu nodded eagerly.

"All the engines are fired up. A couple of these Chin worked the rail line, so they know how to run the engines and what's ahead."

"Remember. Until it's full light, take it slow. If anyone up there's thinking, they'll have broken the track. At each junction or station you pass, make sure you cut the telegraph line. Round up any Chin you meet; if you capture any more trains, take them along."

"We'll go all the way to Huan."

Hans said nothing.

"This is gonna be the hard part, Seetu. I want you to get as far forward as you can. But remember, they might cut you off from behind once you pass. If you can get thirty or forty miles up that track and start tearing things up, it'll buy a couple of days for the men here to get organized."

Seetu said nothing.

"Son, I won't lie. There isn't much hope you'll get through this one. They'll most likely lay a trap, let you pass, cut the rail ahead and behind, then box you in and finish you. Try and spot that, stop, then slowly pull back, tearing up track, burning bridges as you go. If they do trap you," he hesitated, "well, take as many of the bastards with you as you can and smash everything up good and proper."

"I was dead anyhow a year ago," Seetu replied. "Every day you gave me since is extra gift from the gods. Hans, I'm not stopping. Expect to see me in Huan tomorrow."

Hans leaned up and shook his hand.

He rode on. *Strange how we all feel that way,* he thought. *You come back from the grave and after that, well it's a gift.* Hans turned his mount back and slowly trotted out of the rail yard, weaving his way past a skirmish line of Chin moving through the still-burning ruins of a Bantag encampment of wooden barracks.

So they were even giving up their yurts. Strange, the vast circular buildings were wooden replicas of their tents. Yet another changing over to human ways. The Chin were little better than a swarming mob, led by half a dozen of his soldiers, who were desperately shouting orders, trying to create some semblance of organization.

It was the shock of the air assault, the riot of the tens of thousands in Xi'an, that had won this fight, Hans realized. Sheer numbers had dragged the Bantag down. He wondered how many were still lurking out beyond the city and the surrounding warehouses and encampments.

As if in answer to his question a rifle ball slapped past. There were shouts ahead, a flurry of pistol shots. He rode on.

Reaching the base of the eastern wall, he gingerly rode around mounds of Bantag killed trying to retake the city. A damned stupid assault. They should have just sat back, waited for reinforcements, then shelled the place until the defenders panicked. Stupid arrogance to attack like that.

Riding along the wall, he reached the northern side of the city. In the glare of the inferno the airfield was clearly silhouetted. The machines were lined up, engines turning over. Jack, spotting his approach, slowly walked up.

"I'm going to make this formal," Jack announced, while reaching up to help Hans get off his horse.

"I know, I know." Hans sighed.

"My crews and machines are finished. We were circling this damned town half the night while the fighting was going on down here." He gestured to the bodies that littered the perimeter of the airstrip.

"Then we come back in and land again, losing three more ships. Hans, I'm down to twenty-two aerosteamers, an average of two hundred Gatling rounds per gun."

"At least you got fuel," Hans replied, nodding toward the empty barrels that had been saved from a burning train.

"Yeah, great."

Hans wearily sat down on the grass, lowering his head for a moment. Again, the shortness of breath, the flutter of pain.

Jack knelt by his side.

"Hans? You all right?"

He looked up bleakly.

"No. I don't think so, to tell you the truth."

"Hans, you need some rest. Everyone here needs rest. The men are staggering around like the walking dead. I'm going to ask this one last time. We've got Xi'an. Hole up here. I'll take the airships back to Tyre. We'll refit, load up on hydrogen we desperately need, and be back in two days with reinforcements."

"Two hundred more men now won't make a difference here."

He was simply too numb to order, to roar out the order to go. He looked up, half-broken inside, appealing to Jack to understand.

"We'll all die doing this, Hans."

Hans chuckled in spite of his pain.

"Jack, don't you get it?" he whispered. "That day on the Ogunquit, the day we left Earth forever and came here. We died. You know, I bet back home, somewhere up there on the coast of Maine, they've got a statue with all our names on it. We died. We died but then the good Lord caught us as we fell and dropped us here. Maybe this is purgatory, maybe this is the punishment for our sins. I don't know anymore. But I was in their prisons; you weren't. I know that there is the key to our victory."

"They're ready for us by now."

"I don't know. Maybe they are, maybe they aren't. But we'll never have a better chance than at this moment. Tomorrow will be too late. Jurak will react, and it will be too late. Jack, today we can either win or lose this war."

He paused for a moment.

"It's up to you. Yesterday evening I ordered you to do it." He paused, struggling to catch his breath. "I don't have the strength to order you. I'm simply asking you."

Jack stood up.

"Oh, God damn it all, thank you very much, Sergeant Schuder, for the guilt."

Hans looked up and couldn't help but smile.

"One more push," Hans whispered. "That's all I ask, and then you can call it quits. Then we can rest."

It was surprisingly quiet. Standing atop the low ridge, Vincent Hawthorne shaded his eyes, looking to the rising sun. He knew they were out there, the haze of dust rimming the horizon in a vast arc to the north, around to the east and south showed that they were out there.

It had been a sleepless night, curled up by the side of his ironclad, waiting for an attack that never came. They had the advantage on that score. The bastards could decide if and when to attack; they'd most likely pulled back and slept the night through while he and his men had stayed alert throughout the hours of darkness.

Stretching, he scratched the back of his neck. *Two days down here and I'm lousy,* he thought with disgust. *Forgotten just how lousy the army could get,* and he wondered which of his crewmates in the ironclad had passed the damned little critters over to him.

"Your honor, some tea?"

It was Stanislaw, driver of his ironclad, who in spite of his years in the army still hadn't shaken the honorific given to boyars. The man was easily twice his age, drafted out of the locomotive engineers to serve on the front line.

Vincent gingerly took the tin cup, holding it by the edges, blowing on the rim, took a sip. One of the true advantages of serving with the ironclads, he realized, hot tea, drawn off from the boiler water at any time, even though it tended to have an oily taste, plus plenty of rations since the men always seemed to manage to "borrow" a few extra boxes of salt pork, hardtack, and for this expedition some precious jam, butter, and even a few loaves of bread that were almost fresh.

Stanislaw produced a great hunk of the bread, slathered with jam and butter, and Vincent eagerly wolfed it down, squatting in the grass while he ate.

All around him, farther down the slope of the knoll, the army was coming awake, bugles sounding, men milling about, gathering around smoking fires made with twisted-up bundles of dried grass and the ubiquitous dried chips from the bisonlike creatures and woolly elephants that wandered the plains.

Mounted pickets had pushed out from the earthen wall fortress encircling the camp, making sure no Bantag skirmishers had crept up during the night, and men were wandering outside the fortified position to relieve themselves. Vincent wrinkled his nose. Whenever you had ten thousand men camped in one place, it didn't take long truly to stink the place up.

"Think we'll fight today, your honor?"

"Don't know, Stanislaw. It's their choice. They're mounted, we're not. They'll pick the time and place."

Stanislaw reached into his pocket and pulled out a couple of dried applies, offering one to Vincent, who nodded his thanks.

"As long as we got *St. Katrina* with us"—he reached back and affectionately patted their ironclad—"we'll give them a hell of a fight."

"You like your ironclad?"

"Oh, at first no, your honor. I remember when you Yankees first came." He chuckled softly. "I thought you were devils the first time I saw the steam makers, the locomotive you made that went from your fort up to Suzdal."

"Seems like an eternity ago." Vincent smiled.

"Then I was drafted to work laying track to Kev, and from there on to Roum. That was work."

"What did you do before we came?"

"I was gardener for the wife of my boyar Garvilla."

The name somehow registered. One of the boyars who had tried to overthrow the government before the Merki came, Vincent realized.

"Oh, he was a devil he was, but his lady wasn't. She liked the flowers I grew."

He sighed, and Vincent realized that yesterday he had noticed fresh wildflowers tied in a bundle next to where Stanislaw sat down below.

"Well, there was no room for flower growers and gardeners in this new world you Yankees made. Machines and more machines. So I realized that I, Stanislaw, could either lay rails or drive the machine that rode them. I had a nephew who was the driver of one of your new locomotives, and I got him to let me be his fireman. I learned and soon had my own machine to drive."

He sighed.

"I named her *St. Katrina,* same as our big machine of war here. She is the patron saint of gardens. She protected me."

He shook his head.

"Though I wish she'd protected me more and kept me with my steam engine on rails rather than this black thing on wheels that crawls around on the ground."

"Why didn't you stay with the locomotives?"

"Ah, my nephew. He went with these machines and said I was lucky and wanted me with him. He said it would be glorious and perhaps some woman would look upon me with favor in my new black uniform, and I'd finally have a wife. Foolish me, I went."

Vincent tried not to smile for Stanislaw was decidedly ugly—head far too big for his body, a vast misshapen lump for a nose, and he was completely bald. And yet, there was a gentleness to his smile, a certain quiet sparkle in his eyes that was touching.

"I was at Rocky Hill, you know," Stanislaw announced proudly, "in one of the older machines that ate coal rather than the burning oil. That was a good fight."

Vincent said nothing. There was the flash memory of the charge, falling, falling away, seeing the flag bearer staggering past, all of it lost in smoke and fire.

"You were brave beyond the brave there, your honor."

Vincent, embarrassed, said nothing.

"Were you at Capua?" Vincent finally asked.

"No, your honor. Well yes, but I was in the second regiment, the one that didn't go in. Bless Saint Katrina for protecting me," and as he spoke he grasped a small icon which dangled from a chain around his neck, and holding the image of the saint, he crossed himself three times.

"And how do you feel about this?" Vincent asked.

"I go where ordered, your honor."

"No. We're in this together. How do you feel?"

"You Yankees." Stanislaw chuckled. "Asking a peasant like me."

"You are a citizen of the Republic," Vincent said slowly. "You have a right to your opinion."

Stanislaw smiled. "When this war is over, then I will be a citizen, but now I am a soldier who follows orders. That is what my nephew says."

"You're not happy with it?" Vincent pressed.

"Well, your honor. We seem to be driving around to nowhere. The Bantag, the Tugars, all the riders. They own the steppes. They are of the horse, we are not. I wish we could just let them have the steppes and they agree to leave us alone."

"We know that can't be," Vincent replied.

"Yes, yes, I know. If wishes came true, mice would ride on cats."

Stanislaw picked up Vincent's empty tin cup, retreated through the open door of his ironclad. The encampment was now swarming with activity, the buzz of ten thousand men echoing, sergeants barking orders, snatches of conversation drifting; someone was even playing a fife, another an instrument that sounded hauntingly like a banjo. He was glad he had ordered that the march would start late, an hour after sunrise. It gave the men time to relax just a bit longer and have a solid breakfast before moving on.

Stanislaw came out a minute later with the cup refilled, carrying a second cup for himself and sat back down.

"You didn't answer my question," Vincent pressed while nodding his thanks for the refill and a second helping of bread and jam.

"Your honor, if we do make it to their rail line and from there to the Great Sea, then what?"

"Once there we set up a base for any ships that Hans and his men capture at Xi'an."

"I heard the Horde riders have iron ships on that sea."

"Yes."

"Won't the iron ships sink what we capture?"

"Maybe we'll capture some of the iron ships at Xi'an."

"And if we don't?"

"We can still raise hell."

"Suppose the Bantag bring up their own land ironclads to fight us. We shall have only what we carry with us."

"It's what we want," Vincent replied. "If they bring their own ironclads in, we can fight them out in the open. We can have the battle to decide this. Defeat their ironclads, shatter their army here in the south, and keep their leader guessing, that is what we are doing. We want that fight, Stanislaw."

"Then why do I feel like the mouse who is sent to pull the whiskers of the cat so that the old cat will chase him outside and then the others can eat. I wish right now I was one of the mice that was going to eat rather than the one that has to run."

Vincent laughed.

"Back in Suzdal. Suppose they make peace. We heard the rumors of that, you know, just before we sailed. Poor Kal, we had many a drink we did in the old days, trading stories about our boyars."

"We'll win this fight before they can do anything that stupid."

Stanislaw said nothing, then, looking beyond Vincent, he came to his feet and saluted.

Vincent looked over his shoulder and saw Gregory walking up the slope.

"Good morning, sir," Gregory announced, coming to attention and saluting.

"Morning, Gregory. Everything in order?"

"All machines are warmed up except one. We're going to have to leave it behind." He nodded downslope to where a swarm of men were clustered around an ironclad, some of them arguing while others were lugging out shells. Several had torn open the hinges on the top turret and were starting to remove the steam Gatling gun.

"Cracked boiler, can't be fixed out here. I've ordered it stripped."

Vincent nodded. "Not bad so far, only two machines broken down."

"That was yesterday. As we add up the leagues today, more will fail as I warned."

"We'll have enough when the time comes."

Gregory said nothing for a moment, obviously disagreeing with Vincent's assessment.

"Sir, my machines will be ready to roll in fifteen minutes. I think Third Corps is ready to move as well."

Vincent smiled. He was being gently chided for taking the extra few minutes to talk with Stanislaw.

"Fine. Pass the word—fifteen minutes."

Gregory saluted and started back down the slope to where his machine was parked.

"Ah, my nephew, such an officer."

"That's your nephew?"

"Couldn't you tell?" Stanislaw laughed. "Someone had to come along to keep an eye on him."

Vincent finished his cup of tea while Stanislaw disappeared back into his ironclad, shouting orders to the crew to get ready. Exhaust from the kerosene burners plumed from the smokestack, the safety valves for the steam lines popped several times, venting. The engine was hot and ready. A courier came up informing Vincent that the corps was formed. Looking round from his high vantage point, he saw the regiments forming into their loose block formations. Cavalry was already ranging outward in a vast circle a mile across, a few pops of carbine fire forward marking where a minor altercation was going on between outriders of the Horde and the advance pickets. Teams were hitched to the wagons, caissons, and limbers. Bugle calls signaled the call to form ranks, and drummers began to pick up the beat.

Vincent emptied the rest of his cup and climbed through the hatch into the already stifling heat of the lower deck of the ironclad. Slipping around the boiler and its attending fireman, he moved behind the gunner and assistant gunner, who, in the informality aboard ironclads, nodded their greetings since there was little room for anyone to snap to attention.

Stanislaw looked up from his driver's seat and smiled, Vincent noticing a fresh bunch of wild prairie flowers bunched up and dangling by a string from the bulkhead, the brilliant reds and blues adding a gentle touch.

Going up the ladder into the upper turret, he squeezed past the breech of his steam Gatling gun, popped open the upper hatch, climbed half-out, and sat on the rim. Gregory, who was already in position, caught Vincent's eye, and Vincent raised a clenched fist, pointing it forward.

A bugler, riding mounted beside Vincent's machine, sounded the advance. The machine beneath him lurched, great iron wheels churning up clods of dirt and crushed grass as they started down the hill, moving to the fore, passing through the lines of infantry. Fording the shallow stream, they started up the next slope, moving past a lone cavalry trooper coming back, clutching a wounded arm, but still looking game, a cigar clenched between his teeth.

Vincent looked back, watching him ride through the blocks of infantry toward the medical wagons marked with their big green circles. The ten thousand men of the corps were all on the march, regimental columns deployed in a vast hole-square formation, rifle barrels catching the reflected glint of the morning sun so that the army looked as if fire was dancing across the ranks.

"Rows of burnished steel," the words of the "Battle Hymn" came to him.

There are still moments, he realized, *still moments when one can again glimpse the chimera dream of glory.*

*   *   *

He didn't even look back as he rode through the gate. Forgetting himself for an instant, for old habits die hard, he snapped off a salute to the guards standing to either side who had come to attention.

The suit felt uncomfortable, the only civilian suit he had, stitched together by Kathleen, a black coat typical of what was worn back on Earth, at least what had been in style when they left, an unbleached cotton shirt of standard army issue, and black trousers. There was no longer a sword dangling from his belt, though he still had a pistol in a saddle holster. Behind him, in a wagon owned by Gates, rode his wife and the children, following them rode Webster, who had resigned from the government as well, and his young family.

In a way this whole thing felt so damnably foolish, a show play of bluff. The resignation had actually caught Bugarin and his followers off guard; they had expected a coup attempt. He had to go all the way. If he had stayed in the city, it would have somehow conveyed that he was still in the game, waiting down the street for the delegation to come and beg for his return.

He knew that would not happen. Even as he rode out of town the Republic was disintegrating into chaos. The Roum senators and congressmen were packing up to head for home, furious over the murder of Flavius and loudly announcing that they were going to seek a separate peace. It was as if a race was on, for Bugarin was announcing the same intention as well, and the Chin ambassadors sent by Jurak were even then receiving the offer of terms to take back to their master.

He, in turn, had presented them with a dilemma. Vincent was now supposed to be in command, but he was beyond reach. Next after him was Pat, but Pat had apparently cut the telegraph lines to the front, or something was blocking the line just out of Roum. What if they announced a ceasefire but nobody listened?

Mercury stepped onto the bridge over the Vina River, and he looked to his right and the valley choked thick with factories, rows of brick houses. The dam farther up the river was barely visible in the smoky haze. Strange how after ten years it looked far more like Waterville, Lewiston, or Lowell than the medieval city of the ancient Rus. The city he was riding out of was already a memory of an age passed. This was the new Suzdal, if it should survive the madness of its frightened leaders.

Word must have passed that he was leaving. From out of the foundries, rail works, boiler works, gun factories, construction yards, he could see thousands of workers filling the streets, looking his way.

He wondered sadly what it was he had actually tried to create for them. A generation ago they were born, lived, and died on the estates of the boyars, their lives short and brutish, ignorant and filled with fear.

What did they now have? Sons, fathers, brothers, husbands dead or at the front. Twelve hours of laboring in the heat, smoke, and grime of the war factories pouring iron, making steel, casting guns, making machines of war and yet more machines of war. Endless labor and still early deaths but now from consumption or accidents or simple exhaustion.

He wondered if Rousseau was right, and the thought made him smile for an instant, the mind of the professor still there, ready with the random thought of philosophy even in the darkest moments. Yet he had hoped that they would see, that all would see that this was a generation called to the highest sacrifice, that it had to bear the horrible burden so that someday their children, their grandchildren would never know the fear, the filth, the degradation, not just of the hordes, but of slavery and the horror of war.

He realized that he had slackened the reins on Mercury and his horse, as if reading his thoughts, had stopped so that he might look from the bridge and contemplate what he had tried to accomplish and where he had failed.

"Keane . . ."

It was a distant cry, a lone voice, sending a shiver down his spine, reminding him of the moment of triumph at Hispania, his name a cry of victory.

Someone else picked it up, a woman, closer, standing in the open doorway into the rifle-barrel works. She took the kerchief off her head and waved it. The women around her joined in, the name echoing across the valley, accompanied by the cry of a modern age, a locomotive whistle, then another, then the whistles of the factories.

Embarrassed by the outpouring, he did not know what

to do. There was the temptation, to be sure, and he sensed that at this instant it would be all so easy.

Washington at Newburgh, he thought. *But that was easier—the stakes were not the choice between life or annihilation—it was an abstract, an ideal that Washington preserved. Or was it?*

The thoughts raced through his mind. How easy it would be even now to turn Mercury about, point toward the city, and surely they would follow. And then what?

He could sense Kathleen, and looking over his shoulder, he saw her gazing at him, eyes filled with pride.

"Don't you think it's time we pushed on?" she asked softly.

He smiled. Her words were enough.

Without saluting, without looking back, he rode out of Suzdal and headed north toward the great woods.

Stretching wearily Jurak stepped down from the car, taking the dispatches that a courier pressed into his hand. He scanned through them, taking particular note of the last one that had just been relayed up all the way from Huan.

Yankee aerosteamers report, leaving Xi'an. Sighted by station at Chu-lin. Heading east.

Chu-lin? It was the town where Ha'ark had staged maneuvers last year to show the superiority of the new weapons to the clan chieftains. Nearly a third of the way between Xi'an and Huan.

It had to be Hans. So he was going all the way. The airships most likely could get to Huan, but it was doubtful if any would ever be able to get back. This was the desperate bid, not just to disrupt his supplies but to destroy everything.

Brilliant . . . and insane madness.

He skimmed through the other dispatches. The transport carrying thirty new land ironclads was at Carnagan and was off-loading already.

He jotted down two quick notes in the clumsy block print of the Rus and handed them to the telegrapher. Parked a hundred yards north of the track, three aerosteamers were waiting, the fastest of the new twin-engine designs, propellers spinning lazily. At his approach the pilots came stiffly to attention.

"Which one do I fly in?"

"Mine, my Qar Qarth."

He nodded, walking up to the pilot. Strange, most likely five years ago this warrior was horse-mounted, illiterate, never dreaming of what would be.

Jurak slowly walked around the machine, inspecting it. He felt a slight knot in his stomach. He had never much cared for flying, but on the old world it was in vast cavernous six-engine transports, capable of spanning continents to disgorge hundreds of assault troops. Now it was a flimsy hybrid, a sausagelike hydrogen airship with wings tacked on for lift and wheezing steam engines for power. The only factor that even allowed this damn thing to fly was the lighter gravity of this world, and even with that it could barely stagger aloft.

Taking a deep breath, he reached up and pulled himself into the cockpit and strapped into the narrow forward seat, the pilot climbing up to sit behind him.

"My Qar Qarth, the umbrella pack is what you are sitting on. Hook the harnesses over your shoulder. If I tell you to get out, do it quick. You then pull the rope on your left side."

Jurak nodded as he followed the pilot's orders.

"The gun between your feet, my Qarth. You are responsible for shooting that. The hand crank on your right side fires it."

Jurak knew a bit more about this, having sketched out the designs of it more than a year ago, a primitive crank-powered machine gun.

"Are you ready, sire?"

"Ready."

Within seconds both engines were at full power, and the machine slowly lurched forward, bouncing and rolling over the rough grassy field, and finally lifted, heading due west into the morning breeze.

The pilot banked the machine, passing over the locomotive that had carried him two hundred miles back from Capua during the night. As they leveled out, flying low, less than a hundred feet off the ground, he caught a glimpse of one of his two escorts turning sharply, cutting in to come up on their left side. Below, hundreds of Chin slaves stopped their labors for a moment, faces upturned to watch.

He saw the flashing of whips, dark towering forms gesturing, urging the humans back to their tasks. With the wind at their backs, they quickly picked up speed, racing eastward, the single line of track their guide.

They passed a locomotive stopped on the main line, most likely waiting for the train that had carried him to this rendezvous with the air machines to back up onto a siding. The vast open plains were dotted with villas, small villages, all of this once part of the Roum lands, ruled over by the Tugars. The wreckage of war was complete. Not a building was intact. They skimmed over a river, the ruins of a bridge still blackened, a fresh span built by Chin slaves looking dangerously weak. As they slowly continued to climb he could discern the Great Forest to the north and far to the south the rising of the ground into hills and distant mountains beyond.

He settled back. It would be a long day. First to their base at the northern edge of the ocean to refuel. Then the flight across it to a base on the eastern shore to refuel again, and from there by the middle of the night to Huan, where he suspected the true battle was about to be fought.

This day and the next might very well decide everything, all of it. He knew that in his heart. And in anticipation of what was to come he settled back in his chair and let the hum of the engines lull him to sleep.

Chapter Eleven

"Damn!"

Hans snapped his hand back from the shattered throttle controls. His fingers stung, blood seeping out from the wood splinters studding his palm.

"The throttles!" Jack shouted.

A forward windowpane exploded, showering them with glass.

"I knew this place would be hot!" Jack cried. "Under your seat. The master fuel valve, shut it down!"

Hans spared a quick glance up. The place they had chosen to land was an open field adjoining the factory where he had once labored as a slave. So much had changed though over the last year. A new factory, plumes of black smoke pouring out of half a dozen smokestacks occupied the adjoining ground to the west. From the open doors of the compound he could see dozens of Bantag pouring out. Shots were punching into the gasbags behind him, a loud twang announcing that a support wire for the starboard wing had separated.

Grimacing with pain, Hans reached under the seat, fumbling about, his hands coming to rest on a cold brass valve. Hoping it was the right one he turned it, and at the same instant all four engines throttled back.

"Don't shut it completely."

Hans looked up. The open field they had chosen for landing was directly ahead, just to the north of the rail yard where he and his escaping slaves had hijacked a train for their run back to the outskirts of Xi'an.

A thin skirmish line of Bantag ran out into the field, several of them already kneeling, firing, levering breeches open to slam in fresh cartridges.

An aerosteamer passed over Hans, momentarily casting

a shadow. The machine was flying full out, banking over sharply, a stream of fire pouring down from the topside gunner, rounds stitching the field, breaking up the skirmish line, scattering them.

"Fire!"

The scream came from the lower cargo compartment's speaking tube. Hans craned forward, looking out at the starboard wing. A flicker of orange-blue flame trailed from the outboard engine. The fabric around the engine was burning as well, fire tracing with red-hot fingers along the trailing edges of the upper and lower wings.

"Full off!" Jack shouted.

Hans turned the master valve the rest of the way, shutting down all four fuel lines. The machine simply dropped. Jack nosed it down, heading straight for a drainage ditch bordering the west end of the field, pulled up at the last second, bobbled up a dozen feet, then slammed down hard.

The upper wing on the starboard side ignited, fire leaping inward toward the volatile hydrogen gasbags.

"Out, everyone out!" Jack cried.

Hans fumbled with his harness, unbuckling, cursing from the pain as he snatched up his carbine, tossed it out the bottom hatch. Without waiting to unroll the ladder, he dropped his legs through the bottom opening, took a deep breath, then lifted his arms over his head, falling the dozen feet to the ground, knocking the wind out of his lungs.

Stunned, he couldn't move. Jack crashed down beside him. He felt Jack grabbing him under the shoulders, dragging him clear even as he continued to clutch his carbine.

A long staccato burst of fire roared. As they cleared the side of the ship he saw that their top gunner was still firing. Pouring a continual stream of Gatling rounds into a column of Bantag storming out from the two compounds, he dropped dozens of them.

"Get out!" Jack screamed, as the flame from the starboard wing hit the side of the forward gasbag. Within seconds the fire bored a hole through, hitting the hydrogen that spilled out, combining with the surrounding oxygen and flaring into a dull ghostly blue light. The entire side of the airship peeled open.

The boy topside continued to fire, sweeping his Gatling around, pouring fire across the rail yard, tearing apart the small warehouse that had served as the exit for the escape tunnel Hans and his men had dug. As the rounds punched through the flimsy wooden structure Hans could hear the Bantag screaming inside.

The gun fell silent, the steam line hooked to the inboard starboard engine having burned through. The boy stood up to jump clear even as his cockpit collapsed into the burning bag.

A round exploded out the back of his chest. He tried to stagger clear, the cockpit disappearing, falling into the roaring inferno, and the boy disappeared. Cursing, Hans looked away.

He heard Ketswana shouting and caught a glimpse of the enraged Zulu, followed by his men, pouring out from under the burning airship, one of the men somehow dragging clear a precious crate loaded with revolvers and extra ammunition.

A second airship skidded to a stop behind Jack's burning machine, disgorging its assault team, the top gunner emptying his Gatling in support fire as well. A third machine crashed into the left of Jack's machine, pivoting about as its forward wheel collapsed from the hard landing. A fourth airship, coming in too low, crashed on the top of the third machine, crushing the topside gunner, nosed over the bow of the third ship, and slammed into the ground, forward cockpit disappearing, wings snapping off and pivoting into the gasbags, which exploded. Half a dozen men tumbled out of the cargo compartment.

Another airship, abandoning the approach, soared overhead, banking sharply, starboard wing almost clipping the warehouse, which had been shredded by Gatling fire. The topside and forward gunners let loose a stream of fire as they pivoted over the landing site. Another airship, clearing the pileup of the first four, touched down smoothly, followed seconds later by another and yet another.

Ketswana and his skirmish line were already past the warehouse, which was beginning to burn, screams of dying Bantag echoing from within. The building suddenly detonated with a thunderclap roar, bits of lumber, bodies, and kegs of powder soaring up, bursting like shells at a Fourth of July celebration, the explosion enveloping an airship overhead and knocking down several of Ketswana's men.

Debris rained down; Hans crouched into a tight ball, and Jack threw himself over the old sergeant. Peeking out, Hans saw a burning barrel plunge down next to the airship that had landed behind Jack's machine, blowing a few seconds later, destroying that ship as well, catching the pilot and copilot as they tried to scramble away.

"We've landed in a madhouse!" Jack roared. "I'll handle the landings! Secure this area, otherwise, we'll all be slaughtered."

Letting go of Hans he came to his feet, ignoring the debris still tumbling from the heavens, and raced out into the field, waving his arms, trying to flag the other airships off from their landing approaches. Hans saw two machines banking hard to the north, turning away, but another one came straight in through the spreading plumes of smoke, clearing the confusion, touching down, men from the cargo hold tumbling out before the ship had even stopped.

Numbed, Hans slowly came to his feet, his mind a mad jumble of confusion. A squad of troops, Chin dressed in uniform, sprinted past, their lieutenant shouting for them to press into the first factory. He fell out, coming up to Hans.

"Sit down, sir."

Hans looked at him, confused.

The Chin officer gently helped Hans down to the grass, undoing a red bandanna tied around his throat and started to wipe Hans's face. Hans flinched. Shards of glass from the exploding window, he vaguely realized. The officer talked softly, as if soothing a child, falling into the dialect of the camps, the strange combination of Chin, Rus, Zulu, a polyglot language of the slaves.

"We're back now, now we're back with guns. Listen, listen."

The blood cleared from his eyes, Hans looked up to the smoke-shrouded gate. Ketswana stood silhouetted in the gateway into the factory where they had once been slaves, carbine held overhead, his battle chant serving as a rally cry. There was something else as well, though, a loud roaring cry, the screams of thousands of men and women.

Legs shaky, Hans got to his feet, the Chin lieutenant, who was nearly his own age, helping him along.

"We free our brothers here, then we rest, old friend. We drink cha, and then we watch the Bantag slave." He chuckled.

He stepped around the bodies of two of the men caught when the warehouse blew, both of them torn and horribly burned. On the main rail line the wreckage of the aerosteamer destroyed in the explosion was a piled-up ruin, burning fiercely. Miraculously, most of the men in the cargo compartment apparently had survived, though badly shaken, and were huddled to the side, staring blankly at the inferno.

"Get in, get in!" the lieutenant cried, pointing toward the gate. Several still had their carbines; the others drew pistols and woodenly shuffled off.

As Hans reached the gate he recoiled in horror. First there was the stench, the sickening cloying stench of the camps, the unwashed bodies, the steamy heat of the foundry, the musky smell of Bantag, and the deeper underlayer of rotting food, human waste, death, and a strange surreal sense that one could also smell terror.

The camp inside the compound was a scene of murderous chaos. Ketswana had wisely stopped his men just inside the barrier, drawing them up into a volley line. Occasionally one of the men raised a carbine to fire, but it was the thousands of slaves inside the compound who were doing the job. The prisoners were in full riot, swarming like a writhing host of maddened insects, tearing apart the remaining Bantag in the main courtyard. They had charged across the dead space that separated the perimeter wall from the barracks and were now up on the battlements. Frantic Bantag backed up along the upper walkway, furiously trying to keep the enraged host back. From down inside the camp, prisoners were pelting the trapped Bantag with lumps of coal and hunks of twisted rocks from the slag heaps until their comrades moving along the battlement walkways closed in. Four, six, sometimes a dozen died, until finally one overpowered a Bantag and knocked him off his perch to fall screaming into the waiting grasp of the mob below.

Hans spotted a knot of several dozen Bantag cutting their way through the compound, fighting to gain the doorway into the vast cavernous foundry building that dominated the center of the compound. Hans shouted for Ketswana to cut them off. Together Hans, Ketswana, and several squads of his troops pushed their way through the surging crowd.

The Bantag gained the door just ahead of them, his own men unable to fire owing to the press of Chin slaves between the two groups. The first couple of men to gain the entryway were dropped by fire from within the building. Hans pressed against the warm brick wall of the building, edged up to the huge open doors, which were wide enough that a railroad boxcar could be rolled in, and peeked around the corner. The Bantag were inside, deploying into a line not a dozen feet away. One raised a rifle, and Hans jerked his head back, a spray of brick fragment snapping out as the Bantag fired.

The Chin swarming around the door backed away as a concentrated volley tore into them. Hans looked over at Ketswana, who nodded without having to be told. A second volley slashed out; more Chin dropped. Ketswana seemed to be counting, he held his carbine up. Another volley flared.

"Charge!"

Ketswana leapt from the side of the building, carbine leveled, firing from the waist. Others charged after him, firing as they came around the side of the building. Hans tried to follow, but the Chin lieutenant pushed him back, stepped around the corner, fired, and was knocked backwards by a ball that caught him squarely in the face.

Hans stepped over the body, firing blindly, and caught a glimpse of a Bantag crumpling only feet away. The Chin mob, which had been recoiling from the hammerblows, now turned in a mad frenzy and charged into the warehouse, knocking Hans up against the wall, Ketswana and the men who had followed him disappearing in the crush.

The thin Bantag line collapsed, the warriors breaking, running in panic, some turning to go up the north wing of the foundry, others running to the south. Hundreds of Chin pushed in. Hans dodged around the side of the first furnace just inside the door. Looking up at the wall he saw that the damnable treadmills were still there, their human occupants still locked inside, bony hands clutching the side, all of them shrieking in rage.

A Bantag dodged past Hans, running blindly, stumbling straight into a stoking crew. Long iron stoking rods were now weapons. The Chin slaves fell upon the Bantag, the first one dying from the Bantag's bayonet thrust. One of the Chin, grasping the rod like a club, caught the Bantag across the knee, breaking his leg. The Bantag went down like a felled tree, then tried to scramble back up on his one good leg. Another one caught him across the back, and he collapsed, rolling over. Screaming with insane rage, one of the Chin straddled the Bantag, held his iron rod up like a spear, and drove it down straight into the Bantag's face. Then all of them started to beat the still-trembling corpse.

It was madness, and in that place, with all that he remembered, he felt the madness take hold of his own soul as well. Ignoring the pain of the splinters in his hand, he cocked open his carbine, chambered another round, and pushed forward, moving along the wall, dodging around the backs of the furnaces.

It was all so chillingly familiar, furnace number eleven. He wondered if it still drew poorly. He stepped wide of a fresh pour from number eight, several tons of molten iron still boiling hot, slowly congealing in the channels cut into the floor, a dead Chin lying half in the pour, clothes and hair smoldering. As always the windowless foundry was a stygian realm, illuminated only by the flare from the open hearths and the glow of hot iron, echoing with screams, gunshots, the hissing of hot metal, cloaked in a dark gloom so that all seemed ghostlike in the shadows.

He pushed down toward the end of the corridor, stepping out from behind a furnace, dropping a Bantag in the back as the warrior was backing up. Chin ran past, eyes wide with terror and rage, screaming incoherently.

He caught a glimpse of a ragged Chin, a skeletal form, naked except for a filthy rag tied around his waist, pointing. Hans spun around and catlike jumped backwards just as a heavy cauldron of molten iron upended, the glowing silvery cascade exploding into steam as it vomited out onto the pouring floor. Half a dozen Chin who had been next to Hans were caught in the boiling river, the men stumbling, falling, flames exploding as the liquid splashed onto their clothes, hair, and skin.

The two Bantag behind the upended cauldron ran out from behind the overturned vat. The charging mob skirted around the spreading pool and fell upon the two. The fight was horrifying. Hans watched, torn between rage at his old tormentors and pity for two living beings about to die agonizing deaths. The crowd simply beat the one half to death, then pushed him out onto the slowly congealing pool of molten iron. The second one was hoisted up by a dozen Chin, who carried him, kicking and flailing, to the open door of a glowing hearth.

Often enough Hans had seen a Bantag pick up a slave with a single hand and toss him into a furnace over some minor infraction, or simply for no reason at all other than to serve as a minor amusement. The half-conscious Bantag, realizing his fate, started to kick and scream as they tried to plunge him headfirst into the flames. His arms snapped out, trying to block the entry. Blows from stirring rods broke his limbs.

Screaming, he was thrown in, and, to Hans's terrified amazement, the Bantag, wreathed in flames, stood up inside the inferno, bellowing in agony. A single shot from Hans's carbine ended the agony, the explosive shot ending the horrific nightmare.

The shot reverberated through the cavernous room, and there was a strange silence for a moment. The mob, stunned by what it had done, seemed to collectively pause for breath.

"Hans."

Startled, he turned. It was the Bantag dying in the molten pool of iron still slowly spreading out on the floor of the foundry.

The Bantag, kicking weakly, was looking straight at him.

My God, was this one of my captors from so long ago? Hans wondered. *What torments did he inflict upon me, upon my comrades?*

"Hans." It was a rattling gasp of agony, and he could sense the pleading supplication in the alien guttural voice.

Hands shaking, he ejected the spent round. He couldn't stop the shaking as he fumbled to pull another round out of his cartridge box, dropped it, and, cursing, tried to retrieve it from the blood-soaked floor. The Chin surrounding the still slowly spreading puddle gazed in mute silence at the agony of the Bantag and the apparently vain attempt of Hans to end it.

At last he chambered the round, cocked the hammer, and raised his carbine, aiming straight at the head.

"No, no!" It was several of the Chin, gesturing angrily, motioning for him not to shoot.

"Hans . . ."

Tears filled his eyes. Snarling, he raised his carbine, aiming straight at the forehead. The Bantag, twitching spasmodically, appeared to dip his head in acknowledgment.

He squeezed the trigger.

Lowering his gun, he looked at the mob.

"We are men, damn it," he cried. "Not like them. We are men."

He felt an infinite exhaustion, a wish simply to crawl away to a dark corner, to collapse into oblivion. His gaze swept the mob, eyes lingering on the very spot where only a year ago he had cowered in fear as a Bantag, perhaps the very one he had just shot, had almost uncovered the secret tunnel that had led him back to freedom.

"We are not like them," he cried, again his voice breaking. "Fight to be free, not for revenge, not to be like them!"

And yet he knew the rage, the horror of slavery, the secret wish, buried in one's heart, to if nothing else kill one of them, to kill one of them in the most frightful and agonizing way possible, willing to trade one's own life for that terrible instant of freedom, the freedom to kill before dying yourself.

"We're here to win freedom for all the Chin," Hans said, his voice now not much more than a whisper, speech beginning to slur from exhaustion, his heart feeling heavy and leaden, again the spasm of pain. He took a deep breath trying to will the pain away, still it lingered.

"We are from the Republic. I was a slave here as you are now."

Several of the Chin nodded, and he heard them whispering his name in their lilting singsong voices.

He took another breath.

"Furnace captains and barracks leaders. Organize your people. Round up all weapons taken from the Bantag. Find the camp leader and his assistants, I want them out by the gate in ten minutes."

The group seemed to freeze.

"Smash this whole damn place," he cried, "smash it all, burn the barracks. We leave here, forever, within the hour."

*   *   *

Vincent watched in glum silence as flames blowtorched out of the turret of the abandoned ironclad, its crew standing sadly to one side. A medical orderly was by the side of the boiler operator, smearing ointment on his scalded hands and face. It was the fifth ironclad to break down that day, a steam line splitting wide-open. Two or three hours' work, and they could have torn out the line, replacing it with a spare, but there was no time for that. The rear of the vast marching column had already passed and was a quarter mile to the east. He could see that the cavalry pickets bringing up the rear were getting nervous, wanting to push on.

The injured driver was loaded into a two-wheel ambulance wagon, the driver snapping the reins, urging the horse into a slow trot. A second wagon, loaded with the salvaged ammunition and Gatling gun, fell in behind the ambulance. The crew stood silent, not sure what to do, and Vincent motioned for them to get moving. They would be walking, and he could sense their unhappiness over the demotion back to the infantry.

A rifle ball fluttered past his face, another one pinged against the rear of his turret. He looked back to the west. A heavy skirmish line of mounted Bantag, several of them armed with rifles, was less than four hundred yards away.

Throughout the day the pressure on all sides had been slowly building. Most of the Bantag were still older formations, armed with traditional bows, but apparently several regiments, perhaps a full umen, armed with rifles had shown up. They had brought up two batteries of rifled pieces and several batteries of mortars as well, which were becoming something of an annoyance.

A mortar round arced overhead, bursting near the ambulance, the startled driver urging his draft horse into a plodding gallop to regain the protection of the square formed by 3rd Corps. A captain from the trailing cavalry unit rode up beside Vincent's ironclad and saluted.

"Ah sir, they're starting to press a little close."

Vincent nodded, and shouted down to his driver to get moving.

He spotted the puff of smoke as the mortar fired again, back and just behind the cover of the Bantag skirmish line sweeping in behind them. Though it was against orders to fire at long range, he pivoted his turret around, slipped back inside, raised the elevation on the gun, opened the steam cock, and fired several long bursts. Several mounted riders dropped.

Stanislaw engaged the engine and the ironclad lurched forward, wheels cutting into the dry turf. Standing up in the turret he watched as the cavalry skillfully pulled back, one troop reining about, covering, as a second troop a hundred yards farther back broke off, rode through their covering line, then came about in turn to cover. The men were good, skillful, always keeping the Bantag at bay. Twice during the long day of marching the Bantag had attempted to mount a serious charge. The cavalry then pulled in, letting the ironclads cut them apart.

They crested a low rise. Again the vast panorama ahead . . . 3rd Corps in a huge block formation, a thousand yards to a side, inside the hollow square the supply wagons, ambulances, a reserve brigade to plug any hole, and a dozen ironclads. Spread in a vast circle several hundred yards out around the square were mounted units and five ironclads per flank, the forward V formation of the previous day abandoned as the Bantag increased the pressure.

A Hornet came sweeping in, strafing the mortar crew that had been harassing them, the tracer rounds igniting the crew's limber wagon. The mushrooming fireball triggered a ragged cheer from the men at the rear of the square. The Hornet pulled up sharply and continued west, heading back to Tyre to reload and refuel.

The farther east they traveled, the more difficult it was maintaining air cover since the airships now had to fly nearly a hundred-mile round-trip before getting into action. The continual flying and fighting of the last three days was undoubtedly taking a toll on maintenance as well; there were long stretches of time now when no airships were overhead.

He thought about school, so many years ago, at the old Oak Grove in Vassalboro. Memory of Plutarch and the last campaign of Crassus against the Parthians. Much the same, the circling riders. Only two differences, though. The first, his force had gunpowder. But the disturbing second one, unlike Crassus, who actually outnumbered the Parthians, he was facing odds of maybe six to one, the only thing holding them back the ironclads and the Hornets circling overhead.

His driver below turned slightly, and Vincent looked forward again, where several men, dead infantry, lay twisted in the high grass. He hated leaving them to the bastards. A scattering of dead Bantag and horses were in the grass as well, having tried to dispute the possession of the ridge when the head of the column had swept it half an hour ago.

They pushed on, a gust of dry wind from the west blanketing him in a choking cloud of smoke from the ironclad's exhaust stack. Coughing, he waited for it to clear. A courier came out of the smoke, reined in beside his machine, and rode at a slow canter, keeping pace.

Vincent returned the salute and took the note. Still perched atop the turret he unfolded the paper, ignoring the occasional hum of a bullet snapping past.

It was from Gregory, riding at the head of the column, announcing that water had been sighted. He shaded his eyes and looked back to the west. Still a couple of hours of sunlight. There was no need to look at the map, another watercourse was still five or six miles beyond. According to the map that was also the head of the Bantag rail line, which was being constructed from the Great Sea. A Hornet had flown all the way east earlier in the day and dropped a message that two Bantag transports were off-loading land ironclads and additional troops. Two Hornets had been lost trying to strafe the ships and locomotives, and the equipment was being loaded onto several trains, but had yet to move out.

Well, that is what we wanted, he realized. But still it was a chilling thought that somewhere up ahead a warm reception was being planned.

He knew the men were getting tired, they'd been on the march for nearly fourteen hours, a hard thirty miles that day, a little more than halfway to the coast. They'd still have to dig in once stopped for the night. The enemy would come to them. It was best to have the boys as rested as possible for the next day.

"Tell General Timokin to hold at the stream. Tell Stan to halt the corps as well and dig in. Whether we take the railhead today or not doesn't really matter; they'll just simply off-load farther back."

He could sense the boy's disappointment as he shifted uncomfortably in the saddle, then saluted and spurred his mount forward.

He looked out at the circling host. After months in the siege lines they had to be exhausted as well. *No, they won't press it yet, they'll wait for ironclads to come up. Then there'll be hell to pay.*

The aerosteamer touched down lightly, bounced once, then settled back down, quickly rumbling to a halt.

Jurak pulled open the hatch and swung down, barely acknowledging the bows of the aerosteamer ground crew. It was an out-of-the-way position on the northeast shore of the Great Sea, near the realm of Nippon, a little more than halfway to his destination. The only purpose for the station was to act as a refueling depot for the occasional aerosteamer flying the great route from the realm of the Chin, northward to Nippon, then northwest, skirting the flank of the Sea, then finally to turn straight west to the front, now three hundred leagues away. He regretted not setting up stations on the western and eastern shore of the Sea, so one could simply fly across the water, but after too many of the precious ships had disappeared making the transit, Ha'ark had forbidden such overflights, and he had never bothered to rescind the ban.

As it was he had witnessed firsthand the wisdom of that choice. Thirty leagues back one of his two escorts had simply quit, an engine shutting down, the aerosteamer spiraling down to a semi–crash landing along the rail line that ran the length of the northern shore.

"Any messages?" he shouted, looking over at the station commander, who stared at him as if he was a god who had tumbled from the sky.

A sheaf of papers was pressed into his hand, and he scanned them, yet again cursing the fact that the script of his own world had not been introduced rather than the damnable writing of the Rus.

So it was Huan after all. He had at least guessed right on that; otherwise, this trip would be a foolish waste. He jotted down half a dozen messages on a pad of rice paper, tore them off, and handed them back to the station commander. Without a word, he looked back at his pilot.

"How are the engines?"

"My Qar Qarth, they need work."

"Can they take us to the next stop?"

"Tonight?"

"Yes, damn all, tonight. We'll have moonlight, just follow the damned rail line. We're almost around the Sea. The rail line will turn southeast down toward Nippon. It'll be open steppe soon."

The pilot said nothing.

"Shouldn't we wait for our escort?" He nodded toward the small dot that was now winging in from the west.

"He can catch up. Let's be off."

Grabbing a waterskin and satchel of dried meat offered by a trembling cattle slave, Jurak returned to the air machine and climbed in, impatiently waiting for the pilot, who checked as the last of the tins of kerosene was loaded into the fuel tank.

The pilot finally climbed back through the hatch and before it was even closed Jurak leaned over and pushed in the throttle lever, propellers stuttering up to a blur. Turning back out onto the grassy strip, they took off, clearing the towering trees at the far end of the field, heading back for a moment toward the setting sun. Banking hard over, they continued to climb, Jurak catching a glimpse of the Sea off the starboard side. Straight ahead he could see where a shallow arm of the ocean finally played out into a bay ringed with low hills, a place where a year ago the first actions of the campaign had been fought in a vain attempt to lure the Yankees eastward before the attack across the ocean came two hundred leagues to the west.

Huan. The war had leapt all the way back to there. Chaos all the way from Xi'an to Huan, half a dozen factories in enemy hands. A mob though. A disorganized mob led at best by two or three hundred trained troops. They still most likely thought that there was only one rail line. The one that ran from Huan to Xi'an. With luck they didn't know that throughout the winter and into early summer he had pressed the completion of the second line, the one that ran northward out of Huan, up to Nippon, and then finally connected to the route the Yankees had been cutting along the northern shore of the Great Sea. And on that road, even now, he had reversed every train, over thirty of them carrying two entire umens of troops who had been sent back after the siege of Roum to refit and train with the newest weapons.

It had been his plan to keep them in reserve at Huan, an inner warning perhaps that the vast encampment areas for the old, the young, and the females, more than three hundred thousand yurts spread in a vast arc across hundreds of leagues between Huan and Nippon, were too vulnerable.

Pat O'Donald furiously shredded the paper, tearing it in half, then again, and yet again until it was nothing more than confetti. Rick Schneid, his second-in-command for the Capua Front, said nothing, having read the note over Pat's shoulder.

Pat looked down at the telegrapher who had transcribed the note.

"That thing still operating?" Pat asked.

The boy nodded, wide-eyed and uncomprehending of the long stream of English and Gaelic imprecations that had poured out of Pat while reading the note.

Pat looked around the room; half a dozen men of the signal corps were at their telegraphs, which connected to the various commands along the river, and the main line back to Roum and Suzdal beyond.

Unholstering his revolver he grabbed the weapon by the barrel, and slammed the butt down on the receiver, smashing it to pieces.

"Well, now the son of a bitch is broken," he snarled.

The room was silent.

Reversing the revolver he held it casually in his hand, not pointing it at the telegrapher but not quite turning it away from him either.

"If a word, if a single word of that message slips out of this room, I'm going to blame you personally," he paused, his gaze sweeping the others, who stared at him nervously. "I'll blame all of you. Do we understand each other?"

No one answered; there was simply nodding all around.

"I expect it'll be at least a day before you can find a replacement for that machine."

"Ah, yes sir, days more likely."

"Fine."

"Sir, I have to enter something into the official logbook."

"Damn the logbook to hell," he shouted, as he reached over, tore out several pages, and shredded them as well.

"A shell hit this place, damn lucky anyone got out alive, damn lucky. Do we understand each other?"

"Sir, you're right."

"What the hell do you mean I'm right?"

"Just that, sir."

"Don't ever say that, boy, or you'll hang with me. The rest of you keep me posted. We can maybe expect action by dawn. I want to know."

Tossing the pieces of paper on the packed-dirt floor he stalked out, tearing aside the blanket that acted as a curtain. Climbing out of the command bunker, he walked up onto the battlement and with a sigh leaned against the earthen embankment, gazing blankly at the rising moons.

"You can't keep it back forever."

It was Schneid, coming up to join him, proffering a lit cigar, which Pat gladly accepted.

"I want good troops, old veterans we can trust," Pat said. "Make it the First Suzdal. Be honest and tell them what's going on. Get 'em on a train and head back up the line toward Roum. Turn command of your corps over to your second and go with them."

"Me? Pat, we both know those bastards over there are fixing to attack, maybe as early as tomorrow. I'm needed here."

"No, you're needed more back there. Pick a good spot, say the bridge crossing that marshy creek about thirty miles back. That's a good enough spot. Block the track, tear the bridge up a bit, then stop anyone who comes up that line. If the Chin ambassadors should happen to show up, arrest them or shoot them, I don't care which it is at the moment."

"You sure you know what you're doing?"

"Look, Rick. The government might not send anybody up at first, other than a couple of mealymouthed senators. If they do, arrest them as well."

"On what charge?"

"Damn all, Schneid, I don't care. Littering, soliciting for immoral purposes, public drunkenness, I don't give a damn."

Leaning over, he rubbed his temples.

"Sorry, I don't mean to blow on you."

"It's all right."

"I just can't believe that after everything we've been through it's come down to this."

"I know."

"They might send troops, then."

"I know that, too. I'll leave it up to you at that point. I don't want our people killing each other, I'm not ordering you to do that."

"Pat, you can only keep this under wraps a day, two days at most. The army's bound to find out. You can't tie up every damn supply train coming this way. Word will finally get through."

"Two days, make it three, that's all."

"For what?"

"If need be, I'm going to try one more time."

"Try what?"

Pat nodded toward the east.

"To get across that damned river."

"Don't even think it, Pat. You have no orders."

"Rick, everything's breaking apart. The Republic, Andrew resigning, that last damned telegram telling us to inform the bastards on the other side of the river that we want a cease-fire. It's all breaking apart. Well maybe it's breaking apart over there, too. I'm willing to make one more try at it. I think they'll hit first, then I plan to hit back with everything I have."

"Pat, give it another day. We still don't know what's happening with Vincent or Hans. Maybe they've succeeded. If so, the bastards here will have to pull back, and that could reverse the whole political situation at home."

Pat said nothing, staring at the rising moons.

"All right then, one more day, but then, by God, I plan to go down fighting."

"With an army that's no longer supposed to fight?"

Pat smiled.

"They don't know that yet now, do they?"

"You're talking rebellion."

"Only you and I know that, my friend, and maybe a bit of rebellion is exactly what this country needs at this moment."

Chapter Twelve

He had seen cities burn before, Fredericksburg, Suzdal, Kev, Roum, and only this morning it had been Xi'an. None of his nightmares, however, had prepared Hans for the apocalypse spreading from horizon to horizon. Huan, the great city of the Chin, was dying.

It had started at dusk, a column of smoke to the east, a beacon, a warning, the column of smoke by day, and now the pillar of fire by night, and it seemed as if the world, the entire world, was doomed to a purging by flame for its sins.

Even before nightfall the first refugees had come into his advancing lines seeking refuge. No one could explain how or why they knew to head west, it was as if a primal force of nature, chained for ten thousand years had been unleashed.

While a slave he had learned something of the mystery, the Chin called it "wind words," the strange almost supernatural way that news flowed through the slave camps, leaping like the chimera wind, bearing with it tiding of death, the choosing of who shall be next for the moon feasts, the distant whispers of wars. Before the Bantag even came to a barracks to lead someone away, already the news had arrived as "wind words."

Hans knew that in the world of master and slave, the slave was always present, standing by every table, every entryway to a yurt, always there were slaves, mute, dumb-looking, but always listening, and from mouth to mouth the word would spread of what had been decided. That was the only explanation he now could find. "Wind words" had floated into the city of Huan, miles away from where he had landed, bearing with it news of the spreading rebellion.

Some of the refugees claimed that the Bantag garrison

of Huan had started it, rounding up the appointed leaders of the city, taking them out beyond the walls to slaughter them all, that one of the leaders slew a Bantag, and thus the killing frenzy had started in the streets of the city. Others, that the Bantag were in a panic, fleeing the city, setting it aflame and sealing the gates with the intent of murdering the hundreds of thousands within. And yet others said that Cu-Han, the great ancestor god, had ridden into the city upon a winged horse and struck down Ugark, the Bantag Qarth of the city, the flaming light of his sword blinding the Bantag, and then proclaimed that the hour of liberation had come.

He suspected he knew the truth. That all the stories were true. When word arrived of the air assault on Xi'an, and the following day the strike on the factories west of Huan, the garrison commander had panicked and ordered the roundup of all the Chin who were collaborators and managed the daily running of the millions of Chin who labored as slaves. Perhaps it was merely to interrogate, maybe even to take hostages to ensure that the people did not rebel, or stupidly it was with the intent to kill them all in retaliation. As for the god, that was a fascinating irony, the similarity in names, and if at the moment it helped to feed the rebellion, so be it. But as he looked at the thousands staggering past he could see the panic as well.

Panic would feed on panic, the Bantag beginning the slaughter, and the population, after years of occupation, slavery, and terror, sensing that liberation was at hand, but now confronted by the death they had sought so long to avoid, would then turn like cornered rats, believing that the gods themselves would now come to their aid.

Sitting on the side of the wood tender of a Bantag locomotive, which was slowly pushing up the main line toward the city, he nursed the cup of tea given to him by the locomotive engineer, a Chin slave freed when they had seized the engine works adjoining the foundry where they had landed.

The tea and a dirty chunk of hard bread were reviving him, and to his amazement he had actually managed to snatch a few hours' sleep, the first in two days. Seeing that the cup was empty, the engineer gently took it from Hans, opened a hot water vent, filled the cup, then, reaching into his pocket, he pulled out a dirty rag, scooped out a precious handful of leaves, and threw them in, swishing the contents around.

Hans nodded his thanks. Setting the cup down on the floor of the tender to let it cool a bit, Hans leaned out of the cab. A firefight was flaring up ahead, yet another walled-in compound; one of the men reported that it was a powder works. The complex stood out sharply, the burning city, still several miles off, illuminating the world. His skirmish line, deployed a half mile to either side of the tracks, was hotly engaged, beefed up now by thousands of Chin, some armed with cumbersome Bantag rifles, others with the precious pistols carried in on the aerosteamers and not left behind at Xi'an. Most were just a surging, milling horde carrying clubs, pitchforks, stoking rods, knives, heavy Bantag swords, and spears.

Right through the middle of the fighting an endless column staggered to either side of the track, women clinging to screaming infants, frightened children clutching their mothers' skirts, old men, women, lost children, all of them confused, terrified, moving west, trying to get out of the madness.

He had detailed off a few precious troops to cull out anyone, man or woman, who seemed capable of fighting. In any other setting the gesture would be obscene, for all of them were little more than emaciated skeletons, the final dregs of the pit after years of existence in hell and the death of millions in the monthly feasts or dying to prop up the empire of the hordes.

He tried to ignore them, to let his gaze linger for even a second on a lost child, or an exhausted mother lying in the mud and surrounded by screaming children would sap his will to continue the madness. He had come to try and free them, for they had become his brothers and sisters, yet now to free them he could do nothing but watch them die, and it was destroying him.

They were all dead anyhow, he had to remind himself of that. For surely, once the Republic was destroyed, the Bantag would annihilate everyone here and then move on. Yet rather than feeling like a liberator he felt as if he was the angel of death, realizing that as he looked at the inferno enveloping the world, a hundred thousand or more must be dying this night.

A blinding light ignited. Where the powder works had been a harsh white glare, brighter than a hundred suns, erupted, rising heavenward, the flash brilliance of it seeming to freeze everyone. By the light of the explosion the entire world came into a sharp-etched reality. Far to his left he could see the end of his battle line, a milling confusion, mounted Bantag swirling into a tangled mass of humanity. Straight ahead the track was clogged with people, all of them frozen, then falling, their cries drowned out by the earth-splitting thunderclap. The ragged line of infantry circling about the walled compound were turning, running back, flinging themselves to the ground.

The fireball soared thousands of feet heavenward, the brilliant glare darkening into a sullen red hell, spreading out. The concussion stunned him. He staggered, leaning forward into the gale, the air hot and dry. More explosions ignited, crates of ammunition thrown heavenward, bursting asunder, millions of cartridges flaring, sparkling, streaks of fire plunging back to earth.

The compound walls were down, blown asunder, providing a glimpse into the inferno. Bantag, looking like flaming demons, staggered out, flaying wildly at the agony that was consuming them, humans, dwarflike beside them, burning as well. A box of rifle cartridges crashed down beside the engine, exploding like a bundle of firecrackers, rounds pinging against the side of the tender.

"Hans!"

It was Ketswana, dragging several Chin behind him, all three dressed in the loose black coveralls marking them as men who worked aboard the locomotives. They were the precious few, allowed extra rations, exemption of their families from the feasting pit, and in the madness of the last few hours more than one had been beaten to death by those lower on the order of survival in this mad world and thus the special order to round them up not only for intelligence but also for their own protection.

Ketswana climbed into the locomotive cab and, exhausted, slumped down to the floor, back against the pile of wood in the tender. Hans offered his cup of tea, and Ketswana greedily gulped it down, nodding his thanks when

Hans offered a piece of hardtack. The three Chin rail workers he had dragged along were in the cab as well, talking excitedly to the engineer piloting Hans's train, their words flowing so fast Hans could barely decipher what was being said.

"They're from the northern line," Ketswana announced, still chewing on the dry bread.

"Northern line?"

"Remember, we knew they were laying a line up toward Nippon."

"And?" He felt a flash of fear.

"We should have flown a few reconnaissance flights that way, Hans, before ordering Jack to take the remaining ships back to Xi'an."

It was a stupid mistake, damn stupid, Hans realized. He should have ordered Jack to circle out for a quick look around, but had yielded to the argument that if any of the aerosteamers were to survive, they had to get back to Xi'an before dark, refuel, patch up, and hopefully find a hydrogen-gas generator at the Bantag airfield. From there they could get back to Tyre the next morning. But now this.

He knew that his releasing of Jack was also motivated by guilt. Jack had finally agreed to the attack, though he had insisted that the other pilots had to volunteer as well and could not be ordered. Of course all of them did volunteer, they were far too green to know when to say no, and none would ever allow himself to be called the coward.

Only nine airships survived the assault intact and in some semblance of flying order. Close to five out of every six Eagle crews alive just two weeks ago were now dead. Jack and his boys were beyond the breaking point, and thus Hans had sent them home. His sentimentality might just have cost him the fight. He had had no idea of the completion of the rail line to the north.

"The bastards didn't just run the line up to Nippon," Ketswana continued, "they hooked it all the way up to the line we were running along the north shore of the Sea!"

Hans lowered his head, saying nothing. Damn! Six, eight hundred miles of track in a year. He didn't think the Bantag were capable of it. Wearily, he looked down at Ketswana.

"They have another route, Hans. Even though we cut

the sea-lane, they can still move supplies by rail! Taking Xi'an means nothing; they can still keep the war going!"

"We should have heard something," Hans replied, his voice thick with exhaustion, his mind refusing to believe the dark reality this intelligence presented. "Prisoners, escaped slaves during the winter, something."

"The slaves working it were kept separate. They only finished it within the last month. Nearly all the supplies were still going down to Xi'an and moving by boat—it was easier. Now for the bad news."

He could already sense what it would be.

"First off, they built some more factories up in Nippon and put the people to work. Hans, even if we smash this place up, they'll still be able to produce weapons."

"We had to figure on that." Hans sighed, trying to hide his bitter disappointment. So this would not be the crippling blow. The thought sank in with a brutal clarity that the war was indeed lost. Jurak would annihilate the Chin, perhaps stop for a while to regroup, then simply press on with the fight. He was afraid that in his exhaustion his despair would show. He lowered his head in order to hide his face.

"And Hans. Those three Chin I rounded up," Ketswana continued, "were supposed to run a trainload of rails north this morning. They told me that even then word was already in the city that we had taken Xi'an. The Bantag were getting nervous, rounding up the families of the Chin rulers as hostages when we hit the factories west of here. That's when all hell broke loose, and the city rioted."

"Kind of what we figured."

"That's not the main point, though. These three were supposed to pull out with that load of rails when suddenly they got orders to wait in the rail yard. One of them, his brother worked on the telegraph line, said that messages were flying north, up toward Nippon, calling back two umens of troops."

Hans tried not to react.

"We had to figure on resistance. If they only had two umens here covering their rear, we should be able to handle it."

"Hans, two umens of troops with modern weapons. They were sent back here after the Battle of Roum to refit. These

Bantag are veterans. They're deploying north of the city right now."

Hans looked back toward Huan. Damn all, it would have been the perfect place for a defensive fight. Like most Chin cities, it was a rabbit warren of narrow streets, laid out with no rhyme or reason. It had once housed over a million people. There was no telling how many were left after the years of occupation and slavery, but even with several hundred thousand he could have consumed half a dozen umens in a street-to-street fight.

The pillar of fire filled the night sky, a vast inferno, a city thousands of years old dying in one final cataclysm. There was a flash of guilt. He knew that everyone who had lived in that city was doomed to die. Once the war a thousand miles to the north and west was finished, everyone here would have been massacred before the Bantag moved on. Yet still, as a slave he remembered far too well the clinging to life in spite of the doom. If one more day of survival could be wrung out of existence, that was all that counted, a day of numbing agony ameliorated by a warm bowl of millet at sundown, the gentle touch of a loved one sought in the middle of the night, the prayer that the night would last forever, the dawn and the agony that came with it banished by a dream.

His coming had shattered that dream, for everyone here this was the last night, and they knew it. Come dawn two umens of the Horde's finest warriors, battle-hardened from bitter campaigning, would be unleashed, and in their frenzy all would die.

He turned to look west, the twin rails glimmering by the firelight. He could back the train down that track right then. Fighting against despair, he tried to reason that at least they had accomplished something. It was a blow that would take months to recover from. Jurak would undoubtedly have to retreat to the Sea, perhaps even as far back as the Shennadoah or Nippon if Vincent's mad thrust won through and thus threatened the southern flank of the Horde armies.

And then what? Ultimately nothing would change, nothing. Jurak would simply build a new war machine.

Hans squatted next to his friend, sighing with the pain as his knees creaked in protest. He looked at the three railroad men who sat hunched up in the far corner of the cab, talking in whispers with the driver of the locomotive. He caught words here and there, whispers about slaughter, death, families lost, fear.

Outside, to either side of the stalled engine, the columns of frightened refugees continued to pass, fleeing they knew not where, but trying to get out nevertheless. Again another short stab of pain.

"Hans?"

"Yeah?"

"You all right?"

"Just tired, so damned tired."

"We've got to do something, you know."

"What?" He could sense his voice breaking. His mind was clouded, and it was becoming too hard to focus.

"Come dawn they'll attack; they're reorganizing not five miles from here."

"I know that."

Ketswana spoke quickly to the locomotive engineer, motioning with his tin cup. The engineer took it, vented some more hot water, and threw some leaves in. Ketswana took the cup and pressed it into Hans's hands, which were trembling.

Hans took a sip, set the cup down, and leaned his head back against the woodpile.

"We've got six hours or so till dawn," Ketswana announced. "We have to dig in and get ready. Build a fortified line anchored on this rail line, use the factory compounds we've taken as bastions."

"I know, I know," he whispered.

So many years of struggle, so many long hard years, and now it seems to all end here. His mind drifted, the prairie, the starlit nights: Antietam, the road to Antietam, cresting South Mountain, looking back across the valley, the blue serpentine columns stretching to the horizon, afternoon sun glinting on fifty thousand rifle barrels; Gettysburg, when the sun seemed to stand still in the heavens; and these strange heavens. He looked up, the Great Wheel overhead, again wondering which star was home. To have run the race so far, so far, and now to fall at the last step and see it all washed away.

He closed his eyes, a prayer drifting through his heart, *God, let this all be for something.*

"Hans?"

Ketswana leaned over, a moment of fright, his hand gently touching his friend's forehead, drifting down to his throat, feeling for a pulse.

He sighed and leaned back. Let him sleep, he needed sleep. Always trying to carry all the burden, forgetting just how many he had inspired and trained. No, let him sleep.

The engineer was looking over, and Ketswana motioned that Hans was not to be disturbed.

"Ketswana?"

He looked down from the cab. Through the confused press milling about he saw Fen Chu, one of the old guard, a survivor of the Escape.

"There's not much left of the powder mill," Fen reported. "All blown to hell it is."

"The next compound?" He motioned up the tracks toward Huan.

"Told by some of the slaves that escaped that the guards started to shoot everyone, then fled. It was a cartridge factory for their rifles."

Ketswana looked back to the west. The factory compounds were strung like beads along the track for miles, most of them basically laid out the same, brick buildings housing foundries, mills, works for cartridges, shells, bullets, rifles, artillery barrels, land ironclads . . . the brick building surrounded by wooden barracks for the slaves, and those in turn surrounded by a palisades, usually of logs or rough-cut planking.

Most of them were burning.

He looked back toward the city. No, that hope was finished.

South? He knew next to nothing of the land, just rumors. From his days of slavery he occasionally was allowed outside the compound on some errand, southward was nothing but open farmlands, vast rice paddies and pastures before the coming of the Bantag. Most of the farms were abandoned now. He remembered that on a clear day, from the roof of the factory one could see hills rising up, the distant hint of cloud-capped mountains beyond.

"Can't go south," Fen announced, as if reading Ketswana's thoughts.

"Why?"

"People are fleeing from that way as well. They said most of the Horde's encampments are down that way, hundreds of thousands of them, their old ones, women and cubs, yurts as far as you can see. That's their summer pasturing grounds on what had once been farms before everyone was herded into the compounds or slaughtered."

That was out then.

No. The anchor was the railroad. *We try to flee south, this mob will spread out run, in panic, and it will turn into a hunt.*

"All right, pull our men together; we start retreating back along the tracks. We'll push the trains back up the line three or four miles. We string the trains along the tracks between three or four of the compounds and upend them. Loot out what weapons we can. Get into the cartridge works, for example, and drag out as much ammunition as you can. Start culling out this mob, tell them reinforcements are coming up the rail line but we have to hold out."

"Are they?"

"We both know the answer to that, but we got to give these people some hope, some reason to turn and fight like men, rather than be hunted down like the cattle they were. If we can get ten hours, even eight, we should be able to fortify a good position, and then let's see what those bastards will do."

"You're talking about hundreds of thousands of people out here," Fen cried. "They'll all die once the Horde recovers and attacks."

"Fen, a year ago we all figured we'd die anyhow. All I asked then was to die killing the bastards. I still feel that way; how about you?"

A grin creased Fen's weary face, he came to attention, and saluted.

"Fine, let's get to work."

Fen raced off, disappearing into the mob, shouting orders. Ketswana looked over at the engineer and motioned for him to start backing the train up. As the machine slowly lurched into reverse, he looked down at Hans. Picking up a dirty blanket from the corner of the locomotive cab he gently draped it around his friend's shoulders.

"My friend, today will be a good day to die," he whispered.

It felt like the old days, the assault on Caradoga, the fifth year of the War of the False Pretender. The city had been hit by the third atomic to be used in the war, the air assault was dropped upwind to seal off the retreat of the refugees and drive them back in to the inferno, since Caradoga had been a center of stiff resistance. That was the battle where he had lost faith in the cause. Ha'ark had joined the unit shortly after that fight. Perhaps it would have tempered him more to have seen it, Jurak thought.

The Chin city of Huan looked the same now. It had been their beacon for the last fifty leagues of the flight, first a glow on the horizon, then a soaring pillar of light, so bright that it filled the cockpit of the aerosteamer with a hellish red glare. It reminded him as well of the Sacred Texts, the destruction of the city of Jakavu for its sinful ways.

Explosions ignited in the city, entire blocks of cramped derelict homes, abandoned as the population had been driven to work in the factories, rail lines, or to the feasting pits, were now consumed, flaring to explosive incandescence. From the north to southern wall the entire city was burning. By the glow he could make out snakelike columns moving out of the gates to the west of the city, where more fires burned.

Even as his attention turned to that direction a glaring white-hot explosion ignited, soaring heavenward in a giant fireball. It was the powder mill. Damn all, so they were into the factories. A dozen plants or more, foundries, cannon works, powder mill, cartridge works, rifle works, all of them burning.

It was hard to see the works to the east and south. He never should have left old Ugark as umen commander. He was far too much of the old ways, and bitter as well for not having command at the front. For that matter those who were there were, in general, warriors not fit for the front anymore, or those who were never fit, willing enough to torture a defenseless cattle, but not so willing to face one that just might be armed.

It was always the same mistake, to group together the less competent, then send them off to some forgotten front.

And yet the war was so damn close to victory, he could feel it within his grasp. The raids, both here and across from Tyre, though brilliant, were indicators of a final desperation. All that was needed now was to hang on, to contain this madness, save the factories that were left. Once that was done, return to the front and make a final push as if nothing had happened at all. That would shatter their morale once and for all, and they would give in.

The wind was building; the column of smoke ahead rose ten thousand feet or more to the heavens, then spread out in a dark mushroom cloud that blotted out the Great Wheel. Even from two leagues out bits of ash and smoldering embers were raining down. The machine lurched, bounced.

Firestorm, the outer edge of the winds being sucked into the heart of the inferno, he realized, and ordered the weary pilot to turn about and find a spot to land along the railroad tracks north of the city.

He could see the troop trains lined up, over two dozen of them. In the distance the headlight of another one came down from Nippon, winked, and shimmered. The pilot spiraled down, deciding to alight on what appeared to be open land parallel to the track where the long line of trains were parked.

A volley of bullets slashed through the cabin. A red mist sprayed into Jurak's eyes as the machine lurched over. Wiping his eyes clear he saw the pilot, the side of his head a shattered pulp, slumped over the controls.

More bullets slammed into the cabin as Jurak leaned over, trying to push the pilot to one side and free the wheel.

He caught a glimpse of a locomotive, sparks soaring up from the stack, winks of light flashing behind it, rifle fire, and for an instant he wondered how the damned humans had gotten this far, then realized his own men were shooting at him in blind panic.

Jerking the wheel back he banked sharply, closing his eyes for a moment and turning his head away as the forward glass panes exploded, showering him with fragments.

Damn, after all this, to be killed by your own warriors, he thought grimly as he opened his eyes, caught a glimpse of several yurts straight ahead, pulled back up to go over them and felt the shudder of a stall shaking his machine. The controls were mushy, and the machine started to settle, tail first, then slapped down hard.

The forward cabin snapped off from the front of the machine, and, covering his face, he fell.

There was a moment of stunned silence, and then he felt the heat. The hydrogen bags were burning.

Kicking, clawing, he tore himself free of the tangled wickerwork of the cab and crawled out onto the grass. A clump of dirt sprayed up into his face, the crack of another bullet whined overhead.

"You damned fools, it is your Qar Qarth!" he roared.

Another bullet snicked past so close that he felt the hollow sucking pop of it as it brushed his face and then the shouts of a commander echoed, screaming to the warriors to cease fire.

Hesitantly, he came to his knees, knowing that to cower on the ground would be a loss of face. He stood up, brushing himself off. A commander of ten raced up, slowed, turned to shout for everyone to ground arms, then fell to his knees.

"Forgive us, my Qarth." His voice was trembling.

"We thought . . ."

"I know, that it was a Yankee airship."

"Yes, my Qarth. Take my life in atonement."

Jurak reached down and grabbed the commander by the shoulder, pulling him up to his feet.

"If I killed everyone who made a mistake, I don't think I would have much of an army left."

The commander looked at him wide-eyed, and nodded.

"Your umen commander, where is he?"

The trembling leader of ten pointed to the train. He could see that hundreds were coming over out of curiosity. In the long history of the hordes, he realized, never had a Qar Qarth arrived in such a manner.

"Take me to him."

Jurak followed as he was led to the long line of trains. Word had already spread of what had happened and all were on their knees, heads lowered in atonement and fear.

Bokara, the commander of the umen of the white-legged

horse, came forward at the run, stopped, and went to his knees.

Jurak motioned for him to stand.

He started to sputter an apology, and Jurak cut him off. "Will your warriors be ready by dawn?"

"Yes, my Qarth. The last of the trains is coming in even now."

"The situation?"

Bokara looked south toward the flaring inferno.

"The truth, my Qar Qarth?"

"What I would expect and nothing less."

"Ugark panicked, my lord. When he heard the Yankees had landed at Xi'an he ordered all the cattle leaders of the city to be rounded up and slaughtered. I am told rioting was already breaking out even before the Yankees landed here early in the afternoon. Rumors had swept through the Chin that their liberator, the god Hans, was coming to free them."

"Slaughter the leaders? I didn't order that."

"I know that, my Qar Qarth."

"Go on."

"I am told that last night the Chin telegraph operators in the city received your message. I know that it was correctly relayed through Nippon, for I was there and received it, making sure it was passed on."

Jurak nodded, sensing that Bokara was also being careful to wash his hands of this mistake.

"It is apparent the cattle operators did not give the messages to Ugark but did spread the word among their own kind. Thus the riot which actually started before the Yankees even landed here."

Jurak nodded. *Again it shows our weakness,* he thought. *Our very messages carried by our enemies.* He should have realized that given what his message to Ugark contained, of course the cattle operators would hide it and use it against him. And the way Bokara said the word rioted carried with it a certain disbelief, that the Chin slaves, dumber than the dumbest beast, were incapable of such rebellion.

"My train arrived here just before dusk. I heard Ugark was already dead and that Tamuka had seized command."

"The Merki?"

"Yes, my Qar Qarth."

"How, damn it? I wanted him detained."

"Sire. He wears the crest of a Qar Qarth and said that you had given him authority."

"Where is he now?"

"I don't know, my Qar Qarth. Reports are he is west of the city, fighting, rallying the warriors that survived. They say he fought well."

Jurak caught the note of admiration in Bokara's voice. Was this also a subtle way of conveying his disagreement. Far too many of his own Horde actually admired Tamuka's fanatical manner and hatred of the cattle.

"Then let him fight there for the night," Jurak finally announced, deciding that dealing with Tamuka could wait.

"I arrived here just as the cattle started to swarm out of the burning city. It was like waves upon a great ocean, my Qar Qarth, no one could stop them, driven in panic as they were by the flames behind them. I abandoned my attempt to try and link up with those rallying to Tamuka, thinking it best to pull back, form my umens here, to the north of the city, and wait till dawn to move in strength."

Jurak nodded in agreement.

"The second umen?"

"Already forming as well. We'll have twenty thousand warriors well armed, with artillery support and half a dozen land ironclads I managed to get out of one of the factories before it was taken."

"Very good."

"My lord."

"Yes."

"The encampments of the clans of the black horses and of the gray-tailed horses. Our people are in the summer encampments to the south in the hills."

Jurak did not quite grasp for a moment what he was driving at.

"The cattle, my Qar Qarth. They are between us and a hundred thousand yurts of my own clan. The cubs of my own young, all that is left of my blood, are but a day's ride south of here."

He caught the edge of fear in the old warrior's voice.

"They are armed," Jurak replied, trying to reassure.

"Only with bows, my lord. Many of the Yankees and the cattle they've freed now have guns."

"We defeat the Yankees tomorrow morning, then that fear will be put to rest."

"Yes, my Qarth."

"I'm exhausted; I need some food and a place to rest."

"This way, my Qarth." Bokara started to lead him toward the train.

He stopped for a moment and saw a dark form lying on the ground, then another and another. Ten of them in all. Other warriors stood in silence. It was the commander of ten and his warriors, all of them dead, having performed the ackba, the ritual of forming a circle and simultaneously slitting the throat of the comrade to their right in atonement for a failure by the unit.

He wanted to denounce such madness; it had been a mistake, but ritual had to be obeyed. He said nothing, the ten were fallen, it would not be seemly for him to comment upon those who should be beneath his notice. His gaze swept the circle, warriors carrying rifles, yet still wearing the horned and human-skull-adorned ceremonial war helmets of old, the train venting steam while Chin slaves, moving furtively so as not to draw notice, tended to it, feeding wood into the firebox, while another was oiling the driveshaft. What acts of destruction might they be secretly planning at that very moment, he wondered.

Ahead the city still burned, silhouetting the spreading encampment of his army, fieldpieces lined up next to felt-and-hide yurts, a dozen warriors gathered round a fire, roasting what appeared to be the legs and arms of a human while another casually cracked open the severed skull to scoop out the brains.

To make them modern, he now realized with grim certainty, was impossible; one could not expect them, in the span of a few short years, to leap generations. Somehow the humans were more adaptable, or was it simply more desperate. Did his own people truly realize just how desperate they were at this moment?

He felt a twinge of fear. *No, not now, I can't lose my nerve now though the dark foreboding is ready to consume me. Victory first, then let the rest fall where it may.*

Chapter Thirteen

Sitting atop his ironclad, Vincent Hawthorne raised his field glasses, scanning the horizon to the east, which was silhouetted by the dawning light.

"See them?" Gregory asked. "I count at least twenty-five plumes. They must have brought them up by rail during the night. And there, see it, four, make that five flyers are up as well."

Vincent said nothing, slowly sweeping the line of the horizon. Gregory's eyes were undoubtedly far better, and he was trained for this through a year's hard experience.

"Fine then. They're going to make a fight of it," Vincent announced, lowering his glasses.

A sharp rattle of rifle fire, sounding sharp and clear in the early-morning air, ignited. Directly ahead a line of cavalry skirmishers was drawing back from the opposite ridge. Ever since the men had dug into camp just after sundown, the ridge had been a source of contention throughout the night. If the bastards were allowed to deploy artillery up there, they could fire right down into the fortified camp of 3rd Corps.

Standing up, he slowly turned. The dawning light was starting to reveal the encircling host. It was hard to tell, but he sensed that more Bantag had come up during the night. The odds were running steep, at least six to one, perhaps even seven to one, the advantage held by having thirty-eight ironclads offset by the arrival of the enemy machines.

This day would be the day, then, and for all he knew, in the greater world beyond, the war might already be over. There was no word from Hans, not a single flyer had come back from Xi'an with a report. He was beginning to suspect that it would prove to be a very bad day.

"Should we move up to meet them?" Gregory asked.

Vincent shook his head.

"Get the men digging in. We've got fresh water here." He nodded to the oasis-like spring that was in the center of the camp. "Even if the water is somewhat bitter, they can't block it off. We dig in and let them come at us. As for our ironclads, we move up onto the ridge east of here to keep their artillery back. That's where we'll meet their ironclads coming in."

"They could wait us out, you know. We're down to five days' rations."

"They don't know that. No, I think their pride is hurt, us getting this far through territory they felt was theirs. No, once those ironclads come up the fight will be on."

"Wonder if this is all futile anyhow." Gregory sighed.

Vincent looked over at him.

"Sorry, but word is getting around with the boys. Somehow rumors are floating about a coup back in Suzdal, that the war might already be over, and we've surrendered, that Hans and even Andrew are dead."

"And what do you think?"

"If we surrendered, how long do you think those hairy bastards would let someone like you or me live. We know too much."

He laughed, shook his head, and slapped the ironclad they were sitting on.

"We're all doomed to die anyhow; if given the choice, I want to go down fighting in one of these. I was nothing before you Yankees came. You trained me, gave me a chance to command, gave me a machine I could master and even learn to love. That's a pretty good life, I think, and something worth dying for today."

"I wish we had another corps though," Vincent whispered.

"Air cover, that's what I want. What the hell do you think the Hornets were doing last night?"

Vincent shook his head. At least twenty machines had flown directly overhead in the middle of the night. One of them had circled several times and then pressed on. He had hoped that someone would have found a dropped message streamer, but so far nothing. Perhaps they were attempting a moonlit strike on the enemy ships off-loading the ironclads. If that was their mission, the smoke just over the next hill was indicator enough that the mad scheme had been a failure.

"Anyhow, the fewer men, the greater share of honor," Gregory continued with a smile, and the two chuckled softly.

"Well, I guess we're the bait. We wanted a stand-up fight, and we're going to get one. Let's make the most of it."

"Hans."

The voice was gentle but insistent, waking him from a soft floating dream. It was Maine. Funny, he had actually spent very little time there, but even after all these years it still haunted his memory and dreams. Pulled from the Regulars, he'd been sent to Augusta to help form up a volunteer regiment, 1030-odd farm boys, lumbermen, clerks, students, fishermen, boat builders, craftsmen, railroad men, factory hands, and a lone history professor who would become the 35th Maine. He'd arrived early in July. By the end of August they were already heading south to join the Army of the Potomac in Maryland. Less than two months, and yet somehow it had made its stamp upon his heart. He remembered the day he and a nervous and still-young lieutenant hiked their company from the parade field below the Capitol to the village of Belgrade. The lieutenant allowed the boys to strip down for a swim in Snow Pond while the two sat on a grass-covered hill and first questions were asked. "What's the war like . . . how good are the Rebs" and the startling admission . . . "I hope I don't fail these boys."

He had grown sick of officers who only seemed concerned with rank, privilege, clawing to promotion and this shy volunteer, voice near breaking, wondering aloud if he would "fail his boys."

He'd been dreaming of that, but it was different. His own wife, Tamira, their baby Andrew, and with them Andrew, Kathleen, and their children. It was like a dream of heaven. No fear, a soft lazy summer day in Maine where, though the sun was warm in July, there was always a cool breeze stirring off the lake.

Even in the dream he wondered if he was wandering in Andrew's dream realm, for the colonel had told him of his feverish morphine-twisted visions of death, of lingering by a lakeshore with all the dead who had gone before.

No. This was different, and he wondered if it was a foreshadowing, a dream of heaven.

"Hans."

It was Ketswana, hand lightly on the shoulder, shaking insistently.

Hans opened his eyes and saw the dark features, the shaved head, eyes that were so transparent, like windows into the soul, and the look of concern.

Hans sat up, disoriented. He had sat down on the woodpile, the city was burning, the powder works had blown.

He sat up, feeling light-headed, unsure of where he was. The air was heavy with the smell of burned wood, rubbish, and the ever-present clinging smell of the camps. He looked around. He was off the train, inside a brick building, roof burned off and collapsed. There was a chill; it was all so familiar in a distorted way, the foundry where he had once slaved.

Everything was a mad scurry of confusion, men using stoking rods were cutting into the brick wall, chiseling out firing ports through the heavy wall. He was near the main doorway, dead Bantag from storming the building were dragged to one side and piled up, and had been half-consumed in the fire.

He stood up. "How did I get here?"

"You don't remember?"

Hans shook his head.

Ketswana looked at him closely.

"You all right?"

"Sure. Now tell me what's going on."

Ketswana motioned for him to follow as he climbed up a ramp that had once been used by labor crews pushing wheelbarrows of crushed ore, coke, and flux up to the tops of the furnaces. Most of the heavy-beamed walkway had survived the fire but was badly charred.

The walkway rimmed the inside of the factory walls just below the roofline and men and women were working feverishly, clearing away rubble from the collapsed roof, and to his amazement a couple of dozen were slowly dragging a Bantag light fieldpiece, a breechloader, to the northeast corner.

"Where the hell did you get that thing?"

"At the cannon works. A dozen of them brand-spanking-new. We even found some shells. I got one posted down by the gate, the rest of the guns are in the other compounds."

A couple of Chin, a single rifle between them, looked up as they passed, one of them holding up a half-charred piece of flesh and, grinning, nodded his thanks. Directly below, on the floor of the factory compound, Hans could see the burned remains of the Bantag he had shot yesterday, baked into the frozen pool of iron.

Ketswana, knowing what he was thinking, shook his head and laughed.

"I've had crews working all night. We found a herd of horses. I ordered them slaughtered and, using the wreckage of a barracks compound, we roasted tons of the stuff."

He grimaced.

"Well, most of it was damn near raw, but I remember a time when you and I wouldn't have turned down raw meat, as long as we knew what it was. That was the lure, word spread, and we must of had them coming in by the tens of thousands. Anyone who could do anything we organized off with their compound leaders, village elders, even some of their princes.

"We fed them and made it clear, if they ran off, everyone would be slaughtered come dawn. Hans, they all know that. Did you hear who's here?"

"No, who?"

"Tamuka."

Hans said nothing.

"Word is he's the one that fired the city. They went crazy yesterday, started murdering everyone, as word spread that we had taken Xi'an and were coming this way."

Hans nodded, but said nothing. There was no hope of trying to turn these people into a trained cadre, that'd take weeks, months, and months of simply feeding them right as well. Though it was hard to believe he felt they actually looked worse than what he had experienced a year ago. The simple knowledge of what was coming that day would give them the courage to go down in a final mad frenzy.

"Hans, they were organizing for this day, did you know that?"

"What do you mean?"

"You think we were the only ones?" Ketswana chuckled, as he reached out and moved Hans aside as a work crew, carrying a crate of ammunition for Bantag rifles, slowly moved past, pausing by the pair consuming their meal so that they could grab several dozen cartridges before moving on.

"Hans, they had a whole network put together. Word of our breakout a year ago spread from one end of the Chin realm to the other. They say even the people up in the Nippon lands knew about it. The 'wind words' are that rioting is erupting in Nippon as well. The Bantag couldn't stamp it out. Hans, you're something of a god around here."

"What?"

"Legends that we would return, that we wouldn't let them be massacred. They're right, you know."

"Yeah." He sadly gazed at the skeletal crew laboring to roll the fieldpiece into position so that it wouldn't recoil right off the platform the first time it was fired.

"So they had a network, every compound linked together by the railroad crews and track laborers. Telegraphers kept the leaders informed of everything the Bantag did. With rumors that the Republic had surrendered sweeping the city, they were actually going to try and stage a mass rebellion even before we flew in to Xi'an."

"Madness."

"Well, what else could they do? Even if they traded lives a hundred to one, it would have stirred things up at the end. They knew just as well as we did that once the war was over they'd all be slaughtered. Some were talking about moving on the encampment areas south of here."

"What?"

"The old ones, their women and children."

He said nothing, the dark thought repulsive.

"They say there's a hundred thousand yurts less than thirty miles from here."

The way Ketswana spoke chilled Hans, and he shook his head, silencing him.

Ketswana motioned Hans forward as the last of the ammunition carriers hauling up shells for the fieldpiece passed. Gaining the corner of the foundry building, Hans stepped up onto a raised observation platform and sucked in his breath.

The enemy host was coming. They were still several miles off, but in the cool morning air they stood out sharply. These were not mounted archers, aging guards, cruel slave drivers who could whip a terrified Chin to death but might step back from one armed with a stoking rod or pick. They were coming on slowly, deliberately, open skirmish line to the fore. Somehow Ketswana still had a pair of field glasses, and Hans took them, fumbling with the focus. One of the twin barrels had been knocked out of kilter, so he closed one eye.

These were good troops, Hans could see that, black-uniformed, rifles held at the ready. A scattering of Chin were drawing back, refugees who had wandered out into the fields northwest of the burning city. The Bantag were not even bothering to waste a shot on such prey. If their steady advance overtook one, the victim was simply bayoneted and left. There was no looting, tearing apart of bodies, just a cold dispatching and then continuing on.

Behind the double rank of skirmishers he could see the main body of troops, advancing in open order of columns, well spread out, half a dozen paces between warriors so that each regiment of a thousand occupied a front a half mile across and a hundred yards deep. Gatlings had finished the days of shoulder-to-shoulder ranks, and Jurak knew that, as he seemed to know far too many things.

Sweeping the advancing columns he could see their left flank, his right, reaching all the way to the walls of the still-burning city, while their right flank overlapped his left by at least a mile or more. Several thousand Bantag were mounted, ranging farther out into the open steppes. These troops were not black-uniformed, many wearing older style jerkits of brown leather. He caught a glimpse of a standard adorned with human skulls.

It was a Merki standard.

He lowered the field glasses, looking over at Ketswana, who nodded.

"The bastard is here, Hans. During the night he pulled to the west, organizing the survivors of yesterday's fight."

Hans raised the glasses again, but the standard had disappeared in a swirling cloud of dust.

There was nothing to anchor his own left flank on; it simply ended at this factory compound. It was obvious that within minutes after the start of the fight the mounted Bantag would be around his left and into the rear.

Moving with the advancing host he picked out half a dozen batteries of fieldpieces, and several dozen wagons, which were undoubtedly carrying mortars. Except for a few pathetic guns such as the one mounted next to where he stood, they had nothing to counter that. Worse yet, though, in the middle of the advancing line half a dozen land ironclads were approaching as well, while overhead several Bantag aerosteamers were climbing, passing over the infantry and coming straight for him.

As for his own aerosteamers, there was nothing left. The wreckage of his air fleet cluttered the field, bits of wicker framing, scorched canvas, and dark lumps of what had once been engines all that was left of the air corps of the Republic. He spared a quick thought for Jack, wondering if any of them had even made it back to Xi'an.

Turning his field glasses away, he scanned the position Ketswana, his few veterans, and the Chin had attempted to prepare during the night, and he struggled not to weep. The rail line, cutting straight as an arrow from west to east, heading toward the burning city, was the rally point. During the night track had been torn up, crossties and ballast piled up to form a rough palisades.

The dozen compounds that were strung along the track were the strong points; unfortunately, most of them had been severely damaged in the fighting. The powder works, several miles to his right, was still smoldering.

What made his heart freeze, though, was the humanity huddled and waiting. Along the palisades he could see the occasional glint of a rifle barrel or someone holding a precious revolver, but most were armed with nothing more than spears, clubs, pickaxes, iron poles, a few knives, or rocks. And there were hundreds of thousands of them.

Terrified children wailed, old men and women squatted on the ground, huddled in fear, their voices commingling into a mournful wail of forlorn terror. Looking to the south, he saw tens of thousands who, with the coming of dawn, were already quitting the fight, heading out across the open fields, moving through what had once been prosperous villages and hamlets but had long ago been abandoned as the Bantag drew off the populace for labor and for the pits. They were heading God knew where, for there was no place to hide, and once the mounted riders were into the rear they would be hunted down like frightened rabbits.

He knew with a sick heart that his coming had triggered the final apocalypse. After what had happened the day before, Jurak would not suffer a single person to live. They had killed Bantag, they had destroyed the factories that were the sole remaining reason for their existence. They would all have to die.

One of the Bantag aerosteamers lazily passed overhead, the pilot staying high enough to keep out of range of rifle fire. He banked over, making several tight turns. Hans looked back over the wall and saw a sea of upturned faces, hands pointing heavenward.

Now it was not the ships of the Yankees, coming like gods from the heavens, bringing a dream of freedom. It was the dreaded Horde, and as if to add emphasis, the bottom side of the machine was painted with the human-skull standard and there were cries of fear. Yet more Chin started to break away. There was a scattering of rifle shots, a few of his men posted to the rear, holding their weapons overhead, firing not at the ship but to scare the refugees back into the line. Some turned about, but he knew that once the real fighting started, there would most likely be a panic.

The machine turned one more time, nosed over, a puff of smoke ignited. A second later there was the almost lazy pop, pop, pop, of the slow-firing Bantag machine gun. Between his compound and the next one up the line the rounds hit, half a dozen Chin falling, panic beginning to break out. The machine finally leveled out and flew on toward the city.

Hans looked over at Ketswana.

"My God, this will be a massacre," Hans whispered.

Ketswana looked at him, eyes narrowed.

"If they realize they're all going to die anyhow, they'll fight. They have to."

"Fight? With what."

"Their bare hands if need be."

"Against rifles and artillery."

"Hans, they only have so many bullets, so many shells. They can kill a hundred thousand and still we'll outnumber them."

"My God, what have we become to talk like this?" Hans sighed.

"What they have made us become in order to survive."

A whispering flutter interrupted them. Hans crouched instinctively as the mortar round arced over head, crashed down in the middle of the foundry compound, and detonated, the explosion instantly followed by screams of pain.

Looking back over the wall he saw where several dozen mortars had been set up on a low rise, a thousand yards ahead. The advancing skirmishers were already past that position, still relentlessly advancing.

Puffs of smoke ignited all along the low ridge.

"Here it comes," Hans announced, his voice filled with resignation.

Seconds later the factory compound was blanketed with explosions.

Jurak, sitting uneasily astride his mount, said nothing to the subordinates around him. He could sense their bloodlust. This was no longer war; it was an act of extermination. The advance to the jump-off point had carried them across fields where the previous day pathetic bands of guards, fleeing the rioting, had been swept up and torn apart by the Chin mob. It had stirred him as well, and that thought troubled him. He had almost grown immune to the sight of the humans being slaughtered, devoured, but it was now evident that more than one of the Bantag dead had been mutilated after death, or, perhaps, while still alive. He wondered if the cattle had sunk to eating Bantag flesh, and the thought chilled him. Looking down at three aging guards who were sprawled in a ditch, he saw that the arms had been hacked off one, the limbs missing, and the sight of it set the hair on his back to bristling.

He wondered if this was indeed what the humans felt at the sight of the slaughter pits. Did it create that same visceral fear? Was that not as well, then, the reason for their fanatical resistance? He suddenly remembered how during the War of the False Pretender he had learned that the two most influential factors in a soldier's morale had nothing to do with generals, causes, and leadership. The first one was knowledge of how well you would be tended to if wounded. Second, what would happen if you were taken prisoner. On this world there was no such thing as prisoners, and, therefore, though the humans facing him were a disorganized rabble, still each of them might very well fight with the fury of despair.

He rode forward to join the mortar batteries deployed on the low ridge, their steady coughing thumps echoing across the battlefield. The factory compound on the left flank of the human line was smothered under a steady hail of exploding shells. Far to his own right he could see mounted units swinging wide, advance elements already across the tracks moving to get into the rear.

He had sent a courier over ordering them to hold and stand in place. The humans had to believe there was an escape route so that the panic might set in. If their line was flanked too soon, it might hem them in and cause further resistance.

There was a puff of smoke from atop the compound wall and seconds later a hissing roar as an artillery shell streaked past, the round startling him and causing his mount to rear.

"Disgusting way to die, Jurak."

He looked over his shoulder and saw Tamuka behind him, trailed by his small retinue.

Jurak said nothing. Tamuka reined in beside him, slumping forward, hand resting on the pommel of his mount.

He knew the Merki was watching, judging, figuring he could do better. Though enraged at him, now was not the time to express it.

"That is Hans over there," Tamuka finally announced.

"What makes you think that?"

"I can sense it. It would be like him to come back. The greatest mistake I made was turning him over to your Ha'ark. I should have kept him for my own pleasures. I could have made of him a moon feast that would have lasted for days."

"No. Your greatest folly was in losing as you did," Jurak snapped.

Tamuka turned, eyes filled with cold fury.

"Repeat that."

"You heard it right the first time. If you had done your job correctly as Qar Qarth, you would still have your Horde."

"I weakened them for you."

Another round screamed past, but they both ignored it.

"Weakened them? You aroused them. You murdered the rightful Qar Qarth and seized power for yourself and used the war as an excuse. You let your hate blind you. Now it is my people who must pay for this, perhaps all those of our race."

Tamuka reached to his side, scimitar flashing out. The gesture was met with the clicks of half a dozen rifles being raised, cocked, and pointed straight at him by Jurak's personal guards.

"You are not of this world," Tamuka hissed.

"Exactly! That is why I see more clearly than you. They"—and he pointed to the compound disappearing under the rain of artillery fire—"they are not of this world either. They brought change. Now I must, too. The old ways are dead forever, Tamuka. Even if we win this day, we lose. Can I rebuild all this in a month, even a year?

"No. I must slaughter every human here for their own folly of believing in freedom. With luck, back at the front their political will shall collapse and we can attack, finishing it. But if so, I fear this is nothing more than a pyre for both our races."

Even as he spoke the advancing phalanx of infantry started to pass, breaking formation to maneuver around the wagons and caissons of the mortar batteries.

The warriors were well-trained veterans, moving with casual ease, rifles poised, bayonet-tipped, but most still carried their traditional scimitars strapped to their hips. When the real killing started that would be the weapon of choice. They seemed lighthearted, eager for the fray, unlike the weary, exhausted warriors he had watched being shoved into the inferno at Roum. This was sport to them, almost like the field exercises Ha'ark would hold when a Chin town would be singled out and stormed just to give the warriors a taste of modern combat.

The skirmishers far ahead were already engaged, firing, advancing slowly. Several of them were down, a spattering of fire opening from the Chin position. To his left the traditional signalers of the hordes, the giant nargas trumpets and kettledrums were coming up, the deep rumble of the horns and heartbeat thump of the drums setting his hair on end.

He looked back over at Tamuka.

"If you are so eager for the kill, why not ride forward and join in?" Jurak asked.

Tamuka looked at him angrily.

"And you shall stay here?"

"I am the Qar Qarth. This is a modern battle."

Tamuka snarled. Nodding to his renegade followers, he viciously spurred his mount and galloped off.

Jurak, glad to be rid of his presence, dismounted, tossing the reins of his horse to one of his guards. The day was already hot, made worse by the grass fires ignited by bursting shells, the pall of smoke hanging over the entire front.

After I win here, then what? he wondered.

The advancing column slowed, reaching the skirmish lines forward. Tearing volleys started to ripple up and down the length of the front as twenty thousand warriors, the elite of two umens, began to fire into the hundreds of thousands of Chin huddled behind the railroad embankment. The day was turning into a slaughter.

"You've got your mission," Vincent shouted. "I want their ironclads kept back from this square. If they can bring us under fire, they'll break us up."

Gregory, sitting atop his machine, grinned and nodded.

Saluting, he raised a clenched fist, waved it over his head, and pointed due east, toward the advancing column of Bantag ironclads.

Slipping down inside the turret, he buttoned the hatch shut, machines lined up to either side of him already lurching forward. Vincent, trying to ignore the pain, mounted a horse held by an orderly and swung it around, galloped back down the sloping hill and into the fortified camp of 3rd Corps.

The battle was about to explode. After years of fighting the hordes he could sense the building tension. They were the bait, the focal point to divert Jurak. And now the bill was coming due.

The Horde completely encircled their position, but it was

easy enough to see that most of their strength, at least four umens, were poised to the north, though there were more than enough of them ringing the other three sides of the square to keep his forces pinned down. The ironclads held the rise to the east, but he still had to keep troops along that side, in case their infantry or mounted units swarmed in behind Gregory and attacked.

When it finally hit there were no preliminaries, no softening-up bombardment. They knew that if the ironclad battle should go against them, any hope of exacting vengeance was lost. Even if they did win the ironclad fight, the artillery well dug in at the four corners of the square, and in reserve at the center, would chew the precious machines apart. They were going to try it in one sharp push.

From a mile out he saw them emerging out of the cloud of dust kicked up by the tens of thousands of horses. It was a solid wall of Bantag, dismounted, advancing with long-legged strides.

His heart swelled at the sight of them. It was like the old days once again, and to his own amazement he felt a surge of emotion. This is the way they looked before Suzdal, on the Potomac Front, and at Hispania. From all that the older veterans told him, it was the same at Cold Harbor, Gettysburg, Fredericksburg, and Antietam. A full frontal assault, thrown in regardless of loss.

A murmur swept through the men along the northern flank of the square. Some of them stood up, ignoring the bursting of mortar shells raining down. A ripple of excitement swept up and down the line. Young captains scurried back and forth, carrying teams hurried back to supply wagons, bringing up extra boxes of ammunition. Sergeants paced behind the firing line, a division commander, swept up by the moment, jumped his horse over the sod earthwork embankment and galloped down his line, waving his hat, men breaking into cheers at his display of foolish bravado.

"Damn if it isn't like Pickett's Charge!"

It was Stan, reining up beside him, his voice shrill with excitement.

Vincent said nothing, raising his field glasses, studying the enemy advance. Red umen standards were at the fore, a few of their commanders mounted. At regular intervals down the line human-skull totems for regiments of a thousand were held aloft, surrounded by towering bulky warriors armed with rifles. The rest carried the powerful war bows of two hundred pounds pull, arrows already notched.

Batteries at the northeastern and northwestern flanks opened up on the advancing enemy, case shot burst over the lines, but that was merely an annoyance. A standard of a thousand went down, caught by a direct burst, then came up again. The range was down to less than a thousand yards, then nine hundred, then eight hundred.

Sergeants along his own lines were shouting orders, telling the men to lever their sights up to full elevation. There was a scattering of shots, the sniper company armed with Whitworths and the new long-barreled Sharps heavy rifles. Some of the men armed with lighter guns opened and were soundly cursed by their officers.

Good. Wait until four hundred yards. It was a still morning, the smoke would cling, killing visibility. Better to wait.

The range was at six hundred, and then they stopped.

There was an eerie moment of silence, and then he heard the chanting, the weird spine-chilling cries. Harsh, guttural words. He had seen it before, Horde riders who knew they were going to their deaths, and before the charge made this final gesture to their enemies and their gods . . . the chanting of the names of their clans, their ancestors, and their own names and battle honors.

The strange rumbling cries rolled across the steppes, joined by the nargas and war drums, a thunderous roar. Bantag stamped their feet to the rhythm of the chant, the ground shaking. The effect was hypnotic, the chant rising to a crescendo, dropping off, rising even higher.

Again men were standing up, watching, awestruck. For a brief moment all hatred died in Vincent's heart. There was almost an admiration for such insane raw courage. Individual Bantag began to step out of the line, unsheathing scimitars, many of them drawing the razor-sharp blades across their own forearms, then holding the blood-soaked steel up again, their individual chants drowned out by the thunderous roar.

Along his own line he could hear the men mustering a response, the surreal sound of the "Battle Hymn of the Republic" sung in Rus. All this was counterpointed by the continual crump of mortar shells exploding, artillery thundering out case shot, and then, off to his right, a mile to the east of the square, the ever-increasing roar of the iron-clad battle.

He looked heavenward. The air machines were up, nearly twenty of them. They were holding back, flying high, waiting most likely for the square to break apart before swooping in. He caught a glimpse of just two Hornets dropping like stooping falcons, tearing into the enemy machines. He wondered where the hell the rest of the Hornets were.

The roaring chant dropped down to a deep growling bass, and then in a matter of seconds swirled up to a high shrieking crescendo . . . "Bantag hus!, Bantag hus! Bantag hus!"

Umen standards held aloft twirled about in tight circles. Mounted commanders rode out ahead of the line, urging their horses into a slow canter, drawing scimitars. As if controlled by a single hand twenty thousand bows were slung over the shoulder, then twenty thousand scimitars were drawn and held heavenward, catching the morning sun. A collective gasp went through his lines.

"My God, they're going to charge straight in!" Stan cried.

Vincent turned to a courier.

"I want the reserve brigade in the center deployed out now!" Vincent shouted.

The boy saluted and galloped off. Vincent grabbed another messenger and sent him to the commander on the east flank of the square, telling him to get ready to shift half his men to the north and sent yet another galloping with the same order to the west side.

Even as the three couriers raced off, the red banners fluttered down, pointing straight at the center of his line. A mad, howling roar erupted. There was no stepping off at a slow steady march, no subtle maneuvering.

With a mad passionate scream twenty thousand Bantag flung themselves forward at the run, their giant strides consuming the distance between the opposing lines at a frightening pace.

"At four hundred yards volley fire present!" the cry echoed along his own line.

Men hunkered down behind the sod breastworks, hammers clicking back, fingers curling around triggers.

The charge swept across the first hundred yards in less than twenty seconds, Vincent estimated, and they were still picking up speed, the bravest and fleetest moving to the fore. Mounted commanders, carried away by the mad frenzy, were far ahead, some nearly half the distance to the line.

"Glorious!" Stan cried.

Startled, Vincent looked over at his old comrade, but something was stirring in him as well. He remembered many a night so long ago back on Earth, hearing the old veterans speak with awe, describing the rebel charges sweeping toward Seminary Ridge and across the Cornfield at Antietam. My God, this is what it must have looked like, sheer insane courage unleashed in a wild, all-consuming explosion.

"Take aim." The cry echoed up and down the line from a hundred sergeants and officers. "Aim low, boys, aim low!"

Vincent held his breath.

"Fire!"

The volley ignited in the center of the line and within a couple of seconds swept down the flanks.

A billowing white cloud exploded, temporarily blinding Vincent. There was the collective metallic ring of thousands of breeches levering open, shell casings ejecting, fresh rounds sliding in, breeches slamming shut, officers and sergeants roaring to lever sights down to three hundred yards.

Vincent felt a swelling of pride. These were veterans. There was no panic, just a steady professional pace.

Those who were quickest waited, bracing their barrels on the embankment.

"Take aim!"

Individual companies and regiments fired, sheets of flame swirling out. Already the dry grass in front of the works was igniting, puffs of thick white flames clinging to the ground. In the brief instant before the smoke from the second volley shut down all vision forward he saw the deadly effect of the volley, scores of Bantag going down, yet it barely stilled the pace of the mad charge, as the wave leapt over the fallen and pressed in.

A jarring concussion swept the square, a caisson exploding in the center of the position, the mortar round detonating several hundred pounds of shot and shell, sending a fireball a hundred feet into the air.

He caught a glimpse of the battery anchoring the corner to his right, the crew feverishly cranking the elevation screw, even as their companions tore breeches open, swabbed out bores, and slammed in loads of canister.

"Independent fire at will!"

The command echoed above the cacophonous thunder, men cheering as they were released from the constraints of waiting and within seconds the measured heavy volleys were replaced by a continual rattle.

There was just enough of a breeze that the curtains of smoke lifted so that the shadowy wall of the advancing charge was visible. They were down to less than two hundred yards and still coming at a terrifying pace.

They were going to come straight in.

Stan broke away from Vincent, spurring his mount forward, drawing his revolver.

Vincent felt pulled in as well.

No, here, stay here. He looked to his left, his guidon bearer was stock-still, sitting tall in the saddle, but the boy's jaw was actually hanging open in shocked amazement.

Suddenly from out of the smoke a lone rider emerged, blood streaming from half a dozen wounds, his face a pulp, dead but still charging, the horse in its mad frenzy actually leaping the earthen stockade before going down under a hail of bullets. Another rider shot out of the smoke, this one still alive. With his hands off the reins, both arms extended wide, a scimitar in his right hand, his horse leapt over the barricade. The rider's wild shriek of battle frenzy sounded above the roar of battle. He seemed to hang in midair, men recoiling back as if he was a mad god.

The horse touched down, the rider coming straight for Vincent. He drew his own revolver, started to raise it, and then a volley riddled the berserker. He tumbled from his horse, sprawled faceup on the ground, the horse going down beside him.

Magnificent courage, Vincent thought.

Then he noticed it, a dark cloud rising up from beyond the pall of smoke. An arrow volley. It was the old Horde tactic of bringing up mounted fire support behind a charging line. In the smoke and confusion forward he could barely see them, towering high above the line that was still charging forward and now less than a hundred yards away.

Few of the men actually saw, so intent were they on pouring in the fire. Thousands of arrows arced down, so that in an instant it looked as if thousands of young feathered saplings had sprouted from the earth. The volley was short, but enough arrows slammed into the lines to cause a startled cry to go up as men fell, clutching pierced arms, legs, or simply collapsed.

Vincent turned to yet another messenger, shouting for him to find the commander for the four batteries of mortars and tell him to set the range at two hundred yards and pour it on.

Another volley rose up and then another, this one longer. The bastards were sweeping high, sending the deadly shafts into the center of the square. At nearly the same instant the charge emerged out of the billowing smoke, a solid wall of Bantag, running straight in.

Wild cries went up, commanders urging their men to stand. Directly in front of Vincent, a regimental commander holding the flag of the 15th Suzdal and showing remarkable poise, had firm control of his unit, having ordered his men to cease fire and wait. With the wall of Bantag less than thirty yards away the command was given to present and take aim.

The Bantag charge barely hesitated. At ten yards the volley of four hundred rifles erupted. It struck with such force that the front ranks of the Bantag seemed to have run into a wall, collapsing, thrashing, some picked up bodily and flung backwards into those behind them.

He could actually hear the volley hit, bullets smacking into bodies, swords, accoutrements, helmets, bows . . . equipment, parts of bodies, and blood actually showered up and backwards. As one the regiment slammed open breeches, slapping cartridges in. A few Bantag struggled through the confusion and flung themselves up and over the battlement, swords flashing. Vincent saw a human head tumbling into the air. Another soldier was lifted into the air, scimitar driven through his body to the hilt, the Bantag shrieking in triumph. A lieutenant leapt forward, driving his own blade up into the throat of the warrior.

More Bantag surged forward, the next volley cutting

them down at ten paces. The flanks of the 15th started to cave in as the regiments to either side were pushed back from the embankment, curving inward like a drawn bow. A dark wall of Bantag surged over the top of the battlement, swords flashing. Men still down behind the embankment slashed upward with their bayonets, stabbing their towering opponents in the legs, groin, and stomach. Scimitars rose and fell, blood splashing.

A reserve regiment to Vincent's left stormed forward, dozens of men falling as hundreds of arrows soared down from straight overhead.

The batteries in the corners and dug in at the middle of the line were anchor points, the gunners all having gone over to double canister, each gun discharging a hundred iron balls at waist-high level every twenty seconds.

To the left of the 15th and the center battery the entire line started to peel back, men stumbling out of the fight, the insane charge pushing in.

Vincent caught a glimpse of Stan in the middle of the fray, still mounted, revolver out, firing into the host as reserves from the west flank stormed in, counterattacking. Toward the center of the square, men were upending empty supply wagons to form a barricade while the battery in the center, now unlimbered, wheeled about in preparation to fire, but so thick was the tangled press of Bantag and humans that they didn't dare shoot.

A tearing volley erupted behind Vincent, and, looking over his shoulder, he saw that they were charging against the south side of the square as well, this one a combined mounted and dismounted assault. An orderly to Vincent's right was lifted out of his saddle and collapsed, caught in the back by a rifle ball. Vincent could see puffs of smoke from the south . . . *so that's where they are committing their rifle-armed troops.*

Bantag skirmishers by the hundreds were pressing in on the south side, and though his own men had the advantage of earthworks, they advanced relentlessly, falling down into the knee-high grass, popping up to shoot, then disappearing again.

Then the final blow came in. Overhead the first of the Bantag air machines started into a steep dive, the slow-firing machine gun thumping, bullets stitching into the center of the encampment.

It was now time to unleash his one reserve for this, and the two specially equipped ironclads parked in the center of the square went into action. The canvas tops of the converted machines were pulled back, revealing the open center and the twin Gatling guns positioned to fire straight up. The gunners inside the two machines waited, letting the Bantag machines get well in range, then opened up.

Tracer rounds soared heavenward from the center of the beleaguered square. Within seconds both gunners had the range, rounds tearing into the first of the machines, which instantly ignited. The gunners shifted targets to the second machine, then the third and fourth in line.

One after another Bantag airships exploded, the pilots of the other airships breaking off the attack in sharp, banking turns. One of them banked over so sharply that the machine hung vertical on its side, seemed to hover, then slowly rolled over on its back and went straight in.

Wreckage rained down on the square, parts of burning ships, wings, howling engines, causing dozens of casualties, but the sight of the feared Bantag air fleet shattered so completely in a matter of seconds heartened the beleaguered defenders, a ragged cheer erupting from the square.

But the position was starting to collapse in spite of the victory overhead. The 15th Suzdal was all but surrounded, forming its own small square, men backing up, rear ranks firing, front ranks standing with poised bayonets to impale any who broke through. Hundreds of Bantag were swarming in on Vincent's right, a wild confused melee swirling about not fifty yards away. Arrows by the thousands continued to rain down, now catching as many Bantag as humans, sowing confusion on both sides.

As for the ironclad battle to the east, it was impossible to see anything because of the confusion and smoke.

Vincent heard a shouted warning. It was his guidon bearer, arrow buried in his leg, but still astride his horse, screaming, pointing, with his free hand.

Around the edge of the 15th Suzdal several score of Bantag, led by what he assumed to be a umen commander, who miraculously was still mounted, were coming straight at them.

Vincent leveled his revolver and deliberately fired. Still they came on.

He turned his mount; the charge pressed in. A Bantag, scimitar held high overhead with both hands, charged straight at him. He caught the warrior in the face with his next to last round. Letting go of the blade it tumbled end over head, flashing past Vincent's face. Another Bantag, this one on foot, came in low, aiming to hamstring Vincent's horse. He dropped that one, raised his revolver to fire at the umen commander, and clicked on an empty cylinder.

The commander, roaring in wild triumph, blood streaming from wounds to the face and chest, slash viciously, Vincent ducked low, the blade whistling past his ears. Their mounts collided, nearly unhorsing Vincent. He reeled back, throwing his revolver aside, clumsily trying to draw his own sword but barely getting it out in time to parry the next blow, which sent a numbing shock through his arm.

He caught a glimpse of his guidon bearer, sword plunged through his chest, reeling in the saddle, vainly clutching the guidon as dark eager hands reached up to grab it.

The umen commander easily recovered from the parry and started a backhanded swipe. Vincent tried to turn, awkwardly raising his numbed arm and blade to block the blow.

A staccato roar ignited, sweeping past Vincent, hot tracers stitching into the commander. There was a moment when they gazed into each other's eyes, the Bantag suddenly looking infinitely old and weary, cheated at the last second of the prize he had so bravely and now so vainly sought. He tumbled over backwards and a loud cry rose up from those around him, a cry of anguish and of fear as one of the two land ironclads that had so completely devastated the air attack now clattered forward, twin Gatlings depressed to fire into the charge.

Tracer rounds tore across the flank of the 15th, two, three, four heavy .58 caliber bullets striking each warrior. Within seconds the breakthrough disintegrated and receded over the wall.

The machine, wheels churning up the thick sod, creaked past Vincent, still firing. He tried to block out the guttural screams of the Bantag wounded as the heavy iron wheels rolled over them, crushing their still-twitching bodies into the ground.

A long burst of fire swept along the battlement, dropping the charge that was still breaking in. A cheer went up from the 15th, and the counterattack was on as men turned and pushed forward with the bayonet. Again it was the old trade-off, the massive size and strength of the Bantag, offset by the smaller but far more nimble humans, who could dodge the heavy blows, rush in, and slash upward with the bayonet.

Gradually the embankment was regained, the ground for a hundred yards inside the square paved with the dead, wounded, and dying. As the ironclad gained the embankment it turned its fire outward, slashing into the mounted archers providing fire support, and within seconds created havoc.

Bantag were fleeing, stumbling back out of the square; knots of defiant survivors trapped inside grimly traded their lives. Those who were wounded in a final gesture of contempt struggled to cut their own throats rather than suffer the agony of death at the hands of the humans.

Vincent, still numbed from the brief sword fight, rode up to the embankment. The attack was breaking apart, broken fragments falling back like a wave shattered by a rock-bound coast.

"Did you see 'em, did you see 'em!"

It was Stan, blood streaming from a saber slash to his left cheek. He was shouting hysterically, aiming his revolver, squeezing the trigger. Its hammer fell on empty cylinders and yet he was still trying to shoot.

Rifle fire struck into the mounted units as the last of the dismounted assault fell back. Horses reared up, falling, the volume of arrow fire dwindled, then they reined about, retreating, joined by the surviving infantry.

Vincent gazed about in numbed awe. The ground was carpeted black with Bantags. The charge had been an annihilation. Yet as he surveyed his own line he saw that he had received a terrible blow as well. Well over a thousand, maybe two thousand or more of his own men were down, their bodies tangled in with the Bantag along the battlement line and far into the center of the square.

The center battery had been completely overrun, its entire crew annihilated in hand-to-hand fighting, an infantry officer was already at work, shouting for his men to stack their rifles and clear the guns. Walking wounded were heading back into the center of the square, stretcher-bearers were already at work, and the cries and shrieks from the hospital area could be heard throughout the square.

"Damn. We beat 'em, we beat 'em," Stan cried in English. "Like Fredericksburg, except it was us behind the wall this time."

Vincent said nothing, his gaze turning back to the east, where the roar of the ironclad battle rumbled. A machine, one of Gregory's, ignited in a fireball, turret blowing off and rising straight up as the kerosene and ammunition inside blew.

Burning machines, both human and Bantag, littered the next ridge as both sides fought for possession of the high ground. Hundreds of Bantag infantry were filtering into the flanks of the battle outside the square. He saw several Bantag rocket teams maneuvering, running through the grass, trying to get close enough for a kill.

"We got 'em by the tail and really twisted it," Stan gasped.

Vincent wearily shook his head. Raising his field glasses, he looked straight ahead. The broken charge was falling back to get out of range, but there were still thousands of them. If they had sent three umens instead of two into the infantry assault, he suspected they most likely would have broken clean through.

Looking to the west and around to the south, he could see signal pennants flying, dust swirling up, mounted warriors by the thousands moving. They could harass from the south, but the steep bluff along that side was too good a position to take by storm. No, they were shifting around.

"Stan," Vincent snapped, "get your division commanders here now. They're coming back, and we don't have much time."

Stan, calming at last from his battle frenzy, looked around at the wreckage of his corps and finally nodded toward the west.

"That way, the ground is still clear."

"We don't have much time."

Time. He looked back to the east at the ironclad fight. It was slowly dragging out. The Bantag not closing for the kill, Gregory wisely not going too far in for fear of being overwhelmed by the infantry. If this kept up, the infantry would be annihilated and then the ironclad battle would no longer matter.

He gazed at the sun, which was now bloodred from the battle smoke. It seemed as if it hung motionless in the morning sky.

Chapter Fourteen

Hans looked overhead to the red sun that seemed to hang motionless in the noonday sky.

The compound below him was a shambles, packed wall to wall with the wounded and terrified refugees. Mortar shells fell inside with terrifying regularity, and there was nothing he could do to stop it. The one artillery piece had fallen silent, shells exhausted, the survivors of its crew reduced to prying loose bricks from the wall and hurling them as the Bantag surged outside the wall. All along the railroad embankment the Chin, after hours of insane resistance, were falling back, retreating into the ruins of the factory compounds lining the rail line. In the fields to the south, tens of thousands of refugees were stumbling away, desperately trying to escape. Mounted units of Bantag rode back and forth, cornering and slaying them.

Hans knew it was hopeless. The compound could not hold much longer. The only thing that was slowing the Bantag was the sheer number of people they had to slay. Yet they were paying as well. Their first assault, which had come on with such self-assured cockiness, had stormed up over the embankment and then been swarmed under as tens of thousands of terrified Chin, desperate when they realized they were cornered by cavalry closing in from behind, turned and in a spontaneous surge rushed forward, crushing the Bantag by sheer weight of numbers.

That had given him several thousand more rifles and ammunition, enough that when the second charge came, the single volley at a range of less than a dozen paces so that his inexperienced riflemen couldn't miss, dropped hundreds more.

Jurak had then pulled back. Letting firepower, his unrelenting artillery and aimed rifle from several hundred yards out, do the deed. The Chin, defenseless against such an onslaught, had held through midmorning, but now were finally beginning to melt away.

Risking the enemy fire, Hans looked up over the east wall back toward Huan. Rumors had come that tens of thousands of survivors, still huddled in the south end of the burning city, were pouring out, enveloping the flank of the enemy, but it was impossible to see what was occurring there.

Nargas sounded, and seconds later there was a ragged cheer. Leaning over the wall he saw the Bantag infantry pulling back.

Ketswana, eyes wide with battle frenzy, trailed by his two surviving Zulus, came up to Hans's side and pulled him back down from the exposed position.

"They're retreating!" Ketswana cried.

Hans, exhausted, absently rubbed his left arm and nodded.

"You know why?"

"Artillery; he's shifting his artillery over here, the same treatment as the rifle works."

The next compound up the line had been swarmed under after the Bantag rolled a dozen guns up to within a hundred yards and blasted a hole through the wall.

Hans stood back up and saw the two batteries riding into position out in the middle of the field where the airships had landed. Even as he watched, the first of the guns unlimbered, its crew swinging it about, aiming it straight at him. Other guns fell into position.

They were so close he could see the gunners opening their caissons, pulling out shot and powder bags. Hans rested his carbine on the battlement wall, took careful aim, and squeezed, dropping what he suspected was the battery commander. It barely slowed the crew.

He fumbled in his cartridge box. Only one round left.

One final round, and as he chambered it he knew what that had to be saved for.

The first gun fired, the shock of the solid bolt hitting the wall beneath his feet nearly knocking him off-balance. The other guns opened, bolt after bolt slamming into the wall beneath them. In less than five minutes the first round cracked clean through the brick barrier, the spent bolt careening into the foundry. The platform they were on swayed, a huge crack in the wall opening up from the ground all the way to the top.

"Down!"

Hans followed the rush as they abandoned their position, swarming down the ramp. More bolts slammed into the building, the vast room echoing with shrieks of terror as thousands of Chin, with no place to hide, huddled on the ground; the few with weapons clustered behind furnaces, upended cauldrons, piles of coke, slag, and iron ore.

"They'll charge as soon as the artillery stops firing! So get ready," Ketswana roared, trying desperately to be heard. Few paid attention.

Ketswana unholstered a revolver, opened the barrel, dropped the empty cylinder, and, reaching into his haversack, pulled out a loaded cylinder and clicked it in. He looked over at Hans.

"Figured to save the last six rounds."

"Got one for myself," Hans said, trying to smile as he patted his carbine.

"So we have come full circle." Ketswana sighed. "Until you gave me hope I always figured I'd die here."

Hans looked around at the terrified mob, remembering all too painfully the same sight of not much more than a year ago, when he had fought his way through this same building to gain the tunnel and escape, leaving thousands of others to die. Perhaps this was atonement.

"At least we smashed this place," Hans announced grimly. "Smashed the whole damn place from here to Huan and beyond. Took their port of Xi'an as well and smashed that up good and proper. It'll be months, a year or more, before they can even think of recovering."

The artillery fire slackened and stopped. The cries from within the building hushed. Horrified, Hans saw that some of the Chin were already making their final choice, more than one turning a blade upon themselves or loved ones rather than endure the horror of the final butchering.

The nargas sounded the charge.

"Damn Tamuka," Jurak roared. "Damn him. I wanted the flank kept back, give them room to run, let them break."

Jurak stalked back and forth, angrily shouting at no one in particular. He knew he should have slain Tamuka. It was undoubtedly he who urged the charge forward that had cornered the Chin into a fight. He wondered if Zartak had somehow foreseen this, and wished that his old friend was here now.

The losses had been appalling. Nearly half his warriors were down, most of them dead, swarmed under in the slaughter. Now word had come that Chin by the tens of thousands were coming up from beyond Huan and out of what was left of the burning city. In another hour they'd be into his flank, forcing him to disengage. He had already passed a signal all the way up to Nippon to bring down yet another two umens. But every train available had been used to bring the forces he now had. It would take at least two days, perhaps three, to bring up the reserves. As for the vast encampments to the south, he had dispatched a flyer to them. The females, cubs, and old ones had to be prepared to defend themselves, and that was his true concern. A hundred thousand yurts with nowhere to go farther south because of the mountains and jungles. If he broke off the fight, if he allowed those still dug in along the line a breathing space, they'd rally the hundreds of thousands of Chin still alive and it would be massacre if they turned south. He had to kill the core of resistance now . . . or lose the war.

The wall of the factory finally collapsed under the incessant pounding. That, at least, was a relief. His battery commander before being killed by a sniper had already informed him that they were digging dangerously into their reserves of ammunition. A ragged cheer erupted from the warriors who had been ordered back, and they surged forward again, closing in for the kill. Soon it would be finished.

Somehow word had spread into his army that it was the legendary Hans who was leading this fight. A Chin demigod, a legend returned to liberate. And something now told him that directly ahead was where Hans was cornered. He had already passed the word to his warriors that if Hans could indeed be captured and brought to him alive, the warrior would be promoted to command of a thousand.

It wasn't that he wanted Hans to die in agony as Tamuka muttered about. True, Hans would have to die, and the

Chin had to see him die to crush their hope of resistance forever. And then the Chin would have to die as well.

Hans would have to die, but first he wished to speak to him. Ha'ark had had that privilege a number of times. He had but observed him from a distance. If one was to understand Keane, Hans was the teacher. He was, as well, a consummate foe, a warrior worthy of respect for what he had accomplished, escaping, leading the flanking attack that finished the campaign in front of Roum, and now this.

So he would feast him once and talk long into the night. Perhaps he would learn something from him, perhaps not, but still he wanted that moment, and then with the coming of the following dawn he would offer him the knife or the gun so that he could finish it with his own hand. Then, after the Chin were brought forth to see the body, he would burn and scatter his ashes to the wind out of respect.

The charge reached the wall and within seconds gained the entryway, a desperate hand-to-hand struggle erupting in the piled-up rubble.

And then he saw them.

A commander of a thousand had just ridden up to ask for orders and his gaze, locked on Jurak, drifted, looking past him, eyes going wide. Raising a hand, he pointed.

Jurak turned and looked. For a moment he refused to believe, and then the enemy aerosteamers began to fire.

Hans, standing by Ketswana's side, waited just inside the shattered wall. The first of the Bantag were up and over the barrier, crouched low against a hail of thrown bricks and chunks of iron ore. They slashed into the defenders, the killing frenzy upon them. Several, looking in his direction, shouted to each other and came on, as if recognizing him.

Instinct took hold and he raised his carbine, aiming straight at the chest of the nearest one, and fired, dropping him. He heard a revolver let go, several rounds, dropping the next two.

Ketswana was by his side.

"Two rounds left," his friend cried, looking at him questioningly.

Hans smiled.

*   *   *

Skimming the ground, Jack Petracci bore straight in, aiming directly at the tall standard adorned with horse tails and human skulls. An umen commander at least, perhaps even Jurak, he thought grimly.

There was no need to tell his copilot to open fire. Crouched behind the steam-powered Gatling in the nose, his copilot fired the forward weapon. A steady stream of bullets stitched into the low ridge, slicing through a mortar battery, walking up along the hillside, the standard-bearer collapsing.

Continuing to fire, the gunner shifted aim, slashing into the open-order columns of Bantag infantry. As they raced past the first compound, which was blanketed with smoke and fire, he saw a charging column gaining a shattered wall. Looking down from above, he saw the thousands huddled inside and knew what was about to happen.

Hoping that the other aerosteamers were not following too closely and would continue to press toward Huan, he banked his Eagle hard over, shouting to his top gunner to bring the column under fire as they turned.

Swinging about to the south, he spared a quick glance back to the west. Twenty Hornets, flying nearly wingtip to wingtip, were coming straight in, joined as well by the four surviving Eagles. The arrival of the Hornets in Xi'an just before dawn had left him stunned. The Eagle he had sent back to Tyre had actually survived and touched down. The pilots of the Hornets clamored to be released, to go up and save Jack and Hans. The fact that they had actually made the audacious jump from Vincent's position all the way to Xi'an, burning nearly every ounce of fuel they had to make it, had filed him with awe. As it was, nearly half of them had been lost in transit. Never had he known such pride in his command as he did at that moment.

The twenty Hornets and four Eagles were all that was left of a force of over eighty that existed but a week before. From the looks of what was going on below, once they expended their ammunition there would be no place left to land. He might be able to get back to Xi'an, but with the increasing wind out of the west the Hornets were doomed. Yet still they came on, sweeping low over the ground.

Behind them, half a dozen miles back, he could still see

the eight trains. He had almost strafed them coming in until he spotted a makeshift flag of the Republic fluttering from each of the locomotives, and then realized that the thousands packed aboard the flatcars were in fact Chin. What they proposed to do was beyond him.

He bore straight in at the compound, top and forward gunners both firing continual blasts of Gatling rounds into the attacking column. Within seconds the enemy began to dissolve, looking up in panic, turning aside, and running.

As he winged up over the compound he wagged his wings, hoping all below would see the stars of the Republic painted on the bottom of his ship. And in spite of the noise of battle, he could hear the cheers.

Banking hard up to the left, he winged over sharply, turning to head straight toward the artillery batteries that had been pounding the makeshift fortress only minutes before. Gatling fire from a Hornet flying across his own path at a right angle slashed into the position, decimating the crews. As the Hornet passed he added his own fire into the balance. A caisson blew, and he winged over yet again to avoid the exploding mushroom cloud.

He was behind the advance line of Hornets, who now that they were into the fight had poured on full throttle and were quickly surging ahead at nearly a mile a minute.

Smoke poured out from underneath as twenty Gatlings fired, sweeping the Bantag lines, tearing them to shreds. The enemy quite simply broke apart from this unexpected pounding from above. Chin started to pour out from the beleaguered compounds, racing forward, a human wave of tens of thousands, moving like a swarm of locusts.

He circled back around once more to check on the first compound. But the countercharge was already up and over the broken wall, some of the Chin were nearly into the Bantag artillery positions.

And then he spotted him, a ragged guidon, several Zulus around him standing out in dark contrast to the surrounding Chin.

And then he saw him fall.

Jurak stood motionless as the burst of fire swept past him, knocking over his standard-bearer, and he wished at that instant that it would take him as well, ending this horrible burden forever.

The rounds stitched past, clumps of sod kicked up in his face, then the machine passed. Another one soared by, skimming the ground so close he could look straight into the cab and see the human pilot.

Around him was chaos. A mortar battery annihilated, a caisson erupting in a fireball. He could see his warriors falling back, not giving ground doggedly but running, frightened of the mob, the tens of thousands of Chin pouring out from their beleaguered positions sweeping all before them.

Looking back to the west he saw the plumes of smoke, and for a brief instant there was a renewed flash of hope, but he knew in his heart that it had to be Chin coming up from Xi'an. If it had been his own warriors, the Yankee aerosteamers would have strafed them.

At that instant he knew that he had lost a war.

Warriors raced past him in panic, and press of the crowd forced his horse to turn. Suddenly his mount reared, screaming in pain. Never a trained horseman, he panicked, sawing on the reins rather than letting go and jumping off. The horse went down heavily on its side, pinning him.

Cursing, he gasped for breath, trying to pull himself free and then was shocked by the explosion of pain from his broken ankle, which was twisted in the stirrup.

Warriors continued to run past, not noticing him. Suddenly there was a shadow, and looking up he saw an emaciated Chin standing above him, holding a broken rifle tipped with a bayonet. The Chin gazed down at him, eyes wide with lust and hate. He raised the weapon up. Jurak looked straight at him, not resisting, at the moment not caring.

"No!"

A man, a black man, grabbed the Chin by the shoulder, pulling him back.

Jack's aerosteamer had barely rolled to a stop next to the wreckage of the factory compound when he was already out. He had passed over once more to check, and what he had seen convinced him something was wrong and caused him to venture the landing. Running across the field he made his way through the press of advancing Chin.

He spotted Ketswana, kneeling by the side of an artillery piece, and he pushed his way forward.

They had Hans sitting up, jacket torn open. No blood, but his features were deathly pale, beads of cold sweat on his forehead. Ketswana, obviously frightened, was holding his hands.

Jack burst through the crowd, cursing at them to move aside. He knelt by Ketswana's side and to his relief saw that Hans's eyes were open, though dull.

"What happened?" Jack cried.

"We thought it was finished," Ketswana whispered, "I had two rounds left, I was saving one for him, one for me, and then you soared over us. Never have I seen him smile like that, and laugh, the first time in so long he laughed from the depths of his soul.

"We followed the charge out. He had just spotted Jurak, pointing him out, when suddenly he stopped, grasping his chest and fell."

Ketswana lowered his head, a sob wracking him.

"Still here, my friend," Hans whispered.

Hans stirred, life coming back into his eyes.

"Jack, that you?" he spoke in English, the words slightly slurred.

"Here, Hans. I couldn't leave you out here. A lot's happened, Hans. Word reached Tyre last night that the government wanted an armistice. The damn stupid Hornet pilots decided on their own to fuel up and see if they could reach Xi'an. They touched down just after dawn. I was getting set to come back here anyhow, and they wanted to come along."

"You broke them with that."

"No, you did. We just mopped up."

Hans chuckled softly, then was silent for a moment, obviously wracked by another seizure of pain.

"Damn, hurts worse than getting shot."

"What's wrong, Hans?"

"I think the old heart finally decided to give it up."

Jack tried to force a smile.

"Hell, if that's all it is, we'll have you up and around in no time."

Hans looked up at him, his silent gaze frightening Jack. There was a stir behind Jack, a confusion of angry voices.

Ketswana stood up to see what was going on, then barked out a sharp command. Jack saw several of Ketswana's men dragging a Bantag toward them. He instantly suspected who he was, the gold trim to the uniform, the gilting on the bent horns of the war helmet.

"Hans, is that him?"

Hans stirred again.

"You got him?"

"I think so."

"Help me up. Don't let him see me like this."

Ketswana grabbed several Chin, placing them around Hans, blocking the view.

Jack was down by his side.

"You need rest. Don't move."

Hans smiled.

"Son, I've been in this war for how long now? I'm not going to miss the final act. Now button up my jacket for me."

Jack didn't move for a moment.

"Do it now, son," he gasped through clenched teeth.

Jack let his hand rest on the narrow chest. It was the chest of an old man who had been filled with unstoppable strength in his youth but was now sunken, flesh sagging, as if ready to begin the final breaking away. The skin felt cold, clammy, and though not a doctor, he could tell there was something wrong with the heart fluttering beneath the ribs.

"All right," he finally whispered, and he buttoned the jacket, the buttons still the old eagles from his Union Army uniform, the gilding long since polished off.

Hans nodded his thanks.

"Now help me up."

Jack took him by the arm and there was a gasp of pain as Hans stood. He swayed uneasily for a moment, took a deep breath, and it seemed as if by sheer strength of will the heart continued to beat.

He slowly brushed the dirt off his jacket and stepped out of the surrounding circle. Jack wanted to stay by his side, to help him walk, but Ketswana held him back.

He fought to block out the pain, the strange, empty sensation that part of him was floating away. He focused on the warrior before him, leaning awkwardly against the wheel of an artillery caisson. Though he had only seen him from a distance, Sergeant Major Hans Schuder knew he was facing Jurak, Qar Qarth of the Bantag Horde.

He approached slowly, warily. Except in the heat of combat, the last time he had been this close to a horde rider he had still been a slave, and he was ashamed that the old instinct almost took hold, to lower his head and avert his eyes until directly spoken to.

He maintained eye contact. Jurak shifted slightly, and there was a slight grimace of pain.

"Are you wounded?" Hans asked, speaking again in the tongue of the Bantag, the mere act of it sending a chill through him as he carefully sorted out the words.

Jurak said something in reply, a bit too quickly, and Hans shook his head, a gesture they used as well.

Jurak spoke again, more slowly.

"The ankle is broken; it is nothing. You look wounded as well."

Hans paused for a moment on the mental translation, startled to realize that in the language of the Horde, Jurak had used the personal form of *you*, used only when addressing another of the same race, rather than the contemptible *kagsa*, their form of the word *you* for speaking to cattle.

It took him a moment to regain his poise from that. The pain in his chest was still there, coursing down his arms; he forced the recognition of it away.

"Knocked down by an explosion. It is nothing," he lied.

Jurak stared at him and Hans wondered if the ability to see into the thoughts of others was with this one. He realized he had to be careful, to stay focused.

"Though enemies, we must talk," Hans announced.

He felt light-headed, knew that Jurak was in pain as well. Finally, he motioned to the ground. Jurak nodded and, with leg extended, sat down, Hans making it a point of not waiting to be invited to sit as well.

"You've lost," Hans said.

"Today yes, but not tomorrow. I have two more umens arriving by train even now."

He waited, forming his words carefully so as to not imply that Jurak was lying and therefore automatically dishonorable.

"My eyes see differently," he finally said.

"And what is it that your eyes see that mine do not?"

Hans looked straight at him. Less than an hour ago he assumed it was lost. They had damaged the Horde, perhaps fatally, but it would still be lost for him and his comrades. Now there was a glimmer of light.

Again the flutter of pain, but he ignored it. *Even if I don't survive this day, those whom I love will.*

He tried to pierce into the mind, the heart of Jurak. The Horde believed their shamans could read into the souls of others. Andrew claimed it was true as well, having resisted the leaders of the Tugar and Merki Hordes. He, in turn, had been in the presence of Tamuka and Ha'ark. There was something about Tamuka that had been coldly troubling, a sense that he could indeed see.

As for Ha'ark, he was simply a warrior. A shrewd one at times but nevertheless easy to pierce. There was something about this one, though, that was different yet again.

Hans reached into his haversack, Jurak's gaze fluttering down. Hans slowly withdrew the small piece of tobacco and bit off a chew. There was a soft grumbling chuckle from Jurak.

"Now I remember," Jurak said. "You chewed that dried weed. Disgusting."

Hans could not help but laugh softly as well.

He continued to stare at Jurak. As with most of the Horde there was no discomfort in silence, the feeling that one needed to fill the emptiness. As horse nomads they were a race long accustomed to silence, to days of endless riding alone.

The air reverberated around them, distant explosions, the chatter of a Gatling. From the west the shriek of an approaching steam train, the neighing of horses, guttural cries of mounted warriors. Hans looked up. Less than half a mile away he could see a knot of them forming up, the fallen standard of the Horde held aloft again as a rally point. They most likely knew that their Qar Qarth was fallen; he wondered if they knew that he was still alive and a prisoner.

A Hornet circled in on the forming ranks, opening fire, scattering them.

Hans looked over his shoulder. Several hundred men

were gathered behind him, watching in open awe and curiosity.

"Jack, do you have some sort of signal to tell those flyers to cease fire? And Ketswana, I think they understand a white flag. Get some men out there, men who can speak Bantag. We're not surrendering, but we are offering a cease-fire. Tell them we have their Qar Qarth."

He looked back at Jurak who sat, features unreadable. *That has always been one of the damned problems with dealing with them,* he thought. *Can't read their faces, their subtle gestures; it's like dealing with a statue of stone.*

"I am telling my men to stop firing while we talk," Hans said.

Jurak nodded, then looked around. Groups of Chin were wandering about the battlefield. Whenever they spotted a wounded Bantag they closed in with shouts of rage, and of glee and fell to tormenting him before finishing it with a bayonet thrust or a crushing blow to the head.

"And Ketswana!"

His comrade came up to his side, looking down at him, eyes still filled with concern.

"I'm doing fine now. But tell our people to stop that," Hans said in the language of the Bantag. He nodded to where, less than fifty yards away, a mob of Chin had fallen on a Bantag warrior. "It's despicable. This is a cease-fire, damn it, not an opportunity for a massacre. I want our people to halt where they are and hold. The wounded are to be left alone; if they can get out on their own, let them pass."

"Their blood's up," Ketswana replied in the same language, his voice filled with bitterness. "It's time to remember and take vengeance. They wouldn't offer us mercy if it was you who were now prisoner."

"And that's what's different between us," Hans shouted, the effort of it leaving him dizzy and out of breath.

Ketswana's gaze locked on Jurak. He finally nodded, formally saluted Hans, and ran off, shouting orders.

"Are we really so different?" Jurak asked.

"I would like to think we are, at least when it comes to how we wage war."

"And tell me, Hans. After all this, after all the thousands

of years of this, if your race gains the upper hand, can we expect any different?"

"I can't promise anything," Hans replied. "For myself, yes. For those who've lived here all their lives, who know nothing different. I don't know."

"So we shall continue to fight. Kill me if you wish. But I was always an outsider. Few will truly miss me. I was Qar Qarth because they were afraid of you and believed in Ha'ark, who claimed we were sent by the gods. They will select one of their own blood to continue the fight."

"What I assumed," Hans replied wearily.

There was a long blast of a steam whistle. Looking over his shoulder, he saw a train easing to a stop. Shocked, he saw that Seetu, one of Ketswana's men was leading them. They had actually made it all the way from Xi'an. Dismounting from the locomotive, hundreds of Chin, all of them armed with Bantag rifles, jumped down from the string of flatcars and formed up.

"They're from Xi'an," Hans announced proudly, "and there will be thousands more."

Jurak said nothing.

If what Jurak said was true, Hans realized, it would simply go on. He might have saved the Chin, but who would be next after that? And so the war would continue.

"You said your eyes did not see my new umens," Jurak said, interrupting Hans's thoughts.

Hans looked back at him absently rubbing his left shoulder.

"I know enough of cat . . ." Jurak quickly stopped, "of humans to know you are ill."

"I'll be fine."

"It is your heart, isn't it?"

Surprised, Hans nodded.

"You are very ill, Hans Schuder."

"Not too sick to see this through to the end."

Jurak laughed softly.

"Ha'ark once told me you were indomitable. I remember once telling him that if he sensed that in you, perhaps it was best to kill you before you created trouble."

"One of his many mistakes," Hans said with a soft laugh.

"Yes. I know."

"What do I see that your eyes do not?" Hans replied.

"I know two umens were brought up by rail last night from Nippon. It must have taken near to every locomotive and piece of rolling stock within three hundred leagues to do that. Even if you had half a dozen umens in Nippon, it will still take you two days to turn those trains around, run them north, load them up, then another two days to bring them all back.

"As you can see, I now control the rail line between here and Xi'an."

Jurak looked past Hans and nodded.

"I will not speak an untruth. I don't know how they got through. Perhaps they control the line. Perhaps you had few if any warriors between here and Xi'an to stop them."

Jurak was silent for a moment.

"Obviously not enough to stop them."

"We captured supplies in Xi'an. Powder, artillery, guns." He hesitated, remembering the barges of ammunition exploding. "Millions of cartridges, thousands of shells, even some of your steamships and land ironclads.

"By the time you are reinforced, I can arm fifty thousand Chin."

"Then it will be a mutual slaughter."

"I could also pull back, tearing up track. Burn the factories that are left before leaving. Then you will have yet another front and hundreds of thousands of Chin armed and eager for blood by the time your umens reach Xi'an."

Jurak shook his head wearily.

"Then we are doomed to fight. You and I will not be here to see it, but it will continue."

Hans sighed and lowered his head.

"I know."

There was a long moment of silence. He looked back up at Jurak. Here was a warrior of the Horde. Eight feet or more in height, black-and-brown mane matted, dirty, the same as the black uniform. Visage that for a decade had filled him with horror. There was the memory of slavery, the terror, the brutality, the moon feasts and slaughter pits. And all so many comrades of the 35th and 44th New York. Men of Rus, his friend Marcus, those whom he had suffered bondage with. All caused by this race.

He fought down the urge to find a weapon, a knife, anything, to gut Jurak right there, to make it a signal for the slaughter to continue to the death. For he did indeed have the upper hand at the moment.

He looked to his left and saw Ketswana standing over a wounded Bantag, ordering the Chin back. They were ready to fall on him with drawn knives.

He thought of the rumors of yesterday, that in the frenzy of killing, Bantag had been mutilated beyond recognition; and some were even whispering that a few had even taken their flesh and consumed it.

He looked closely at the wounded Bantag and realized that it was barely more than a cub, about the same height as the Zulu standing over him. He was on his side, gutshot. Looking up at Ketswana.

The Chin fell back. Ketswana started to turn away, and the wounded Bantag said something. Ketswana hesitated, then unslung his canteen, pulled the cork, knelt, and offered the Bantag a drink.

Jurak was watching as well.

"In spite of what my race did, still one of yours will offer a drink to a dying child."

Hans said nothing for a moment. He was ready to shoot back with a sarcasm, an enraged comment about how many human children had died in agony, watching parents murdered before they themselves were slaughtered. He sensed, as well, that Jurak had an inner revulsion for what this world was. And the thought formed as he continued to watch Ketswana, holding the canteen to the cub's lips.

"Jurak."

He was looking straight into his opponent's eyes.

"Yes, Hans."

"Your tribal camping areas. Your old ones, your children, your women. Do you know where they are camped now?"

Jurak seemed to stiffen slightly, the first true gesture Hans felt he could read accurately.

"Yes."

"Many are south of here, toward the Shin-Tu Mountains."

There was a moment's pause.

"Yes, some are there. Others to the north and east."

"But many are there. A hundred thousand yurts, two hundred thousand perhaps."

"I cannot count them all."

Hans smiled. Jurak could try to bluff, but somehow he wasn't.

"My forces here are between them and you. Troops moving along this rail line are between them and you. For that matter, I have a score of airships that could be over them within the hour."

"What are you saying?"

Hans made it a point of dropping eye contact for a moment. He slowly stood up. Jurak remained seated, but now it was he looking down on Jurak rather than the other way around.

"I am ordering that all of them are to be put to death."

Jurak said nothing, gaze becoming icy.

"The umens you see that I do not can come up if you want. But in two days' time I will have a ring closed in around a hundred thousand yurts. The flyers will be over them ceaselessly from dawn to dusk. Arrows fired by women and old ones will fall back to the ground. Bullets and firebombs slashing down from the skies will slaughter by the tens of thousands.

"And once armed Chin are amongst them, once I tell the Chin that this is their destiny, that the gods seek revenge, the slaughter will continue until even the ground can no longer drink all the blood, and the rivers will turn red.

"You might bring up two umens, a dozen umens, but they will find themselves to be childless, fatherless, for their seed will be extinguished from this world forever.

"This is the war your race started and I shall now finish."

As he spoke he was aware that Ketswana had come back and was standing by his side.

"When do we begin?" Ketswana asked, his voice a guttural challenge.

Jurak looked at the two of them and wearily shook his head.

"Am I to believe you, a warrior I had come to respect, would do this thing?"

"You did it to us first."

Jurak visibly flinched and lowered his head.

He was again silent, and then ever so slowly he grabbed hold of the wheel of the caisson he had been sitting against and pulled himself up, flinching as he gingerly tried to put weight on his broken ankle.

"It is over," he finally whispered. "I would like to believe that you do not wish this murder to continue. I am asking you to spare them."

Hans said nothing, keeping his features hard.

"Your terms?"

This was a leap ahead for Hans which momentarily caught him off guard. Two hours earlier he was hoping Ketswana had saved one final round to prevent the agony of capture, now he was negotiating the end of a war. He wished Andrew was here; his friend would be far better at this than he.

"Immediate cease-fire on all fronts. Immediate withdrawal from the territory of Roum, Nippon, and the Chin."

"To go where?"

"East if you want, south. I've been told that there's a thousand leagues east of here with barely a human on it. That is range enough for your people to live upon."

"You'd suffer us to live?"

"It's either that or kill all of you." He held back for a second then let it spill out. "And if I did that, if we did that, in the end we would become you."

Jurak stood with lowered head and finally nodded.

"I offer no apologies for what this world became."

"Then change it, damn it. Change it."

"And what is to prevent war from starting again?"

"I don't know," Hans said, his voice weary. "I promise you this, though, if you go beyond that thousand leagues of open prairie, if word should ever come back of but one more person dying, of being slaughtered for food, or put into bondage, then I, or Andrew, or those who come after us will hunt your people without mercy."

"You will have the factories, the flyers, the machines. We will not," Jurak replied. "I know what the result of that would be."

"Fine. I will keep the Chin back from your encampments. I will order the release of ten thousand yurts immediately to start moving east. Once I have word that the last of your troops are out of Roum territory, twenty thousand more. Once out of the realm of Nippon and the Chin, fifty thousand more, and a year from today the remainder. Any violation of what we agree upon here and all of them will die without mercy."

"Would you really do that?" Jurak asked.

Hans stared straight at him.

He knew there was no sense in bluffing, but he could not betray his own doubts either.

"I don't think either one of us wants to find out what we are capable of doing."

Jurak nodded.

"Perhaps someday we can talk more, Hans Schuder. You might not believe this, but I sense your Andrew and I are more alike than each of us realizes, the same as Andrew has you, there is an elder for me."

Hans did not know what to say.

In a way it had all been so simple, and yet all the years of agony and suffering to reach this moment, and all the millions of dead.

Strange, he suddenly thought of Andrew, and knew that what had happened here Andrew would have agreed to.

"I will signal that the attack is off at Capua."

Hans looked at him quizzically.

"There were rumors that your government had collapsed, that Andrew was going into exile. We were to start the attack this evening, just before sundown."

Hans tried to quickly digest all that he had just learned. Andrew in exile? Suppose the government had already thrown in the towel. Then what? If this fighting was to end, he had better move quickly. He had already decided to let Jurak go, but he had to get him back to where he could telegraph out orders of a cease-fire before the government back home surrendered first. If they did that, some other Bantag leader might be tempted to press the attack anyhow.

"Ketswana, bring up a couple of mounts."

The two stood in silence, waiting as Ketswana left them to find horses.

"Twenty years from now I wonder," Jurak said.

"Wonder what?"

Jurak fell silent again as Ketswana came up, leading two horses, one of them sightly wounded and limping.

Hans motioned for Jurak to take the better horse. He hobbled over. Grimacing, he grabbed hold of the pommel, swung his injured leg up and over, then slipped his good foot into the stirrup.

Hans, still feeling light-headed, though the pain had subsided somewhat, struggled to mount and was embarrassed when Ketswana and several others came to his side to help.

"Hans, where the hell are you going?" Ketswana asked.

Hans looked down at his old comrade.

"Just for a little ride, that's all."

"Wait for me."

"I can't wait for you, my friend."

Hans suddenly reached down and took Ketswana's hand.

"Thank you. I don't know how many times over I owe you my life."

"I owe you my freedom," Ketswana replied, his voice suddenly choked.

"No man owes another man his freedom," Hans replied softly. "That was, and always will be, your right. Remember that."

He nudged his mount gently, not wanting to hurt it.

"Wait here; I'll be back soon enough."

The two rode off, side by side, heading to where Bantag survivors of the bloody fight were rallying. Overhead a flyer circled as if keeping watch. Chin infantry, coming off of the trains, was fanning out to envelop the flank of the Bantag. Eastward, toward the still-burning city, the sound of battle continued to thunder, though it seemed to be dying away, falling into a final spasm of slaughter.

The pain had abated; he wondered for a moment if that meant that he would survive the day after all, or was it the final ringing down of the curtain and that soon he would slip away.

At the moment it really didn't seem to matter. He felt a sudden lightness, a gentle floating, a sense of peace. Back home, back in Suzdal, for that now was home, Tamira would most likely be out with his young Andrew, the boy leading his mother on their daily walk through the meadows to the east and south of town. The thought of it made him smile. In the last year he had shared not more than half a dozen days with them, but each moment had been a blessed treasure, each night a reawakened dream.

They would be safe, and ultimately he knew that a man

could not ask for anything beyond that, to know that those whom he loved were safe.

"What are you thinking about?" Jurak asked.

Hans stirred.

"My family."

"You had a child, I remember that."

"Yes."

"And they are safe?"

"You mean did they escape safely with me?" Hans asked, a touch of anger flaring into his voice.

"No. I know that. I was there, I saw her lead the escape carrying your child. She was brave. To be proud of."

Surprised, Hans nodded his thanks.

"They are safe now?"

"Yes, as far as I know."

"You are lucky."

"Why so?" Surprised he turned to look at Jurak. Strange, for a brief instant he had almost forgotten who he was talking to.

"My home world. My family, parents, the one that I . . . what you called married."

"Yes."

"They all died. A type of bomb I pray to the gods is never known on this world. They all died. That was just before I came here."

"I'm sorry."

Jurak looked over at him, surprised. Hans as well felt a mild shock. The two words had slipped out of him so easily. Never did he dream he could feel sorrow for a Bantag. Yet in Jurak's voice he had sensed the pain.

There was an awkward moment of silence.

"Do you have a family here?" Hans asked.

Jurak shook his head.

"No. They cannot replace her."

"Perhaps someday. I lived alone nearly all the days of my life and did not find her until . . ." He let the subject drop, given how he and Tamira had met.

"Perhaps someday."

They were approaching the Bantag formation. Hans could see them stirring as they recognized that their Qar Qarth was still alive. Jurak reined in, gaze sweeping the battered ranks.

"The war is finished," he shouted. "We withdraw."

Excited murmuring erupted. Hans could sense rage on the part of many, but there were others who seemed relieved, nodding, grounding clenched rifles.

Jurak looked over at Hans.

"I will order my troops pulled back north of the city at once. Tomorrow, at noonday, let us meet on the rail tracks going north out of Huan. We both have to assume that there will still be fighting until word reaches all, and we can separate from each other."

Hans nodded.

"Noon then."

To his surprise, Jurak extended his arm in the gesture of clasping. Hans reached out tentatively, then grasped Jurak's wrist, and felt the tight grip on his own forearm.

"No!"

Hans looked up. A rider, followed by half a dozen, broke out of the ranks and approached. There was something darkly familiar about him, and then the recognition hit, the scarred disfigured face. It was Tamuka.

"No! That is the path of a coward. Press the fight now and slaughter them all."

Jurak drew himself up stiffly.

"They are between us and the yurts of our clans. In agreement for our ending the war and withdrawing, they will harm no one and let our families live. If this madness continues half a million or more of our sires, females, and cubs will die."

With the announcement of that Hans could see that yet more were now glad that it was ended. He suddenly realized that the Bantag had been terrified that over the last day the Chin would even now be swarming southward to initiate a massacre.

"They have made the gesture of letting our old ones and young live, even though they now have the power to kill them all. We all know that we are powerless to stop them. There is not one more warrior between Xi'an and Nippon capable of resisting them. It will take days to bring down what we have left in Nippon. By then, all our families will have been slaughtered."

That admission startled Hans. So it was a bluff. They had stripped themselves bare.

There was a sidelong glance from Jurak and Hans felt he could almost smile, as if Jurak had finally revealed that he didn't have a pair of deuces, let alone a full house.

Tamuka turned to face the Bantags.

"Fight! Kill them all while there is still time! One more charge, and we break through and slaughter them all!"

His screams were met with a stirring. More than one again gave himself over to the lust for battle, some raising their rifles in response, shouting agreement.

Hans could not understand all that was being said, the words were spilling out of Tamuka so quickly, yet he could sense the rage that was out of control. He looked over again at Jurak, who sat motionless. This wasn't a leader who could win by overpowering. It had to be a display of calm in the face of madness.

He knew that if Tamuka should somehow win the argument, then it was over. Jurak would die, they would attack in a mad frenzy, and the Chin would unleash a massacre against hundreds of thousands in a final orgy of mutual destruction. Madness, to be so close and then have it all plunged back into madness.

"Kill them all!"

The world seemed to be shifting like sand swept away by a tidal wave. The lust was coming back. Jurak sat impassive, undoubtedly knowing he could not shout down the mad leader of the once great Merki.

"And kill this traitor from another world first!" Tamuka cried.

Hans barely understood the words, but he recognized the gesture as Tamuka dropped his reins and reached for a saddle-mounted holster. Like a snake striking, the revolver flashed out.

"No!"

Hans kicked his own mount forward. He saw the revolver going up, thumb cocking the trigger back. He fumbled with his own holster . . . and grabbed nothing but thin air. There was a flash memory of throwing it away after firing the last round. Time seemed to distort, he felt his heart thumping over, wondering if it was finally shattering. Or was it fear.

He saw the gun coming down, Tamuka squinting, one eye half-closed, the other sighting down the barrel, aiming it straight at Jurak. He caught a final glimpse of Jurak, knew the Bantag, at heart, was not a true combat soldier. He was reacting far too slowly, just then recognizing the danger, starting to recoil in anticipation of the crashing blow.

There was a final instant, a wondering, a sense that somehow this was a vast cosmic joke. This wasn't Andrew, or Pat, or Emil, or even a simple Chin that he was trying to save. It wasn't anyone, yet it was, as well, a warrior whom he had learned in the last few minutes to respect. He was someone who had offered an ending to the madness, a way out, a way for Tamira and the baby to live in peace . . . and that peace was about to die if Jurak died.

Time distorted, and he knew there was but one last thing he could do. Without hesitating Hans lunged forward across the neck of his horse. He saw the gaping maw of the revolver, the eye behind the barrel, face contorted in a mad scream . . . and then the flash.

"No!"

It was Jurak screaming, as Hans, lifted out of his saddle, tumbled over backwards and crashed to the ground. The dirty yellow-white smoke swirled in a cloud, and through the cloud he saw Tamuka. There was a momentary look of surprise that he had shot Hans, and then, even more enraging, a barking roar of delight.

Jurak drew his scimitar, blade flashing out, catching the light. He caught a momentary glance of those watching. This was now a blood challenge for control of the Bantag Horde. He raked his spurs, the pain in his leg forgotten. His mount leapt forward.

Tamuka, thumb on the hammer of his revolver, cocked the weapon and started to shift aim.

Screaming with a mad fury Jurak charged his mount straight into the flank of Tamuka's horse. The revolver swung past his face, going off, the explosion deafening him, the flash of it burning his cheek.

Their eyes locked for a second. Even as he started his swing, there was a final instant, a flash of recognition. His rage, a rage which surprised him, for it was a mad fury over what had been done to a human, added strength to his blow.

The look in Tamuka's eyes turned in that instant to disbelief as the blade sliced into his throat, driven with such force that it slashed clear through flesh, muscle, and bone.

Tamuka's horse, terrified as a shower of hot blood cascaded over its back, reared and galloped off, ridden by a headless corpse still showering blood.

Jurak was blinded for an instant, not sure if he had somehow been wounded after all by the pistol shot. Then the mist started to clear as he blinked Tamuka's blood out of his eyes.

He viciously swung his mount around, gaze sweeping the assembly, wanting to shout his rage at them, at all their insanity and bestiality. And in their eyes he saw something that had never quite been there before. It wasn't just that he was their Qar Qarth. It was that he was their leader. Some went down on their knees, heads lowered.

Something snapped inside and he screamed incoherently at them, holding his bloody scimitar aloft. More went down on their knees; within seconds all were down, heads bowed.

He reined his horse around and looked down. Cursing wildly, he swung off his mount. As he hit the ground his broken ankle gave way and with a gasp of pain he went down on his knees. None dared to rise to help him.

He slowly stood back up and limped the half dozen paces over to where Hans lay. Looking up he saw humans, hundreds of them, running up, led by the dark Zulu. He held up his sword so they could see it, then threw it down by the severed head of Tamuka. The humans slowed, the Zulu turning, shouting a command. They stopped, and, alone, Ketswana came forward.

Tamuka knelt down by Hans's side, Ketswana joining him.

"I'm sorry," Jurak gasped. "And thank you for my life."

Hans looked up. Strange, no pain. The dark specter who had trailed his every step across all the years, and all the worlds, had him in hand at last, and, surprisingly, there was no pain.

Still he wondered why he had done it. *Was it because I knew I was dying anyhow?*

No.

A gallant gesture then? And he wanted to laugh over the irony of it, but no laughter came.

He saw them gazing down. Jurak was saying something, but he couldn't hear him. He saw Ketswana, tears streaming down his face. He tried to reach up, to wipe them away, as if soothing a child, but for some strange reason his arm, his hands would no longer obey.

They were kneeling side by side, and he fully understood what it was he had been fighting for all along, and what he was now dying for. And he was content.

Then they slipped away . . . and Hans Schuder smiled as they disappeared into a glorious light.

Exhausted, he stood alone, watching as the sun touched the horizon.

The last of the gunfire died away and he felt cold, alone, empty. Throughout the long day the square had slowly contracted inward, drawing closer and yet closer after each successive charge until the backs of the surviving men were almost touching.

The ground was carpeted with the dead and dying, tens of thousands of Bantag and humans tangled together.

If ever there was a killing ground of madness, this was it. He stood atop the low rise of ground, watching as half a dozen ironclads, the survivors of the daylong fight wove their way up the hill, maneuvering slowly, looking for an open path through the carnage.

The lead machine ground to a halt fifty yards short of the square, the turret popped open, and he saw Gregory stiffly climb out then half slide, half fall to the ground. He looked at the other machines. *St. Katrina?* No, he had seen that one blow up . . . the gentle gardener was dead, and Vincent blinked back the tears.

Walking like a marionette with tangled strings, Gregory slowly made his way up the hill. The men around Vincent parted at his approach.

Coming to attention he saluted. Vincent, exhausted beyond words, merely nodded in reply.

"They're leaving," Gregory announced, his voice slurring.

"What?"

"What's left of them, the poor damned bastards. They're mounting up now, heading north."

Even as he spoke there was a ripple of comments along the battered line. Vincent looked past Gregory and saw a lone rider appear on the next rise half a mile away. The Bantag rider stood out sharply against the horizon. He held a horse tail standard aloft.

He waved it back and forth and Vincent watched, mesmerized. The Horde rider slammed it down, the shaft sinking into the earth. The rider held a clenched fist aloft and he could hear a distant cry, desolate, mournful. Vincent stepped out from the battered square, removed his kepi, and held it aloft.

The Bantag rider turned and disappeared, leaving the standard behind.

Gregory came to his side, and Vincent turned to face him.

"I hope this was worth it," Gregory whispered.

Vincent's gaze swept the wreckage, the tangled mounds of dead. All he could do was lower his head and cry.

"Pat!"

"It's started?"

Instantly, he was awake, sitting up in his cot. All day long he had been anticipating the attack. Praying in fact that it would come, come before someone finally got through from the west with the orders to stand down or he finally made the suicidal gesture and attacked instead. Rumors had been floating through the army ever since Pat had dropped the telegraph lines and all trains from the west had ceased to arrive.

Only that morning Schneid had come back up to the front, personally bearing a report that rioting had erupted in Suzdal and Roum.

Rick stood in the doorway of the bunker, the sky behind him glowing with the colors of sunset.

"Where are they hitting?" Pat cried, stumbling up from the steps and out onto the battlement.

He was stunned by the silence. There were no guns firing, not even the usual scattering of shots between snipers. Then he heard it, a strange distant keening.

He stepped up onto a firing step and cautiously peered over. He saw though that men were now standing up, some atop the earthworks, fully exposed, and not a shot was coming from the other side.

"What the hell is going on?"

"I'm damned if I know. It started an hour or so ago. This weird chanting. I thought they were getting themselves built up for the assault. I figured to let you sleep as long as possible, though, and waited. Well, this chanting kept on going and going and then about five minutes ago I saw the damnedest thing."

He suddenly pointed across the river.

"There, another one!"

Pat looked, not sure for a moment what he was seeing. It was darker on the far shore, and then he saw where Rick was pointing. Two Bantag were standing, fully exposed. They were holding something. It was a mortar . . . and they flung it over the side of their fort and down into the mud of the riverbank. And then, without any ceremony they turned and simply walked away.

All along the riverbank he could now see them, not just a few, but hundreds upon hundreds, climbing up out of the trenches, still chanting, then walking off into the darkness.

Suddenly a flare ignited on the far shore and in the flickering light he saw a mounted Bantag, war helmet off, white mane catching the light. The Bantag was holding the flare and Pat looked at him mesmerized.

He felt a strange stirring within, as if this one could somehow reach into his soul and touch his heart. There was no hatred, only an infinite sadness.

"It's over," a voice seemed to whisper inside.

By the light of the flare he saw a rider moving down into the river, holding a white flag aloft, in his other hand waving what appeared to be a piece of paper.

"Send someone down to get that," Pat shouted.

The rider reached midstream and waited, and a minute later a mounted artilleryman galloped into the shallow river, approached the messenger, and took the paper.

At the same instant the flare was thrown heavenward. He traced its flight as it bisected the Great Wheel, which even then was rising in the east. It fell into the water, and all was darkness.

Pat, unable to speak, simply looked over at Rick and smiled, though in his heart he sensed, at that same moment, that something was lost forever as well.

Andrew Lawrence Keane, his wife riding beside him,

rode into the Great Square of the city. The entire populace was out cheering his arrival, chanting his name, but he ignored the tribute.

He saw Father Casmir standing on the steps of the White House, and as Andrew reined in his mount, Casmir made the gesture of taking off his skullcap and offering the traditional Rus bow, right hand sweeping to the ground.

Andrew smiled and dismounted. He started to raise his hand in a formal salute, then remembered he was no longer in the army and instead he simply held it out. Casmir took it.

"Welcome home, Colonel Keane."

Andrew did not know what to say. The courier, a young priest, had arrived at his retreat, a country house on the edge of the Great Forest, near the old Tugar Ford, only that morning. Breathless, he had announced that Father Casmir insisted that he return to the city immediately.

All Andrew's questioning would not budge the youth, who insisted he was sworn to a vow of silence. The only news he would divulge was that Kal had emerged from his coma and asked for him as well.

Leaving the children under the protection of several young men from the 35th who had gone with him into exile, he rode south, back to the city along the old ford road, Kathleen insisting that she come along, too. The ride with the silent priest and Kathleen was a flood of memories . . . the battles around the Tugar Ford, the first skirmish in the woods against a raid by boyars, the ambush of the Tugar column just north of the city. As they cleared the lower pass he was stunned to see thousands outside the gates, lining the road.

There had been no cheering, only an awed and respectful silence. As he passed, all offered the old traditional bow of the Rus, bent at the waist, right hand sweeping to the ground. He wanted to ask but sensed all had been told to wait, to let Casmir explain.

He looked into the eyes of the Metropolitan of the Rus.

"I will never forget the night that I, a young priest, ran barefoot through the snow to where you and your men were camped below this city," Casmir began, his voice echoing across the plaza, and Andrew realized that this was all part of some elaborate ceremony.

"I knew you Yankees were voting that night whether to stay and fight the Tugars or to take ship and leave and seek safety. I came bearing the news that we, the people of Suzdal, had rebelled against the boyars and wished to fight the Tugars as well.

"Colonel Keane, you could have turned your back upon me at that moment. You could have left, but you decided to stay and to fight for our freedom.

"Those men that were with you that night," and his voice faltered, "how few now remain."

Casmir paused, and Andrew saw the emotions and felt a knot in his own throat.

"You did not leave us, Andrew Keane. It was we who left you."

Andrew wanted to say something, embarrassed. He felt the touch of Kathleen's hand on his shoulder, stilling him.

"We left you. You tried to teach us that though you fought to give us freedom, we ourselves must have the strength to defend it. When you rode out of the city, alone, we finally learned that.

"My friend, I now beg you. Pick up your sword again. Take command of the armies. Be Colonel Andrew Lawrence Keane once more."

As he spoke the last words the chanting resumed, "Keane, Keane, Keane."

Stunned, Andrew was unable to respond for a moment.

"What about Bugarin, the vote for an armistice?" Kathleen asked.

"Those buggers. We loaded them onto a ferry across the river. They're packing it on the road west of here," Emil announced, coming down the steps to join them.

At the sight of him Andrew brightened, reached out, and grasped his hand.

"It started down at the factories," Emil continued. "Oh this priest might deny it, but his monks were organizing it. By yesterday evening the entire city was on strike. They cut the telegraph lines repeatedly, blockaded the Capitol and the White House. The poor damned Chin representatives didn't dare set foot outside for fear of getting torn apart."

"They didn't overthrow the government, did they?" Andrew asked.

Emil smiled.

"Let's call it vox populi. Some of the senators got a bit roughed up, maybe a couple of them were told that if they voted the wrong way, they might not get reelected because they wouldn't live long enough to make reelection. But the people of Suzdal made it clear they would fight to the end rather than go down, and communicated that real clear to the Roum as well."

"What did Bugarin do?"

"It came to a head last night. He tried to order some ruffians he had rounded up to fire into the crowd gathered right here. They lined the steps, and then Casmir here steps out, arms extended, and tells them to aim at him first."

Andrew looked at the priest, unable to speak.

"That finished it. There was a bit of roughness, a few black eyes, busted ribs, broken arms, and a few lads singing soprano, but the people of this city took the White House. I declared Kal competent to resume office. There was talk of a treason trial and that was it, ten senators and a couple of congressmen quickly resigned and got the hell out of town."

"My role is somewhat exaggerated," Casmir intervened.

A wild cheer rose up in the square, laughing, belying Casmir's statement.

"I doubt that," Andrew cried, trying to be heard above the roaring of the crowd.

"You know, Andrew. Maybe it's a good thing for a Republic to clean house occasionally and throw out a few cowardly senators now and then."

Andrew said nothing, shaking his head with disbelief.

"Flavius, and the shot at Kal. Who did it?"

"I don't think we'll ever really know, but if my sacred vows did not prevent it, I'd bet on Bugarin even though he vehemently denied it."

"I'd like to see Kal," Andrew said. "He is the president, and he alone can appoint the commander of the army."

"I told you he would say that," Emil interjected as he led the way up the steps and into the White House.

Following Emil, he could not contain himself any longer and asked the question that had been tearing his soul apart ever since he had let go of the mantle of command.

"Any news from the front?"

"Nothing," Emil replied. "I think Pat cut the lines, though we've been trying to reach him all day. Of course, nothing from Tyre, though we have to assume a courier boat from Roum carrying the cease-fire order reached there last night."

"Not even a flyer?"

"No, nothing."

"I hope these people realize that by doing this they've most likely condemned themselves to death."

"Andrew, they know that. They know as well that what Bugarin offered was death as well. A coward's death. It might have given them an extra month, maybe a year, maybe even five years, but in the end, without freedom, it would be death anyhow. At least now, if we're doomed, we go down with heads held high. I think that alone is worth fighting for."

They reached the door to Kal's sickroom. He stepped in, following Emil's lead. Kal was propped up in bed, features pale and drawn. The Lincolnesque beard was still there, and the unofficial symbol of his office, the stovepipe hat, was back by his side on the nightstand.

Andrew approached the bed, and Kal, smiling weakly, patted the covers.

"Sit down, my old friend."

Just the tone in his voice broke away all the tension of the last months. Andrew sat down and took his friend's hand.

"Once I'm out of this damned bed we should go off together, have a drink, and perhaps buy that pair of gloves we're always talking about."

Andrew chuckled at the clumsy joke, for Kal had lost his right arm and Andrew his left.

"How are you, Kal?"

"Better than I've ever been. Perhaps that bullet knocked some sense into my thick skull."

"You know what you are letting yourself in for?"

"I know. Most likely a bloody end. But then again, my boyar often told me that would be how I finished."

"For everyone," Andrew whispered.

"That was our difference, my friend. I wanted a way out, any way out to stop the slaughter. You saw that the only way out was to endure it, to have the courage to fight your way through it. When I thought of Bugarin crawling before them, again offering us up, something finally changed in my heart, as if I was throwing off a sickness. Oh, he would be spared, perhaps even I would be spared, but I swore an oath to myself, long before the Republic, long before I was president, that never again would I see a child go into the slaughter pits. That I would die first, that I would rather see us all die than endure that again.

"You knew that all along. I had to relearn it. So if we are doomed to die, we'll die as free men. And as long as you are by my side, Colonel Andrew Keane, I will be content."

"Fine then," Andrew whispered, squeezing his friend's hand. "Together, and perhaps we can still win."

Kal smiled.

"Actually, I think we shall. This afternoon I had a dream. You often told me that Lincoln was famous for such things."

"And?"

"Strange. It was even like his dream. A ship, far out to sea, coming toward me. It sailed past, and I felt a strange wonderful peace."

"Good. Perhaps it will come true."

"There was something else, though. Someone was standing on the deck. I couldn't tell who. He was alone, but then he wasn't. The deck was crowded, so very crowded. I felt that it was the *Ogunquit,* the ship that bore you to this world, sailing one last time, perhaps back to where it came from, bearing with it all those who gave the final sacrifice. The lone man raised his hand, and then the ship disappeared into the mist."

Andrew said nothing.

"Sleep, my friend. Perhaps you'll have another dream."

"I think I will. Knowing you're back, I feel safe again."

"I never really left."

Kal winked. "I know that, too."

Andrew looked up at Emil, who nodded, and with Kathleen quietly withdrew. Andrew sat by Kal's side, watching as his old friend drifted off.

It was a peaceful moment. A strange mix of feelings. On the one side an infinite sadness, knowing what was still to come, the sacrifice still to be made. On the other side, though, there was a tremendous swelling of pride. Win or lose, the people of Rus, of Roum had come together, mingled their blood, and out of that mingling a republic was born. And now, even if they should lose, they would not crawl basely into the night but would go with heads held high. The legend of it would then live on as well, and in the turning of years be remembered, be reborn, and finally triumph.

His thoughts drifted to Hans, wishing he was there to share the moment. As Hans had taught him, he had passed that strength and vision on to others. Everyone pointed to him, and yet actually it had been Hans all along who had shaped and guided him, and, in turn, he had created the Republic.

He heard renewed cheering outside, a wild tumultuous roaring that thundered up. Embarrassed, he stood up, gently releasing Kal's hand. They were most likely cheering the news that he had accepted reappointment; he would have to go out and give yet another speech, something he did not want to do just now.

And then he saw Kathleen in the door, tears streaming down her cheeks.

"It's over," she gasped.

"What?"

"The war Andrew! It's over."

He couldn't speak, and then he sensed something else.

"The telegraph line just went back up to the front. Pat reports a message from the Bantag side. They are withdrawing. The Chin have revolted."

"Glory Hallelujah," Andrew gasped.

"Andrew."

And then he knew, even before she whispered the words and fell into his arms crying.

"Andrew, darling. Hans is dead."

He couldn't speak. He held her tight, trying not to break. He saw Emil and Casmir in the doorway.

So strange, such joy, and yet such pain in their eyes.

"Emil, stay with Kal. Let him sleep; if he wakes up, tell him, but don't say anything yet about Hans."

"That dream—I think he already knew." Emil sighed.

He tried to step past Emil. The doctor touched him on the shoulder.

"The year, this year was a gift, Andrew. He came back to lead us one last time. Now the job is finished."

Andrew nodded, unable to speak.

He stepped out of the room, and Kathleen stopped him. "Andrew."

"Yes?"

She nodded to Casmir, who was holding a package.

"I brought this with me; I thought you might want it."

Casmir opened the package. Inside was Andrew's weather-stained uniform jacket, his Medal of Honor still pinned to the breast.

He nodded in agreement, and Casmir and Kathleen helped him remove his simple brown coat. The feel of the tight uniform somehow reassured him, and he wordlessly nodded his thanks.

Holding Kathleen's hand, he walked down the corridor, passing the reception room where he and Hans had first stood before the Boyar Ivor, and at last gained the steps to the White House.

Out in the square there was wild rejoicing, and though he was filled with grief, he could feel their joy as well. They had made the decision to stand and fight, redeeming their souls at that moment, and now they had discovered that it was not just their souls that had been redeemed, but their lives as well.

At the sight of him the cheering redoubled into a thunderous tumult, so that it seemed as if the very heavens would be torn asunder.

He stood silent, and then gradually the wild celebration died away. As if sensing his thoughts and his pain, a new chant emerged, "Hans, Hans, Hans."

There was no rejoicing in it, only a deep and reverent respect.

Alone he stood, eyes turned heavenward, imagining the ship Kal had dreamed of.

"Good-bye, Hans," he whispered. "Good-bye and thank you, my comrade, my friend."

Chapter Fifteen

"As he died to make men holy, let us die to make men free . . ."

The final refrain of the song echoed across the open steppes.

Colonel Andrew Lawrence Keane, commander of the Army of the Republic, stood stiffly at attention as the last chorus drifted away.

The ceremony was nearly done. All the dignitaries had spoken, as had he. Now there was only the final ritual.

A company of soldiers, cadets of the 35th Maine, came to attention, the first rank making a sharp half turn.

"Present . . . fire!"

The volley made him start. There was a momentary flash of memory, the first volley crashing into his line at Antietam.

"Present . . . fire!"

He lifted his gaze. The ruins of what was now simply called the Foundry were before him. In front of it was the cemetery, neat orderly rows with simple stone slabs, thousands of them. Some were for single bodies, most marked mass graves, the thousands upon thousands who had died in the final battle of the war.

"Present . . . fire!"

In the middle of the vast graveyard there was a lone cross. Some had wanted a towering monument, others a vast mausoleum, but his quiet insistence on what he knew his friend would have wanted had swept away all the grandiose proposals. Hans Schuder had tasted slavery, rose up, and cut free the chains, and then died coming back to liberate not just the people he called his comrades, but the world. To rest among those who had died with him that day was all the tribute he would want.

As the last volley died away, a lone bugler, concealed inside the ruins of the Foundry, blew the first notes of taps.

It was yet another ritual from the old world. It was a tune born of the Army of the Potomac, written by Dan Butterfield as nothing more than a signal for lights-out. Butterfield's lullaby many had come to call it. Hans had once said he was partial to it, and Andrew now thought it would be a fitting gesture.

As the bugler hit the final high note, a shiver seemed to go through those assembled. He could hear President Kal choking back tears. The note echoed and died away.

"Stand, at ease!"

The order, given by a young Rus colonel who now commanded the 35th Maine, cut through the air. Andrew lowered his hand from the salute, the boys of the 35th slapping rifles from the present salute down to at ease.

Andrew swept the assembly with his gaze. They were all here, having made the journey by rail from Suzdal to Roum, where the delegation of Roum senators and congressmen joined them. Then by rail all the way to Nippon, where yet more newly elected senators and congressmen joined in, and then finally to Chin.

It had been a year to the day since the ending of the war, and at last he had come to visit his friend and say a final farewell.

They had passed through the Roum lands devastated by the wars, and he was pleased to see new homes going up, tangled vineyards being cleared and replanted.

They had passed through the battlefields around Junction City, Rocky Hill, and the Shennadoah, and already monuments were going up to honor the regiments that had fought and died there. He had seen as well the orderly cemeteries at each place of battle and had stopped at each of them to offer his salute and his prayers.

There would still be four more. Tomorrow they would complete the long train ride and go to Xi'an, and from there take a boat to Carnagan, to visit the battlefield that still haunted Vincent, and from there to where Hans had made a stand in the retreat to Tyre, and, finally, a last stop at Tyre.

But this was the place that had been central to his tour of the battlefields of the war and the dedication of the cemeteries. The week before the Chin had held their first election, and Kal had made it a point to come to this place to witness the swearing in of the new senators and congressmen and congresswomen. Politics was even returning to normal, he realized. Kal had been up for reelection, and somehow it seemed like the admission of Nippon and Chin into the Republic didn't quite come until after the votes had been counted and the Republican Party had swept back in. Though the way feelings were at this moment in the first heady days of peace, Kal had nothing to fear; every last citizen, Chin, Roum, Rus, and Nippon would have voted for another term.

The amusing part of the admission of the Chin though was that they had indeed elected several women to office. It was an action which delighted him, though the election had scandalized some of the more straitlaced from Roum and Rus. He had pointed out that in the Constitution there was nothing that said a woman could not serve thus, and it was Kathleen who triggered even more of an uproar with a statement in *Gates's Illustrated Weekly* that there should be an amendment to the Constitution granting women the right to vote, and she planned to organize a movement to see that it was done.

So much in a year, he thought. Only this month the last of the Horde had been released by the terms of the treaty with Jurak and escorted to the border. A report had just come in as well that the remnants of the old Tugar Horde were joining them. So far there had been an uneasy peace, but he would feel far better when the expedition dispatched to make contact with those living a thousand leagues to the east returned with a report that the depredations of the Horde had indeed stopped along that distant border as well. Of the last of the horde clans, those who rode south and east of the Bantag and passed through the region half a dozen years ago there was no news; apparently they had simply ridden on, ignoring the conflict to the north. He sensed that someday they might have to be dealt with, but that was years, maybe even decades, off.

He had come to trust Jurak, having met with him twice in the months after the war, but unfortunately Jurak was a lone individual moving to break thousands of years of tradition. All reports indicated, though, that at least for now the moon feasts were finished, the riders of the Horde turning instead to hunting of the bison and the wool-clad elephants of the steppes.

There had come other reports, these from the south, beyond the realm of the Cartha, who only now were beginning to make the first overtures of peace. A Cartha merchant reported that there was a vast ocean in the southern half of the world, a realm few humans had seen. Andrew wondered what was out there, but for the moment that could wait.

He suddenly realized that he had been daydreaming again. Kathleen jokingly said that he was already beginning to slip into the mode of being a professor, a career he still promised he would return to once the demands of running the army diminished and he finally felt comfortable with letting go.

He stepped forward, his gaze sweeping the dignitaries gathered on the dais, the indomitable Father Casmir, Kal, Emil, Pat, Vincent, the other corps commanders, senators, and congressmen. As far as he could see, completely encompassing the Foundry and the graveyard stood hundreds of thousands of Chin, all of them silent, filled with reverent respect for this ceremony dedicated to their departed ancestors and to the one they now considered to be their eternal guardian in the spirit world above.

He waited. There was one final touch, and it was running a bit late. Finally, he heard them. The crowd shifted, looking to the west.

A squadron of aerosteamers, half a dozen Eagles, followed by half a dozen Hornets winged straight in and a loud roaring cheer erupted, for these were the fulfillment of prophecy, the coming of the gods, the Yankee gods coming from the sky bringing redemption.

The aerosteamers soared overhead, and he caught a glimpse of Jack Petracci leaning out of the cab, snapping off a sharp salute. They continued on eastward.

Andrew returned the salute. The cheering was deafening, and there was no sense in announcing that the ceremony was ended. His voice would never carry. He simply saluted the crowd, the gesture causing the wild cheering to redouble.

The fireworks, which had been carefully saved until after

the aerosteamers were well out of range, started soaring heavenward, and even though it was the middle of the day, the crowd still clapped and cheered. Andrew turned to salute Kal, who, grinning, lifted his stovepipe hat in reply.

Andrew looked over at Kathleen and nodded.

Smiling, she came forward and took his hand. Together they stepped off the dais and carefully walked out into the graveyard. The band picked up a patriotic air, the marching song of the army, "The Battle Cry of Freedom," and the music cut into his soul.

So many times I heard that, he thought wistfully, *on the parade ground in Maine, on the road to Antietam as we crossed South Mountain, again on the road to Gettysburg, in the camps around Petersburg, then through so many hard-fought victories on this world. And now yet again here.*

"Mind if we join you?"

It was Pat, Vincent, and Emil trailing behind.

Andrew smiled.

Together they walked to the middle of the cemetery. They stopped together before his grave. Andrew looked down at the mounded earth, finding it hard to believe that here was the final resting place of his oldest friend. No, not here, he tried to reason, and he thought again of Kal's dream. Kathleen let go of his hand, and he looked back and saw that Tamira, leading her son, was quietly approaching.

Kathleen put her arm around her shoulder. Andrew and the others respectfully drew back.

She knelt by the grave, placing a flower upon it, the boy doing the same.

"Papa here?" the boy lisped.

"No," she replied softly, "Papa in heaven."

The boy smiled and, as two-year-olds will, started to wander off.

Kathleen looked over at Andrew, eyes bright with tears, and again there was the deep unspoken understanding of love.

He nodded, and she turned, putting her arm around Tamira's shoulder, and led her away.

"You old Dutchman. Damn how I miss you." Pat sighed as he stepped forward, looked around awkwardly, wiping the tears from his eyes, and saluted. A bit self-consciously he reached into his pocket, pulled out a flask, raised it in salute, and took a drink. Recorking the flask, he laid it on the grave.

"Farewell, sir, and thank you." Vincent stepped forward and saluted. Gone were the rakish kepi and the Sheridan whiskers. The boy was clean-shaven, wearing a standard-issue slouch cap. Andrew studied him carefully and smiled inwardly. Hans always liked the lad, and he sensed that in Vincent he saw the same things Hans once saw in him. The icy fury of war had been purged out of the boy. He had seasoned into a commander who could lead, earn respect, and show compassion. Vincent shyly laid a single flower on the grave.

Emil stepped up to join his friends. He started to say something, but couldn't. Lowering his head, he gently reached out and touched the headstone.

Andrew caught a whisper of an ancient prayer in Hebrew. "Yisgadahl, v'yiskadash . . ." With head still lowered, he finally stepped back.

As if by unspoken agreement, the three looked back at Andrew and nodded. They turned, Pat in the middle, the other two with hands on either shoulder, and walked off, leaving Andrew alone.

There was nothing more to be said, Andrew realized. The tears were all but gone, replaced with a sad yet happy memory of all that had been, of all they had done and all the dreams still to come.

Here at last the Lost Regiment had found a home and a country. He reached into his pocket and pulled out a precious keepsake of the other world.

"It was always yours, Hans," he whispered through his tears. "I just hung on to it for a little while."

He placed the object on the grave, stepped back, and saluted.

"Good-bye my old friend."

As he started to turn he saw the colors passing by the edge of the cemetery, the regiment following in close order, accompanied by the band still playing the "Battle Cry of Freedom."

Coming to attention he saluted the passing of the colors of the 35th Maine, the 44th New York Light Artillery, and the flag of the Republic.

Colonel Andrew Lawrence Keane, commander of the

Army of the Republic, quietly left the cemetery to rejoin his friends . . . leaving behind, on the grave of Sergeant Major Hans Schuder . . . the Medal of Honor given for heroism above and beyond the call of duty.

<u>*Coming Next Month From Roc*</u>

S. L. Viehl

Stardoc

Anne Bishop

Queen of the Darkness

Book 3 of the *Black Jewels* trilogy